"I am many things," Lord Sheene said. "Kind is not one of them."

Beautiful Grace Paget has no reason not to believe these words. After all, she was kidnapped, spirited away to a remote country manor, and told she is to grant this man his *every* desire . . . or lose her life. But Grace is no common trollop. So she risks everything to save her virtue by planning a daring escape, even though she finds herself tempted by this dangerously handsome man. There is something in his eyes that makes her wonder if he is as cruel as he would have her believe.

Sheene knew nothing of the plan to bring him this woman. Locked up as a prisoner, called "mad" by all the world, he will do anything to reclaim his life, and Grace's sensuous beauty has distracted him from his goals. And although he finds her irresistible, he is horrified to hold her against her will. Now, together, they must both revolt against the strange set of circumstances that has forced them together—for only then will Grace truly surrender to him . . . forever.

ANNA CAMPBELL

UNTOUCHED

An Avon Romantic Treasure

AVON

An Imprint of HarperCollinsPublishers

This is a work of fiction. Names, characters, places, and incidents are products of the author's imagination or are used fictitiously and are not to be construed as real. Any resemblance to actual events, locales, organizations, or persons, living or dead, is entirely coincidental.

AVON BOOKS
An Imprint of HarperCollins*Publishers*
10 East 53rd Street
New York, New York 10022–5299

Copyright © 2007 by Anna Campbell
ISBN: 978-0-06-123492-7
ISBN-10: 0-06-123492-3
www.avonromance.com

First Avon Books paperback printing: December 2007

Avon Trademark Reg. U.S. Pat. Off. and in Other Countries, Marca Registrada, Hecho en U.S.A.
HarperCollins® is registered trademark of HarperCollins Publishers.

Printed in the U.S.A.

10 9 8 7 6 5 4 3 2

Acknowledgments

Firstly, a huge thank you to the many readers who contacted me about my first book, *Claiming the Courtesan*, to say how much you enjoyed Verity and Kylemore's story. It really meant a lot to this debut author to know that characters so dear to me found a warm welcome in your hearts.

With *Untouched*, I'd like to thank everyone at Avon Books, especially Lucia Macro, my fantastic editor, and her wonderful assistant, Esi Sogah. The brilliant members of the Art Department have excelled themselves once more with a gorgeous cover. I'd like to thank Sales and Publicity for their hard work on my first book and for their enthusiastic efforts on behalf of my second. Gratitude also to my agent, Paige Wheeler, of Folio Literary Management.

My writing friends are a continual source of encouragement and support, especially Anne Gracie, Christine Wells, Vanessa Barneveld, Sharon Arkell, and Kandy Shepherd. Above all, I'd like to thank my long-suffering critique partner, Annie West, who is an endless font of wisdom and patience and insight. You're the best, AW!

I dedicate this book about a man of honor to another man of honor, my beloved father, Leslie.

Chapter 1

Somerset, 1822

"**T**his lass is nowt like any whore I ever seen."

The man's thick Yorkshire accent pierced Grace's agonizing return to consciousness. Through the pounding ache in her head, she recognized the sound of home.

If she was back on the farm in Ripon, why did her stomach cramp with pain? Why couldn't she move her hands or feet? Fear iced her blood, froze the voice in her throat.

Remember, Grace, remember.

When she tried, she met only a terrifying wall of blackness.

"No question she's a whore!" a different man insisted from her other side. "What were she by the docks for if she's not a bloody whore? You heard her ask the way to the Cock and Crown. She'd want nowt there but to pull a gent with brass in his pockets."

A whore? They couldn't possibly be talking about her. Confusion eddied through the fog in her mind. How could anyone mistake respectable Grace Paget for a woman who sold herself on the streets?

Instinct stifled her protest. Something told her it was vital that these frightening strangers believe her still unconscious. Keeping her eyes shut, she battled the throbbing headache and forced her sluggish mind to function.

Stray details, each more mystifying than the last, filtered into her awareness. It was day. Light penetrated her closed eyelids. She was strapped to some sort of cushioned bench and she lay flat on her back, arms by her sides. Stout ties fastened each wrist and ankle and a thicker band stretched across her chest, restricting breathing.

For one suffocating moment, the broad strap seemed crushingly tight. She felt faint for lack of air. Sweat broke out on her skin, chilling her to the bone, although the room wasn't cold.

And still she stayed as mute as a stone.

Bewildering memories of violence and duress swam up through her nausea and dizziness. Her head filled with chaos. Chaos and swirling, acrid dread.

Clawing back from smothering panic, she forced herself to breathe. Where was she? Without benefit of sight, she could only collect jumbled impressions. No rumble of traffic. So a room in the country. Or at least in a quiet part of town. The reek of unwashed males mingled with an incongruous hint of spring air heavy with blossom.

The first man made a doubtful sound deep in his throat. "No self-respecting ladybird would be seen dead in them black rags. And she got a wedding ring."

His cohort gave a scornful laugh. "Mebbe she's new to the game, Filey lad. Mebbe the ring is part of the act like her la-di-da chitchat. Them toffs at the Cock and Crown go for that. If she's fresh to the trade, all the better. Lord John said make right sure we plucked a nice clean tart, not some clapped-out old jade."

Appalled disbelief flooded her. She was a lady, even if a lady with threadbare clothes and holes in her shoes. People treated her with respect, deference. Men didn't accost the virtuous Mrs. Paget for a quick fumble in the hedgerows.

Except if these brutes had troubled to abduct her, they must want more than a brief tumble.

Had they already raped her in her sleep?

Oh, please, God, I couldn't bear it if they touched me while I lay unaware.

The weight of her shabby dress was familiar. Hard to be certain without moving, but she seemed unharmed. *So far.*

But what now? A nightmare vision seized her of these thugs raping her again and again. Sour bile flooded her mouth. Only with the greatest effort did she remain silent when every nerve screamed to shriek and struggle and fight.

As she'd struggled and fought when they'd kidnapped her in Bristol.

Oh, yes, she remembered now. Everything.

Cousin Vere had offered her a home to save her from destitution but he'd failed to collect her from the mail coach. After hours of waiting, she'd gone out into the night to seek him. She'd never found her cousin. Instead, she'd met these two devils in human flesh.

Monks and Filey.

They'd been brazen enough to introduce themselves.

Desperately, she strove to recall that short, terrifying encounter in the darkness. She'd asked the two hulking brutes for directions. Lulled by their familiar Yorkshire accents, she'd accepted their escort back to the coaching inn. She'd been so frightened, lost in the labyrinth of dockside streets, that any help had been welcome.

Stupid, stupid, stupid.

They'd trapped her in a narrow alley. Filey had held her while Monks forced laudanum down her throat. Filey's foul stench, repulsive, unforgettable, lingered in her nostrils. Now the noxious odor grew stronger as he lumbered closer.

"Aye, she looks right fresh. She's bonny enow to catch the marquess's fancy. But I still don't reckon she looks owt like a whore."

Monks grunted. "Any road, she'll play a whore's part until his lordship tires of her. Hope she knows a trick or two to keep a lad happy. Or she'll not last out the month."

"Happen we should have fucked her while we had the chance." Filey's regretful musings tested Grace's tenuous control on her roiling insides.

"The watch would have been on us. You'll get your turn after his lordship's had his fill. Let's go. The laudanum'll wear off soon. If she comes to and sees your ugly mug, happen she'll be in a right state for the marquess."

"I care nowt," Filey said. "She's got a grand pair of tits. I lay a penny to a pound her slice is even sweeter."

Stale gin-scented breath puffed into Grace's face. Rough hands wrenched at the high neckline of her dress. Horror kept her paralyzed as Filey ripped at her buttons. A meaty hand shoved under the edge of her stays to palm one breast with bruising force. He was so intent he didn't seem to notice that every muscle in her body tensed with revulsion.

Her heart raced like a half-broken horse given its head. A scream hovered behind her teeth.

Still she dared not make a sound.

This couldn't be happening. It couldn't. Not to her.

"Leave the slut, Filey," Monks snapped. "If the marquess reckons you fucked her first, he'll cut up rough."

"He don't need to know." The encroaching, clammy hand tightened cruelly around her flesh.

Monks gave an unimpressed grunt. "He will if she blabs. I never seen a lass keep her gob buttoned."

"Aye, happen you're right," Filey said regretfully. One last vicious pinch, then he withdrew his hand.

He'd pawed her only for a few seconds but it felt like his hands had violated her for hours. She felt dirty, contaminated.

After another revoltingly drawn-out moment, Filey shuffled away. Dimly through the pounding in her ears, Grace heard the door shut.

Finally she was alone. She gave a great sobbing gasp and opened her eyes.

She was in a pleasant room with white walls and two doors. The first was closed and the other opened onto a sunlit garden. Her sensation of unreality heightened. Surely she hadn't been abducted off the public street and brought here to service strangers.

The laudanum's mind-dulling effects ebbed. Some dissolute aristocrat meant to use her before handing her to his abhorrent henchmen.

She needed to get away now, before her jailers returned. Before the mysterious Lord John who'd ordered a nice clean tart—she cringed at the description—arrived to see what his minions produced for his delectation.

The opiate still clogged her senses and the vile taste filled her mouth. She desperately wanted a drink of water.

No, she desperately wanted to be back at the Cock and Crown waiting for Cousin Vere.

Panting and sobbing, she began to struggle against the leather ties.

"That won't do you any good." As if to confirm what she'd already guessed, a man spoke from the garden doorway. "I should know. I've tried to break those bonds often enough."

She whipped her head around in his direction. Light dazzled her. All she could make out was a tall figure with broad shoulders.

But she heard the voice clearly.

A deep voice smooth and rich as the cream she scooped from the new milk on her farm in Yorkshire. That beautiful cultured baritone frightened her more than all Monks and Filey's ribald speculations.

Then she realized what he'd said. "They've tied you to this table too?"

The man stepped into the room. "Of course," he said mildly as if the admission held no consequence.

The gold-limned shadow resolved into a gentleman in his middle twenties wearing a loose white shirt and buff breeches. He was more than six feet tall and overly slender for his height, although she didn't mistake his physical strength. He might be lean, but it was sinewy leanness.

He was the most beautiful man she'd ever seen. Even terrified as she was, she couldn't help measuring each detail of his appearance.

Fine dark hair grew back from his high forehead. A long straight nose. Sharply cut cheekbones, prominent because of his thinness. His eyes remained downcast under his winged dark brows. He looked like one of God's angels humbly awaiting direction from the Deity.

Except no angel would study her prone body with quite that level of curiosity.

The heated inspection licked its way up her form with leisurely thoroughness. It lingered at her breasts, making her burningly conscious of her gaping neckline. Every muscle contracted in fear and refusal.

Grace had lived with fear long enough to know facing it down was her only strategy. She glowered at the man. "Are you Lord John?"

His mouth quirked in an unamused smile. "No. Lord John is my uncle."

"If you're not Lord John, will you help me? Your uncle has brought me here for . . ." Words failed her, although she doubted any description she chose would shock this superb and lascivious angel.

That ghost of a smile again. Like the rest of him, his mouth was perfect. Wide enough to be expressive. A sharply defined upper lip. A generous sweep of lower lip.

"His amusement?" The deep voice darkened with irony as he chose the innocuous term for something they both knew was anything but innocuous. He shifted closer so his shadow fell across her. She fought another wave of panic.

Her fingers curled beneath the restricting straps. "Yes. You must help me get away."

"Must?" The young man stretched out one long-fingered hand to stroke her cheek. His touch was cool but she jerked away as if scalded. He took her chin and held her for his scrutiny. "Hmm. Pretty."

He terrified her. But he was her only chance of escape before the unknown Lord John arrived. She moderated her tone. "Please, sir. Please help me."

She'd closed her eyes. Although somehow she knew that fleeting smile flickered and vanished again.

"Better. Much better."

The monster toyed with her. He'd toyed with her from the first. She swallowed nervously. "I appeal to your honor, sir. You cannot . . ." No, insistence hadn't worked. "I appeal for your help."

"Ah, I knew you could manage the right note. I find myself moved, madam. That slight break in your voice is a masterstroke. Well done."

Her eyes snapped open. Strange to be both so annoyed and so scared at the same time. "I protest, sir. You speak like I'm an . . . an actress trying out for a part."

"Do I indeed?" He bit out the words. With a flick of his fingers, he released her as though touching her offended him. "How remiss of me when it's quite clear you've already been cast for this particular role."

He swung away from her with a restlessness she noticed even through her fear. Knowing as she spoke that she'd fail, Grace made one last try for this singular young man's help. "Your uncle means to rape me. You cannot just abandon me."

He turned back to her, his remarkable face a mask of well-bred contempt. "This confusion charms, madam. And almost convinces. But we both know you're here for my use, not my uncle's. Unless one discounts your purpose as his cat's paw."

She licked dry lips. "You must be mad."

He gave a short huff of humorless laughter and met her gaze for the first time. He had rich brown eyes marked by a sunburst of gold. Beautiful, unusual eyes, colder than anything she'd ever seen.

He spoke quite gently as those strange striated eyes stared into hers. "Of course I am, my dear. Unquestionably and incurably mad."

Chapter 2

Damn his uncle. Damn him to hell, Matthew silently cursed.

His heart flooded with despair as he looked down at the girl tied to the table like some blasted pagan offering. Somehow, Lord John had invaded the secret corners of his soul and read the longing there. From that longing, he'd fashioned a woman of moonlight and darkness. A woman who matched every lonely dream that had ever tormented Matthew.

How the hell had his uncle known?

And if he knew so much, did Matthew have a shred of a chance of defeating him?

The jade's terrified gaze, dark blue shadowed under a thick fan of black lashes, hadn't wavered from him. Whatever else she feigned, he'd wager good coin—if he had any—she was genuinely frightened.

He wanted her frightened. Frightened, she'd be off balance. Off balance, she was likely to make mistakes. Too many mistakes, Lord John would discard her.

If Matthew relied on anything, it was his uncle's eternal ruthlessness.

She swallowed and, against his will, his attention snagged on the movement of that pale slender throat. Then inevitably his focus slid lower. The top of her dress was artfully undone, showing mounded flesh and the white edge of her shift. His fingers clenched into fists at his sides.

Oh, yes, he needed to get rid of her. And quickly.

"You . . ." Her husky voice faltered. The incongruous air of authority had vanished. "Surely you jest, sir."

His lips twisted in a bitter smile. "Surely I don't, madam."

The smile didn't reassure her. It wasn't meant to.

"I assume it will do me no good to scream." Like so much else about her, the sound of her voice was unexpected. It was low, and soft enough to turn her clipped upper-class accent into music.

"Well, you can try," he said idly. "I've never found it particularly effective. You've already gained my attention and Monks and Filey will have orders to grant us privacy. I suspect, if anything, a clamor from you will only reward them with a moment's gratification."

"In that case, I won't scream." The little color that remained in her face had leached away to pure ivory.

"I commend your wisdom." He inclined his head slightly as if acknowledging a point in a fencing match.

She was a universe away from what he'd imagined when his uncle first broached this revolting scheme. Lord John had offered to get him a tart to while away his hours. Matthew had pictured a much-used doxy hardened to her profession. However desperate he was—and desperation near seeped from his skin—he'd been sure he could withstand the tired blandishments of a painted harpy.

His arrogant assurance had been misplaced. For, of course, Lord John was a subtle man and had eschewed the obvious.

Instead, his uncle had found . . . *perfection.*

God, he couldn't stay, suspended by the power of pleading cobalt eyes. Almost blindly, he made for the door.

"Wait! Please." He couldn't misunderstand her frantic tone. "Don't leave me here. Untie me at least, I beg of you."

He swung his head back toward her. "I believe it to my advantage to have you constrained."

To untie her, he must touch her. The memory of her satiny cheek under his hand still burned like acid, fleeting as the mocking caress had been.

"Please. I . . . I think I'm going to be sick."

She dragged in a shuddering breath that made her breasts rise, round and enticing, against the loosened front of her faded black dress. He resented the fact that he noticed.

"Don't practice your tricks on me," he snarled.

"No. I mean it," she said unsteadily.

In truth, the wench's alabaster complexion showed an alarmingly green tinge. She'd closed her eyes and dark marks beneath them stood out like bruises.

He paused. Perhaps this wasn't a ruse.

Reluctantly, he strode across to that cursed table where he'd spent so many hideous hours. All the way, he derided himself for a soft-headed fool. This slut was his enemy and in league with all his other enemies.

Even while the litany ran through his mind, he tugged swiftly at the tapes that held her. As soon as she was free, she struggled into a sitting position.

"Sir, I'm afraid I . . ."

Yes, the ashen skin definitely held a sickly hue. While she lied about so much else, she was definitely ill. He scanned the room and found what he wanted. Fortunately, just an arm's length away.

"Here." He shoved a large blue and white bowl into her shaking hands.

She mumbled something that might have been thanks then bent to retch miserably into the dish. Her physical discomfort awoke grudging sympathy, despite what Matthew knew of her. When finally her stomach settled, he sat with his arm around her to keep her from collapsing.

He tried to ignore the warm, womanly feel of her, but it was impossible. She fit against his side as if created to curve into him. His hand automatically conformed to the sinuous shape of her body, so different from the hard masculine angles of his. The deep V of her unbuttoned bodice revealed shadowy glimpses of her breasts. A clever touch, he thought bleakly, trying to distance himself from the urge to see more.

She trembled and laid her head back on his shoulder in a gesture of absolute exhaustion. The braids circling her head were untidy and soft tendrils of hair pleasurably tickled his jaw.

"Rest for a moment," he murmured into that silky black mass of hair.

Gently, he reached across to disengage the bowl. He set it beside him on the table. She hadn't brought up very much. He guessed her stomach was empty. Certainly, the body he held so unwillingly was thin to the point of emaciation. She felt fragile, as if the slightest pressure might shatter her.

"It must be the laudanum they gave me last night," she whispered. "It's never agreed with me."

Laudanum? The word, with its hint of compulsion, hovered as a question on the edge of his mind. Then his concentration returned to the woman lying bonelessly in his embrace. He angled himself so he could see the round smoothness of her forehead and the straight, oddly aristocratic nose. She was beautiful. He'd recognized that immediately.

Recognized and railed against it.

The oval face with its exotically slanted cheekbones reminded him of etchings he'd seen of Italian Madonnas.

His uncle had been generous in giving him books to make up for the Grand Tour he'd never undertake.

His gaze fastened on where delicate color returned to her lush mouth. Its fullness belied the impression of purity. That mouth made even such a sorry excuse for a man as Matthew dream of sin.

Oh, she was skilled at this game. In a matter of moments, she had him just where she wanted. His uncle had coached her well. Although why a woman with her looks and acting talent should whore herself to a madman remained a puzzle.

If he didn't know better, her show of vulnerability and hard-won courage against overwhelming fear would take him in. Any theater management would vie for her services. Any predatory nobleman would vie for services of a more intimate nature.

Abruptly, he felt sullied by his pity.

She fumbled in her skirts—for a handkerchief, he supposed. He suppressed another curse and thrust his own in her direction. "Here."

"Thank you." She wiped her mouth with a trembling hand.

"Can you sit without help now?" he asked grimly, for once not caring if his genuine emotions emerged without subterfuge. He'd determined to remain cool and uninvolved, but some things were beyond mere mortals. He'd been angry for years, but this cruel charade honed his rage.

"Yes, I think so." Gingerly, she drew away.

Immediately, he missed her warmth and teasing female scent. She smelled of sunshine and dust and the faintest trace of lavender soap. Another subtle touch. This whore didn't use heady scents of the Orient to draw a man's attention. Instead, she smelled fresh and natural and real.

Ironic, given she was nothing but falsehood.

She braced herself by hooking her fingers around the

edge of the table. He was close enough to see the tremors that racked her slim frame. With difficulty, he resisted the urge to lend her his hand.

He damned his uncle yet again. And just as fruitlessly.

Even in boyhood, Matthew couldn't pass a sick or injured animal without trying to help. Lord John must have decided the best way to destroy his nephew was through this weakness. That fatal sympathy for the brave, the hurt, the gentle was meant to be his undoing.

The girl looked at him fully for the first time since he'd released her. The laudanum had shrunk her pupils to black pinpoints, leaving her irises impossibly blue.

Nice touch, Uncle, he thought sourly. Drugging her makes her appear so much more the victim. He had to remember this woman's frail gallantry was an act.

"Forgive me, sir. I have inconvenienced you and embarrassed myself."

Still that strange courtly demeanor. The discomfort over her loss of control befitted any fine lady. He could have told her she wasted her time. He knew exactly what she was. His uncle had promised him a tart. A tart she most definitely was.

He shrugged, unfazed by her nausea. "It is of no importance."

What right had he to be squeamish? In his fits, he'd lost control over his bodily functions. Why else should the bowl be kept convenient to the table where they'd strapped him so often? Although, thank God, he hadn't required that particular treatment for a long time.

She cast him an uncertain glance under those wickedly luxuriant lashes. "Still, you were kind. Thank you."

He had to shatter this damned enthrallment she so effortlessly exercised. Holding her had been too sweet. But then, it was years since he'd either given or received comfort. The insidious pleasure was a purely animal reaction and nothing to do with the actual woman in his arms.

Or so he tried to tell himself.

"I am many things, madam," he said coldly as he stood. "Kind is not one of them."

He saw her face change. Briefly, her physical crisis had swamped fear. Fear flooded back as she remembered she was alone with a self-confessed madman. Her trembling fingers rose to clutch her loose neckline together.

What a masterly performance. Why was such an accomplished actress rusticating in darkest Somerset? She should be dazzling a packed house at Drury Lane.

"I have to get out of here," she muttered, more to herself than him, he thought. She rose to unsteady feet and backed toward the door. His handkerchief fluttered onto the floor to lie like a lost banner of surrender.

"There's nowhere to run," he said mildly. Oh, she was good, but he was on to her deception. "The estate is walled. Filey and Monks guard the only gate. And I doubt my uncle will release you from your engagement so early in the play's season."

She frowned as if she didn't understand. Her beautiful eyes were glassy. Her unsteadiness developed a distinct sway. An alarming sway.

"Christ!" he bit out as she began to crumple.

He dived across the short distance and caught her before she crashed. Immediately, the heady and jarringly innocent scents of sunshine and soap flooded his senses.

"Sir, would you kindly restrain your language?" she whispered against his throat. Her breath on his skin set his blood leaping with awareness and it took him a second to realize what she'd said.

He gave a disbelieving snort of laughter. For God's sake, she had more important things to worry about than his manners. But his hold was careful as he gathered her up and carried her through to the salon.

"I insist you put me down," she said with a woeful lack of force.

"If I put you down, you'll only fall at my feet."

He waited for an argument but none was forthcoming. She was near the limit of her resources, he saw.

After this last year, he wasn't as strong as he had been. But her slight weight posed no difficulty. Again, his attention caught on the signs of deprivation. The outdated dress. The thinness. Even her shoes were worn and cracked.

He settled her more comfortably and stoically ignored the way her breasts brushed his chest. She might be insubstantial as a wraith. But he'd immediately observed she was without doubt a *female* wraith.

He laid her on the sofa near the empty grate, brushing the open book he'd left there to the floor. "Lie back," he said softly, sliding a red velvet cushion behind her tousled dark head.

She tried to draw away but weakness defeated her. Her perfect profile stood out in austere clarity against the rich material. His breath hitched in his throat at her beauty.

"Don't touch me." She closed her eyes and a tear slid down her smooth cheek.

Her terror and unhappiness called so strongly to his compassion that it was an effort to speak with disdain. "You're safe enough." Then in a harder voice, because she was his enemy, however lovely and vulnerable she seemed, "You couldn't fight me off now, even if you wanted to."

A startled cobalt glance darted up to his face. He kept his expression implacable as he turned toward the sideboard to pour her a brandy.

He returned to the couch and extended the small crystal glass. She barely had strength to lift her head. She was shivering and he could hear each ragged breath she took.

"Sweet Jesus," he muttered and leaned forward to support her as she drank.

She flashed him a disapproving look under her lowered dark brows but refrained from censuring him. She took a sip and started to choke.

He swore again and pulled her up against him so she could catch her breath. How his uncle would preen if he were here. Matthew had sworn he'd never lay a finger on any woman Lord John found. Yet he coddled and cosseted this conniving baggage as if she were an ailing princess. It had taken the wench only minutes to wheedle her way into his arms.

He had to admire her cleverness, if nothing else.

Oh, be honest, he derided himself. So far, you admire everything about her apart from the fact that she's on Lord John's side and not yours.

"Drink, damn you," he growled, snatching the glass which she was about to drop and pressing it to her bloodless lips.

"After an invitation like that, how can I refuse?" she replied breathlessly, then took a few small sips. "Could I have some water, do you think?"

He almost smiled as he added sheer bravado to the growing list of things he admired about her. "Whatever madam desires. I exist but to serve."

Her drawn features didn't lighten. He had a sudden burning need to see her smile. Savagely, he stifled the urge.

What did he care if a whore chose to smile? He had enough trouble when she was on the brink of collapse. He returned the brandy glass to the sideboard and filled another glass from the pitcher of water.

"Thank you," she said with that odd politeness.

He stood and surveyed her as she drank. One of her protectors must have had pretensions to gentility. Or perhaps she was the wayward daughter of a good family. She spoke with the smooth cadences of the wealthy classes and he couldn't fault her courtesy.

She leaned back against the sofa. The temptation was raw to take her in his arms again. To comfort and support only, he told himself desperately. Although as he'd held her, he hadn't missed the supple indent of her waist or the winsome arch of her hip or the firm roundness of her bosom. And her damned evocative scent lingered, luring him closer and closer.

He gazed down at her with a mixture of helpless wonder and furious denial. He wanted to curse and insult her. He wanted to rage and rant and tear the room up like the madman he was supposed to be.

Instead, he found himself asking, "Are you hungry?"

She closed her eyes and inhaled deeply as if the air itself offered sustenance. The rise and fall of her chest only made him more aware of the beautiful shape of her breasts. They weren't large but on a woman of her extreme slenderness, they seemed miraculously voluptuous. His fingers curled at his sides as if he already tested the weight and shape of her.

"Madam, when did you last eat?" he asked more insistently.

She roused from her uneasy doze. "I had some bread and cheese at breakfast yesterday," she said dully.

"I'll get you something," he said, more relieved than he wanted to admit at having a valid excuse to escape her presence. That shaming relief was graphic demonstration of how dangerous she was.

He was a man of unfailing will. Will was all that kept him alive. But half an hour in her company threatened to turn him into her creature. And she hadn't even started to work her seductive wiles. She'd been too sick.

God help him when she regained her health. She'd have him on his knees in five minutes flat.

No, damn her, she wouldn't win.

He'd fought his uncle all these years and not given up. No mere scrap of a girl would vanquish him.

Still, only when he went through to the kitchen did he manage an unconstrained breath. His first unconstrained breath since he'd discovered her.

"It's more bread and cheese. There wasn't much else in the larder." He angled the laden tray through the door.

The girl didn't answer. He supposed she was asleep. She'd looked weary to the point of exhaustion. Quietly, he came round the end of the sofa.

He wasted his consideration. The sofa was empty.

He set the tray on the dresser with a thud. So the strumpet had run off. The estate was impossible to escape. He could vouch for that after years of trying to break free.

Clearly, she'd decided no amount of money compensated for sharing her bed with a lunatic.

He couldn't blame her. The assignment had probably sounded promising when his uncle outlined it. He knew how persuasive his guardian could be when he concentrated that magnetic personality on someone he wanted to charm or manipulate. Charm and manipulate, Matthew thought with a bleak laugh. The two were the same to John Lansdowne.

Well, let her try to run. She'd tire soon enough and come back. Even if she didn't, it was nothing to him. He'd intended to rid himself of her intrusive presence. He should be glad he'd achieved his goal so easily.

Glad? He should be bloody well chanting hallelujahs.

She'd flee to Monks and Filey and they'd take her back to where they'd found her. This distasteful farce would end.

Except Monks and Filey had gone to a deal of trouble to fetch the trollop. They wouldn't be pleased to discover she'd changed her mind. When they weren't pleased, they were inventive in expressing their disappointment. He carried scars from occasions when their inventiveness had exceeded even its usual bounds.

The girl would be at their mercy.

The girl was here to spy on him.

He bent to pick up his book. She'd involved herself in his uncle's schemes. She deserved whatever happened to her.

But as he sat and found his place on the page, his mind focused not on the Latin treatise but on large dark blue eyes that silently begged for his help.

He should abandon her to her fate but she'd be frighteningly defenseless against his uncle's thugs.

"Christ," he grated out, slamming the book shut.

He had a sudden piercing memory of her disapproval for his uncouth language.

The chit had courage but courage wouldn't save her from his jailers. Knowing he was a fool, but unable to stop himself, Matthew surged to his feet and went in search of his unlikely harlot.

Chapter 3

Grace buckled over at the waist and struggled for breath. Late afternoon sun shone warm on her bare head while bitter hopelessness sapped her determination. Since her husband Josiah's illness, despair had become a familiar visitor. But never before had despair dug its icy fingers so deep into her craven soul.

She'd hardly believed her luck when her unsettling companion had left her alone. Fear had lent a spurious strength when she'd leapt from the sofa and run. Since that euphoric moment, she'd searched doggedly for a way out.

There was no way out.

The decorative but hostile marquess took no risk in letting her go. The boundary wall stretched before her as it had stretched since she'd reached it. High, white, and polished to a slippery smoothness that offered no handholds. Even so, she'd tried several times to deny the evidence of her eyes and scale it. Now the harsh truth battered at her that someone worked extremely hard to keep the young man a prisoner.

And she was as trapped as he.

The walls enclosed a small estate, mostly woodland, although she'd noticed well-tended gardens and orchards close to the house. In other circumstances, she'd find her surroundings appealing, even beautiful. In this nightmare of compulsion and dread, the burgeoning spring growth encroached and threatened.

The sheer efficiency of these walls was most terrifying of all. This prison indicated wealth, endless resources, cleverness, determination. It indicated someone formidable enough to take an innocent woman captive and ruthless enough never to release her.

This place was impregnable. She'd passed only one gate, chained and barred, constructed of solid oak. Near the gate there was an untidy huddle of buildings, barns, stables, yards, a cottage.

Her jailers had been sitting on a bench against the cottage wall, passing an earthenware jug between them. The purposeful intensity of their drinking had been obvious even from where she crouched in the bushes a hundred yards away. Their laughter held a lewd note that made her shudder. Although she couldn't hear what they said, she knew they gloated over what they imagined the marquess did to her.

She didn't fool herself they were inebriated enough to let her slip past. Living in a poor farming community, she'd met men of their ilk, although she'd never encountered quite their level of viciousness. Pigs like her abductors didn't become insensible with spirits, they became mean.

She'd taken a deep breath in a futile attempt to quell her rioting stomach. Then she'd crept away to continue her search.

Now she was back where she'd started. No closer to escape than when she'd fled the beautiful madman with his cold voice and hungry eyes.

The wretched realization battered at her that she could die within these walls and nobody would know. Her aching belly cramped with another surge of panic. She was lightheaded with hunger and thirst, and her stomach still heaved with nausea. Under her now-buttoned collar, sweat prickled uncomfortably at her neck.

Dear heavens, she was weary to her very soul. She slumped to the dusty ground. Even if her unsteady legs carried her further, there was nowhere to go.

"Think, Grace, think," she whispered, seeking courage in the sound of her own voice.

The words faded to nothing. Trembling with exhaustion and fear, she bent her head to stave off tears. Her eyes were still scratchy from the crying she'd done over Josiah and the loss of the farm. Tears had done no good then. They'd do no good now.

She desperately needed food. Even if her stomach revolted at the mere idea. Perhaps after dark, she could sneak closer to the house and steal from the gardens.

Was it likely she'd remain free to wander the park? Her captors would flush her from the greenery like beaters flushed pheasants for the hunters' guns.

She smothered a bitter laugh. Josiah Paget's penniless widow had thought she'd measured disaster. She hadn't known what trouble was then.

"Pleasing to see you haven't abandoned your sense of humor," a deep, subtly mocking voice said.

She raised her head and met the lost, compelling eyes of the man who had held her while she vomited. He stood before her with rangy ease. A wolfhound sidled close to him. One elegant hand lowered and negligently stroked the dog's shaggy head.

"No!" she gasped, scrambling to her feet. Logic told her she lacked the strength to evade him. Her galloping heart insisted she try.

"Wolfram," he said quietly. The huge hound bounded forward to bring her to bay against the oak behind her. "There's no point running. You must know that by now."

Over the animal's rough back, she glowered at the picturesque monster who tormented her. "If it delays your assault on me, that's point enough," she said in a voice that shook no matter how she fought to steady it.

The accusation was meant to sting. But the honey mosaic gaze didn't waver. "If the client isn't to your taste, I can only apologize. Although I wouldn't have thought a whore could be too fussy about who she opens her legs to." Acid contempt laced his words.

She drew herself up to full height. This time, her voice was firm and edged with outrage. "I am no whore. Those swine you employ brought me here against my will. Any man with a shred of honor would do his utmost to restore me to my family."

"But I am not a man of honor." His mobile mouth curled in the already familiar sardonic smile. "I am just a poor helpless lunatic."

He stepped forward with a loose-limbed ease that Grace couldn't help noticing and rested his hand on the dog's neck. The movement brought him dauntingly close. She edged away until the dog's soft growl forced her to freeze.

Her brief defiance evaporated. "Please let me go," she said brokenly.

His brows drew together in irritation. "I pray you, madam, cease this charade," he snapped, his long fingers tightening in the dog's brindle coat. "My uncle, Lord John Lansdowne, paid you to come here and ply your trade. It was clever to invent this fanciful tale of abduction. But the widow's weeds, the panic, the pleading, even the induced sickness, none gull me into believing your story. I am wise to your trickery."

"You're mad," she breathed, as the nightmare closed around her in a blinding fog.

He shrugged. "Surely my uncle cannot have neglected to inform you of that. What other reason could he offer for my confinement?"

She shook her head in bewilderment. The impossible thing was he looked as sane as any man she'd ever known, even while his words made no sense. She focused on the part that was easiest to deny.

"I've never met your uncle."

An expression of haughty displeasure crossed his features. "You cling to your lies. No matter. You'll tire of the masquerade." He turned away. "Come, Wolfram." Obediently, the hound trotted after him as he strode off.

Disbelievingly she watched the retreat of that straight back in its loose white shirt.

"You're leaving me here?" She cursed the words for emerging as protest rather than demand.

"Follow me back to the house or stay out here for Monks and Filey to find when they check the grounds," he said without looking at her. His tone was indifferent and his manner was dismissive as he walked off.

Her trembling fingers dug into the rough bark behind her. "But you mean to rape me," she said shakily.

He paused to send her an unreadable glance over his shoulder. "Perhaps not immediately."

She looked into those odd eyes and wondered why she was convinced that at least for now, he posed no physical threat.

Which was absurd as he admitted he was mad, he'd made no promises, and he clearly harbored misconceptions about what sort of woman she was. All she had to weigh against these facts was that he'd been kind when she was ill. And he was yet to hurt her.

"Who are you?" She straightened and lifted her chin.

Again, that grim smile. "Why, I am the master of this pathetic kingdom, my lady."

She swallowed sick nervousness. "Does this master have a name?"

He faced her fully so the sun gilded his high cheekbones. "Didn't my uncle tell you?"

"Indulge me," she said unsteadily.

"As you wish." He bowed as though they'd been introduced at a ball. The elegance of the sarcastic gesture made the breath catch in her throat. "I am Matthew Lansdowne, Marquess of Sheene."

She frowned. Could she trust what he said? The Marquess of Sheene was one of the richest men in England. What was he doing here, locked away from the world?

His henchmen called him the marquess. The luxury of his surroundings indicated someone with gold to ensure comfort. Perhaps he really was who he claimed to be.

His attention fixed upon her as though she were a botanical specimen. It was unnerving. Or would have been if her nerves didn't already jangle. "Will you do me a similar favor?"

"What do you mean?"

A shadow of impatience darkened that striking face. "Your name, girl. What is it?"

She spoke without thinking. "Grace Paget, my lord."

"Grace," he said musingly, his eyes never leaving her.

She had no illusions about what he saw. A faded woman in shabby clothing who had endured too much sorrow and witnessed too much privation.

Then she wondered why she minded. She didn't want him to notice her as a man noticed a woman. Her situation was precarious enough.

She waited for some comment on her name, perhaps a remark that it didn't suit her. The recollection of how she'd been sick in front of him revolted her. She had a sudden sharp memory of his care for her. Surely someone so considerate in such circumstances wouldn't use her against her will.

But what did she know of men her own age? Josiah had been old and the blood had run sluggishly in his veins. She recognized the virile strength in the marquess's lean, youthful body. And if he spoke true, he was a great lord, used to getting what he wanted at the snap of his fingers. As if to prove her right, he clicked his fingers to summon the dog who nosed at a pile of last year's leaves.

This man offered a buffer against Monks and Filey. Her only buffer.

What he'd want in return she didn't dare contemplate. If his sole purpose was bed sport, he could have had her when she was bound to the table.

She didn't trust him. But what alternative did she have?

Wondering if she cast her lot with the Devil, she straightened away from the tree and followed him.

Grace trudged behind the marquess until they reached the clearing around the house. During the long walk from the boundaries, her panic faded into a haze of weariness.

The man—Lord Sheene, she supposed—paused at the edge of the trees and waited for her to catch up. The sun sank in the west and gold rays etched his tall figure with brilliance. She blinked. Something about his stance struck her as ineffably sad.

He looked magnificent standing there. And lonelier than anyone she'd ever seen.

The unwelcome perception vanished as Wolfram turned back to sniff at her skirts. A soft exhalation of surprise escaped her.

"He won't bite." Lord Sheene's eyes were intent on her. Clearly, he'd forgotten in his isolation that it was rude to stare.

Her lips flattened in self-derision. Rude to stare? This man could claim use of her body. His eyes were the last things she needed to worry about.

Banishing the disturbing thought, she looked down into the dog's intelligent yellow gaze. "I like dogs."

She'd had dogs on the farm. At times, they had seemed

the only beings in creation capable of unconditional love. She reached out to let the impressive beast sniff her fingers before she scratched behind his ears. Wolfram's eyes closed in rapture. It was the first normal reaction she'd received from anything or anyone in this strange prison. She smiled down at the hound.

Whenever she was with the marquess, unsettling currents of awareness swirled around them. Now the soft air shivered with a sharp turbulence that made the fine hairs stand up on her skin.

She whipped her head up in confusion. Lord Sheene glared at her, his gaze fixed on her mouth as if poison dripped from her lips. Her smile faltered and disappeared. She whipped her hand away from Wolfram. What had she done to arouse this savage displeasure?

"You've made a conquest, I see," the marquess said harshly. "Don't expect everyone here to come to heel at your merest simper."

Open-mouthed with shock, she watched him stalk off as if he could no longer bear the sight of her. Wolfram immediately pulled away to trail after his master.

Grace stayed behind, dizzy with fear and confusion. The marquess's mercurial shifts of temperament frightened her, left her floundering and disoriented. Perhaps he truly was mad. He was certainly angry. Was he an ally? Was he a threat? Right now she couldn't have said.

Gradually, her heartbeat slowed. She watched Lord Sheene stride toward the house, then turned to observe her surroundings. An unlikely setting for one of the nation's greatest noblemen. The large cottage wasn't imposing. It basked before her, the old red brick glowing in the mellow light. The house looked warm and welcoming. The house looked like home.

And danger thickened with every second.

She'd already realized that in this place, appearance

and reality engaged in eternal battle. She must keep her wits about her that she didn't mistake one for the other and come to destruction.

She shivered. Without Lord Sheene, the trees behind her held an ominous air, for all their beauty. A sudden fancy took her that her abductors ogled her from the thick woods. She dredged up the energy to stumble across the smooth green lawn after the marquess.

Grace looked into the mirror in the charming bedroom that the marquess had indicated was hers. Terrified eyes stared back and she chewed nervously on her lower lip, a childhood habit she'd never broken.

"You've survived so far," she whispered to her reflection. "You will keep surviving."

If only she believed it.

Swallowing her dread before it strangled her, she picked up one of a heavy set of silver men's brushes from the dresser and hurriedly rebraided her hair. She'd managed a wash and she'd removed the worst of the dust from her dress but she still looked tired and hungry and poor. And far too frail to fend off lecherous noblemen.

In the glass, she saw Lord Sheene prowl into the room behind her. The fear Grace had struggled to dam flooded back. The large bed in the corner suddenly loomed as the most significant object in the room. She snatched up the brush like a weapon and whirled around.

He gave a bark of contemptuous laughter. "Do you intend to groom me to death?" He turned back to the door. "Monks has brought dinner in. If you're contemplating murder, you'll need to keep your strength up."

How she hated his effortless superiority. Was this just a game to him? Her fear. Her helplessness. Her resistance. Reviving anger flowed hot through her veins, swamping her earlier cowardice.

Nothing and no one in the last years had defeated her. And nor would this ramshackle lunatic.

She raised her chin and gave him a frosty stare. She might be a Paget now but she'd been born a Marlow and a Marlow had every right to look a Lansdowne in the eye. He'd learn she wasn't a woman to trifle with. She wouldn't collapse in abject terror because he had the gall to mock her.

"If you'll lead the way, my lord?" she said coolly.

With deliberate firmness, she replaced the brush on its silver tray laced with ornate engraved Ls. For *Lansdowne*, she supposed. Although the letter would better stand for *lout* or *lecher* or *lunatic*.

His gaze sharpened on her face as if he tried to solve a puzzle. She braced herself for more derision, but he merely gestured for her to precede him down the narrow staircase.

In the cottage's main room, the room she'd escaped earlier with such futile hope, candlelight flickered on polished wood and rich fabrics. The table was laid with gleaming china and crystal.

The whole cottage was furnished in the most expensive taste. The only hint of its real purpose—as a madman's cell—was that horrible bench where she'd been restrained. The rest of the house conjured ideas of a wealthy man's love nest.

She blushed. Even if this place were a voluptuary's hideaway, that didn't mean she must accept the role of voluptuary's plaything.

He came up behind her. "The food grows cold."

Her nerves tightened. She was alone with a powerful and unpredictable monster.

Although when she took her place at the table, she thought he looked anything but a monster. He'd troubled to put on a black coat and a neckcloth. Above the snowy folds, his face was intent and thoughtful. And guarded. Those heavy-lidded eyes and strong bones hid secrets.

Was one of those secrets that he'd lost his mind?

No, he freely admitted that, didn't he?

He slid a filled plate in front of her then returned to the sideboard for his own meal. The elegance of his movements distracted her and she took a moment to realize she hadn't seen food like this since she'd run away from her father's house at sixteen.

When the marquess sat opposite, he must have caught her dazed wonder. Again, she marked how he studied her. She hid a shiver of fear and despite her exhaustion, sat ramrod straight. He must never guess how close to breaking she was.

"Is the fare not to your liking?" he asked.

Her hesitation over the elaborate dinner stemmed from complex reasons which she refused to share with this terrifying stranger. Her chaotic, disastrous past was nobody's business but her own.

When she didn't answer, he went on almost conversationally. "Mrs. Filey tempts my appetite which in recent months has been uncertain."

It could have sounded like a spoilt aristocrat's whining complaint. Except she'd noticed immediately that he was too thin for a man of his height. "Filey's wife does the cooking?"

"Yes. And the cleaning. She, Filey, and Monks are the extent of my staff."

Grace had already remarked the scarcity of servants. Surely even a mad marquess merited a larger household.

Another mystery.

The greatest mystery of all arched a supercilious brow. "Eat. You have no reason to fear poison. Monks and Filey brought you here for a purpose. They certainly don't want you dead before you accomplish it."

"And what do you want?" she asked bravely, while fear danced a wild tarantella along her veins.

He smiled briefly as if at a private joke. "Keep looking at me like that and I'll tell you."

She flushed. Clearly, he wasn't the only one guilty of staring.

He frightened her with his unwavering gaze and barely veiled resentment. But she couldn't deny his masculine beauty. She'd been married to an old man for nine years. Despite her dread and anger now, she couldn't resist drinking in the sheer magnificence of the marquess's physical presence.

Still blushing, she lowered her eyes and sliced into her *bœuf en croûte*. Her hunger was stronger even than her fear.

As the rich and familiar flavors filled her mouth, she closed her eyes and fought tears. She refused to start bawling just because her captors gave her a decent meal. That would be too pitiable.

The delicious food brought back so many memories. Memories she'd crushed deep inside through years of deprivation. Memories that now surfaced to make her dangerously vulnerable.

Control yourself, Grace, she told herself sternly, or you'll be lost. With a shaking hand, she reached for her wine and took a gulp. But even the cool flow of claret down her tense throat reminded her poignantly of her past.

"The gowns didn't meet with your approval?" the marquess asked idly after a long silence. He raised his wine to his lips and sipped. "Surely you must realize by now that the grieving widow hasn't disarmed me."

She ignored the taunting jibe. "What gowns?"

He gestured contemptuously with his heavy crystal glass. "Your costumes for act two. The bedroom coffers overflow with silks and satins."

"I didn't look." Her heart sank under the desolate

knowledge that someone had made elaborate preparations for her arrival. And if they'd made such effort to get her here, they'd make doubly sure she didn't leave.

She drank more wine to bolster her failing nerve. Questions might anger her companion but she had to take the risk. Ignorance rendered her utterly defenseless.

"My lord, where are we?"

He'd combed his thick dark hair away from his face and she had no trouble reading the suspicion that settled on his features. "Madam, what profit is there in continuing this pretense?"

Nothing shook his belief that she worked against him in some plot.

Weren't madmen always certain the world conspired to achieve their ruin? Apart from his own avowals, it was the first indication that he was indeed insane.

Still she didn't give up. "What harm to tell me?"

He surveyed her for a disturbing interval while his fingers toyed with the stem of his glass. He had beautiful hands, she noticed inconsequentially. Slender, strong, long-fingered, sensitive.

Would those hands soon be on her skin, hurting her?

He sighed with impatience. "No harm compared to what has already been done," he growled eventually. "If it amuses you, by all means let's play this little scene. You are in an isolated corner of Somerset about twenty miles from Wells."

"How long have you . . . how long have you lived here?"

The wry smile flickered and died. "How long have I been out of my wits, do you mean?" When she didn't answer, he went on in a terse voice, "I contracted a brain fever when I was fourteen. I am now five and twenty."

They were the same age, she realized with astonishment. She couldn't imagine why that created a bond, but it did.

"So you've been a captive for eleven years?"

Eleven years of incarceration, eleven years of his warders' brutality, eleven years of madness. The misery he must have endured didn't bear thinking about.

He shrugged. "It could have been worse. My uncle in his kindness," he bit out the words, "saved me from confinement in an asylum. I doubt I'd have survived otherwise."

"Even so, eleven years a prisoner," she said, aghast.

Abruptly, the fine food lost its flavor. With trembling hands, she set down her knife and fork. She noticed the marquess had eaten even less of the extravagant meal than she.

He shrugged. "I believe it was for the good of all concerned. At the time." This last with a caustic edge.

"You speak of your uncle. What of your parents? What of your brothers and sisters?"

"My parents died before I fell ill. They had no other children. My uncle was my legal guardian when I was a boy and as I never regained my wits, he has continued in that role." He frowned across the elaborately set table. "Didn't Lord John explain this? Surely he'd want you in possession of the basic facts, if only to stop you bolting in hysteria when faced with your client." He paused. "But of course, you did bolt, didn't you?"

"I wasn't hysterical," she snapped. "And for the last time, I don't know your uncle."

His face tautened with disdain. "And for the last time, I tell you I don't believe you." He shoved back his chair and stood. "I weary of this conversation, madam. I bid you goodnight."

Just like that, he stalked out of the room. She heard his firm footstep cross the hall then the slam of the door as he left the house.

Thank heaven she was alone at last. The aching tension that had knotted her muscles since he'd fetched her from the bedroom eased a fraction and allowed her an unfettered breath.

Perhaps the marquess's mistrust was part of his affliction. Josiah had definitely gone a little strange toward the end. But he'd been old and sick. She didn't have the experience to judge the marquess's sanity. In her untutored opinion, he appeared disconcertingly intelligent. Certainly nothing escaped those perceptive eyes.

Was it possible to be both mad and coherent at the same time?

The urgent question, though, wasn't whether he was mad but what he intended to do. Until now, he'd only touched her to help her. Nor had he indicated he meant violence.

Until now.

She shivered and stared bleakly into the shadows. He was so much stronger than she. She remembered the latent power in his muscles when he'd carried her. If he threw himself upon her, she had no hope of fighting him off.

Should she flee? She couldn't escape the estate. But the night was fine, if cool. Sleeping outdoors wouldn't hurt her.

Outdoors she risked running into Monks and Filey.

Dear Lord, she couldn't face that. Whatever the marquess did, it had to be better than the degradation she'd meet at their hands.

She rose and staggered, grabbing the table for balance. She hadn't touched a drop of wine in years. On her empty stomach, even the small amount she'd imbibed made her head spin. She sucked in another deep breath and strove for clarity.

Why hadn't she been more careful? The last thing she needed was alcohol slowing her reactions. She was such a fool. She bent her head and waited for the dizziness to pass.

Her bedroom. That was her only sanctuary. She'd bar-

ricade the door. When the marquess returned, at least he
wouldn't find her waiting like a dog expecting its master.

How long did she have? He'd marched out in a huff but
he might decide roaming the night wasn't the only way to
work off his bad temper.

She had to make herself safe. And quickly.

She needed a weapon. Her trembling fingers curled
around the knife she'd used for dinner. It wasn't sharp
enough to do real damage, but it might slow him down.

Clutching the knife, she hurried upstairs so fast that her
candle threatened to flicker out. She hurled herself into the
elaborate bedroom and kicked the door shut behind her.
Then she slipped her knife into her pocket and raised her
candle to find the bolt.

No bolt. No lock of any kind.

Of course, this house was a madman's prison. His jailers would need continuous access. She should have realized
there would be no way to secure the door. With unsteady
hands, she slid the candle onto the dresser.

A heavy oak chest sat against the wall. She could pull
it in front of the door then pile other furniture on top. The
marquess was strong but she'd make sure not even Samson
could break into this room to ravish his reluctant Delilah.

She ranged herself against the far side of the chest and
pushed hard.

Nothing. No movement at all.

She took a deep breath and tried again. The chest didn't
budge. Again and again, she pushed. Eventually, she realized nothing would shift it.

Perhaps the dresser would serve. She straightened and
moved across to set her shoulder to the bulky piece of
furniture.

It didn't move an inch.

She pushed until the breath sawed in her lungs and her
muscles cramped with effort.

Her heart heavy with a dread she didn't want to face, she checked the rest of the room. The furniture was nailed to the floor so firmly that without heavy tools, she couldn't hope to pry it loose.

Fighting tears, she sank onto the bed's high mattress. All she had to show for her efforts were broken fingernails and aches and bruises where she'd slipped and fallen in her desperation.

She couldn't bar the door against the marquess. She was as defenseless up here as she'd been when her kidnappers had drugged her.

No, not quite. She fumbled for the knife. Although the grim truth was that it provided only the flimsiest protection.

She hadn't heard the marquess downstairs. Even as she strained to shift the room's heavy oak fittings, she'd listened avidly for his return.

Now it was late and she was stupid with weariness and fear. Her eyes stung with exhaustion but she couldn't allow herself to sleep. Clutching her knife in damp hands, she lay back against the pillows and stared into the candlelit room.

Grace stirred from her troubled sleep. It was dark. The candle must have burned out. She had the strange fancy she was a child again, safe in her room at Marlow Hall. The large bed, fine sheets, soft pillows under her head.

Then she realized *safe* was the last word she should use.

The faint breeze from the open door must have woken her. This puzzled her briefly as she knew she'd closed it when she came upstairs. She curled shaking fingers around her knife.

Her eyes adjusted to the darkness and she saw the tall silent man on the threshold. His stare burned unerringly through the darkness to where she lay.

Chapter 4

Matthew stood in the bedroom doorway, breathing heavily. Lust thundered through his veins and his heart hammered as though he'd just fought off a powerful assailant.

The room was dark and still, but he knew instinctively the woman was awake. And watching him.

He could see a pale glimmer where her face turned toward him. She didn't speak. He couldn't even hear her breathing. Every nerve in his body sensed that she waited for him to cross to the bed.

He could go to her now. He could have her. It was what she was here for.

She'd open her arms and offer up her body's secrets. He grew hard thinking about it. He'd lose himself in her honeyed depths and she'd give him the ease so long denied.

He braced his arms against the doorway on either side as if only physical effort stopped him surging across to take her. She wouldn't refuse him. She'd been paid to do this. Whatever her distaste for him, she'd honor her contract or face his uncle's wrath.

He'd paced the dank woods for hours, battling his baser self. And God help him, his baser self had won.

What man could resist when defeat was so sweet?

He shook his head as a drop of water traced a chilly path down his face. It had started to rain while he was outside. He hadn't cared, had hardly even registered the wet. It did nothing to douse the raging fire inside him.

Dismissing his uncle's plan had been easy when the doxy remained an imaginary creature. Faced with this defiant beauty, his resolution wavered, disintegrated.

Yet here he hesitated like a beggar at the kitchen door.

Why didn't she say something? Scream? Protest?

Invite him to touch her?

She must know her collusion with his uncle no longer mattered. All that mattered was she was female and he wanted her. Wanted her with every beat of his yearning heart.

As his uncle had known he would.

He curled his fingers so hard against the wood that the edges bit painfully into his flesh.

Jesus, had it come to this? Eleven lonely years of struggle to retain his humanity. Then one whiff of female and he forgot everything else?

He would not do it. He would not.

His uncle hadn't yet won. Although he came damned close with this latest sally.

Matthew could hold out against temptation.

Just.

Brave words. Only with the greatest difficulty did he straighten and step back.

He'd honed his mind as his weapon against Lord John. Only to find his body threatened to prove his downfall. His body and one exquisite strumpet.

As he retreated, she released her breath in a sobbing gasp.

She was frightened of the madman. Well, let her stay frightened. If she kept her distance, he might have a chance against her. Despair blacker than the surrounding night weighed his heart as he trudged downstairs to his mean, makeshift bed in the salon.

He was trying to accommodate his ungainly height to a sofa never designed for sleeping when he heard a sudden flurry of footsteps on the floor above.

The door to the bedroom slammed shut with enough force to rattle the windowpanes.

Late the next morning, Matthew worked in the walled courtyard, grafting his new hybrid to some rootstock. He felt an electric shift in the air and looked up to find the wench staring at him from the red brick archway. She looked in better health than yesterday, although her face was still stark with suffering and her cobalt eyes still cut to his soul.

"Good morning," he said stiffly. The hand holding the grafting knife dropped away from the rose bush.

"Good morning, my lord," she responded with those damnably perfect manners.

Her gaze fixed on the knife but she didn't retreat. Even after one day, he was used to her daring. She took a wary step from the shadow of the ivy and entered the heart of his private kingdom.

Then he noticed what she wore and he almost groaned aloud. The teal dress hung loosely on her slight frame and slashed perilously low across her magnificent bosom. He could see the rounded tops of her breasts and the intriguing valley between them. The neckline drooped so all he could think about was how easily he could bare that creamy bounty.

Manfully, he dragged his gaze from her cleavage to meet her accusing glare.

Well, what could she expect when she flaunted herself in whore's regalia?

Last night, he'd sworn never to touch her. But it was

only human to look, wasn't it? Looking couldn't hurt. But looking led inevitably to touching.

If he touched her, he was lost.

She wrapped her arms around herself to hide her eye-catching décolletage. An attractive flush lay high on her cheekbones. He had to give his uncle credit for unearthing the only whore in Christendom who remembered how to blush.

He returned his attention to what he was doing. It took him a hellishly long time. For once, his thoughts were far from his botanical experiments.

Any conversation had faltered after the greeting. What did he know of entertaining the fair sex? Nothing. And right now, he told himself with no great conviction, he was glad.

He waited for her to accept the dismissal. She merely hovered near the archway as if she were as ill at ease as he.

Nice touch, he thought grimly. And snagged his thumb on a thorn for his trouble.

He wiped the spot of blood on his linen shirt and glared at her. Against his will, he made a detailed inventory of the figure the dress displayed. The narrow waist. The way the shiny material skimmed the outward curve of her hips. She wasn't wearing petticoats—indication enough of her lack of virtue—and the light behind her offered glimpses of her legs through the skirt.

Every drop of moisture in his mouth evaporated as his gaze traced their slender length. He clenched his hands at his sides to stop himself from reaching for her.

After a tense silence, she moved. Unfortunately not away, but closer. Closer so the faint breeze carried drifts of her scent to torment him.

She still smelled like sunshine. But today her soap hinted at the heavier perfume of jasmine. He wished he didn't like it. He closed his eyes as he enumerated his reasons to despise and mistrust this woman.

"My lord," she began. She sounded nervous, an impression fortified when he opened his eyes to see her fingers laced together in an unsuccessful attempt to hide their trembling.

The gesture was disarming. He steadfastly refused to be disarmed.

"Mmm?" He wished she'd disappear. He wished she'd take one short step and press all that flower-scented loveliness against him.

"My lord," she said more firmly, staying exactly where she was, confound her. She hitched at the dress's neckline but it slipped down immediately. "We need to talk."

Matthew's mature experience of women was sketchy to the point of nonexistence. But he was acute enough to know those words from a female promised trouble.

"I'm busy." He studied his new rose as if it held the secrets of the ages on its barren stalk.

She sighed with impatience. "This won't take long."

Startled, he lifted his head and looked into her eyes for the first time. "You're not frightened anymore."

A steady blue gaze met his. "Of course I'm still frightened," she snapped. "But cowering away at the mere sight of you won't do any good. And I've worked out that if you meant to hurt me, you'd have done so already."

She raised her chin in a brave gesture that stirred his heart. My God, where had his uncle found her? She was a miracle.

"I might be lulling you into a false sense of security," he said dryly. He had to remember her candor and courage were weapons she used against him.

"Believe me, secure is a long way from how I'm feeling." Her eyes didn't waver. "I want your help to escape."

He threw his head back and laughed. She was so earnest, yet she must know her request was ridiculous.

Her fine dark brows had lowered with annoyance when he finally regained his breath. She'd even forgotten to fiddle with her dress. "I am overjoyed I provide your lordship with such amusement," she said with heavy sarcasm.

He sobered immediately. "That is your purpose, is it not?" he responded in a silky tone.

He turned his back to go to the greenhouse for more binding to finish the graft. Perhaps his deliberate rudeness would chase her off. But of course, it didn't. Instead, she came after him, close enough for damned jasmine to mingle with the other scents that surrounded him, of spring flowers and freshly turned soil.

"Lord Sheene, I suspect our . . . intimacy is as unwelcome to you as to me."

That made him pull up so suddenly that she crashed into his back, every luscious inch of her.

He turned on her, fighting the urge to sweep her up in his arms, and barked, "What makes you say that?"

She stepped away, thank God, before he could grab her and consign his war with his uncle to Hades. Her color was even higher and she breathed in gusty little mouthfuls. A perfect portrayal of an innocent woman who found a man's proximity disturbing. He'd have applauded her performance if he hadn't been so disturbed himself.

She went on in an unsteady voice. "Your manner, for one thing. You clearly resent my presence. Also last night, you didn't . . ."

"Force my disagreeable person upon you?" he finished for her and saw her flinch.

"If you were in a fever of lust, you'd have already had me. I told you I'm a widow and not unacquainted with men and their . . . needs."

He nearly laughed again. She sounded prim as any spinster schoolmistress. All the time, she stood there arrayed like an expensive tart and driving him out of his mind with her nearness.

As if he weren't out of his mind already.

He folded his arms and surveyed her down the length of his nose. "Madam, if I could get you out of here, I would. But your only hope of leaving is my uncle. And having brought you here, he'll be less than eager to let you go."

She made a curiously defeated gesture. "I know what you think. But I truly am a victim in this. I lost my way in Bristol and wandered into a rough quarter of town. Monks and Filey caught me and drugged me. Surely you cannot doubt I was dosed with laudanum to ensure I didn't struggle."

He gave her credit for sticking to her story. "Both the constraint and the drug could be tricks to convince me of your innocence."

"You still don't believe me," she whispered. Then more strongly, "Look at me, Lord Sheene. Do I look like a . . . a whore?"

"You look more the part today than you did yesterday," he said frankly.

She went back to plucking unhappily at her dress but it continued to cling like a loose green skin. "I know, but this was the least revealing thing I could find."

His curiosity roused. The rest of her wardrobe must be provocative indeed. He stifled the ribald images flooding his brain.

Still she fidgeted with her clothing. She certainly gave a realistic show of someone uncomfortable in what she wore. She ended up folding her arms across her bosom again, to his unwilling regret.

"There was a woman. Mrs. Filey, I suppose. She drew

me a bath and took my black dress. I assumed she meant to brush it down but she didn't bring it back. She wouldn't answer me when I asked her what happened to it. And she wouldn't return my petticoats."

"She's deaf, has been for years," he said flatly. "I believe Filey clouted her too hard about the head after one of his drinking bouts. I see no reason why she can't speak but I've never heard her do so."

The girl whitened until he could almost see the veins beneath her skin. "That's awful."

"I don't need to tell you the man is a brute."

"Then I don't need to tell you why I need help," she said with a hint of asperity. She reminded him briefly of the shabby duchess he'd met yesterday with her threadbare gown and her imperious manner. "Will you ask your uncle to let me go?"

This time his laugh held a grim tinge. "Mrs. Paget, my uncle pays no heed to my wishes. I expressed abhorrence of this latest scheme before your arrival."

"Well, perhaps I could ask him."

He shrugged and turned away, heading toward his greenhouse. "If you can get a message to him, you're welcome to try. He's a man who follows his own notions. His current notion is that I need a woman to share my delightful idyll. You're unquestionably a woman so I doubt he'll stir himself to find a replacement."

"I cannot accept we're stuck in this impossible situation."

Yet again, she pursued him. Couldn't the blasted chit take a hint?

He didn't pause nor did he look at her. "You will."

This time he managed to escape by going into the greenhouse and shutting the door firmly after him.

He should have known she wouldn't leave the matter there.

* * *

That afternoon Matthew wandered through the woods with Wolfram. He remained blind to the beauty of dappled sunlight breaking through new leaves. Instead, his mind fixed on his problem.

The woman.

Mrs. Paget.

Grace.

He'd been little more than a boy when he was confined. Even so, his recollection of the world beyond these walls didn't include whores who spoke in cultured accents and deliberately played down their attractions. She was a beautiful woman but she didn't use paint and she insisted on that unbecoming hairstyle.

He had a sudden intense urge to see her hair down. It would be long and shining as it tumbled about her naked shoulders. Even the severe braids around her head couldn't conceal her hair's luxuriance.

He drew a tight rein on his imagination. She was dangerous enough to his control fully dressed. Or as close to fully dressed as that green gown allowed.

If she wasn't a common prostitute, what was she? Why would a woman like her agree to this scheme?

Was she indeed a temporarily unengaged actress? It was possible. With destitution as the alternative, the prospect of tupping a madman might be attractive. His uncle mightn't even have given her so much information.

When Matthew had told her he was insane, her shock had almost convinced him.

If she didn't know he was mad, why did she think he was held prisoner? She must have known, which meant all her show of dismay and fear was just that—a show.

Perhaps she had another reason for falling in with his uncle's machinations. Perhaps she wasn't here for money, but for love.

He swore under his breath and kicked discontentedly at

the leaf litter on the path. If the woman were his uncle's cast-off mistress, a great deal made sense.

Like her air of innocence. His uncle wasn't above corrupting a respectable woman. His uncle, for all his public probity, wasn't above much. Eleven years of captivity had taught Matthew that.

This could explain why she set out to diminish her beauty. In her heart, she remained loyal to her original protector. Maybe she was unable to face bedding another man.

His uncle was unprincipled enough to ruin an innocent and turn her to his purpose. Any enjoyment Lord John got from the woman would be a bonus. What became of the jade afterward wouldn't worry him.

The snag with this perfectly logical explanation was that Matthew found it even more unpalatable than the unpalatable alternatives. Hellish images hurtled through his mind. His uncle thrusting between the woman's pale thighs. His uncle's hands stroking her bare skin. His uncle's mouth tasting that smooth white flesh.

"Christ!" He crashed his clenched fist into the smooth gray bark of a beech.

Pain wrenched him back to reality. He hadn't suffered one of his fits for years. He couldn't go on like this. He'd make himself ill. And he'd kill himself before he descended into that shuffling, mindless, quaking wretch again.

Wolfram's cold nose pressed into his dangling left hand. Matthew absently stroked the dog's head, finding comfort in the animal's steadfast affection.

The woman was here until his uncle chose to remove her. All Matthew could do was avoid her. Difficult when they shared a house. Still, it counted as a strategy of sorts.

Feeling more in control, he headed back to the cottage, only to watch his pathetic plan crumble before his eyes.

Monks and Filey were in the yard behind the house.

That in itself was nothing unusual. But when Matthew
paused in the shade of the trees, he caught a glimpse of
bright green satin against the bricks. His brawny jailers
were ranged between the girl and Matthew so he could see
no more of her.

What was the fool woman up to?

Matthew signaled Wolfram to stay. Monks and Filey
closed in on their prey and didn't notice as he edged up
behind them. What he heard as he came within earshot
froze his blood to ice.

"Happen there's only one way you're leaving, lass.
That's dead as a doornail. Do it now or wait until his lordship has his fill. Any road, it's up to you." Monks spoke
softly but clearly. Matthew could have told her the quieter
the thug became, the more lethal he was.

"And first, I'll have my go." Filey stepped to one side of
the girl so they had her boxed against the brickwork. "I'll
not throw away such a grand chance."

"I'm trying to tell you you've made a mistake. I'm a
respectable widow, not a . . . a whore."

Matthew still couldn't see Mrs. Paget past the broad
backs. But he heard how she struggled to maintain the
sweet reasonableness of her tone. Good God, she spoke to
these two unpredictable curs as if she invited them to tea.

Monks snickered. "All lasses are whores. Any road,
whatever you once were, you'll learn to play a whore's part
right fast."

Her voice developed a pleading note. "Let me go. I
won't tell anyone what you've done. You have my word."

Did she know the danger she courted? Anger at her
recklessness tasted sour in Matthew's mouth.

Monks laughed again. Even Matthew, who knew his
adversary of old, couldn't restrain the shiver that ran down
his spine at the pure evil of the sound. "Your word, eh?
That's worth nowt to me. No, you stay and keep his sod-

ding lordship happy. He might be out of his head but he's right pretty, I reckon."

"He doesn't want me," she said.

Matthew closed his eyes in despair. Christ, what had she done? Whether she was a willing instrument in Lord John's schemes or merely an innocent swept into this fiendish game—and at this precise moment he couldn't say for sure—she'd just signed away her life.

"Eh, the lad's nowt but shy," Filey said coaxingly. "He'll get over that soon enow."

"No, I'm not to his taste," she persisted, idiot girl.

"Eh, then it's daft to keep you," Monks said in a businesslike tone. "Filey, use the wench until tomorrow then I'll finish her off."

"No," she protested frantically. "You don't understand."

Filey chuckled with lascivious eagerness. "Oh, we understand right well, flower. It's you who's a mite confused. His lordship has you, then I do, then we shut you up good and proper with a hit on the head or a knife to the neck. If his lordship's not interested, we skip the first step." He grabbed her arm and dragged her toward him.

"Let me go!" she cried out, writhing in her captor's grip.

Even if she was a lying trull, Matthew couldn't help but pity her terror and helplessness. Terror and helplessness he'd felt often enough himself over the last eleven years. He resented but couldn't stifle his swift empathy. It no longer mattered whether she conspired against him. All that mattered was that she was small and defenseless and the only champion she could call on was Matthew Lansdowne.

"What is the meaning of this?" he snarled, stepping forward. He signaled to Wolfram and the dog loped up, his hackles rising.

Monks turned toward him and sketched a bow. These

days, his jailers preserved superficial respect for his rank. When they'd had him bound before them, they hadn't been so careful. Perhaps they thought in his raving, he'd neither register nor remember their cruelty.

"My lord. This slut hasn't met with your approval. We'll take her away and get you a new one."

"I'm not a toy," the woman snapped, still trying to wriggle free of Filey's bruising hold.

"Shut your gob, bitch," Monks said. "Or I'll shut it for you."

"You have no right to speak to me like that," she objected in her cut-glass accent, a perfect match for Matthew's.

"I warned you." Monks raised a clenched fist.

Matthew got there first, his arm upheld to fend off the blow. Staring fixedly into Monks's small dirt-colored eyes, he stood like a barrier in front of the frightened girl.

"Damn you, let her be." He summoned every ounce of Lansdowne arrogance. And still knew it mightn't be enough.

It was enough for Filey. He released the chit and shifted away. "Beg pardon, your lordship," he muttered, keeping a nervous eye on Wolfram.

Matthew wasn't so sure of Monks. For a long space, the brute stared with obstinate hatred into his face. Eventually something—fear of future consequences, unwillingness to break the fragile but long-held truce between them— made Monks's eyes flicker away.

The girl was still at Matthew's back. He reached behind to snatch her arm and tug her forward to stand beside him. He didn't look at her but he felt the convulsive tremors that ran through her. Thankfully, for once she'd decided silence was her best tactic.

"This lady is under my protection. If harm comes to her, my uncle will hear. I promise you, he won't be pleased."

Monks might be in retreat but he was far from defeated.

His lips stretched in a leering smile. "So I take it the bitch is mistaken and you do want her, your lordship?"

Matthew hesitated. Admitting he wanted the woman meant he enlisted in his uncle's foul scheme.

If he didn't claim her, she would die.

Triumph glowed in Monks's eyes. He was far from stupid and he was party to many of Lord John's plots. He knew the significance of this moment.

Matthew couldn't say it. To save his soul, he couldn't.

At his side, the girl choked back a terrified sob. She stood close enough for the scent of jasmine to lure his senses. She was warm against his body. Warm and alive.

He looked steadily into his enemy's eyes and spoke with calm certainty. "Yes, I want her. She is mine."

The words wouldn't have been nearly so difficult to say if they hadn't been the absolute truth.

Chapter 5

~~~~~~~~~

Grace heard the marquess speak from a great distance. The actual words hardly registered. Shaking with sick relief, she pressed against his side. He was all that shielded her from unimaginable horror. His ruthless grip on her arm anchored her to reality, stopped her screaming out her fear.

Her disbelieving heart thundered two words over and over. *I'm safe, I'm safe, I'm safe.*

Monks grinned at Lord Sheene in a horribly knowing way that made cold sweat break out all over her body. "I wish your lordship good sport. Eh, I'll be right glad to give you tips on pleasing a lass."

The marquess's smooth baritone dripped ice. "Keep a civil tongue in your head, Monks. Treat this lady with respect or by God, you'll answer for it."

Lord Sheene's arm slid around Grace's shoulders and drew her into his body. Like an elixir against panic, the clean smell of his skin wafted out to tease her. It was familiar although she'd have thought herself too disoriented yesterday to notice his scent.

"That goes for you too, Filey." He sounded like a man who commanded armies, not a poor captive lunatic. "Now leave us."

The aura of authority must have convinced. Filey and Monks scuttled off in bowing confusion. Only when they were out of sight did Lord Sheene untangle himself and step away. Grace immediately missed his heat and strength.

"Are you all right?" His hauteur had vanished. He sounded concerned, kind. The hostility for once was absent.

Grace wrapped her arms around herself to control her shaking but they didn't provide the warmth she'd found in Lord Sheene's embrace. Her legs felt like they might collapse under her. She needed a couple of attempts before she could control her voice enough to reply. "They . . . they didn't hurt me."

"They would have. It was foolhardy to confront them." Intent golden eyes ranged over her. Eventually, he gave a nod as if he accepted she was unharmed. "I believe your story about the kidnap."

Well, hoorah for you. Good honest anger swamped her dread. Renewed energy made her straighten and glare at him. "I appreciate your condescension, my lord. Any man with eyes in his head could see I was telling the truth."

His lips curved in another of his wry smiles. "You forget you're dealing with a poor mad fool, Mrs. Paget."

His show of charming self-derision made her angrier. Unless she got away, she'd pitch something at his handsome head.

"I think you are precisely as mad as you wish to be, my lord." She whirled around and marched toward the house, cursing every male born into this miserable world.

By the time she came downstairs for dinner, Grace regretted her temper. It had been reaction to her paralyzing fear when Monks spoke so dispassionately of killing her. She shuddered anew at what could have happened if Lord Sheene hadn't saved her.

If Lord Sheene hadn't claimed her as his.

Of course, it meant nothing. He didn't want her. If he wanted her, he could have her. What stopped him extending those elegant hands and taking her? He'd even come to her room last night, then hadn't been able to stomach the act.

When she quietly entered the salon and saw him standing at the window, her heart began to race. She told herself she trembled because she was scared. But years of endurance and unhappiness had taught her unflinching honesty. Along with fear, other emotions stirred. Her wariness of the marquess held none of the gagging revulsion Filey aroused.

Lord Sheene kept his back to her as he looked out into the twilight. Yet again, his isolation struck her. His physical isolation. And also his spiritual isolation. Perhaps that alone constituted his madness. So far, she'd seen little other sign of his affliction.

He spoke without turning. "Stay away from Monks and Filey. They don't make idle threats."

Again, that instinctive animal awareness of what happened around him. Were all madmen so attuned to their surroundings?

She wouldn't have thought so.

A sudden memory pierced her of his intense concentration on the spindly rose bush that morning. His hands had been so deft, their very sureness breathtakingly beautiful. Her wayward heart dipped into an unsteady dance at the thought of those hands on her skin.

Grace, stop it! You're in enough trouble as it is.

Heavens, she must regain self-control and quickly. The last thing she needed was an infatuation with her fellow captive. She hadn't thought about a man touching her for pleasure in years. Certainly not since her marriage and the collapse of her girlish fantasies.

She stepped up to stand beside him. The window faced

the darkening woods. The day had been clear. Now the first stars shone in the cloudless sky. It could have been a landscape by Claude, if one didn't know an unscaleable wall circled the trees or two homicidal devils guarded the gate to this perilous Eden.

The silence allowed her to say something she was guiltily aware she should have said earlier. "Thank you, my lord. If you hadn't come . . ."

"Don't think about it." He focused those uncanny eyes on her. Except that after a day and a half, she noticed their strangeness less and their beauty more.

"I can't help it." She'd been frightened and wretched for so long, even before her abduction. But nothing matched the horror that had gripped her when Monks stared into her face and promised rape and death. Compared to that, the mad marquess was a bastion of security. The clinging ghost of today's panic made her speak more freely than usual. "You were magnificent."

A bleak smile tilted his generous mouth. "Hardly."

He swung away from the window. He clearly couldn't bear standing so close to her. Perhaps her gaudy clothing disgusted him. She hitched at her amber silk gown's neckline but it remained as provocative as when she'd put it on upstairs. A clashing pink sash cinched it around her waist but she hadn't been able to fix the loose bodice.

She'd turned the bedroom upside down seeking her widow's weeds. No black bombazine, but she'd found plenty of gowns to make a cyprian blush. She lacked nothing a whore required for her trade. Slippers dyed to match the tasteless dresses. Drawers full of filmy underwear such as she'd never seen, even in her days at Marlow Hall. A coffer overflowing with cheap jewelry. Boxes of cosmetics.

She'd also found a chest of the marquess's clothes.

There was something unbearably intimate, almost marital, in having his personal belongings under her hand.

As if he could pop in at any time to select tonight's shirt or neckcloth. She'd quickly slammed the lid down on the neatly folded attire. The idea of him making free of her bedroom wasn't quite so easy to shut away.

After a long search, this tent of a dress was the best she'd come up with. It threatened to slide off into a slippery pile, leaving her clad in only her shift. She could just imagine how the marquess would turn his well-bred nose up at that.

Why should she care for his approval? They were strangers flung together in an impossible situation. Whether he liked her was irrelevant. Already she spent too much time thinking of him in ways she shouldn't.

Running the farm, she'd dealt with men from dawn to dusk. Workmen, farmers, tradesmen, merchants. She was used to men. Why was she in such a flutter over this particular one?

She took a deep breath, smoothed her voluminous skirts and turned to find him pouring two glasses of wine. Still keeping his distance, he extended one toward her. "Do you want to tell me again how you came here? I dismissed your earlier explanations as lies cooked up with my uncle's conniving."

She stared into his face, automatically noting its pleasing arrangement of planes and angles. This . . . relationship between them might be simpler if he were less physically compelling. The impact of his appearance was distracting, dangerous, frightening.

His gaze remained intent upon her. "Unless you'd rather not speak of your ordeal." He gestured her toward the sofa.

"Thank you." She sat down, watching him take his place on a chair opposite. It was all so civilized, she had to remind herself they weren't in a London drawing room.

Would he seem so extraordinary if she'd met him out

in the world? Through her churning tempest of emotion, a voice insisted she'd notice his quality anywhere.

As she glanced across to where he lounged like a decadent dark-haired angel against the tapestry chair, she felt curiosity but no apprehension. This evening, he looked fearsomely elegant, the complete aristocrat. Even someone as woefully out of touch with fashion as she could see his black superfine coat had cost a fortune. It fit him with the smoothness and ease only the best tailoring gave. The splendor daunted a woman who had lived in poverty for so long. She felt at a distinct disadvantage in her ill-fitting harlot's costume.

She took a deep breath to quiet her nerves. "My lord, I'm a widow from a farm near Ripon in Yorkshire."

He still watched her. She should be used to that by now. But a scurry of awareness up her spine told her she was far from indifferent to that unwavering gold stare.

His gaze dipped into her gaping cleavage before he looked away with a tight expression. Dear Lord, he couldn't think she meant to entice him, could he? No wonder she aroused his disgust.

"Ripon is a long way from Somerset," he said neutrally. "The other end of the country."

"I know, but . . . financial necessity forced me to accept a home with my cousin who is a vicar near Bristol." Because her pride smarted at admitting her indigence, she went on quickly. "Vere didn't arrive as arranged. I waited and waited and still he didn't come. So I went looking for him."

"And in the process ran into Monks and Filey. You were unlucky."

Unlucky. Such a paltry word to describe the disaster she'd tumbled into.

"Yes. And stupid." Looking back, she couldn't believe

she'd accepted their company so easily. "It will sound absurd, but I heard their voices and the sound reminded me of home." To hide her disintegrating composure, she sipped at her wine.

As the marquess toyed with his glass, light caught the rich red depths of the claret. He'd hardly drunk at all. She'd already noticed his abstemious habits.

He glanced up at her from under his slashing brows. "How long have you been widowed?"

Turning her head, she blinked away tears. "A month." She paused to strive for composure. "Five weeks on Thursday."

She looked back swiftly enough to catch the anger that contorted the marquess's face.

"Sweet Jesus, you've hardly had time to mourn your loss before my damned uncle dragged you into this catastrophe." Burning gold eyes focused on her. Yet she shivered under their heat as though an icy wind howled around her. "When he broached this appalling scheme, I knew he'd moved beyond all restraint. He should be put down like a rabid dog."

"It's not your fault," she said helplessly, sensing the guilt that underlay his outburst.

"Yes, it is," he said bitterly. "I should have died years ago, when I first fell ill."

"No." Why did the idea of his death cut so deeply? "Never say that."

His eyes sharpened on her. "Do you have children?"

She found herself blushing and stammering as if he'd made an improper suggestion. "No, we didn't . . . We never . . . We couldn't . . ." She sucked in a breath as old sorrow rose to choke her. "No."

She waited for the inquisition. Country folk had no qualms about discussing reproduction, animal or human.

She was used to people prying into her barrenness. Not that familiarity made the questions easier.

Lord Sheene merely nodded and rose to disentangle the glass from her deathly grip before she tipped claret over her awful gown. "Mrs. Filey's dinner grows cold."

Again he served her. Chicken in brandy cream sauce. Fresh vegetables. A beef and mushroom pie that smelled like heaven when the marquess placed it before her. How unlikely that slimy Filey had a wife capable of creating this feast.

No more unlikely, she supposed, than that prim Grace Paget should be mistaken for a whore.

The reminder erased the brief well-being provided by fine wine and good food. "My lord, I'm the victim of a misunderstanding. Surely your uncle will release me once he realizes I'm a respectable woman."

Not so respectable, a sly voice whispered inside her. Your husband lies dead just five weeks, yet here you slaver over the marquess.

Lord Sheene frowned and laid his knife and fork on his plate. Yet again, she noticed he lacked appetite for the sumptuous fare. "Mrs. Paget, I'm afraid it's you who misunderstands. After this afternoon, you must realize your circumstances are hopeless."

Grace set down her own cutlery with much less finesse than the marquess. "Sir, for nine years, people have informed me my circumstances are hopeless. I didn't believe them and I certainly don't believe you."

A humorless smile curled his lips. How would he look if he smiled properly, without restraint, with genuine joy? Her heart gave a strange stutter at the thought.

"That's very commendable, madam, but I'm afraid reality has finally caught up with you. Hopelessness is the essence of life here."

"I don't accept that."

"You will."

He sounded so sure. The food she'd eaten congealed into a cold lump in her stomach. With shaking hands she reached for her glass. "There has to be a way out," she said unsteadily, lifting her wine, then replacing it before she spilled it.

"If there is, I've never found it." Fierce pity lit his eyes.

"Perhaps if I speak to your uncle . . ."

The grim smile still hovered. "You belong to this secret kingdom now. Once that happens, there's no escape."

"But you believe my story, don't you?" For some reason, his faith in her was vitally important.

He studied the cooling food before him as if seeking the best way to offer a denial. But when he looked up again, his gaze didn't waver. "Yes, I believe you."

Grace relaxed slightly. "Thank you."

"Virtuous woman or not, you cannot leave." He paused then spoke in a low voice laden with emphasis. "Let me assure you, Mrs. Paget, I swore to my uncle I wouldn't lay a finger on any woman he found. That's as true for the grieving widow as it is for the harlot."

She should be grateful to hear that. But the tangled skein of emotion within her permitted no such uncomplicated reaction.

He frowned at her silence. "You have my word. I know you don't trust me. There's no reason you should."

Actually, she did trust him. Which probably meant she was as mad as he. So far, he'd done nothing but help and protect her. Even when convinced she conspired against him, he hadn't hurt her.

And he'd saved her from Monks and Filey by lying, even though the lie played right into his uncle's hands. She already guessed that if the marquess used her body, he somehow ceded victory to the unknown Lord John. There were longstanding tensions and currents here she couldn't hope to understand. It was clear Lord Sheene and his uncle engaged in a war. Lord John had tossed her over into the marquess's lines like a *grenado* primed to explode.

Her hand trembled as she lifted her napkin to her mouth. "I find I am a little tired."

"As you wish, Mrs. Paget. Sleep well." He inclined his head and candlelight glanced across the shining black wing of hair. The breath stuck in her throat. He was so beautiful. And so hurt. He made her want to cry.

He rose when she left, as if she were a lady and not his unwilling whore. For that's what she was, whether he chose to avail himself of her services or not.

Only as Grace lay awake—and alone—in the great bed upstairs did she acknowledge the feeling that burned her like acid. Not fear. Not anger. Not desperation. Although all those emotions seethed endlessly inside her.

When the marquess had sworn he wouldn't touch her, her principal reaction had been aching disappointment.

Chapter 6

Lord Sheene's acceptance of Grace's story should have eased their interactions. That, and his stated intention not to touch her. But after three days, she was near screaming with the tension that thickened the air, a tension that lay strangely separate from her perpetual fear of her jailers. A tension based on how her pulse surged when she saw the marquess, heard the marquess. Heaven help her, even thought about the marquess.

Grace told herself to ignore his lordship the way he ignored her. He made no secret of his lack of interest. No matter how early she rose, he was always gone from the house. Unless she'd known better, she'd think he'd left. If every day didn't convince her he'd been right to dismiss any chance of escape.

They still met for dinner. But her attempts at conversation led nowhere. What could one speak to a madman about? Even if she was increasingly sure that, for all his reticence, his wits were in perfect working order.

Last night, she'd allowed him to guide the conversation. Silence begat more silence and she went to her bed after speaking only the few words politeness required. *Good evening, my lord. Thank you, my lord. Goodnight, my lord.*

Yet despite his unhidden reluctance for her company, she itched to be with him. Only in his vicinity did she quiet the panic that threatened to overwhelm her.

From her place on the sofa, she surveyed the stuffed bookcases lining the salon. Josiah had been an unsuccessful bookseller before he became an unsuccessful farmer. She knew to the penny what a fortune all this gold-embossed Moroccan leather and creamy paper constituted.

Grace put down the novel she'd hardly glanced at through the afternoon. The marquess must be a committed reader. Books in several languages and on hundreds of topics surrounded her. Unlike other libraries she'd seen, these books had been read, some many times over if creases on the bindings spoke true.

He was a great annotator. She sought out books he'd made notes in, although she was horrified that anyone would scribble over such fine volumes. The comments gave her some clue to his character, clues his continual absence kept to a minimum.

She'd also been through his desk, an unforgivable breach of privacy, but she was too desperate to contain her curiosity. She'd found letters from Lord John Lansdowne, short, curt, discreet, unless one knew what occurred on this enclosed estate.

More interesting had been drafts of articles in English, French, and Latin by someone called *Rhodon*. She assumed *Rhodon* was the marquess. Correspondence from editors of learned journals throughout Europe. Admiring notes from fellow scientists. Figures and notations that made little sense to her. Packages of papers forwarded from a London solicitor. *Rhodon* communicated via intermediaries with his intellectual cronies. She'd even found volumes of what at first she triumphantly decided were diaries. They'd turned out to be meticulously kept records of botanical experiments.

The marquess's writing was clear and beautiful. Not at all how she imagined the jottings of a madman.

She excused her behavior by saying it was perfectly natural to pry. He was the only other denizen of this well-appointed hell and she was at his mercy.

But she admitted in her heart she was obsessed with the marquess. Did he avoid her because he sensed her unhealthy interest? No virtuous woman should be so physically aware of a man who wasn't her husband. He was young and beautiful and she'd been trapped for months in a world of decay and death. Her blood warmed at the sight of a strong hand reaching for a wine glass. A hand that didn't shake, a hand unmarred with the brown stains of old age.

She sighed, impatient with herself. She could pursue evidence in margins like a hunter tracking deer through a thicket. Or she could try and catch her quarry in the open. The sun shone, the day was fresh and she was sick to death of her own edgy company. Perhaps if she spent more time with him, the mad marquess would lose his fascination and become just another man.

Perhaps.

As she rose, she straightened her shoulders the way her brother Philip always had before a fencing lesson. Lessons the young Grace would sneak into the ballroom to watch. The memory of her glittering older brother brought the usual grief. Even though it was two years since she'd learned of his death, she still hardly believed all that shining promise lay in cold earth.

No more sorrow. It was time to act. "*En garde*, my lord," she whispered, and left to face her enigmatic opponent.

Grace found the marquess holed up with his roses. He had his back to her and did something abstruse with what looked to her uneducated eyes like a dead stick.

"What do you want?" he growled without glancing up.

How did he know she hovered in the brick archway behind him? She wiped her damp palms on the skirts of her garish yellow gown. She'd been busy with needle and thread so at least this dress fitted, even if it was too tight across the bosom. Mrs. Filey had returned the black bombazine but in this warm weather, it itched.

Determined to start as she meant to proceed, she raised her chin. "A charming greeting, my lord."

He still didn't turn, but the long muscles of his back tensed under his loose white shirt. "I'm occupied, madam. Perhaps whatever it is can wait until dinner."

"Yes, it probably could, but I'll have lost my nerve by then," she muttered, hoping he wouldn't hear. But his hearing, like all his other senses from what she could tell, was preternaturally sharp.

"Well, all right, say what . . ." There was a pause, a sharp crack, then, "Damnation!"

She flushed at his language but didn't retreat. "You should know by now swearing at me won't chase me off."

At last he faced her. As she'd expected, his expression was stiff with well-bred annoyance. At such times, she had no difficulty picturing him as the haughty cynosure of society. "I've just wasted three hours' work."

"What?" Her attention fell to what he held. The dead stick was now two dead sticks. She raised mortified eyes to his. "I'm so sorry."

He met her gaze and she wondered what he was thinking. Then his lips twisted in a grimace and he tossed the sticks onto his rubbish pile. "Hell, what does it matter? It isn't as if I haven't time to do it again. Time is all I've got in this bloody cage."

The glimpse into his torment sent black shame swirling through her. She bit her lip. What right had she to badger him like a child demanding an adult's notice? He didn't owe her anything.

Bending her head, she started to leave. "I shouldn't have disturbed you."

He swore again under his breath then took a couple of paces after her. "No, wait."

His hand circled her arm. He hadn't touched her since he'd lied about wanting her. Through the thin barrier of yellow silk, his fingers burned like flame.

Shocked, her gaze flew to his. She thought she caught equal astonishment in the golden eyes. Then he masked his expression and his hand dropped away as if he couldn't bear to prolong the connection. He looked uncomfortable. "Mrs. Paget, forgive me. I'm in a filthy temper. Nothing's gone right for three days."

Her flesh tingled from his touch, brief as it had been. She hid the flash of hurt his persistent rejection aroused. "I'm sorry."

He shook his head and managed a rueful smile that she found far too beguiling. "No, I'm sorry. What do you want to talk about?"

Alone in the salon, she'd been sure she was right to accost him. Confronted with his lean strength, she was no longer so confident. "It doesn't matter."

"Yes, it does."

She sucked in a deep breath then spoke in a rush. "I know you don't want me here. I don't want to be here either. Can't we call a truce?"

He arched his eyebrows in perfect aristocratic hauteur. "I wasn't aware there was a war."

She felt her cursed color rising. With her fine, clear skin, she'd always been quick to blush. She thought she'd outgrown the habit. Apparently not, or at least not when she cornered supercilious noblemen.

Having come so far, she couldn't back out now. She twined her hands together and plowed on. "You'd have to spend time in my company for us to engage in hostilities, my lord."

Swift comprehension swept his striking features. "You pine for attention."

She felt like stamping her foot. "No, I pine for something to do. I pine for normal interaction."

"You're imprisoned with a lunatic, Mrs. Paget. Normal interaction isn't on offer."

Yet again, he used his affliction to keep her at bay. The words lost more of their edge every time he used them. "There are two people in this cage. Doesn't it make sense to try and be friends?"

His eyes closed. She supposed the prospect of friendship with a humble creature such as herself offended his sensibilities. After all, he was the great marquess and she was a poverty-stricken widow of no particular distinction, whatever grand setting she'd been born into.

"Friends?" he repeated faintly.

She resisted the urge to hit him with one of his flowerpots. "I realize the barriers of rank, my lord, but here we suffer a kind of equality, don't you think?"

His brows contracted as if he were in pain. "As equal as a madman and a sane woman can be."

She made a dismissive sound. "I give you leave to doubt my sanity, sir." She looked around helplessly, searching for inspiration in the neat beds of leafless rose bushes. "I'm used to being busy. On the farm, I did most of the labor as well as nursed my husband. If you don't want a friend, what about an assistant for your experiments?"

He looked surprised that she'd guessed his occupation. He looked unhappy that she insisted on his company. He looked resigned as if he recognized it was easier to relent. What he didn't look was pleased to accept her help.

She told herself she didn't mind. He was obviously inured to solitude. But another prickle of hurt jabbed at her.

As if to confirm his reluctance, he said, "The work's unexciting. And uncomfortable and dirty for a lady."

Good Lord, what did he think? That she was made of sugar?

"I assure you running a sheep farm was both unexciting and dirty." She met his eyes with a challenge. "If I find my delicate temperament overset, I promise I'll trot back to the house and never bother you again."

He didn't exactly smile but some of the tension drained from his expression. He'd looked brittle to the point of shattering when she'd come through the archway. "You're an obstinate scrap of a female, aren't you?"

Startling that the tragic marquess had it in him to tease her. But this was the first genuine amity he'd shown, so she let a smile touch her lips. "Not exactly a scrap."

"No, perhaps not."

Did she imagine that burnished gaze skimmed where her dress strained across her breasts? Her nipples tightened as if he'd touched them. Pray God, he didn't notice.

Now, when it was too late, she wondered if demanding his company was wise.

Dear Jesus, she wanted to be friends. *Friends*. And she looked at him so sweetly, he couldn't deny her, whatever his common sense screamed.

For three days, her nearness had driven Matthew mad, so mad that he'd feared a relapse. He'd struggled to stay away but nothing banished her from thoughts and dreams. Or stopped her presence permeating his haunts on the estate, places where he'd only known unbearable loneliness. Those lonely vigils seemed like lost paradise now Grace Paget had crashed into his stagnant existence like a boulder into a pond.

He spent as little time with her as he could, blocked her from all intimacy. Yet she was with him as he trudged unhappily around the woods. A single visit from her had shattered the hard-won peace he'd always found among his roses. Worst of all, she'd made the cottage hers in a way eleven years had never made it his.

How had she done it? She kept signs of her occupancy to a minimum. But the moment he crossed the threshold, the heady essence of Grace overwhelmed him.

The essence of Grace kindled desires he could never satisfy.

Every night, he lay awake and restless on that infernal sofa, knowing he only had to climb the stairs to fulfill every longing.

He had no right to climb those stairs. Grace was a virtuous woman imprisoned against her will. He couldn't use her as his whore.

Grace Paget was permanently beyond his reach.

Rapacious desire gnawed at him. The sight of her, the scent of her, the sound of her—oh, Christ, the touch of her, the effects of that thoughtless clasp on her arm still hurtled through his veins—were worse torture than anything Monks or Filey had ever perpetrated.

He stared wordlessly down at the source of his anguish and his delight. His silent ineptitude probably terrified her. He was, after all, a madman.

Although her manner toward him was remarkably free of fear. Even harping on his insanity didn't daunt her any more. Perhaps he should have tried harder to convince her he was dangerous. But after years of suffering real madness, he'd be damned before he assumed sham lunacy.

She stared up at him, her large eyes dark and questioning. Her breath emerged in soft huffs between her parted lips. Wanton color flushed those full lips.

He almost groaned. This awareness of every detail of another person was new. He resented it. He fought it. But he couldn't block it.

"My lord?"

She sounded breathless. It was an effort not to let his attention stray to her bosom again. He'd relinquish his hope of heaven to cup her warmth in his hands.

"You'll need a hat," he said abruptly, noticing the sun already added a pink tinge to her pale skin.

She must have realized he'd surrendered because she smiled. His wayward heart gave a great thud of despair as her lips stretched over white teeth and her blue eyes glowed.

He'd only seen her smile once and not at him, but at Wolfram. The memory plagued him, kept him awake on his uncomfortable bed. Christ, how was he going to survive?

"Thank you." She sounded far too glad to receive this small concession. Clearly, the lack of occupation chafed. She must be used to people and activity. A reminder of the barriers between them. Barriers he could never cross, however his soul wailed with misery in its cold wilderness.

Then the screws tightened further. She extended one slender hand in his direction. He stared down at her in horror.

As he hesitated, a frown shadowed her happiness and she started to withdraw her hand. "I'm sorry, my lord. It's habit. Whenever I made a bargain with another farmer, we always shook on the deal."

Ungraciously, he thrust his hand out and clasped hers. The contact lasted a second. The contact lasted a century. Long enough to feel the roughness of calluses. She hadn't exaggerated her familiarity with physical work. Again, he wondered about this woman with a duchess's manner and a navvy's hands.

Now they were *friends*—he silently damned the word—perhaps he'd find answers. And with every new secret he uncovered, it became more impossible to conceal his own dark secret. That he wanted her with every shred of his being and he had only his fragile honor to protect her.

The marquess really didn't like her. She should leave him alone. But she was weak and she wanted to be with him. She promised herself she'd be as unobtrusive as possible. Silent helpmeet was a role she'd perfected for Josiah.

Grace lowered her head with familiar meekness and said softly, "I'll go and put on something more suitable, my lord."

"You do that." He turned away as if he'd already dismissed her from his thoughts. Clearly, she was less important than all the vegetable matter around him.

Josiah had often accused her of vanity. If her dead husband could read the pique in her heart now, he'd know he was right. It was dangerous and sinful, but something in her begged the marquess to notice her as a woman, to admire her, to . . . *desire* her.

Then what, Grace? You were kidnapped to be his whore. Is that a part you want to play? Are you willing to embrace shame in return for pleasure?

And what makes you think he'll offer pleasure? You know what men do to women. There's precious little to entice you.

As she watched the marquess retreat, she admitted she was enticed. Very enticed indeed.

Five days in this place and already she questioned everything she believed about herself. She had to get away before the Grace Paget she'd created so painstakingly over the last nine years crumbled to nothing.

Troubled, she made her way back to the cottage.

"Eh, there you are, lass."

Her churning thoughts had stopped her noticing Monks in front of the cottage. He wore his usual surly expression. For once, there was no sign of Filey.

"Mr. Monks," she said warily. She hadn't spoken to him since that horrible afternoon when he'd threatened to kill her. She took a shaky step back, ready to flee. "What do you want?"

"His lordship asks to see you."

She frowned. "I've just left Lord Sheene."

Monks gave a grunt of humor. "Not the pretty marquess. Lord John Lansdowne. And if you'll take a word of advice for nowt, you won't keep him waiting."

In spite of the warning, she stared open-mouthed at him. Salvation arrived just when she gave up hope.

Surely when she told Lord John who she was, he'd let her go. She'd be free, free of this luxurious prison, free of danger, free of temptation.

"Well, take me to him." She was unable to suppress the lilt of relief in her voice.

Monks glanced at her doubtfully but gestured for her to precede him inside. The unknown Lord John's influence extended even to lending his unpleasant henchmen manners, it seemed. Grace hurried through to the salon where rescue awaited at last.

Chapter 7

"**H**ere be the wench, your lordship," Monks said with a bow, then left them.

Grace blinked as her eyes adjusted to the gloom after the bright sunshine. The room with its closed curtains was stuffy. For the first time, a fire burned in the grate, although it was a warm day.

A man sat almost unnaturally straight at the table where she and Lord Sheene took their meals. He wore a heavy brown wool coat. How could he bear the oppressive temperature?

She stepped forward and sank into the sweeping court curtsy she'd been taught as a girl. "My lord."

He didn't stand. As she rose, she met eyes of gelid gray in a long face. He bore a strong resemblance to his nephew although his features, while handsome, lacked Lord Sheene's striking beauty.

From the marquess's description, she'd expected a villain from a fairy story but this could be any well-to-do gentleman of her acquaintance. He was in his middle years with graying dark hair. Surely such a man couldn't countenance kidnap, rape, and murder. He seemed to embody respectability. His manner expressed disdain, certainly. She was both a woman and his social inferior so that hardly counted as a mark of irredeemable evil.

She cursed the yellow dress that proclaimed her a whore. If only she'd worn the black bombazine. At least its shabby black supported her story.

"You are the doxy Monks and Filey found in Bristol?" His voice was deep and unexpectedly pleasant.

"My lord, I protest the description." Instinct told her poised control would gain more headway than pathetic groveling. "My name is Grace Paget and I'm a virtuous widow. There's been a grievous mistake. I throw myself upon your mercy."

His eyebrows arched with surprise, she supposed at her cultivated accent. "Madam, this lie is absurd. My men said you were drumming up custom on the docks."

He spoke as if Grace were lower than dung in the gutter. Her fleeting hope contracted into a hard knot of despair. Did she think he'd remedy the error the moment she identified herself? What made her imagine he'd even believe her? What an idiot she was. She'd find no easy salvation here. Lord John had ordered her abduction. Monks and Filey had told her so. Lord Sheene had told her so.

She struggled to keep her voice steady, although with every second, this quietly spoken man frightened her more than his minions ever had.

"I got lost seeking my cousin who had arranged to meet me off the mail coach." With repetition, the tale became more threadbare than her widow's weeds. "I beg you to restore me to my family."

"This concoction could be an attempt to avoid an uncongenial client. Monks informs me you've yet to crawl into my nephew's bed."

Color rose in her cheeks at Lord John's casual, contemptuous reference. "Surely if I were the sort of woman who . . ." She swallowed and tried again. "Surely, a woman off the streets wouldn't hesitate to do your bidding."

"Perhaps." Frowning, he stared into the distance and tapped his fingers on the polished wood of the table.

The pause extended. And extended.

Eventually he focused on her with a disgruntled expression. "If what you say is correct, your presence is problematic. Monks was right to alert me to the difficulties." He didn't sound shocked, he sounded annoyed. He pointed to a chair opposite. "Please sit. Mrs. Paget, is it?"

She remained standing. Ignoring the fear prickling the back of her neck, she spoke with all the firmness she could muster. "I shall go and change into the clothes I arrived in. I've been missing nearly a week. My family will be concerned about my whereabouts."

Lord John's lips stretched in a humorless smile that reminded her sharply of the marquess at his most difficult. "They must continue to be concerned, my dear lady."

Surely he knew he had no right to hold her as his nephew's unwilling plaything. For all her poverty, she was a lady, deserving of his respect, his care. It was heinous enough that he'd planned to abduct a woman of easy virtue. To subject a female born to his own class to this treatment was unthinkable.

"I can't stay here." Dread and the airless room made her lightheaded. She curled her fingers over the back of the nearest chair for support. "Please let me go."

He tilted his head to study her. His reptilian eyes slid over her and she fought the urge to shield her breasts.

"Out of the question, Mrs. Paget. You could bring charges of abduction against me."

Her fingers clenched hard against the chair. "What if I give my word never to mention this house or what you've done?"

"Tempting, I'm sure." She saw he didn't mean it. "I find myself reluctant to rely on so fragile a prop as a female's promise."

Her voice broke. "I'll beg on my knees if I have to."

Aristocratic displeasure crossed his face. "Histrionics will only extend this embarrassing scene."

Inside her tight chest, her heart thudded the inexorable message that he'd never let her go, no matter how she cried and pleaded. "There must be something I can do. I don't belong here."

The disdain on his face hardened into ruthlessness. "Your life outside these gates matters not one whit, madam. Your fate was decided when my servants found you. The only way you'll leave this estate is in a shroud."

The gray stare was pitiless and unwavering. How could he threaten her with death and ruin and remain as emotionless as a monolith? In spite of the close atmosphere, she shivered as fear chilled her soul.

"I don't understand," she whispered. Her heart drummed a frantic rhythm and breathing became a struggle.

"Don't you?" His voice was calm. When she didn't say anything, he went on with a hint of impatience. "Monks should have explained. If he failed to clarify your situation, my nephew should have exerted himself to outline your duties."

Rage swept in and bolstered her faltering courage. "I am aware why I am here, my lord. But you must see I'm no whore."

The man opposite made a slight moue of distaste. "You must learn to act one then, Mrs. Paget. I brought you here to entertain Lord Sheene. If you fail to gain his approval— as from all reports you have, I hear he goes out of his way to shun you—you are of no use."

"Then let me go."

His impatience became more marked. "Do you not listen, you tiresome young woman? Once your usefulness is over, so is your life. If my nephew finds you diverting, you live as his mistress until he wearies of you. If you cannot stomach a madman's touch, your end comes without delay. I don't store tools with no function."

"He's not mad," she said in a thin voice, then wondered why, given all the threats she faced, defending the marquess should be her first response.

Lord John laughed softly as if she'd made a witty remark at a society event. "He's gulled you into thinking he's sane, has he? I must say he can be quite convincing. Until he starts to shake and drool and lose control of his bowels. I doubt you'd be so quick to defend him then."

The picture was so graphic, nausea rose in her throat. She wanted to call Lord John a liar. But what did she know? She'd been here five days. His uncle had known the marquess all his life. Still, she spoke through stiff lips. "I don't believe you."

"It is of no importance what you believe." His tone hardened. "You have one week to lure my nephew into your bed."

She stepped back from the chair and straightened her shoulders. Even in the overheated room, the sweat on her skin was cold, although not as cold as the bleak knowledge seeping into her mind. *There was no escape. There would never be any escape.*

"And if I don't?"

Lord John's expression became, if anything, more condescending. "You die and I instruct Monks and Filey to locate a replacement. Hopefully, one with a greater sense of self-preservation."

"This is monstrous." She sought but failed to find guilt or regret in his impassive face.

"Yes, perhaps it is." He sounded unconcerned.

She pressed one shaking hand to her roiling stomach

to calm it. "So it's death or dishonor?" she said with false bravado.

"Death in any case," he said negligently. Then he paused and a calculating light entered the flat gray eyes. "Although if you prove your trustworthiness and bring my nephew up to snuff, we needn't be so final about your eventual fate."

"What do you mean?" she asked, even though she knew he played with her to gain obedience and had no intention of negotiating concessions. She'd been a naïve fool when she rushed into this room, but she was a naïve fool no longer.

He shrugged. "Just that I reward those who serve me well. This past year, Sheene hasn't been himself. If I see you've taken my wishes to heart and my nephew returns to his former health and vigor, you may rely on my gratitude."

She was past guarding her words. "So if I prostitute myself, the payment is freedom?"

He didn't even blink at her biting question. "I offer the suggestion merely as incentive." He stood. He was tall, but not as tall as the marquess. "You have a week. One guarantee I will make is if you fail, next Saturday is your last day on earth. After Monks and Filey have taken their turn at you, of course. They blundered in this scheme, but they're faithful. As I said, I reward loyalty."

"You're a devil." The words seemed to come from a long way away. She sucked in a gulp of heavy air but her vision remained cloudy. While a suffocating sense of unreality rose to crush her, one memory remained cruelly clear. Filey's hands mauling her breasts and his foul breath in her face as he promised degradation.

Death she could bear if she must. The prospect of Lord John's foul henchmen raping her made her want to scream until she had no voice left.

The monster came around the table and gripped her

arm in merciless fingers. "Think upon what I've said, Mrs. Paget. You're comely enough to snare my nephew if you try."

He trailed one white hand down her cheek. She tried to flinch away but subsided into shuddering stillness when he pressed his thumb hard into the base of her throat. She gagged on a strangled whimper.

He continued in the same reflective tone even while his thumb pushed and pushed at her windpipe, choking her. "Don't imagine lack of cooperation will meet with lenience. Replacing you presents only minor inconvenience."

He released his bruising hold. She stumbled free. Through an aching throat, she struggled to breathe.

"Don't touch me," she managed to rasp, blindly fumbling for the wall to keep herself upright. A little while ago, she'd offered to kneel. Now she couldn't countenance the idea of collapsing in front of him.

He clicked his tongue in disapproval as though at a naughty child. "You must rise above such fastidiousness, madam. You have a week."

"I won't do this," she said in a low shaking voice.

"Then face the consequences." He nodded in her direction. "Good day, Mrs. Paget."

She couldn't bear to turn and watch him leave. She listened to the even tap of his cane as he crossed the floor, then the gentle click of the closing door. Lord John had done everything carefully and softly. His voice hadn't risen above a murmur when he promised her destruction.

Grace raised a quivering hand to her lips and stared sightlessly down at the table. Danger crowded upon her from all sides of this darkened, stifling room.

Suddenly, she craved air and light. She lunged across to rattle back the curtains and fling open the windows. Great lungfuls of clear spring air brought her rioting stomach under control. But nothing shifted the leaden weight of hopelessness and fear. She suspected that burden would remain until the day she died.

The day she died might only be a week away.

"Congratulations," the marquess said from behind her, his tone edged with lacerating contempt. "My uncle must be so pleased with you. He looked even smugger than usual when he left."

Through her panic, she hadn't heard him come in. She didn't shift from the window.

"Did you speak to him?" The words scraped over her sore throat. She didn't need to look at Lord Sheene to know the bristling animosity was back.

"No. He finds my company uncongenial." Again that acerbic drawl. "But I'm sure he enjoyed his coze with you, Mrs. Paget. Particularly when you told him how easily you gulled me."

She barely believed what she heard. Surely he must guess Lord John's *coze* had involved only threats and terror.

Slowly, she turned. Lord Sheene leaned indolently against the wall near the door, his arms folded across his chest. His expression was shuttered but she read the anger blazing beneath his sangfroid.

He was her only ally against Lord John's evil. She needed him to trust her. She needed an hour unshadowed by fear. Futile to list what she needed. The stark reality struck that what she needed above all was survival.

What would survival cost?

"You cannot think I'm in league with your uncle," she said in a broken voice.

"I cannot think otherwise. You and he shared a long, apparently fruitful conversation and he reeked of self-satisfaction when I saw him step into his coach a few moments ago. Tell me—what's the next scene in this farce?" He sounded as though he didn't care but a muscle jerked spasmodically in his lean cheek, eloquent witness to temper.

She felt as though she'd been shaking forever. She was too distraught to dissemble. "I am to cozen you into my bed."

His haughty expression didn't alter. "Surely that was your cause from the start. No need to exert yourself with this show of desperation. Your terrified act duped me once before. The repeat performance isn't nearly so effective. Perhaps eschew the vulnerability and adopt a more seductive manner."

Grace flinched. He sounded like he hated her. If he truly believed she connived with his uncle, who could blame him? She met the marquess's burning eyes, frantically searching for some goodwill, some trace of the man who had been almost cordial less than an hour ago. "My lord, I'm in trouble."

He smiled, a grim twist of his beautiful mouth. "You most certainly are, Mrs. Paget. Especially when my uncle realizes I stand by my vow not to touch you."

"You won't help me." The words emerged as a thread of sound. Something clenched inside her like a cold hard fist. She felt lost in an endless desert.

His inimical gaze flicked across her as if she were eternally beneath his notice. The look was terrifyingly similar to the one his uncle had cast upon her. Then a smile conveyed rejection and triumph in equal measure. "Help you, madam? How may a poor madman help you when he cannot help himself?"

"You have to believe me when I say I don't conspire with your uncle."

His response bit at her like a whiplash. "On the contrary, my dear Mrs. Paget, I don't have to believe anything you say."

"I'm telling you the truth," she insisted in helpless despair.

"Truth?" He gave a short, contemptuous laugh. "You don't know the meaning of the word."

"I beg of you, my lord, help me."

His expression hardened and his mouth flattened with implacable rejection. "You waste your time with these theatrics. I told you—I'm awake to your deceit."

Weak, useless tears welled up. She could see that nothing she said would convince him she wasn't his enemy. All hope was lost. All hope had been lost from when she'd set out to find Vere in Bristol.

She stumbled toward the door. She didn't have the strength to argue with the man she must seduce. The man who had never liked her, most emphatically didn't want her, and who now quite obviously loathed her.

He turned his head as she reached him and spoke with a detachment she knew was feigned. "Just tell me one thing, Mrs. Paget—are you my uncle's lover?"

She stopped as if she collided with an invisible barrier and stared at him aghast. For the first time, she really believed he was out of his mind.

Another woman might have slapped him. But she was too astonished for outrage.

As her shocked silence extended, he straightened away from the wall and brushed past. She didn't move as she listened to him stride out of the cottage. His rapid steps suggested he couldn't bear to breathe the same air as she did for another second.

Chapter 8

Matthew stretched out as far as he could—not bloody far enough—on his awkward sofa and listened to Grace pace in the room above. It was late, past midnight. As if to prove him right, the hall clock chimed two. He hadn't slept. From what he heard upstairs, neither had she.

They hadn't met since he'd challenged her with being his uncle's mistress. For the first time, she hadn't come down to dinner. He wondered if she'd eaten, then chided himself for caring about the artful trull's well-being. She could sulk up there until Kingdom Come as far as he was concerned.

Burning anger still choked him. Anger with her. And with himself for allowing her to sneak under his barriers. He'd always known she was his uncle's creature, a superb actress ready to go to any length to convince her unwilling audience of one. God knows she'd even drugged herself to nausea to achieve that last touch of verisimilitude.

Yet she'd gained his cooperation, his friendship, his trust. Or at least she'd been on the verge of gaining those things. If he hadn't emerged from the courtyard in time to see his uncle drive away, he might have fallen into her warm, fragrant trap.

He'd wanted to kill her then.

He rolled over on the couch, but five nights' experience told him there was no comfortable position for a man of his height. Savagely, he punched the cushions under his head.

What use lying awake and stewing over her duplicity? He should be inured to treachery. Betrayal had dogged him for the last eleven years. Hers was just one more instance, and scarcely the most significant.

Although that wasn't how it felt.

A step creaked. What the hell was she doing? Perhaps she wanted a walk, unlikely as the hour was. He'd welcome surcease from her damned endless pacing.

She paused outside the salon. The door squeaked faintly as she pushed it open. Immediately, he lay still, feigning sleep.

His senses were always abnormally sharp around her. He heard the uneven saw of her breath, the rustle of her clothing. Not the rasp of the silks or satins that seemed to constitute her wardrobe. No, this was something softer that whispered as she moved.

She crept inside, then paused in the center of the room. He dared a quick look under his lashes. She wore something pale and filmy so he had no trouble locating her.

She'd never approached him at night. Clearly, Lord John's visit had incited her to take the initiative. What other purpose could bring her here silent as a ghost? His uncle had ordered her to bed him and like a good little puppet, she danced to the tug of the strings.

The reminder of his uncle stirred his anger. Thank Christ. Otherwise, he'd have leapt to his feet and grabbed her, damn the consequences.

Her scent called to him, tempting him to forget everything except that she was close enough to touch. His hands balled against his sides.

If he touched her, he'd take her.

He resented her. He mistrusted her. But he couldn't deny he wanted her.

He didn't know how long they waited. He, pretending to sleep. She, trapped between fleeing and advancing. All the time, his unruly flesh swelled and rose, insisting she was his for the price of reaching out his hand.

"I know you're awake," she said huskily.

"Yes." He gave a heavy sigh and sat up, placing his bare feet flat upon the floor. Although it was dark, he dragged the blanket across to cover his nakedness. "What do you want, Mrs. Paget?" he asked wearily, running his hands through his hair.

"I don't know."

That was a lie. They both knew why she was here. She was his uncle's obedient cipher. But God help him, she sounded so innocent and bewildered. He tried to revive his earlier rage but he was too dizzy with lust.

"Sweet Jesus," he muttered to himself rather than to her. He couldn't take much more. He stood, hitching the blanket more securely. She gasped and lurched back. Copulation might be her goal but she seemed less than reconciled to the idea.

The darkness was dangerously intimate. He leaned across and lit a candle to dispel the web of awareness between them.

A futile hope. He was always aware of her.

She'd tied her thick dark hair into a glossy plait that fell across one shoulder and dangled between her breasts. Under her transparent ice-blue night rail, the outline of her slender body was visible.

She kept her gaze lowered. Even so, she must have sensed where his eyes dwelt. To his reluctant regret, she wrapped her arms around herself, covering her chest. It was a characteristic gesture she used when she was frightened, or at least pretending to be so.

"You're safe enough," he said in a dismissive tone, praying it was true. "I can restrain my manly passions."

"You don't have any manly passions," she said sullenly.

"What?"

He stared at her, startled. A flush of color seeped under the creamy skin of her face.

"No, I meant . . . That is . . ." She took a deep breath and at last looked at him. Unbelievably, he watched the beautiful eyes widen and fix on his bare chest. Her color rose higher and her tongue flickered out to moisten her lips. Her arms dropped loosely to her sides as though she offered herself. If he hadn't known better, he'd believe she found him as compelling as he found her.

She wrenched her gaze up to meet his. "I'm sorry. I referred to your interactions with me. I mean, I'm sure you have manly passions. Every man . . ." She trailed off. She glanced away and her attention focused on the rumpled sofa. "I didn't know you slept down here."

He shrugged. "You occupy the only bed in the house."

"I know." Again she licked her lips, pink, moist, succulent. The simple action tightened the coil of lust inside him. "Or I know now. I looked for you upstairs but only one chamber is set up for sleeping."

That explained some of the restless movement he'd heard. The picture of her pursuing him through the darkened house was evocative enough to stop his breath. Thank God for the blanket around his waist or his unwelcome visitor would have no doubt about his manly passions.

He bent his head in an ironical bow. "Until your delightful advent into my existence, I hadn't expected to entertain guests."

She flinched at his sarcasm. His brain kept telling him she was a deceitful little cat. His heart stubbornly insisted that every time he attacked her, he should be horsewhipped.

Right now, though, even the most obstinate part of his mind found it hard to credit she was quite the lying witch he believed her. She followed his every move with her drowned dark sapphire eyes as if unsure whether he meant to tumble her or strangle her.

Although if she were genuinely reluctant, she'd cover her body with a robe. If she were genuinely reluctant, she wouldn't be in this room at all. He forced his gaze away from the tantalizing shadows beneath her flat belly.

"I want to talk to you," she said in a reedy voice.

"Do you?" he asked unhelpfully.

She wasn't here to talk. There was only one reason she stood before him in her delightful dishabille. She contrived to seduce him as his uncle had commanded.

Now the time had come, and she was unable to complete the act. He mocked himself for that burning instant when he'd imagined she felt the first sparks of desire.

"Yes." There was a pause while she sought some reason to explain disturbing him in the middle of the night. Then in a rush, "It's not fitting that you sleep here. You're the Marquess of Sheene. You should have the bedchamber."

Aha, he thought, fighting the urge to tell her to stop talking and just do what she'd come for. Perhaps she meant to lure him to her bed first. He cast a derisive glance at his inconvenient couch. She'd certainly be more comfortable under him upstairs.

Then she confounded him as she almost always did. "I could sleep in here."

So she wasn't inviting him to share the bedroom. He had no right to be disappointed. As long as his will held— and it wavered by the second—he had no intention of tupping her.

"No, keep the bed," he said shortly. How could he bear to sleep where she had slept? The idea was too evocative, fatal to his will.

"Your uncle said you'd been ill."

His laugh was humorless. "Of course I've been ill. I went mad."

The serious gaze didn't falter. "No, he said you'd been ill this last year."

"I see you were in the mood for confidences."

She studied him with that damnably steady regard as if she meant to uncover his every secret. He had a strange premonition in his gut that she'd succeed. "Your uncle is an evil man," she said softly.

That startled him. "Most people find him charming. Even I did, when I was a boy." Then an unwelcome thought struck him. "Did he hurt you?"

His uncle rarely descended to violence. He had Monks and Filey and a host of other bullies to enforce his will when he wished to exert physical coercion.

She shook her head so the plait slid beguilingly along the valley between her breasts. Jesus, she was spellbinding. How could he fight her? He reminded himself that she was his uncle's instrument but the idea was no longer so convincing.

"No, he didn't hurt me."

Something in her voice alerted him. "He threatened to, though, didn't he?"

She'd started to turn away. Now she faced him with a stark expression on her drawn face. "He frightens me."

For once, he couldn't doubt her sincerity. He sent her a twisted smile. "He frightens me too."

Surprisingly, she smiled back. "We agree on something at last." She turned toward the door. "Goodnight, your lordship."

"Goodnight, Mrs. Paget," he echoed as she padded across the room and left him to candlelit solitude. While all the time his soul exulted in rusty joy.

He couldn't mistake her revulsion when she spoke of

Lord John Lansdowne. She might be his uncle's cat's paw, but the more he considered it, he doubted it.

In fact, call him a gullible fool, but he believed her to be exactly what she'd always claimed. A virtuous woman dragged into this catastrophe through no fault of her own.

Significant as the perception was, that wasn't what made his heart sing.

He couldn't be wrong. Her feelings were unmistakable.

She wasn't his uncle's lover. She'd never been his uncle's lover.

Grace left the salon at a steady walk, then broke into an awkward run as she stumbled upstairs. All the time one word repeated again and again in her mind.

Coward, coward, coward.

She'd steeled herself to go to the marquess and seduce him. Surely, she could play the siren and make him take her. But when the time arrived, she'd been unable to do it.

Oh, how she wished she could say virtue had prevented her. But the truth was more humiliating.

Fear had stopped her. Fear stronger than the terror for her life that had shadowed her since her interview with Lord John.

She hadn't been afraid that the marquess would take advantage of her. She'd been afraid that he wouldn't. Even if she flung herself naked into his arms and begged.

She came to a panting halt at the bedroom window and stared sightlessly across the dark trees to where she knew the wall stretched. Outside that boundary, the world went on as it always had. Inside, the rules that had governed her life no longer applied.

One of those rules was that she was immune to men and their false promises of physical pleasure.

She shivered, although the night wasn't cold.

She wanted Lord Sheene.

There, she admitted her soul's shameful secret.

When had desire stirred to life? She'd been terrified of him when she woke bound and sick and stupid from laudanum. Even then, some devil inside her had recognized his masculine beauty. That beauty had lured.

That beauty still lured. A searing memory arose of how he'd looked downstairs, his dark hair ruffled and his smooth skin bare in the golden light. Josiah had been an old man, thick through the middle and with a heavy pelt of gray hair over chest and shoulders and back. She now knew Lord Sheene was completely different. Lean with sharply defined musculature and just enough hair to make him breathtakingly male. Supple in the waist. Bony, straight shoulders. Long, sinewy arms.

The devil within lusted to see what the blanket had concealed. The narrow hips, tight buttocks, long legs.

The organ that made him a man.

She curled trembling fingers over the sill, seeking stability in a reeling world. The wood bit cold and hard under her palms. Hunger beat inside her like a ceaseless drum.

She'd never wanted a man before. The relentless physical urgency dismayed her, astonished her.

She fell to her knees and rested her head between her hands on the ledge. It was the position for prayer. But her thoughts were shockingly profane.

Desire for the marquess burned with a raging fire.

She couldn't give in to temptation. Women like her didn't surrender their chastity to any handsome face. Women like her found satisfaction in duty and principle. If she let hunger for Lord Sheene drive her into his arms, she couldn't blame John Lansdowne for turning her into a whore. The guilt would be hers alone.

You'll end up no better than a bawd.

Her father's cruel words when he'd banished her after

her wedding haunted her, as they'd endlessly haunted her during her unhappy marriage. However far she'd fallen in the world, she hadn't yet fallen to selling herself. She was an honest woman, or so she'd believed until these last days.

The marquess disliked and mistrusted her. In that lay her only salvation. Her will was dangerously weak. His will wasn't even engaged.

Her fingers tightened on the sill to the point of pain. Astoundingly, she'd forgotten the most important fact of all.

If she didn't bed Lord Sheene by Saturday, she would die.

Chapter 9

The next morning, Grace found Lord Sheene in the courtyard, staring at a potted rose on his workbench. He was in shirtsleeves and his fine dark hair was disheveled as if he'd raked his hands through it more than once. The bleakness in his face made the breath snag in her throat.

She must have made a sound of distress because he looked up. The blankness receded from his golden eyes and he focused on her. Yet another reminder, should she need one, that she was far from his major concern.

Wolfram, who snoozed in the pale sunlight, lifted his head. When he saw who it was, he returned to his dreams.

"Mrs. Paget," the marquess said neutrally.

"My lord." She descended two worn stone steps to the grass around the rose beds. He looked tired but not angry. That gave her encouragement. She tightened her grip on the straw hat she carried and braced herself to breach the fortress of his mistrust. "I know you don't believe me, but you misunderstood what you saw yesterday. I'd never met your uncle before and I'm not party to his schemes."

That's true now, her conscience taunted. Will it be true by Saturday?

Lord Sheene's expression didn't lighten. "What does it matter what I believe?"

She swallowed but couldn't help her voice emerging as a husky whisper. "It matters to me."

That revealing statement invited questions she didn't want to answer. To her relief, he merely studied her in silence. She wondered what he saw. She wore the yellow gown again. It was still the dress that fit best. She'd pinned her hair into its accustomed severe style. Part of her was a virtuous widow. Part of her was a whore touting for trade. Enough truth lurked in both descriptions to make her cringe.

Did he divine the secret lechery skulking in her heart? Dread had kept her awake after she left him last night. Dread. Humiliation. And forbidden longing to touch his strong, beautiful body.

When he didn't speak, she forced herself to go on. "We're together in this, my lord. If we trust each other, perhaps we can find some comfort."

A bitter light darkened his eyes to caramel. "There is no comfort here."

"Then friendship is a worthwhile prize."

His brows contracted and she waited for him to lash out as he had yesterday. He leaned back against his workbench and folded his arms over his chest. The sudden memory assailed her of that chest gleaming bare and hard in flickering candlelight. A wayward pulse began to beat deep inside her.

He spoke as if he considered every word. "I believe you're genuinely afraid of my uncle."

She gave a shiver as she remembered yesterday's ultimatum. Of course she was afraid. Lord John would order her death and hardly note the event. "Yes."

Lord Sheene still frowned. "I can't save you, Mrs. Paget."

"You make me feel safe," she said, and knew she spoke

a lie. Although with the marquess, her fear wasn't for her life but for what she threatened to become. "Lord Sheene, I'm not your enemy."

"No," he said slowly as if he reached an important decision. "Perhaps you're not."

"So may I stay?" She couldn't retreat to the cottage and her own company. All she did there was relive that hideous conversation with Lord John. His threats buzzed round her mind like wasps trapped in a bottle. With a determined gesture, she placed the hat on her head, although her fingers trembled as she tied the ribbons. "Surely I can help."

Astonishingly, the marquess's expressive mouth quirked in long-suffering humor. "You must indeed be bored if you seek hard labor."

"I told you yesterday that I'm used to working, my lord."

He straightened and stepped closer to take one of her hands. One simple touch and she was undone. A jolt of sensation sizzled up her arm to lodge in her pounding heart, and lower where wanton heat made her slick with need. She shifted to ease the uncomfortable pressure between her thighs. She prayed he didn't notice her agitation.

He inspected her palms with a scientific attention that did nothing to calm her racing pulse. "These hands have done their share."

Mixed with reluctant sensual awareness was chagrin at her calluses and scars. It was many years since she'd had a lady's smooth white hands. Such a ridiculous thing to fret about when her life was at risk. But seeing the signs of wear and work through the marquess's eyes, she wanted to weep for shame.

His thumb brushed a thick white mark. "You cut yourself," he said softly. His face was all somber concentration and she was close enough to catch his scent, healthy male and something citrus that must be his soap.

"The knife slipped when I built a rabbit hutch," she whispered, swaying nearer to catch that elusive scent. Her eyes drifted shut as the delicious mix of male musk and lemon eddied over her. She realized what she did and blinked. She swallowed to moisten her dry mouth.

"Such capable hands." Abruptly, he let her go. He looked shaken and for once the hauteur was absent. She flushed. Had he discerned her hunger? If so, he had every reason to despise her. She despised herself. One short month a widow and already she craved another man.

Lord Sheene became all practicality as he turned to the bench crowded with gardening apparatus. He passed her a pair of gloves. "Try these. They're probably too big but that can't be helped. I'd be grateful if you cleared some weeds."

Wordlessly, Grace reached for a trowel. She was still lost in a longing haze. She'd forfeit her soul for another touch from those elegant hands. She wrenched herself back to reality. Mooning over the marquess only worsened her untenable situation.

For a long time, they worked without speaking. The garden was more neglected than her first impression of order had indicated. She'd sought company as distraction. But looming danger gnawed at her as she dug the cool soil. And her sinful desire for the marquess only reminded her what she must do, willing or not.

Fear inched higher every minute. She had to concentrate on something other than her dilemma or scream. Once she started screaming, she wouldn't stop. She spoke quickly before she thought to censor herself. "Have you been ill this last year?"

His back was to her as he bent over his workbench and she saw his shoulders tense. "Not ill, exactly."

He warned her off. She knew it as surely as if he posted a sign saying *no trespassing*.

"Then what?" she persisted, surprising herself.

Slowly he turned, his lips adopting a sardonic twist. "I see you're in a mood for confidences, Mrs. Paget."

She flinched. They were almost the same words he'd used yesterday when he'd accused her of colluding with his uncle. Of course he had no reason to trust her but the reminder hurt. "I'm sorry. It's none of my business."

"Oh, hell, what does it matter? What does any of it matter?" He glanced down at the knife in his hand and pitched it onto the bench where it landed with a clatter. "What do you want to know?"

Absolutely everything about you.

She caught herself just before the admission emerged. She sought a safer alternative. "There's so much I don't understand here, so much that puzzles me."

He ran one hand through his mass of fine hair. "Damn it, Grace . . . Mrs. Paget . . ."

The sound of her Christian name in that rich, deep voice sent a frisson of perilous pleasure through her. Her ready blush rose but she didn't look away. "You've seen me sick. You've seen me in my nightgown. It's absurd to stand on ceremony."

"Grace, then." He looked squarely at her. "My uncle decided to arrange a mistress for me after I escaped last year."

This was the last thing she expected. Slowly, she rose to her feet, dropping the trowel and stripping off the rough gloves. "You say escape is impossible."

Again that wry smile. "With good reason."

"But you got out."

"Three times in eleven years. But I've never stayed out. The first time I was eighteen. Even after the worst of my illness passed, it took four years before I could speak or read. I could hardly walk. I took occasional fits."

"No longer?" Her mind conjured the specter of the helpless lunatic that his uncle had summoned yesterday.

"Not since before that first escape."

She took the step that brought her to his side. "Seven years health means you're well," she said softly, wanting to take his hand, then noticing she had.

"I don't know." For once, he sounded young and uncertain. Instead of rejecting her, he turned his fingers in hers and gripped hard enough to hurt. The heat of his touch seared her to the core. "Sweet Jesus, I don't know."

She realized the fear he constantly lived with. Fear not of his uncle's cruelty, but that his mind might turn traitor, perhaps this time forever. His strength overawed her. His pain broke her heart. How could she bring herself to destroy this remarkable man?

He drew her down to the old wooden settle under the greenhouse eaves. "My uncle's men caught me within three miles. They thought I'd lost my mind again and tied me down for a few days. I was so angry, I probably was mad." He rested their linked hands on one muscled thigh. Grace tried desperately not to notice the heat and strength that radiated through the buff breeches. "After that, my uncle had the walls treated. It's like trying to clamber up glass."

"I know." She recalled her own futile attempts to climb out. "But you got away again."

"Yes. Two years later, Monks cut himself on an ax so I only had Filey to worry about. I tricked him into the kitchen and locked him in, then I just walked out. I got as far as Wells before the Bow Street Runners found me. There are no locks on the estate now except for the gate."

She'd found the lack of locks frightening until she realized that Lord Sheene would never beat at her bedroom door and demand entrance. "Still you hoped."

"Yes, foolish, stubborn hope. Perhaps madness persisted."

"No," she said with certainty. "What happened last year?"

"I learned the error of my ways," he said bitterly. Pain and shame shadowed his face. "I stole a horse and made it to the family seat at Chartington in Gloucestershire. I knew people there would hide me while I worked out how to prove my sanity."

"They turned you in?" she asked, aghast.

His fingers flexed hard on her hand. "I wish to God they had. My nurse had married one of the estate gardeners and they were overjoyed to see me. But my uncle knew where I'd go."

"You were punished again?"

"No, damn my uncle to hell." Lord Sheene paused, visibly fighting for control. His voice was steadier as he went on, although rage still roughened his tone. "He's the local magistrate and he transported Mary and her husband to New South Wales for harboring an absconded lunatic. My uncle made sure I saw their letters begging for mercy. He's kept any other news to himself. It's possible they didn't survive the journey. Mary was expecting a child and she hadn't been well."

He wrenched away and surged to his feet. The eyes he turned upon her were dark with guilt and self-hatred. "If I hadn't taken advantage of their kindness, they'd be safe. My uncle will use his power against anyone who aids me."

As she looked into his tormented face, an old memory surfaced. When her brother was sixteen, he'd winged a wild hawk with his gun and carried the wounded bird back to Marlow Hall. He'd had some idea of training it to hunt. But while the bird's injury healed readily enough, Philip could never tame its spirit. The hawk had starved in its cage.

Grace had begged Philip to release the bird but he was stubborn. The hawk had died, its fierce yellow eyes staring hatred at her until the end. For a long time, that inimical obstinate gaze had haunted her.

When she looked at Lord Sheene, she saw that same wild spirit. She saw the same will for freedom above all. And when freedom became an impossible dream, life slowly faded.

He extended his arm. The gesture wouldn't have looked out of place in Hyde Park during the fashionable hour. "Walk with me?"

She laid her hand on his forearm. Lord Sheene's shirt was warm under her hand and hinted at the lean muscles beneath. The marquess in full health would be a magnificently powerful man. "What about the gardening?"

"Later. Neither of us is going anywhere."

Perhaps not. Although after Saturday, Grace might no longer be here. An ominous shiver chilled her blood.

He noticed her trembling. "Are you cold? Would you rather go inside?"

"No." Back to the cottage which still reeked of his uncle's overweening evil? Lord, anything but that. She'd rather stay outdoors and freeze. "Why is your uncle so determined to keep you here?"

He gave a grim laugh as he led her under the archway and into the woods. Wolfram stood, stretched, and trotted after them. "Greed. As basic and banal as that."

After the gothic horrors she'd faced, she'd expected some convoluted history of family enmity. "Greed for what?"

"Money, of course. When my parents died, Lord John was named guardian. He's run the Lansdowne interests ever since. For a younger son whose fortune was only respectable, the sudden wealth was dazzling. When I reached my majority, he was set to lose it all."

"But you fell ill." Her fingers tightened on his arm.

"No, I lost my mind," he said with sudden harshness.

He was tense under her touch. "When I was fourteen, I went mad."

"You're not mad now," she insisted. "You haven't suffered an episode in seven years."

"Every year, my uncle sends two doctors to examine me. They confirm I'm unfit to govern myself and, more significantly, my inheritance."

"Lord John must pay them."

The sourness left his expression and he gave a short but genuine laugh. The sound rustled through her like a warm wind. "Mrs. Paget, your cynicism threatens to outstrip mine."

She didn't smile. "Your uncle took little trouble to hide his true nature."

He sighed and turned onto a path Grace had followed just after she arrived. When she'd been terrified of the man with the frightening eyes. How long ago that seemed. Yet it was only a few days.

"While I'm alive and confined, my uncle plays the man of importance."

The word alive struck her. "And if you die?"

"The title goes to my cousin Hector. If he meets his maker, a string of younger brothers line up for the marquessate. My father produced one sickly descendant and Lord John has thrown only girls, four of them. Uncle Charles hatched a brood of six husky boys before he broke his neck in a hunting accident."

"And Lord John returns to being merely a younger son." Her fingers clenched in his sleeve. How could he bear what his uncle did to him? Her belly cramped on a surge of futile rage. "He wants you healthy but under his control? Like an animal in a menagerie? It's obscene."

"Yes, Grace, it's obscene," he said in a flat tone.

"And he thought if he got you a woman . . ."

"I'd accept imprisonment."

The ruthlessness stole her breath. She stopped and looked searchingly up into Lord Sheene's face. She'd always found his features compelling, even when she'd been half-unconscious with dread and laudanum.

Now she saw so much more. Courage that battled for health and competence. Strength to resist his uncle's machinations. Honor, so when his freedom brought harm to others, he resigned himself to imprisonment.

"My uncle thinks to use you to control me," he said quietly.

At that moment, she realized he was determined never to take her. If he came to her bed, he betrayed his deepest principles. She was safe.

And her safety meant she was lost.

What was she to do? Subvert the integrity that sustained him? Or save herself?

She abhorred the choice she must make.

He ran his hand through his hair. She fought the urge to reach up and smooth that silky darkness. The need to touch him fermented in her blood but she couldn't surrender to it. She bent her head so the brim of her hat concealed the lust she knew must shine in her eyes.

"No more dark talk. Are you interested in plants, Grace?" He seemed to like saying her name. She wondered why. When she looked up, he appeared boyish, diffident. It reminded her he wasn't so very old. Neither was she, she acknowledged, as wayward excitement fizzed through her veins.

"I've never had the chance to find out." Growing up, she'd learned a lady's arts, including floral illustration. Another subject to master before she caught herself a husband. Well, she'd caught herself a husband but not the one she'd been groomed for. Since her marriage, she'd been too busy keeping food in her stomach and a roof over her head to worry about much else.

"Orchids grow in the wood, if you'd like to see them."

His smile for once contained no bitterness. Its sweetness surprised her, enticed her. She found herself agreeing to search for wildflowers. He could ask her to paint the sky or dig for hen's teeth and she'd say yes.

Grace left the marquess downstairs before dinner. Foolishly, she wished she had something of her own choosing to wear, like the silks that had crowded her wardrobe at Marlow Hall. For nine years, she'd muffled her feminine vanity. Now she wanted to look beautiful for a man.

Beautiful for a man. . . .

Troubled eyes met her reflection in the cheval glass. Her life hung by a thread. The man she wanted was trapped, tormented, and possibly insane. This wasn't a bucolic flirtation. This was a nightmare of coercion and violence.

If she ever forgot that, she was doomed.

She was doomed anyway.

Her attention fell on the bed behind her and for the first time, she noticed the letter lying on the cover. She turned from the mirror with a shiver and went across to pick it up. There was no name on it but it had to be for her, just as she already knew it had to be from Lord John.

The seal was an eagle under a crown. That must be the Lansdowne badge. Yet again, the ghost of her brother's dead hawk worried at her.

The thick paper crackled as she tore the letter open. There was one word in slashing writing.

Saturday.

Lord John felt a need to confirm his threat. He underestimated how convincing he'd been. She'd never doubted he meant every horrible promise.

"Oh, God," she whispered, crumpling the message into a ball and flinging it to the floor. She smothered a sob and sank down onto the bed, hiding her face in her hands.

There was no escape.

She couldn't do this.

She had to do this.

She rose on trembling legs, hating Josiah for leaving her alone and vulnerable, hating Vere for letting her down, hating Lord John for his greed and callousness.

Above all, she hated herself.

Tonight, she'd betray the marquess. And force him to betray himself. She was no better than his grasping uncle.

She was worse. For she recognized how exceptional Lord Sheene was. The long afternoon with its confidences and companionship had only confirmed his extraordinary quality. He was a man who in other circumstances and at another time she might have loved.

Yet still she meant to ruin him.

Chapter 10

Matthew woke instantly, then realized that to wake, he must have slept. In spite of the couch's incommodious design. In spite of unreliable sleep proving more elusive than ever over recent days. In spite of Grace Paget's presence in the house torturing him on a rack of endless desire.

The room was dark. The unusual run of fine weather had ended at sunset and rain spattered against the windows. It had drummed on the roof during an unexpectedly silent dinner. Mrs. Paget—Grace—had been with him all day and her presence had warmed his soul. But she'd remained withdrawn throughout the meal.

Who could blame her? His story must convince her she'd never escape. Yet he mourned her retreat from brief affinity. For one day, she'd been everything he desired in a companion. Intelligent. Sympathetic. Knowledgeable.

Beautiful.

He couldn't deceive himself that all he wanted was friendship. But friendship, by God, was something. If he could resign himself to captivity, he could resign himself to keeping her at a distance.

One day. Maybe in a thousand years.

Never.

Now Grace hovered in the open doorway.

He was surprised to see her. And dismayed. The electric darkness whispered of all the things he wanted to do to her. He prayed she stayed where she was. If she came any closer, he didn't trust himself.

"What is it, Grace?" he asked in concern, sitting up. "Are you ill?"

"No."

The almost inaudible syllable didn't reassure. He stood and reached for his clothes, close to hand since last night. "Let me light a candle," he said, fumbling for his shirt.

"No." This time with more force. He heard her inhale, the sound rasping like a file over his taut nerves.

"Grace?"

"I'm sorry," she said brokenly.

With a cracked sob, she launched herself in his direction. A warm fragrant bundle of femininity landed hard against him. Automatically, his arms closed around her, his shirt dangling uselessly from one hand.

She was slender and trembling in his grasp and sweeter even than he'd imagined. While he told himself to let her go, his grip firmed, dragged her closer.

"What . . ." he managed to say before she clutched the sides of his head and tugged him down with clumsy force.

"Forgive me," she said, the words muffled. Then her lips, hot and taut with purpose, jammed against his.

The world outside the embrace stopped. His mind ceased to function. His body began to function too well.

She wore the sheer nightdress. He wore nothing at all. Only a flimsy layer of material separated them. His skin burned where it touched hers and he hardened in immediate response. Her womanly scent filled his head. Her heat filled his arms.

Before he could stop himself, he tightened his hold so her lush breasts flattened upon his bare chest. His shirt fell disregarded to the floor as his hand shaped the sinuous indentation of her waist.

She gave a whimpered protest and tore her closed mouth from his. The kiss had been too brief to justify the name. But even such brutal, fleeting contact inflamed his starved senses. He wanted her mouth on him again. He wanted time to discover her taste.

"Kiss me," she said unsteadily, her fingers kneading the muscles of his arms.

Keeping his hands off her was difficult enough when she maintained a decorous distance. Now he found it impossible. Her warmth eddied out to lure him closer until he forgot everything but pleasure.

He moved his hands to her shoulders, as much to contain his own rioting reactions as to hold her off. What little he'd learned about the shape of her, the curves and dips and valleys of her body, scorched his mind, urged him to discover more. But he wasn't totally lost to passion, although he wavered on the brink.

"We can't do this." Regret laced each word he wrested from his tight throat.

Her shuddering inhalation pressed her breasts into his chest. He gritted his teeth and struggled to stop his hands slipping down to weigh and touch and explore.

"I have to," she said hoarsely.

Even in his overexcited state, that response seemed odd. A voice demanding caution screamed at the back of his mind. "God, Grace . . ."

She clasped his head in her cool slender hands. "Kiss me."

The brief flash of clarity evaporated. Under his hands, she stretched up. For one incendiary moment, her mouth clung to his. The intimacy was astonishing. His unruly cock swelled and lifted. Her lips were so soft, like warm satin. Experimentally, he made a slight sucking movement. A shiver ran through her and the fingers clutching his arms dug into his flesh almost to the bone.

He stopped. He must be doing this wrong.

His heart overflowing with self-disgust, he waited for her to recoil from his boorishness. But with a cry, she pitched herself after him as if even that much separation was too much. His hands slid to her back, gathering her closer.

He rubbed his lips across hers. She opened slightly so he drew in her breath. He inhaled, instinctively parting to taste her moisture. She gave another choked sound. Of distress or pleasure, he couldn't tell.

She pushed herself so violently against him that they reeled onto the couch. As her delicious weight landed on top of him, the kiss broke. Her nightdress rode up and one of his hands brushed the curve of her buttock. Her bare buttock.

The feel of her naked skin nearly shattered him. He surged up in a frenzied search for relief. She surrounded him, all hot flesh and seeking hands. She touched him with hectic, clinging strokes as if afraid he'd disappear.

Something was wrong. His dreams couldn't be so mistaken. This wasn't how he'd imagined their embraces.

In a thousand secret fantasies, he'd held her close, he'd kissed and caressed her, he'd thrust inside her. She'd been soft and yielding. She'd relished his possession.

The woman in his arms was stiff with tension and she shook as though in the grip of fever.

He rose on his elbows to kiss her again, then paused. His misgivings roared. He couldn't ignore them any longer. He fell back to lie beneath her and his hands dropped to his sides.

"Grace, why are you here?" he asked sharply, clenching his fists so he didn't snatch what she offered and let consequences be damned.

She scattered kisses across his bare chest. Desperate kisses. Just as her hands were desperate. Her fingers hooked into his biceps like talons and she fumbled to bring his arms around her again.

"Don't talk," she gasped. She raised her head and he felt her eyes burn him through the darkness. "Kiss me. Kiss me properly."

She plastered herself across him as if force alone kept him with her, as if she expected him to fight her off. She smashed her open mouth against his, hard enough to bruise. He tasted blood and fear. He lifted an unsteady hand to her cheek to calm her wildness.

Her face was drenched with tears.

"Jesus!"

He shoved at her and jerked into a sitting position at the far end of the sofa. She tumbled away with a cry then crawled after him until she straddled his legs. He would have read eagerness in her touch, if not for those betraying tears against his fingers.

Christ, this turned his sensual visions into distorted nightmare. In those visions, she'd panted with desire, not cried as if her heart broke. He struggled to rein in the lust rampaging through his veins. He wanted her more than life. But not like this. Never like this.

"Stop," he grated.

"I will make you take me," she said breathlessly. She rested back on her heels so she bumped the arm of the sofa behind her. With ungainly movements so different from her usual fluid grace, she tugged the nightdress over her head and threw it to the floor.

"Jesus . . ." he said again on a low hiss and closed his eyes.

Too late. Even through the darkness, the image of her seared his brain like fire. The glimmer of white flesh, the full high breasts with their darker nipples, the pool of shadow where her legs met.

"Stop it, Grace," he said while the devil inside him shrieked to take her, take her.

Her pale thighs braced his legs as she slid toward him. Her position was excruciatingly suggestive. She paused at a point where if she moved the slightest inch, he'd be inside her. He clenched his jaw so hard it hurt.

"I have to do this."

He heard the despair in her voice. Her shaking hand grazed his erection. Christ, she'd kill him before she finished. Through the fireworks shooting through his head, he heard her shocked inhalation.

She snatched her hand away. "You want me," she whispered as if even with unmistakable physical evidence, she still didn't believe it.

Matthew's control shredded. With a roughness he couldn't help, he thrust her aside so she bounced against the upholstery. He scrambled to his feet.

"Of course I bloody want you," he growled. "God, where the hell did you put your damned clothes?"

He scrabbled for her nightdress but when his hand alighted on a garment, it was his shirt. It would have to do.

"Here, put this on." He thrust the garment at her, then grabbed his trousers and tugged them up. Without looking at her—if he looked at her, his fragile resolution would crumble—he stalked to the desk and lit a candle with hands he could barely control.

Only then did he face her. And wished to God he'd marched out of the room instead. She was in such a state that even so simple a matter as pulling his shirt over her head took far too long. As the loose folds of linen tumbled over her smooth white flesh, his cock strained painfully against his trousers.

Her head drooped on her slender neck and her body formed a despairing curve. Untidy tendrils of hair clung to her damp face. One long tress escaped her plait and snaked down to disappear under his shirt. How his hand itched to follow that shining black line. He clenched hard on the desk behind him to block turning the wish into reality.

The only sounds in the room were her rasping sobs and the patter of rain against the windows. She knelt on the sofa, struggling for breath so his shirt heaved over her breasts. Breasts he now knew were round and white and tipped with small, perfect nipples. Another bolt of desire slammed him and left him shaking.

"Why did you kiss me, Grace?" he snarled.

Tears streaked her wan face as she looked up at him. "I want you to take me," she said flatly.

"No, you don't," he said with an absolute certainty he wished to hell he didn't feel.

"If you want me, why don't you take me?" Her bewilderment cut to his heart.

Because you don't want me the way I want you, damn it.

"You know why. It's dishonor for you. And for me."

"I don't care about dishonor." The same toneless voice. New tears flowed down her cheeks. Her throat moved as she swallowed nervously.

She was frightened.

His heart contracted in anguished denial. "Grace, I'd never hurt you. There's no need to fear me."

Horror dawned in her eyes and she shook her head vehemently. "I'm not afraid of you." A blush tinted her cheeks as she looked away. "Or perhaps only a little."

Of course he scared her. His desire had been immediate and flagrant. And was still rampant, as a married woman would know, although so far she'd studiously fixed her attention above his waist.

"Then what is it?" He gripped the desk like a ship-wrecked sailor gripped a broken spar in a stormy ocean.

Her hands twined in her lap with restless distress. "This was wrong. I shouldn't have come to you. I'm sorry."

He couldn't help himself. Her misery called more strongly than his sense of self-preservation. He shoved himself away from the desk and took the three strides that brought him to the sofa. "Grace, just tell me."

Striving for control, he sat next to her and lifted one of her twisting hands. He wanted her to feel safe, to know he'd mastered his ravening hunger. But his fingers trembled as he touched her.

"Tell me," he repeated, beating back the lust that writhed and screamed inside him.

Her hand curled around his in a gesture of trust he didn't deserve and she sucked in a deep breath. The faint color receded from her face, leaving her even paler. "Your uncle said unless I . . . coax you into my bed before Saturday, he'll kill me."

Jesus, why hadn't he guessed?

Through the humiliation and fear writhing in her belly, Grace struggled for words. "And before . . ." She swallowed again, then spoke in a frantic rush. "And before he kills me, he'll give me to Monks and Filey."

"God blast him to hell," Lord Sheene said viciously, his hand tightening around hers.

"I've betrayed you in the worst possible way." The shame that had shadowed her all night rose to choke her. How could he be so kind when she'd set out to suborn him? She lurched to her feet, desperate to escape to the lonely privacy of the bedroom.

Roughly, he pulled her back down beside him. "What are you going to do about Saturday?"

She searched his eyes for the disgust he must feel. She only found concern and the banked fires of anger at his uncle's machinations.

"I don't know," she whispered, although she shuddered because she did know.

At that moment, she reached a difficult decision. She'd never allow Monks and Filey to touch her. She'd kill herself first. Her death had been inevitable from the moment those foul thugs had abducted her. Better that death came before the final degradation. After tonight's fiasco, she'd never again muster the nerve to try to seduce Lord Sheene.

Her course was set for irrevocable ruin. She wouldn't take him down to destruction with her.

"You should have told me this," he said gently.

"What could you have done? Apart from say there's no hope."

"We could deceive my uncle. If we share a bed . . ." He stopped. "If we share a bed, no one need know we're not lovers."

For one bright moment, rescue beckoned, then she remembered what the ruse would cost him. "Then your uncle will think he's won. After what you told me today, I know the stakes."

"My pride isn't worth your life, Grace."

But pride kept Lord Sheene alive. If he conceded victory to his uncle, he was lost. She couldn't let that happen. "No."

His expression twisted with pain. "I vowed I wouldn't hurt you, Grace."

Useless tears welled up again. She felt so utterly helpless. "Everything's impossible."

Surprisingly, he gave her the sweet smile that made her heart cramp with futile longing. "It won't look so bad in the morning."

The comfort one offered a child. Grace recognized its

essential falseness. Still, when Lord Sheene drew her into his embrace, she slid up the sofa to lean against him. He cradled her upon his bare chest as tenderly as if she were indeed a child. But when she rested her sticky face on his cool skin, the feelings that flooded her were unmistakably adult.

Her failed seduction had opened the doors to forbidden knowledge. After tonight, his smell and his taste had permeated her bones. She wanted his arms to bind her to his side forever. She wanted him to kiss her again and again with his open mouth. The unsatisfactory kisses she'd forced on his unwilling lips only whetted her sinful curiosity. She wanted him to push her onto her back and thrust inside her, solid, heavy, possessive. She wanted him to make her his in a way her husband never had.

He said she could trust him. And she did. It was herself she didn't trust.

Especially now she knew she didn't yearn alone.

Chapter 11

As Grace slept in Matthew's arms, he read exhaustion and unhappiness on her face. She'd come to him tonight to whore herself. The candlelight revealed what that decision had cost. Even in sleep, she looked strained to breaking.

Matthew eased along the sofa so her body curved into his side and her head rested on his shoulder. For once, the cramped space was welcome. Whimpering, she snuggled closer and her bare legs tangled in his.

He'd seen her naked body. He'd touched her skin. The world had changed for him tonight. He groaned softly into the fragrant hair on her crown as he recalled how she'd straddled him. Spending daylight hours with Grace stretched control to the limits. Nights holding her in his arms would test him beyond bearing.

Yet he had to convince Lord John they were lovers.

He had to protect her. What did his struggle with his uncle matter if it meant her destruction? He'd die before he let anyone harm her.

Even asleep, she seemed to sense his turmoil. One slender arm, clad in his shirt sleeve, slid across his naked chest in a protective gesture.

The thought was absurd. He meant nothing to her. How

could he? Malicious fortune had catapulted her without warning or consent into his tragedy.

He lay awake watching her as the candle guttered and gray predawn crept into the room. His eyes traced the pale smoothness of forehead. The elegant arch of eyebrows. The straight, delicate nose. The determined chin.

He'd likened her to a painted Madonna. But this particular Madonna was stubborn. Courage and will tempered her sweetness. Grace was no pliant reed.

Thank God. Or his uncle would crush her.

Or mold her into an obliging puppet.

His eyes rested on her mouth, soft and vulnerable in relaxation. The mouth she'd used on him tonight. He couldn't call that violent meeting a kiss. Although the fleeting possibility of a kiss had trembled between them.

What would it be like if she kissed him in genuine passion?

God help him, he'd never know.

The next morning Grace discovered the marquess standing in a clearing. Unreliable sun glanced across his dark head and gleamed on the boots he wore with black breeches and a loose shirt. Her heart missed a beat at his magnificence.

Apprehension and unquenchable curiosity warred inside her. She'd kissed him. Touched his body. Flaunted her nakedness before him. Cried in his arms. Slept next to him wearing only his shirt. She'd felt the contained power in his long sinewy muscles.

It was a level of intimacy she'd never achieved with her husband. She'd done her duty by Josiah but the act was always quick, furtive, performed in darkness while they remained clothed.

In silent fascination, she hovered behind Lord Sheene. She watched him aim a pebble at a small patch scraped into the bark of a beech about thirty yards away. The sharp ping as the stone struck the makeshift target explained the noise she'd followed to find him.

He bent and scooped more stones from the heap in the wildflowers at his feet. With dogged persistence, he threw each one at the tree, every time hitting the center of his mark. The accuracy was uncanny. And sad. His skill was stark testament to the solitary hours he'd spent perfecting this.

When he'd pitched the last pebble, he glanced over his shoulder. Although she'd approached quietly. Although she hadn't said a word.

"Grace."

Nothing else. Just her name. It lay between them like a challenge.

The potent memory of her naked skin gliding against his rose like lava in her blood. Before she met him, she'd never felt lust, but she felt lust now. It blinded her to everything but her need to touch the marquess.

Cursing her blush, she stepped forward. "Lord Sheene."

He turned slowly. She wasn't sure how he'd react to her. Anger? Disdain? Disgust? After her failed seduction, she deserved all three, although at least he knew now that his uncle had forced an impossible choice.

She was astonished to see unveiled hunger burning in his eyes. She shivered as the charged silence built. Extended.

A soft sound of yearning emerged from deep in her throat. Her heart thumped out an erratic, heavy rhythm. His eyes deepened to dark honey and he made a convulsive movement toward her.

"When you came to me . . ." His voice was ragged.

"No." She flung out a hand to ward him off. How could she find words to express what she'd felt last night? The fear. The shame. *The desire.*

She couldn't. Not in daylight.

"Very well." His jaw adopted a granite line. She suddenly remembered that he stemmed from a long line of ruthless magnates. "But we will discuss it."

"Just . . . just not now." She grabbed a steadying breath. "What were you doing with those pebbles?" Her color rose higher at the question's banality.

He dusted his hands off and stepped closer. "My father taught me to shoot. This keeps my eye in—and helps me think."

She didn't need to ask what he thought about. Lord John's threats still preyed like ravenous leopards on her own peace. His gaze sharpened on her. "What do you want, Grace?"

You.

She bit back the swift answer. Although, heaven help her, it was true. And after last night, she knew he wanted her too. That knowledge lay between them like an unsheathed sword.

She stepped over the invisible but deadly blade. Her lips stretched in an uncertain smile. "We could walk."

"We could." He bent his glossy head in grudging assent but his eyes held an implacable glint as they focused on her. "You can tell me about your life."

She started back as if he'd punched her. She never spoke to anyone about her past. Never. Never. Never.

"I can't." It was the whine of the indulged child she'd left behind with her life at Marlow Hall. The girl who wouldn't practice her pianoforte or do her French translation. That girl was a ghost she'd banished years ago. "It's not an edifying story. I don't . . ."

How could she reveal the depths of her selfishness to this man she admired above all others? She didn't want him to despise her, as he would despise her when he knew the damage she'd caused.

"Grace, your secrets are your own," he said gravely. "Keep them or share them. I have no right to insist."

The calm acceptance in his rich eyes soothed her fears, lured her to contemplate unprecedented confidences. Suffering had granted Lord Sheene a unique wisdom. If anyone could understand her topsy-turvy history, the mad marquess would.

No other man had seen her naked body. Perhaps it was fitting that he should glimpse her naked soul.

She squared her shoulders. "No, I want . . . I want to tell you." Strangely, it was true.

Both were silent as they stepped onto the faint track through the trees. Wolfram bounded out of the undergrowth and trailed after them, although he soon grew bored with their sedate pace and set off on exploratory tangents of his own.

The narrowness of the path meant only a couple of inches separated her from Lord Sheene. Close enough for his warmth to tease. The loamy woodland smells carried a tempting hint of his soap. Even through the anxiety swirling in her mind, she was unbearably aware of him as a man.

"I know you're from a good family," Lord Sheene eventually said, his voice gentle. He'd used the same tone when she was sick and he'd believed her his enemy. Even then, his voice had quieted the screeching devils in her heart. "Were you an only child?"

She'd been struggling to work out how to begin. Although talking about Philip was always painful, she forced herself to answer. "I had one brother. He died two years ago."

"I'm sorry."

"Yes, I am too." And sorrier still for the mess he'd made of his life. Philip had been clever and handsome and charming, but spoiled. He'd died in a duel over another man's wife after a drunken quarrel in a Soho gambling hell.

With an abrupt movement, she bent to pluck a late blue-bell. She nervously twirled the frail flower in her fingers. Heavens, why was it so difficult to find the words? "When I was sixteen, I fell in love with a poor man. Worse, my suitor was in trade and a radical."

She waited for some derisive comment but the marquess remained silent as he followed the shaded track at her side.

Eventually, she went on in a more natural tone. "Josiah was the local bookseller. He used to talk to me about big things, important things. It was so flattering to be treated as an intelligent woman and not just a silly girl. Of course, I was just a silly girl. Conceited and headstrong and selfish and with far too high an opinion of my cleverness."

"You're not the first chit to have her head turned by male attention. You're being too hard on yourself."

"No," she said hollowly. "No, I'm not being too hard on myself. My vanity and foolishness broke my father's heart."

"Grace."

Just one word in that deep, deep voice. He reached out to still the busy fingers that shredded the bluebell. The touch lasted the sheerest instant. Still it scorched her to the marrow. She relaxed her deathlike grip on the ruined flower and dropped it to the edge of the path. She sucked in a steadying breath.

"When Josiah realized I was interested in his cause, he lent me books, books that would have given my father an apoplexy if he'd known. Shelley. Southey. Mary Wollstonecraft. Godwin. Cobbett."

"That's a list to chill the heart of every landlord in the kingdom."

She read his carefully neutral response as tacit criticism. "You disapprove."

"Not at all. The country groans under inequality." He stepped in front of her to hold a dripping branch out of her way. "Although I wonder what sympathy I'd have for the downtrodden if I hadn't suffered my own injustice. My uncle's an unregenerate reactionary who invokes the death sentence for the most minor offenses. I loathe that he uses my fortune to support his merciless conservatism."

She ducked under the branch and waited for the marquess. "When I met Josiah, he was in his fifties but still on fire to save the world. He was like a prophet out of the Bible." How she remembered the vivid excitement of those weeks. Her sheltered existence had never offered anything to match it. "Even after my maid betrayed me to my father, Josiah still smuggled letters to the hall. Wonderful letters about how he and his followers would create heaven on earth. I was so eager to join the crusade."

"Even so, it's a huge step for such a man to offer marriage to a well-born miss of sixteen. Or was he blinded by the family fortune?"

The sardonic note in Lord Sheene's voice made her curious. She cast him a searching glance under her lashes, noticing the severe line of his usually expressive mouth. He claimed to support reform, yet his demeanor reeked of hostility.

Having started her story, though, she found herself determined to finish it, whatever it cost. Something in her was desperate to reveal the sorry, disastrous facts. Perhaps because if the marquess scorned her, it would break the growing intimacy and attraction that bound her to him.

"No, I proposed to Josiah. I couldn't share his quest without the world calling me harlot. That would only harm the great mission. I was a forward baggage. I didn't think how my actions would affect my family. All I cared about was what I wanted."

Lord Sheene hooked his hand around her arm, swinging her round to face him. He dropped his hand quickly. Once she'd have thought that was because he didn't want to touch her. Now she knew better.

"Jesus, Grace, Paget didn't have to agree. You were little more than a child and he was a man in his maturity."

Yes, the marquess was angry. She wondered why he cared about the fate of a harebrained girl and her overbearing old lover. She began to walk again. Motion somehow made words come more easily. When Lord Sheene caught up, she began to speak in a flat voice.

"Josiah wasn't happy about the marriage. Family life distracted him from his glorious task. But I was so dedicated, so avid to learn. Nobody else was. Josiah had such hopes of founding the New Jerusalem. When it didn't happen, he was a disappointed man." In spite of her attempt to sound composed, sadness seeped into her tone. "Disappointment became his stock in trade, much more than his shelves of dusty unsold books."

How it had hurt to discover that her idol was a sanctimonious, narrow-minded prig. She'd soon learned that she'd been tragically mistaken in her judgment of Josiah's qualities. By then, it was too late to undo the harm she'd done to herself and others, including Josiah. She'd exchanged a loving family for a ranting martinet who never forgave her for being better born than he. Her disillusionment and his disappointment had combined into a bitter brew that tainted every moment of her married life.

The marquess frowned at the path ahead but she sensed his vision remained fixed on a purely internal landscape. "Your father must have been furious when he learned what you'd been up to."

"Furious. Frustrated. Disbelieving. He'd planned a great match, a viscount at least. I wasted myself on an indigent shopkeeper forty years my senior and a blasted democrat as well. After he found out, he gave me a terrible scolding. He banished Josiah from the village, easy when you own every stick and stone." She took a breath, striving to reclaim her unemotional tone. "Josiah left and set up in York and we decided to run away, then seek forgiveness. He was never happy I disobeyed my parents—the Bible says you must honor your father and mother."

"So you eloped?"

The marquess still didn't look at her. Was he condemning her as she'd condemned herself so often in the lonely reaches of her soul? He should.

"Yes." How thrilled she'd been. She'd always wanted to see the world. *See the world?* What a laughable notion. She'd consigned herself to nine years of a prison barely less constricting than her present captivity. She stifled the caustic thought. "I'd always been my father's favorite. He'd come round once he recognized Josiah's great soul."

"I doubt rich fathers care for poor men in any guise, even poor men with great souls," Lord Sheene said dryly.

"I learned that with experience. Josiah and I married at Gretna, then returned for my family's blessing. My father granted me five minutes to inform me I was no longer his daughter. Mamma and Philip were forbidden to say goodbye."

"I'm so sorry, Grace," he said softly.

"I deserved it," she said in a thick voice. Then with a sudden burst of passionate self-hatred, "How could I hurt my family like that? Somehow Josiah made me believe his cause was more important than the people who loved me. I soon regretted what I'd done. But I'd made my bed and had to sleep in it." She paused and drew in a shuddering breath. She wasn't far from tears. That last rancorous interview with her father in the library at Marlow Hall still haunted her.

Lord Sheene helped her over a fallen branch. The touch of his hand was fleeting. Even so, it burned. To distract herself from the forbidden tingle in her blood, she pressed on with her story.

"For the next year, the only contact I had with my family was when my mother sent me money. That stopped then, I suppose because my father found out and forbade her to have anything more to do with me. Josiah wasn't just an ineffective prophet. He wasn't a particularly good bookseller either. Without my mother, we'd have starved."

"You didn't think to approach your father again?"

She shook her head, slowing to a stop. "I honestly think Josiah would have beaten me if I had. He hated my father. I didn't dare tell him my family's money paid for what we ate. It never occurred to Josiah that the pittance he gave me wouldn't feed a mouse."

"Still you tried to be a good wife." He sounded so certain as he faced her. She returned from the wasteland of memory and looked at him fully. There was no contempt in the golden eyes. Compassion, sorrow, contained anger that she knew wasn't aimed at her. But no contempt.

"I tried. I didn't succeed." Her lips stretched in a humorless smile. For a man who preached freedom for the masses, Josiah had taken a dim view of liberty for his wife. "I was always too argumentative, disobedient, rebellious."

The marquess's face contracted with outrage. "Dear God, he didn't abuse you?"

"No. Oh, heavens no," she said aghast. "Never." She didn't add that she might have preferred a beating to Josiah's endless self-righteousness.

"So how did you end up on the farm?"

"The bookshop failed after three years. We bought a sheep run with what remained of my mother's money."

How furious Josiah had been. She believed he realized he hated her when she revealed her family's secret support. It smacked too much of aristocratic patronage. Josiah had loathed the Marlows and everything they stood for.

"And did you prosper?" The marquess bent to pick up a stick. Her eyes fixed on the way his hands savagely ripped the twig into tiny pieces. Yes, he was definitely angry.

She gave a sour laugh. "Of course we didn't. It was a catastrophe. Josiah was town-bred and hated the farm and hated me for trapping him there. Then he fell sick."

She paused. The ghost of the grim, relentless, hopeless misery of her last months in Yorkshire grabbed her by the throat. She couldn't talk about those days even to so empathetic a listener as the marquess. He was so compassionate—and she deserved his compassion so little. If Josiah had ruined her life, she had surely ruined his in return. And she knew in her heart, it wasn't Josiah but her own willfulness and stupidity that she must blame for her wretched history.

"Wouldn't neighbors help?" He scattered the last fragments of broken stick at his feet and looked up at her. The steadiness of his voice dispelled the choking miasma in her mind like a stiff breeze.

"Josiah's temper drove even the most well-meaning away. Only the vicar's wife came at the end and then just to help with the house. Josiah had waited his whole life to be tried and illness tried him to the limit."

She lifted a shaking hand to swipe at the moisture that rushed unbidden to her eyes. Why was she crying? She'd long ago admitted she'd never loved Josiah. Yet his memory still filled her with a turbulent mixture of grief and guilt and regret.

For nine years, he'd been the center of her life. Perhaps not beloved but just . . . there. Then he was no more.

"And you lost your home."

"Yes." She inhaled audibly and stood straighter. If she dwelled further on her sorry history, she'd make an utter fool of herself. And she'd done that too many times already in front of the marquess. He had an uncanny ability to probe her vulnerabilities. "You're a good listener, my lord."

"Thank you," he returned dryly. "It's not something I've developed through practice."

He now knew more about her than anyone she'd met in the last nine years. She felt at a loss, unsure if that altered their lethal dilemma or the attraction simmering between them.

Did her confession change things at all? Not in any concrete way, she guessed, although in her heart she felt differently.

"You're sorry you asked." She managed an awkward laugh.

He didn't smile back. "No, never sorry."

Matthew studied her as she walked ahead. He remained behind. Partly because he knew she wanted privacy after her revelations. Partly because he was so angry, he was likely to lash out.

Furious grief for her sorrow gripped him in claws of steel. She was young, close to his age, yet she'd seen so much unhappiness. He'd give his soul to ease her pain. But his soul, he knew to his regret, held no value for her.

He clenched his fists at his sides as he watched her raise her hands to her face. He didn't need to be close to her to know the tears that had threatened during her tale finally overflowed.

Jesus, he hated it when she cried. Every tear ripped at his heart like a blunt butcher's knife.

She'd been determined to cast herself as the villainess in her recounting. He'd heard the shame throbbing in her voice. He could well believe she'd acted thoughtlessly. She'd been a mere chit of sixteen and she'd more than paid the price for her foolishness since. The loss of her family was a wound that still festered.

His parents had loved him dearly. He could imagine no circumstance, however dire, that would make his mother or father repudiate him. Yet Grace had endured long, lonely banishment from her home and those she loved.

Damn bloody Paget to the hottest hole in hell. He hoped the bastard fried forever in his own self-righteousness. How in God's name could a man in his fifties remove a pampered girl from everything she knew and subject her to unrelieved hardship?

It wasn't hard to fill in the details. The misery of life with a man set on crushing her spirit. The unending drudgery on the farm. The despair when she was left destitute and friendless. The fortitude with which she'd faced her trials.

Matthew's outrage boiled up. She'd been reticent about the sordid details of her marriage but nonetheless, he had a vivid picture of the man. Dry, arrogant, sanctimonious, obsessive.

Beautiful, warm Grace had been tied to that canting tyrant for nine joyless years.

He knew already that she'd stuck to her vows to the sour, judgmental old fool. She'd put heart and soul into making the best of the situation. Even if it killed her, which, given her thinness, wasn't far from the truth.

Paget should never have married her. But Matthew could guess how irresistible she'd been in her passionate commitment to a better world. Hell, hadn't she tried to mask her beauty and ardor in the last days? Still he wanted her so badly he couldn't sleep or eat. Old Paget hadn't stood a chance in that dusty old bookshop, God rot him.

The bastard had won an exquisite treasure and he hadn't deserved her.

And Matthew finally faced the shameful truth that lurked in his heart. He was jealous. Jealous of a dead man. In his way, he was no better than that whoreson Paget. Both of them wanted Grace. Neither could do her any good.

His longing gaze followed her as she slowly made her way along the path. While one triumphant chant rang over and over in his heart.

She hadn't loved her husband.

It was late but Grace lay in watchful alertness in the dark bedchamber. Trusting the marquess with the details of her marriage had left her edgy, exhausted. But it wasn't the strain of reliving her painful history that made sleep elusive.

No, furtive lust kept her awake.

Lust all those hours with Lord Sheene had built into a raging blaze. It now threatened to incinerate every principle.

With a feeling of inevitability, she watched the door swing open. The marquess stood on the threshold as he had that first night. She shoved herself up against the headboard and tried to quash the drunken joy surging through her.

"My lord?" The question in the soft rain-hushed darkness was an invitation.

Chapter 12

Holding her in his arms last night had heightened Matthew's senses to an almost preternatural level. He heard her husky uncertainty. He heard the breath catch in her throat. Jesus, he even heard desire thrumming beneath the seemingly innocent words.

Lingering in the doorway, he told himself he'd faced greater challenges than this exquisite dark-haired woman. He wished to Hades he believed it.

Bedclothes rustled and bedsprings squeaked. Damnably suggestive sounds. Then he heard her fiddle with tinder and candle before an unsteady glow bloomed. Briefly he closed his eyes against what the golden light revealed. Grace, all great unfathomable eyes in a pale oval face. Her long plait fell over her shoulder and curved to caress one breast. His fingers curled at his sides as if they followed that sinuous line.

"My lord, what are you doing here?" She leaned forward and the garish green satin nightgown slipped almost to her nipples. Before she hitched the neckline up, he glimpsed the soft pink of her areolas. Desire slammed through him and he bit back a groan.

"We must share a bed," he said curtly, too close to the limits of control to modulate his tone. He should have spoken about this in daylight, but he'd been reluctant to shatter the intimacy her confidences had created.

Emotion flared in her eyes. Fear, certainly. And something else smoky and mysterious that tightened his need another agonizing notch.

He plowed on. He had to. Her life hung upon this moment. He spoke as though drilling soldiers and not talking to the woman he craved above all others. "We have to convince Monks and Filey we're lovers. I mean only to sleep here. You have my word you're safe from my advances."

Surprisingly, that full mouth quirked into a wry smile. "So we lie like Tristan and Yseult with a sword between us?"

Hard as it was, *hard as he was*, he couldn't help smiling at the absurd image. "I find myself currently embarrassed of a sword."

He didn't say that, in the legend, the sword had proven no barrier to passion. He was in enough trouble.

She shook her head. "This won't work."

He stalked across the threshold. The blasted night rail slipped again, revealing a smooth white shoulder.

"Unless I spend my nights here, my uncle will kill you." He watched the color drain from her face. He went on in a more measured tone. "And by here, I mean this bed. I'd offer to sleep on the floor or in a chair but there are no locks. Monks or Filey can check on us any time."

By now, she was pale as a new moon. She moistened her lips again. Jesus, he wished she'd stop doing that. His fists balled at his sides.

"Grace, this is a ruse to save you, that's all," he said in a raw voice.

Without waiting for assent, he headed toward the bed. She slid across, leaving him room. Her voice was subdued as she spoke. "As you wish."

"Christ," he muttered and went on before she protested

his language. "It isn't as I wish. Nothing in my bloody life is as I wish. But I'm trying to keep you alive."

He sat on the mattress and tugged his boots off. He flung them with twin thuds against the wall. He ripped his shirt over his head and pitched it after his footwear.

"Lord Sheene . . ."

He wrenched his head around to look at her, although the picture of her stretched out against the sheets tempted him far too much. She stared aghast at his naked back.

"Your scars," she whispered in shock.

He'd forgotten about his ruined back. It was years since the wounds had healed and he'd exercised like a demon to banish any residual stiffness. He hadn't thought how the sight might affect Grace.

Corrosive shame flooded his face with color. He lurched toward the floor to fumble for his shirt. "I'm sorry. This must offend you."

Her hand, warm, comforting, womanly, on his back turned him to stone. He closed his eyes and let her touch seep through to his bones, although he knew he should flinch away, hide the degrading evidence of his weakness.

"No, I'm not offended." She sounded like she fought back tears. He heard her suck in a shaky breath. "Tell me what happened."

He straightened slowly and opened his eyes to stare down at where his hands fisted on his knees. "One of the doctors attempted to beat the madness out. Monks continued the treatment when he left."

That was as much of a confession as he could manage. He couldn't bear to tell her of other beatings or of the times Monks or Filey had blistered his skin with hot irons as he lay tethered like an animal. Although if she looked closely, the map of welts across his skin betrayed his humiliation.

"I'm sorry." Her hand gently stroked down to his waist. Her touch soothed the old pain even as the brush of her fingers on his skin made forbidden desire flare like a hungry flame.

"It was a long time ago," he said harshly.

That was true, but his soul still suffered from those beatings as though they'd occurred yesterday.

"You think I'm prying." Her hand dropped away and he only just stopped himself begging her to touch him again. For comfort. And God help him, for pleasure.

"I think we have enough difficulties in the present without worrying about past troubles," he forced himself to say.

"You've borne so much and I've brought you nothing but pain," she said sadly from behind him. "How you must hate me."

"You know that's far from true."

He turned and glared at her. She was flat on her back and tears glinted in her long lashes. His heart stumbled to a halt at the thought that he'd made her cry. He was a damned clumsy fool. And he couldn't even trust himself to offer a solacing touch.

Her warmth curled out to entice him nearer. It whispered to let Lord John, Monks, Filey, and the whole damned world go to hell.

He couldn't give in. Even while denial made every sinew ache.

Very carefully, so he didn't touch her, he stretched out and stared fixedly up at the ceiling. He drew the sheet up to hide the fact that he kept his breeches on. His loins ached like the very devil. It was going to be a very long night.

Grace turned her head and studied the marquess. Even in profile, his expression was tense. Frustration and displeasure all but steamed from him. She longed to smooth the hair from his brow, calm the turmoil in his soul. She wanted to kiss every pale scar that marred the golden skin of his back. She wanted to take the agonies he'd suffered into herself and make him whole again. She wanted to save him from any pain to come.

Futile wishes, all of them.

With a stifled sigh, she leaned over to blow out the candle but Lord Sheene spoke first. "Leave the light."

She almost said as you wish, but the innocuous words had already provoked such fury, she stopped herself. Instead, she lay back and tried to pretend nothing out of the ordinary occurred. She'd shared a bed with Josiah. For most of her marriage, the sharing had been chaste. She was used to lying beside a male body with no expectation the body would roll over to claim hers. Where was the difference?

The difference was desire.

Even at the height of her girlish infatuation, she'd never wanted Josiah the way a woman wanted a man.

She wanted Lord Sheene. She'd never experienced the pangs of sexual need. How cruel that they burgeoned in this impossible situation.

Her heart caught as she remembered how he'd looked when he came in. Tall, powerful, commanding. The white shirt loose at the neck, hinting at the shadowy planes of his chest. She now knew the skin there was smooth, with a scattering of black hair. She knew how lean muscles tightened over his belly and ran in sinewy, vein-crossed strength down his arms. He already had more physical actuality for her than Josiah ever achieved.

The marquess was close enough for her to feel his warmth and smell lemony soap mixed with the underlying essence that was purely him. He was close enough for her to sense each breath. His eyes were shut but he was no nearer sleep than she.

As if to confirm that thought, he spoke. "I'm sorry my

presence disturbs you." He opened his eyes but didn't look at her. Instead his gaze fixed again on the ceiling.

Yes, his presence disturbed her. In ways he couldn't even begin to guess.

"You do this for my sake." She watched that sculpted profile. The high-bridged blade of a nose. The mysterious eyes. The passionate mouth. She wanted that mouth on hers. She wanted that mouth on her body. The image was so graphic, every nerve tightened and she shifted uncomfortably.

He said no more. Grace assumed he eventually slept. She stayed awake and restless until dawn stole into the room.

The hurried thud of rough boots on the stairs outside woke Matthew. He barely had time to fling the sheet up to cover Grace before Monks loomed in the open doorway.

"What is the meaning of this?" Matthew asked coldly, his grip firming protectively around her shoulders. He was already holding her. Somewhere in the night, he must have taken her in his arms.

Lascivious appreciation replaced the furious consternation in Monks's blockish face as he took in the couple entwined on the bed. "Beg pardon, your lordship," he said out of habit while his pig-like eyes focused on what little he could see of Grace. "I was right worried when I saw nowt of you downstairs."

Worried because he feared his charge had escaped. The brutal facts of imprisonment never faded into the background. They oozed into the sunny room like a foul miasma.

"Well, now you've located me, remove yourself," Matthew growled. Against his chest, Grace muffled a distressed sound. His arms tightened in silent warning.

"Aye, your lordship. I reckoned you'd get around to spreading the slut's legs one day. Was she good, lad? A wild ride? Or cold and tasteless as barley water?"

Matthew's eyes sharpened on the man who had tortured and tormented him for eleven years. "I'll kill you one day, Monks," he said in a quiet, deadly voice.

Monks remained unimpressed. "Aye, well, that's grand and I wish you luck, my lord. If wishes were horses, beggars would ride, as my mam would say."

"Get out," Matthew snapped. Grace's hands curled like claws in the sheet and her breath was a frightened flutter on his bare neck.

Monks shrugged and turned toward the door. "You'll want to get back to business, I warrant. Enjoy your sport, lad."

"You will grant us privacy, Monks," Matthew growled.

The big man paused in the doorway and glanced back with a gloating leer. "Shy, is she? Or is it your lordship who's a might bashful? Aye, well, if she's keeping you entertained, there's nowt else we need to know. Filey and I will get our turn at her when your lordship's had his fill."

This time Grace's whimper was clearly audible. Matthew didn't shift his eyes from Monks. "If you harm so much as a hair on this lady's head, you will pay."

The mockery in Monks's smile became overt. "His first fuck always makes a lad right brave. Brave and stupid." He bowed his head in a gesture of respect that held no respect whatsoever. "Any road, I wish you a right *good* day." He didn't bother to contain his laughter at the crude witticism as he stumped across the landing and down the steps.

Matthew struggled to restrain his anger. The urge was strong to smash something. Preferably Monks's smug face.

At his side, Grace lay in trembling stillness until the downstairs door slammed behind Monks. Then she scrambled out of bed to stand shaking in the center of the room.

She wrapped her arms around herself, hands clenching and unclenching convulsively on her elbows. Her stance lifted her breasts under the green satin. Matthew's sexual hunger, momentarily submerged in sick anger, returned in a crashing wave.

"That was . . . awful." Her eyes glittered with agitation and she vibrated with tension. "I can't do this."

"Yes, you can," he said implacably. He rolled out of the bed and stood close enough to tower over her.

Her fine dark brows contracted with furious denial and she jerked her chin up until she met his eyes so far above her. "I can't!"

She flung herself into restless pacing. The flimsy satin flowed around her slender body, clinging and sliding over thigh and breast and hip with a fascinating liquidity that reminded Matthew of the sea.

He hadn't seen the sea in eleven years but he remembered the relentless roll and rush of water. He remembered how he couldn't take his eyes off it. He certainly couldn't take his eyes off Grace as she prowled the room like a caged tigress.

"I will not have that filthy creature salivating over what he thinks you and I do in this bed." She reached the end of the room and whirled around with such violence that her plait whipped around her head like a lashing tiger's tail.

"It doesn't matter what he thinks as long as he thinks we're lovers," Matthew bit out while Grace's angry humiliation seethed around him like a stormy ocean.

Such passion she had. How could Monks say she was cold when she invested everything she did with feeling, with heat? Matthew wanted that passion to warm him.

"I can't bear it!" She passed so close that her scent teased him. She'd slept in his arms for two nights and now her scent was part of him, like blood or breath.

Another turn. Another swish of satin. Another flurry of steps toward him and away and back again.

He reached out to tug her around to face him. The skin of her arm was smooth and cool under his hand in spite of her quivering rage. "A few insults from a creature like Monks is small price for safety."

He was edgy and angry. Monks's foul insinuations had ripped at him too. Grace's tempestuous parade around the room only worsened his frustration. He wanted her to devote all that energy to him. If she didn't calm down, he'd tumble her onto the rumpled sheets and forget his rapidly fraying honor.

She nodded once and her wary, unhappy eyes sharpened on his face. "I don't know how you bear living here."

"I bear it because I must," he said grimly. He turned toward a chest and ripped out fresh clothing without paying attention to what he chose. If he stayed within touching distance, he wouldn't lie when he claimed she was his lover. "I'll see you at breakfast. We should spend the day together."

"For Monks and Filey," she whispered behind him.

No, he wanted to say, for me. But he was silent as he left her to her chastity and the sunlit room.

Grace sat back on her heels away from the now-tidy rose bed and found Lord Sheene watching her. That gold gaze heated her to her marrow.

All day he'd watched her, at first covertly. As the hours went on, he'd taken less trouble to mask his interest.

He stood at his workbench potting what looked like another dead stick. He definitely wasn't concentrating on the task.

She blushed and looked down to where his attention focused. Her woefully low neckline drooped, revealing the embroidered top of her chemise.

Perhaps it had been a mistake to pull on this particular gown. So far she'd only altered two dresses and Mrs. Filey had removed both for laundering. She raised a hand to tug her décolletage up when something stayed her. Perhaps the hungry intensity of his gaze. Perhaps the barely hidden desolation beneath the sexual interest.

His uncle had stolen so much from him, even the chance to ogle a pretty girl.

Well, the only girl he had the chance to ogle was Grace Paget and she couldn't bring herself to refuse him.

A decent woman wouldn't tease a man like this. Josiah would be disgusted with her. But Josiah was gone and she was most definitely alive. And in the grip of a physical enchantment beyond anything she'd imagined possible.

She wanted Lord Sheene to look at her.

She let her hand drop to her waist and straightened her spine so her bosom rose high and proud. How she wished there was more of her. Although what there was seemed enough for Lord Sheene. The lines of his face sharpened and a muscle twitched in his cheek. She had no doubt that behind the concealing bench, he hardened. The moisture evaporated from her mouth at the thought.

"You were talking about extending the franchise," he said in a strangled voice.

"Was I?" She vaguely remembered they'd been discussing politics. The marquess, for all his seclusion, was surprisingly well informed, much more than she.

"Yes."

She waited for him to say more. But he was silent while his eyes devoured the curves she paraded like some strumpet hawking her wares in Covent Garden.

The moment spun on. Her nipples peaked. Her breasts swelled and pushed against her flimsy stays. She knew he noted her arousal. Still she displayed herself.

He made a jerky movement in her direction. She waited

for him to circle the bench, cross the few feet between them, and grab her.

As he lunged forward, his hand snicked the pot. It toppled and hit the stone flags with a resounding crash.

"Hell!" he muttered as terracotta smashed around his booted feet.

Grace leapt up. "I'm sorry," she said in dismay. These silly games were dangerous enough in the outside world. Here they threatened disaster.

But it had felt so good when he looked at her, as if he'd die if he stopped.

"It isn't your fault." He dropped to his knees and fished the largest shards out of the scattered dirt. With guilty horror, she saw that his hands shook.

"Yes, it is," she said sadly. It wasn't fair to torment him. Even if tormenting him was so sweet.

She knelt to help and they both reached for the same piece. Their fingers met. It was like touching lightning. Her heart gave a great thud and every hair on her skin stood on end. She gasped and made to pull away. He snatched her hand, gripping hard enough to hurt.

"Grace . . ." he said in a cracked voice.

He dragged her forward, almost overbalancing her and cradled her hand against his chest. His heart kicked violently under her palm. Beneath the fine shirt, his skin burned.

She wanted that heat. She wanted it to envelop her, incinerate her. Only inches separated them. Inches she could bridge with one small tilt of her body. Heavy, liquid desire settled low in her belly.

Wrenching free, he lurched to his feet. He turned his back, his shoulders heaving as he fought for control.

She remained on her knees while she waited for her pulse to steady. Very deliberately, she wiped her damp palms on her skirt and took a deep breath.

Should she give in to what whirled around them? Or

leave him to find composure? Was she ready to take that final step? Could she face the inevitable consequences if she did?

Her heart thundered a mighty *yes*.

Still she hesitated. Through nine years of unhappy marriage, she had guarded her reputation like a miser's treasure. Was she ready to abandon that?

She bit her lip, studying his tense back, his bent head, those clenched fists pressed so stiffly to his sides.

She chose the coward's way.

"I'll take Wolfram for a walk," she said unevenly, rubbing the hand he'd crushed.

She had to get out of this walled garden before she did something irrevocable. Something virtuous Grace Paget couldn't countenance. Something that turned her father's last words to her into an accurate prophecy of her ruin.

The marquess didn't answer. Nor did he look at her as she stood up on legs that threatened to fold beneath her.

"Come, Wolfram."

The dog lifted his head from the shade and rose with a stretch. He obediently trotted to her side.

As she entered the woods, her steps were slow and reluctant and Lord Sheene's ragged breathing echoed in her ears.

Grace clicked her fingers to Wolfram to urge him away from a pile of leaves. She'd walked for hours. She knew she should go back to the marquess but she couldn't bear the tension between them. She just couldn't bear it. She came to a shuddering halt in the middle of the path and strove for clarity, for strength, for courage.

All eluded her.

The huge dog came up and nosed at her hip, clearly wondering why she'd stopped. She pulled gently at his soft ears. "Oh, Wolfram, what am I to do?"

He must have heard her distress or sensed it in her quivering body because he gave a soft whine and butted her softly with his blunt head. She blinked away tears. She'd moved beyond comfort.

And she was so tired.

Tired of fear, tired of fighting her deepest urgings, tired of working out what she should do. She'd wanted Lord Sheene from the first, she recognized. Now controlling her desire was so much more difficult. Now she'd kissed him, held him, touched him.

Now she knew he wanted her.

The immediacy of Lord John's threats had receded with the marquess sharing her bed. As that fear ebbed, fear that she'd succumb to sin flooded in. Desire beat ceaselessly inside her. Nothing silenced it. Not the counsel of prudence. Not the voice of morality. Not even the relentless demands of self-interest.

Her skin still prickled where he'd held her hand. Her hand! She really was hopelessly infatuated.

She sank onto a bed of new grass and lay back, closing her eyes. Monks and Filey wouldn't check the grounds for hours yet. Just for a minute, she'd rest. Before swirling, terrible need stirred again. Before she stepped once more into the turbulent dance of illicit desire.

Lord Sheene moved in her body, his powerful muscles flexing with each entry and withdrawal. She shifted, lifting her hips so his thrusts went deeper. The friction was delicious, wonderful.

Not enough.

She moaned in complaint. He was hot and heavy above her but she wanted more. He said her name softly. She yearned toward the sound.

He said her name again. She opened her eyes to find him standing at her side, staring down at her.

A dream, then. All that lovely pleasure had existed only in imagination. Regret bit so sharply, she almost cried out. Guilty heat flooded her face. The fantasy had been so explicit, so uninhibited, so . . . depraved.

She blinked, but the dream's effects were slow to fade. Her breasts ached full and needy for his touch and she was embarrassingly moist between her legs.

She could smell her own arousal. Could he?

"Grace?" He looked tense and wary. "It's late. Come inside before Monks and Filey find you."

Still trapped in a fog of longing, she let her eyes feast on the man above her. She was so hot for him, she felt as though she trapped the sun inside her.

Then she realized the shadows lengthened. She must have slept for hours in the sweet thick grass.

Dreaming of Lord Sheene's lovemaking.

In her dream, she'd been wanton and welcoming. More wanton and welcoming than she'd ever been with Josiah.

She accepted Lord Sheene's hand to help her up. But her legs buckled and she staggered against him.

"Hell and damnation," he muttered savagely. He grabbed Grace by her upper arms and tugged her into his body. She had a brief, confused impression of strength and heat.

Then his mouth collided with hers.

Chapter 13

Grace's lips mashed painfully against her teeth. Lord Sheene's fingers clenched with bruising force around her arms. Where her breasts flattened against his chest, she felt the wild thud of his heart.

Astonishment held her paralyzed. Then she gave a muffled whimper of discomfort. He must have heard, because abruptly the fierce kiss was over.

Struggling for breath, she stumbled free. She rubbed her arms as the blood flowed back in a tingling rush. Lord Sheene swung away and stared into the trees. His expression was so desolate, it wrenched her heart.

"Christ!" he gritted out.

The self-loathing in the curse made her flinch. Heaven help her, he wasn't the one who should feel guilty. She'd provoked him with her reckless behavior in the courtyard. Bitter shame ate at her.

"This is my fault," she said unsteadily. Her lips still throbbed from his violent ardor.

He turned tormented gold-flecked eyes on her. Their beauty was stark in a face etched with suffering. "No, it's damn well not your fault. You can't hide from what we both know is true. I've wanted to touch you from the moment I saw you tied up on that table like some damned heathen sacrifice."

She shivered under the searing intensity of his gaze.

Yes, she knew he wanted her. His desire called to her most secret yearnings. Yearnings she found harder to deny with every hour. Volcanic heat built between them. But any explosion would leave only devastation behind.

She recognized that. Yet she couldn't block the thrill that crackled through her as she imagined him kissing her again. Properly this time.

Oh, Grace, you're a wicked woman.

She shivered again. He noticed as he always did. "You're cold. I'll take you back to the cottage." He bowed and presented his arm. They could be in Mayfair instead of trapped inside this luxurious cage. Another shadowy glimpse into the life he should have led. The reminder, as always, filled her with a roiling combination of futile anger and piercing compassion.

"Grace?" His eyes darkened with familiar self-mistrust. "Or do you prefer your own company?"

"No." She placed her hand on his arm and was shocked to feel how he trembled. His veneer of control was wafer-thin.

For a few fraught moments, they walked in silence. Grace's lips stung from his attentions, the way they had stung last time he'd kissed her. Regret tightened her throat. Regret for what she drove him to, certainly. But even stronger, regret that he withheld the sweetness of his unfettered kiss.

She knew him well enough to recognize that tenderness formed the bedrock of his soul. Tenderness and strength, although it was the tenderness she longed for most of all. Yet his kisses had been hard, quick, unemotional. Almost cruel.

Her courage faltered but she couldn't suppress the curiosity that gnawed at her. "Why did you kiss me like that?"

He tensed under her hand but didn't, as she expected, pull free. "I told you why. We needn't dwell on it. Unless, of course, you find my humiliation diverting."

The last taunting remark reminded her of his sarcasm when she first arrived. Then his jarring wit had been a defense against the woman he believed his enemy.

What did he defend himself against now?

Her fingers curled against his shirt sleeve, forcing him to stop and face her. "Why were you so rough?"

He flushed under her searching regard. A muscle flickered in his cheek as he jerked free. "I've already apologized. What more do you want? Blood? I'm sure I can oblige."

"You know that's not true," she said softly.

His voice was harsh. "You leave me no pride. You must guess you're the first woman I've seen since I was fourteen. You must guess what that means." He drew in a jagged breath. "Now, for God's sake, leave me alone."

She hardly heard his biting command. Instead, she stood in appalled silence.

Curse her for a blind, insensitive fool. How could she not have known? He'd fallen ill when little more than a boy. Since then he'd been Lord John's prisoner. Every day it became more heartbreakingly apparent how much his uncle had stolen from him.

The marquess watched her, his remarkable eyes filled with despair. "Go on, laugh. I'm twenty-five years old and until I saw you, I've never touched a woman in passion." His expressive mouth twisted in a humorless smile. "My uncle should exhibit me as one of the wonders of the age."

His pain clamored to her. Louder than the demands of self-interest. Stronger than the tenets she'd always followed.

You can offer him recompense.

The insidious suggestion welled up from deep within. From the dark realm where lust and loneliness skulked. She stiffened as though someone aimed a pistol at her head.

She found her voice. "Kissing is simple enough to learn," she said huskily.

"Perhaps." His expressive mouth settled in an unhappy line. "If one has the opportunity."

Grace chewed nervously on her lip. The marquess's eyes sharpened on the movement. For all his inexperience, he was still a man with a man's responses and needs.

The reminder tipped her uncertainty into rash decision. She took a deep breath and spoke before she could stop herself. "I offer you the opportunity."

His vivid face creased in a frown and his eyes deepened to somber bronze. The soft gloaming cast shadows across his black hair and tall, leanly muscled body. She was always conscious of his attractions. Now his masculine beauty transfixed her.

"Are you sure about this, Grace?"

She was far from sure. But she'd traveled too far to retreat. Her heart raced and her hands twisted at her waist in an anxious dance. "A . . . a woman likes to be treated gently, my lord."

Some of the tension seeped from his expression. "Then I'll be gentle."

Grace waited for him to fumble, perhaps betray traces of his earlier ferocity. But his touch was assured and light as he framed her cheeks with his hands and used his thumbs to angle her chin up.

Slowly, so slowly her heart had almost stumbled to a standstill by the time he kissed her, his head lowered. She felt his breath on her lips before he pressed his mouth to hers. Even after those travesties of kisses she'd forced upon him two nights ago, he tasted familiar.

His lips moved, clung.

The contact was poignantly sweet. Then it was over.

It had been a boy's kiss although his eyes held mature speculation as they focused on her face. She didn't know what he saw, but there was no hesitation as his mouth descended once more.

This time, he lingered, tasted, discovered, savored. Astonishing really, how quickly he mastered the basics. Her blood thundered in her ears. His teeth scraped across her bottom lip and the kiss deepened. Her lips parted to the delicious pressure.

Unbelievably she felt his tongue slide against hers, a hot invasion startling in its intimacy. Neither her few stolen kisses in the gardens at Marlow Hall nor her years with Josiah had prepared her for this.

The sensation was glorious, heady, *frightening.*

She gave a moan of protest. Immediately he released her, although he only moved a few inches away. He was close enough for his lemony scent, overlaid with the spice of masculine arousal, to tease.

"Grace?" He sounded shaken to his soul.

A deep breath did nothing to calm her chaotic senses. She raised an unsteady hand to her heated cheek. How could someone so untried make her feel what no man ever had?

"I think perhaps you overestimate my experience," she said unevenly. "Josiah wasn't . . . wasn't physically demonstrative."

"I see," the marquess said slowly.

She wondered if he did. If she became his tutor in the preliminaries to love, he needed to know she was in many ways a fellow beginner.

"So we're more equal in this than I imagined," he said, because of course, he did understand.

As always, his rare smile made her heart somersault.

How could she resist the man who smiled like that? How could she resist the man who now swept her into his arms with such confidence?

She'd never been so aware of his strength. She curved to fit herself to the hard planes of his body. When Josiah touched her, he'd always made her feel like a dirty secret. With one kiss, the marquess made her feel wanted, beautiful, a woman at last.

"My lord?" she asked shakily.

"Matthew," he prompted.

"Matthew." His name flowed over her tongue, smooth as warmed honey. And a hundred times sweeter.

"I like that. I'd like it even better if you put your arms around me."

"We've gone far enough, my lor . . . Matthew." She intended to sound repressive but her words emerged as a breathless appeal. His warm tormenting scent drove her as mad as he was supposed to be. "We should stop."

"No," he said with an arrogance befitting the great Marquess of Sheene.

His mouth swooped down on hers. She gasped astonished pleasure into his seeking heat.

This was no apprentice. This man knew what he wanted and how to get it. The restrained gentleness had vanished. In its place, she surrendered to power and need and demand.

Some long-constrained demon in Grace rose to meet him. Soon her mouth responded as hungrily, her hands clutched him as tightly. He tasted like forbidden joy. He tasted like everything she wanted. He tasted like rapture and passion. She strained upward, craving more, her fingers digging into his muscled back as if she meant him never to escape.

The kiss moved infinitely beyond anything Grace had

experienced. Her breasts were tight and ached for the touch of his hands. Her loins throbbed insistently. With dismay, she recognized her wildness would only quiet if he filled her emptiness with his body.

How had a few kisses created this storm of desire?

Except it wasn't the kisses, intoxicating as they were. The kisses were just an excuse to feed her ever-present longing. Now she'd liberated that longing and as a result, ruin loomed.

Ruin pulled away slightly and gave her a lazy, satisfied, male smile. "Kiss me again, Grace," he said softly.

And despite everything, she made no demur as he gathered her up and found her mouth with his.

This, this was what Matthew had dreamt of through those endless nights. Grace luscious and eager in his arms. Grace warm and supple under his hands. To defy the reliably malign fate which was sure to rip her away, he brought her closer and plundered her mouth.

She tasted delicious. More succulent than the ripest plum. The harrowing encounter two nights ago had hinted at her bounty. But he'd never guessed the riches that awaited when she came to him willingly.

He'd had no idea a kiss could be like this. So all-encompassing. As if when lips met, souls met.

Instinct made him push his tongue between her lips again. Heat sizzled through him as her tongue grazed his, then moved with more purpose. She sighed into his mouth and rational thought deserted him. The kiss lost all restraint. Became an open gateway to other pleasures he had no right to seize.

He raised his head. Her eyes were dazed and dilated with arousal. Wanton color flushed her usually pale cheeks. Her lips glistened wet and swollen. They parted as she sucked in a shuddering breath. He fought the urge to taste that breath. His erection rubbed insistently against the front of his breeches, demanded that he draw her down onto the lush grass where he'd found her sleeping.

No! He must let her go now. Or he'd never let her go.

Slowly, he slid his arms from around her, while every beat of his heart insisted he take their kisses further. Take them to the conclusion his body screamed for.

Stepping away from her was physically painful.

And all for nought.

When she swayed, he caught her again. Only the last shred of willpower stopped him snatching her up for more intoxicating kisses. Instead, he hooked his fingers around her upper arms and held her steady.

She stared at him, lost, dazzled, silent. Masculine triumph surged through him. She looked like the world started and ended with this moment.

"Grace? Are you all right?" His voice emerged as a croak.

She swallowed and her eyes dropped to his mouth. He bit back a groan as another bolt of incendiary desire left him staggering. "Grace?"

She blinked and raised her eyes. He watched as awareness slowly replaced her lost expression.

God knew what she saw when she looked at him with that level cobalt stare. A poor shuffling lunatic? A fumbling brute? An inept boy? Or a man she wanted in her bed?

"That . . . that was a mistake," she said huskily. Her voice scraped along his strained nerves like velvet sandpaper.

"A glorious mistake," he said, before he could help himself.

"Yes."

The murmured admission set his heart racing again. His

clasp on her arms softened, became a caress. She closed her eyes and leaned nearer, tilting her face up.

He couldn't ignore the invitation. Whatever honor required. As their mouths melded, he felt rather than heard her gasp.

His fingers plunged into her thick black hair. He wanted to tear her clothes off and take her. He wanted the rapturous kiss never to end.

He wanted her. He wanted her.

He could never have her. Making her his mistress was wrong. He couldn't do it. He wrenched out of her arms. His hands clenched hard at his sides. He wouldn't do it.

"This was meant to be a kiss only," she whispered, raising a hand to her lips as though she tested the memory of his touch.

"A lesson." Bitterness tinged his voice. She was right to remind him of how this had started. His futile anger betrayed her miraculous generosity. Her kisses had offered a glimpse of paradise. A paradise he could never enter.

Surprisingly, she smiled. "You graduated with honors."

"If not with honor."

Even as he said it, shock slammed his heart against his ribs. He'd trained himself to theorize and experiment and collect evidence. He couldn't mistake his conclusion.

She'd enjoyed kissing him.

Was it possible she wanted him even a fraction as much as he wanted her?

"I can't imagine you doing anything without honor," she said softly but with emphasis, and turned with a flick of her skirts toward the house.

He could imagine it, he thought, watching the alluring sway of her hips as she walked off.

He could imagine throwing her down on the muddy ground and having his way. Or cornering her against a tree. Or chasing her back to the cottage and catching her the minute she was safe from spying eyes.

No honor in any of it. Although there would be pleasure. And shame.

But as he watched her retreat down the path, it was the pleasure he contemplated.

Matthew's mood had soured by dinner. The kiss had been wonderful. The most wonderful thing that ever happened to him. Now he knew her taste and the soft sighs she made in surrender, how could he live without touching her again?

If he touched her again, he wouldn't stop at kisses.

He still had to get through the night lying beside her in chaste misery. The prospect made every muscle tighten in agonized denial.

Grace stood at the window and turned as he entered the salon. His hand clenched hard on the door as he struggled to rein in his urge to sweep her up in his arms. She needed his protection not his passion. The glories of the afternoon were something he must put aside, like an outgrown coat.

Easy to say, harder to do when her smile caught at his poor heart. Why the hell did she have to be so beautiful?

"Lord Sheene."

"You called me Matthew this afternoon."

Her eyes darkened as they'd darkened that afternoon. He strode toward her before he remembered he'd sworn to keep his distance. Only when she nervously backed away did he stop, still several feet away.

"Matthew."

That throaty voice turned his name into an endearment. Oh, yes, kissing her had been a mistake. A mistake he'd pay for in endless pain and frustration. Still he couldn't regret it.

"Grace." He watched the fickle color fluctuate on her milky skin. "Are you hungry?"

Her eyes flared with unmistakable interest before those sinfully thick eyelashes hid her expression. "Yes," she said almost inaudibly.

His fingers itched to trace that flush of warm pink along her cheekbones. He hadn't expected her to be ill at ease. After all, she was a widow and had known a man. Surely a mere kiss couldn't send her into such a flutter. Had Paget, the dry old stick, let her down in this as well as everything else?

She wore a blue silk gown cut low at the neck. His eyes fell to the intriguing shadow between her breasts. She shivered as if he touched her there.

"Please say something," she said on a cracked laugh. "Even if it's only to talk about the weather."

"I believe we're due for rain," he said, unable to tear his gaze away. As if to prove his comment's awful inanity, rain splattered hard against the window. They were in the middle of a downpour. He hadn't noticed. All he noticed was Grace. Her exquisite skin, her slender curves wrapped in silk the color of sky, her lush mouth.

He ripped himself from his distraction and crossed to the sideboard to pour her wine. But invisible wires connected him to her. Wires that tightened infinitesimally with every breath so the effort of keeping his hands off her became more onerous by the second.

Grace picked at her food, in spite of her avowal of hunger. She was hungry, all right. For a man. The man who sat opposite, struggling to make conversation. Struggling not to look at her. Looking all the same. As if no power on earth could stop him.

Just as she couldn't help looking at him.

She'd never felt this way before. A turbulent storm of desire raged within her. Need blazed like a comet. This thirst for a man's touch was unfamiliar. Distressing.

She admired Lord Sheene's mind, she applauded his steadfastness, she was in awe of his courage. But all of this faded in her craving for the slide of his skin on hers, the heat of his mouth, the beat of his heart under her hand.

She'd never understood why women discarded reputation, future, security for passion's sake. That overpowering physical passion had always seemed as illusory as Josiah's fine soul.

She understood passion now. Or its alluring prelude.

She glanced up from pushing food around her plate to catch Lord Sheene studying her. Again. Fire smoldered in his eyes. He no longer tried to conceal his interest. Heaven help her, that very openness stoked her simmering need.

How had she ever imagined he didn't want her? With the freshly opened eyes of knowledge, she realized desire had ignited from the first. Desire laced with fear on her part. Desire laced with suspicion on his.

Now desire emerged naked from the shadows.

And she was afraid.

Grace Marlow had been brought up a lady. Grace Paget had never broken her marriage vows. Had never been tempted.

Five weeks a widow, and temptation entangled her in strands of finest steel.

She wanted the marquess to possess her.

The thought sent a torrent of heat crashing through her. She shifted on her chair as the heat settled, became more specific. Matthew's nostrils flared as if he caught the scent of her arousal. The animal awareness between them was electric, irrefutable.

She tried to tell herself the act would be the usual disappointment. She'd endured Josiah's occasional use of her body, but never found joy in it.

Why should Lord Sheene be any different?

He was a man. He'd rut over her until he finished. Then he'd roll off her to fall into snoring oblivion.

But she remembered the deftness of his hands this afternoon. She remembered the heady scent of his skin and the taste of his mouth.

He was a young man in the prime of life. Josiah had been old, old.

She was the first woman Lord Sheene had touched. The idea held such erotic charge. She'd awoken him to desire. She could teach him pleasure. She could . . .

No, Grace. You can teach him nothing. What do you know about passion?

She clamped down hard on the images of his long beautiful body moving on her, above her, in her. What little food she'd swallowed coagulated into a cold mass in her stomach and she rose, trembling.

He stood when she did. Concern lit his gold eyes as he stared at her. "Are you unwell, Grace?"

She shook her head. "No, just tired."

Greedily, her eyes traced the lines of his face, the strong powerful body. Then she realized what she did and she hurriedly stepped away. She had to get out of here.

Without another word, she fled.

Grace lay unmoving next to Matthew in the silent intimacy of the moonlit bedroom. He was fully dressed. He hadn't even taken his shirt off. She knew why. The ghost of their kisses hovered tangible as a knife.

Hunger stalked her. Hunger radiated from the man beside her. He hadn't moved in an hour but he was no more asleep than she was.

"It was wrong to kiss you," she said dully.

"No."

She waited for him to continue but the tense silence grew.

Grace sucked in a choked breath. Misery, guilt and desire tangled in her heart. She'd already given Matthew more of her real self than she'd given any man, even Josiah. Still it wasn't enough. She suspected only her complete surrender would be enough. A tear trickled down her hot cheek.

The mattress shifted as he turned to look at her. Perhaps the darkness would hide her weeping. A futile hope. She'd long ago noted the acuteness of his senses.

"Oh, my dear." Unerringly, he reached out and captured a tear in his fingers. Another tear, another. She closed her eyes and struggled for composure.

"Crying won't help," she said huskily.

"Sometimes it's all we can do." His voice caressed her like black silk.

With a sigh, he stretched out and drew her close so they lay facing each other. Strong arms locked her to him and he tucked her throbbing head into his shoulder. She folded into his body without resistance and burst into a useless fit of weeping. Nobody had offered care or support since she was a girl. She'd been alone and struggling against a hostile world ever since.

She cried for her foolish sixteen-year-old self. For Josiah who had never found contentment. For the beautiful marquess who wasted youth and strength in this secret arena.

She cried for Grace Paget who, after nine years of marriage, finally learned what desire was. Grace Paget, mistaken for a whore. Who now promised to become one in truth.

"I'm sorry," she blurted out, telling herself she could bear it if he turned away. She'd learned she could bear almost anything. But she didn't believe it. If Matthew rebuffed her, it would hurt more than all of Josiah's unsubtle efforts to belittle her. She sprawled across Matthew's chest, her head resting on his soft linen shirt just below his collarbone.

"I've howled like a lost dog upon occasion," he said in what she recognized was a deliberately light tone. "Why, your few pathetic tears hardly justify the name."

What a brave, good man he was. Although how he'd retained either bravery or goodness through the hell he'd endured, she couldn't imagine. Desire lurched to life again. The chest beneath her hands was broad and powerful. Under her ear, his heart beat steadily. If she shifted the palms that lay flattened on his crushed shirt the slightest inch, she'd touch bare skin. Although she wanted to stay close to him more than she wanted air to breathe, she tried to pull away.

Instead of releasing her, his grip firmed. "Don't go."

She heard the aching need in the soft words. An aching need that mirrored her own. Without speaking, she subsided against him.

Silence heaving with all they felt but could not say weighted the air.

Dear heaven, they couldn't go on like this. Thwarted desire would end in destroying them both.

Eventually, he slept while Grace stared dry-eyed into the darkness.

Her harum-scarum past paraded through her mind like a pageant. Memories of the pampered girl, the unhappy wife, the destitute widow. Cruel memories of a father consigning his daughter to perdition with words that stabbed her soul. Words she'd sworn would never become truth. More recent memories of a madman who frightened her, then saved her, then carried her to heaven with kisses.

Through the last unhappy years, honor alone had sustained her. She was about to relinquish that precious honor. And strangely, she felt not an ounce of regret.

Long dark hours passed while she said farewell to the woman she'd always been. And embraced the woman she was about to become.

Tomorrow night. . .

Chapter 14

$\sim\infty\sim$

Giddy with a heady mixture of excitement and apprehension, Grace waited in the bedroom for Matthew. Downstairs, she'd deliberately kept the conversation neutral, as it had stayed neutral most of the day.

It was late, nearly midnight, and everything was quiet. She'd abandoned him to his port while she dashed upstairs in a lather of nerves. And desire. Desire that swung her wayward heart into a drunken, swaying waltz that played in urgent triple time.

I want him. I want him. I want him.

Anticipation fizzed in her veins like fireworks. A deep breath. Another.

She stood leaning brazenly against the base of the bed so he'd see her the instant he came in. She wore the most beautiful—and most risqué—of the nightgowns his uncle had ordered. A sheer batiste sheath embroidered with a scatter of tiny silver stars.

The garment could almost look virginal, if one ignored its transparency. Or the way it dipped over the unconstrained jut of her breasts. Or that only four tapes held it together, two on the shoulders and two at the sides. A couple of well-judged flicks from a man's fingers and the garment would crumple to the floor.

At last, she heard Matthew leave the salon, cross the hall to the stairs. She listened to each reluctant footstep as his booted feet mounted the steps. He paused on the top landing, striving for control.

How was she so sure what he felt?

Because she'd fought the same battle.

Tonight she yielded.

And gloried in defeat. This outcome had been destined from the moment she'd first looked into his enigmatic eyes.

He waited outside a long time. Finally, he sighed. The sound's sadness added a rich minor note to the lilting music in her heart. She heard him turn toward the bedroom.

One step. Two.

He appeared in the doorway. She watched him absorb the scene with one flicker of those extraordinary eyes.

Bright candles on shelf and chest and windowsill.

Bedclothes folded down so only the sheet awaited. White. Pristine. Provocative.

Beckoning.

The air was heavy with sensual jasmine perfume. She'd used it on her pulse points and anointed the bed linen with its evocative fragrance.

His eyes widened as they lit on her. She watched his long fingers curl at his sides as if he stopped himself reaching out. It was the reaction she'd prayed for. Although whether she begged help from God or the Devil, she couldn't have said.

"What are you doing, Grace?" he asked hoarsely. He didn't cross the threshold. His gaze darkened with accusation—and unwilling hunger. A tiny muscle beat an erratic tattoo in his cheek.

"I'm seducing you," she said with deliberate steadiness.

His face settled into rigid lines. His face wasn't all that

was rigid. He'd hardened the moment he saw her. The loose fawn trousers clearly revealed his arousal pressing against the buttoned frontfall.

She shook her freshly washed hair away from her face. Her hair flowed around her, brushing warm and silky across bare skin. It gave off a sweet tinge of wood smoke, lingering from when she'd dried it in front of the fire. Never before had she taken her hair down for a man. The effect was amazingly erotic, oddly liberating.

A smile curved lips supple with red salve. She'd never worn paint before either. Another freedom.

"I told you this is impossible." His face was ashen and he looked lost, bewildered, unhappy. "Why didn't you say something at dinner?"

"Because you'd try and talk me out of it." She burst into speech before her courage failed. "Your uncle will think he's won when he learns you share my bed. Monks and Filey will believe I've taken the harlot's path. I'll have no reputation to salvage after this." She swallowed, afraid of what awaited, afraid of what she threatened to become. "The world believes me your mistress. What benefit to us if it isn't so?"

"You and I will know the truth."

Her smile faded as she read the despair underlying his hostility. "Lord Sheene . . ."

"Christ, Grace. My name is Matthew. I'm lord of nothing in this hellhole. Least of all myself."

He turned and leaned his forehead on the hand he fisted against the door.

"Matthew," she said softly and noticed how the sound of his name on her lips leached tension from his tall form. Deep within, a coil of nerves loosened, turned liquid.

She took a shaky breath. She'd hoped that the setting and her patent availability would send caution flying. That he'd take one look and carry her away on a tide of passion.

She should have known better. He was so strong. He'd had to be to survive the last eleven years.

"Matthew," she said again, purely for the pleasure of hearing it. She linked her nervous hands in front of her and struggled to dredge up the right words. "This estate is a world unto itself. You may never have the chance to bed another woman."

No, that was wrong. She knew it even before his head whipped up and he blasted her with a ferocious golden glare. Yet again the captive, doomed hawk teased at the fringes of her mind. The haunting, tragic image bolstered her wavering determination.

"You do this out of pity?" he asked sharply.

Composure became more difficult every second. She repressed the urge to scramble to the armoire for a robe to cover her all-but-nudity. Straightening her shoulders, she forced herself to continue calmly. "Not pity." Then the greatest risk of all. "I want you. I think you want me."

His hunted expression didn't lighten. "Yes, I want you. That doesn't make this right."

"Why?"

His jaw clenched. "This is cruel, Grace. And unworthy of you. Stop this spiteful game. I will not fall in with my uncle's plans, whatever my own selfish cravings. I swore you'd suffer no harm. Making you my whore means I'm no better than my jailers."

His attention fixed over her head as though he couldn't trust himself to look at her. She had no such scruples. Her eyes devoured him from the crown of his gleaming black head, down his lean, strong body, to his long feet.

Desperation frayed her tone. "I may never escape. Monks or Filey could kill me tomorrow. I've always been a virtuous woman. I went to my husband a virgin. But my life outside ended when those thugs drugged me." Never had she spoken so frankly. Enough of her old self lingered for hot color to flood her face.

He stared at her now, a troubled light in his beautiful eyes. "What if there's a child?" He sounded almost angry.

"My womb hasn't quickened before."

"Your husband was an old man."

"In nine years of marriage, I never conceived."

"We gamble on the future of an innocent."

She clutched her hands together so tightly that they ached. "Every moment here is a gamble." Then in a voice that shook with urgency, "Joy would be your greatest revenge on Lord John. I believe . . . I believe we could find joy together."

"Joy is a stranger here," he said bleakly.

"It doesn't have to be. This is something to take for yourself, something your uncle can't control. Something true where everything else is false. Don't let pride steal this from you."

"It's more than pride." He stepped into the room at last. A concession, even if he didn't recognize it as one.

"Is it?" She didn't shift from the base of the bed.

"If you touch me now, I'm lost," he said gruffly.

She brushed her hair over one shoulder and watched a flame ignite in the golden eyes as they dwelt on the tumbling mass of black. "The decision is yours. You have little enough freedom."

"While you flaunt yourself before me like every dream I've ever had." Bitterness laced his voice.

He took another step. Soon, if she reached out, she'd be able to touch him. Oh, how she longed to touch him. But the time wasn't yet right. "This could be our only chance, Matthew. Heaven forgive me, but I've never wanted a man before. I want you. Don't make me want alone."

"You know you don't want alone, Grace." Another step.

He extended one hand but let it fall before he made contact. "I may disappoint you. I've never done this before."

The words hung between them as if drawn in flame on the air.

She'd won.

Praise God and all His angels, she'd won.

She dragged in a relieved breath. The painful twist of tension between her shoulder blades eased. Whatever tomorrow brought, she had tonight. For the first time since this nightmare began, she controlled her destiny. She offered him the same privilege, if he had courage to take it.

She'd never doubted his courage.

The gravity of the moment tightened her throat. Should she guide him, tell him what to do? She was a stranger to all but the basics. Ridiculous after nine years of marriage, but true. For the sake of his pride, for the sake of his manhood, she didn't want to play teacher to his student.

"I am at your disposal." She smiled as his final step brought him directly in front of her.

"I love your smile, do you know that?" he said tenderly, framing her jaw in two careful hands. "How is a fellow to make a start with this business, Mrs. Paget?"

Her smile widened while desire bubbled like champagne inside her. "A kiss is always a good beginning."

Matthew stared into her beautiful face while a crowd of chaotic emotions jostled within.

He'd dreamed of a woman for so long. A woman to ease his anguish, his anger, his loneliness.

That animal relief wasn't what he wanted from Grace.

From Grace he wanted . . . *love.*

So his touch was gentle as he cupped her face between his palms. Slowly, he bent his head to brush his lips across hers.

He sipped pleasure, coaxing her to open. Her lips softened, parted. She sighed and gave herself up to the kiss with a swiftness that made his blood leap with joy.

He used his tongue to explore the warm recesses of her mouth, learning again her sweetness, her passion. Her tongue fluttered to meet his and the dizzying pleasure threatened to spin out of control.

It was the same melting delight he'd savored yesterday. But it was also different. Even yesterday, she'd clung to a vestige of prudence. Tonight, she held nothing back. He read surrender in her uninhibited response, in the fluid yielding of her body. Her nipples were hard points against his chest. Soon he'd taste her there. The prospect shot a blinding jolt of lust through him.

With increasing confidence, he intensified the pressure. She hummed low in her throat and drew his tongue deep into her mouth. His heart slammed against his ribs at the glorious sensation. He lashed his arms around her, pulling her tight against him. She gasped and clung closer, her fingers clenching and unclenching in the lawn shirt that stretched across his back. The kiss developed a desperate edge.

Careful, Matthew. Careful.

If he didn't discipline his hunger, he'd hurt her. He tore his mouth from hers and stared helplessly down into her dazed eyes. He craved her so much, he was delirious. But he didn't want to attack her the way a starving man fell on his first meal after a famine.

Although, God knew, he starved for her.

"Oh, my," she gasped, releasing him and staggering back against the bed. She looked like she'd lived through an earthquake. A hectic flush lay along her cheekbones and her lips were red and full. From his kisses, not paint, he recognized with a sharp punch of satisfaction.

She pressed one shaking hand to her chest. Each ragged

breath lifted her full breasts under the sheer nightdress. He closed his eyes briefly and prayed for restraint, while every moment made restraint more elusive.

Even the few inches of space between them tortured him.

"Come here," he said roughly, tugging her into his arms again. All that shining black hair had teased him since he stood in the doorway. Now it slid around him like dark satin.

His mouth plunged down to take hers. She answered with wild ardor. Her slender body was tensile as hot steel.

Her mouth ravished his, hungry, rapacious. The openness of her desire astounded him, made his cock swell and pulse against her belly.

He wanted to devour her. Jesus, he already did a fair job of it.

He tried to hold himself back by concentrating on her responses. But her responses were so willing and ready, they only stoked the heat inside him until he threatened to combust to ashes.

He raked hot, open-mouthed kisses across her cheeks, her eyes, her nose, her jaw, her neck. He wanted to inhale her, ingest her, so he'd never be without her. She tasted like salty honey. She tasted like heaven. He couldn't get enough of her.

The scent of jasmine whirled around him. Heavy. Dark. Whispering of sin and seduction. But beneath her heady perfume, she still smelled like sunshine, like the woman he'd first held and wanted. The woman he'd want forever. The woman as much a part of him as blood or bones.

He traced a line of hard, sucking kisses along the tendon that ran down her neck. She gave a choked gasp and trembled in his arms.

Interesting.

He used his teeth, not hard enough to hurt but hard enough to make her shiver and moan.

How fascinating a woman's body was. How fascinating *Grace's* body was.

He followed her collarbone with his lips. Paused to explore the wildly fluttering pulse at the base of her throat. She sighed and arched into him.

Reluctantly, he left that hollow, so warm and redolent of her, to discover the silken firmness of her shoulder. His lips met one of the fragile knots holding her nightdress.

Soon, soon that knot would loosen to his fingers.

Even while his blood trumpeted the need for haste, he forced himself to linger. He didn't trust how long this joy would be his. His uncle's schemes had caught him out before. He'd experience all he could before fate stole his treasure.

Her scent, sharp with what he instinctively recognized as arousal, intoxicated him. She trembled like a reed in a gale and her sighs and gasps filled his ears with the sweetest music he'd ever heard.

Suddenly impatient with barriers, he pulled away to shuck his shirt over his head and fling it into the corner. He didn't dare remove his trousers. If he did, he'd be on her. The friction of worn nankeen on his tumescent sex already threatened to send him over the edge.

He battled his ravening impulses. Grace deserved better than a rough tumble from an inexperienced boy.

Then he saw her face and good intentions shattered.

She leaned against the bed as she had when he came into the room. But instead of presenting a picture of nervous determination, her cheeks were flushed and her mouth was swollen with kisses. She reached out to touch his chest, stroking the scattered hair across his pectorals.

"You're magnificent," she said softly.

Her thumb grazed one nipple and he shuddered. This was torture. Exquisite torture. The fascination in her eyes made him feel like a king.

"I'm just a man who wants you beyond reason," he said rawly.

Speech evaporated as she touched his belly. He sucked in an agonized breath while those seeking fingers seared his flesh.

Her open curiosity puzzled him. Surely she knew how a man was made, even if her husband had been an unsatisfactory lover. But her face reflected his own wonder as she tested the firmness of abdomen, the dip of navel, the rim of hip.

And lower.

He groaned when her wandering hand settled on his erection. Her fingers took up a hesitant rubbing motion. He closed his eyes so hard that stars exploded in his vision.

If she kept touching him, this would be over in seconds. He still wouldn't know how it felt to lose himself inside a woman.

Inside this woman.

"Grace, no," he said in a strangled voice, grabbing her wrist.

"Don't you like it?"

Her uncertainty brought him back to himself as nothing else could have. "You threaten to unman me, Grace."

Comprehension flared in her eyes, turning them the color of the sea at sunset. Then she smiled, a witch's smile, a siren's smile.

Her hand was steady as she reached up and pulled at one of the negligee's ties. The knot came free. With a slowness that made the breath hitch in his throat, the material sagged. It slipped softly down the slope of one breast to snag on a pebbled nipple.

He stopped breathing altogether.

His attention followed her hand as it rose to the second tie. And gave a short tug.

The soft white nightgown slid down. And down. And down.

A heart-stopping wiggle, then one delicate step to the right.

She was naked beneath the nightdress.

He'd known that. The sheer material didn't hide much. But knowing and seeing were two totally different things.

His eyes feasted on her. Her breasts were breathtakingly lavish. Firm, white, tipped with tight rosy nipples. His brief glimpse in the darkness three nights ago had only hinted at their perfection.

The curves and indents at waist and hip and thigh. The long slender legs, smooth and pale like the rest of her. The delicate ankles and slender feet.

She was Eve. She was Venus. She was Diana.

She was every dream that had disturbed his lonely nights made flesh.

She was more than any of these. She was Grace.

And soon she'd be his.

Soon? Now!

With shaking hands, he fumbled at the fastening of his trousers. He was all thumbs and the material fought him. He bent and tore his short boots off, grappling for control. His hands still refused to obey when he returned to his trousers.

"Jesus!" he swore softly. With sudden ruthlessness, he ripped the garment off, so he too stood naked.

Her gaze dropped to his erection then fell away, but not before he caught the astonishment in her eyes. Astonishment and apprehension. Hectic color bloomed in her cheeks and she bit her lip, a sure sign of nervousness. She was slightly built and he was a large man.

He couldn't wait or he risked humiliating himself. But the reminder of her relative innocence meant his touch was gentle as he tipped her back onto the mattress.

She edged up on the sheet, leaving him room to kneel between her legs. As she opened herself, he caught her musky essence. Jasmine and woman. Richer and earthier than her daytime scent. He'd remember the intoxicating combination the rest of his life.

Slowly, she stroked up his arms then curled her fingers around his shoulders. He shifted forward, taking his weight on his hands.

She was rain in the desert. She was a banquet to a starving man. She was Grace.

Her breasts fascinated him. Carefully he touched the furled bud of one nipple.

She gave a low sigh of pleasure and stretched her back against the mattress. She liked this. He glanced his finger across the tight peak, listening to her breath catch.

He skimmed his hand across her belly, down her ribs, along her arms. She moved into each touch as though asking for more.

Did that mean she was ready?

All he had to guide him were his school friends' smutty speculations. And they were no help at all. Not when he had a real woman in his arms for the first time. Not when the woman was Grace Paget.

He lowered his body against hers and kissed her. But kissing was no longer enough. She moved restlessly as his tongue tangled with hers. Her smooth bare skin slid hot and damp upon his. Her hips tilted in invitation.

He raised himself on both arms and looked down into her face. Her eyes were dark and heavy, almost black.

Was she ready? He didn't know. If she stopped him now, he didn't think he'd survive.

He shifted his hips forward and probed at her entrance. The hot, seeking head of his cock met slick moisture. His heart lurched into a hard, heavy rhythm and every muscle in his body clenched.

He pushed.

She was tight, so tight. Her flesh resisted the invasion.

He pushed again.

She gave a soft moan.

He stopped, still poised at her opening. The desperate lungfuls of air he sucked in left him lightheaded and gasping. Jesus, don't let her stop him now. *Not now.*

"Are you all right, Grace?" he scraped out in a voice he didn't recognize as his own.

She shifted so her wet cleft stroked his straining shaft. Bright lights exploded behind his eyes and he almost lost himself.

"You're too big," she said unsteadily. "This isn't going to work."

Through the blood thundering in his ears, he hardly heard her. He gritted his teeth and battled for control. "Hold on to me," he almost snarled.

What if he hurt her? What if she changed her mind? It would kill him, but he'd have to stop.

Christ, not yet. Don't steal this away from me yet.

He bent his head and closed his eyes, his chest heaving, his cock nudging at her.

"Try again, Matthew," she whispered, digging her fingers into his shoulders to anchor herself.

He raised his head and looked at her. Her eyes flickered with uncertainty and she was shaking. So was he. Every sinew ached with impossible tension.

He tightened his hips and pushed.

Still she remained closed.

His jaw tensed and he pushed again, more powerfully this time. Her fingers clutched hard on his shoulders to the point of pain.

Her flush had faded. Instead, her face was set and pale and her skin stretched tight against the fragile bones. She

closed her eyes in a wince of discomfort. In her distended
neck, the tendons stood out like ridges.

Dimly, from the back of his mind, the voice of conscience told him a man of honor would leave her be.

Damn honor. Damn conscience.

He braced on one hand, using the other to angle himself
better. He surged forward.

Resistance. Resistance.

Then suddenly, a marvelous yielding.

He slid into her with a long, shuddering exhalation.

She cried out at the intrusion. Then muscles that had relaxed to allow his incursion clenched hard around him. The
pressure was delicious, like nothing he'd ever felt before.

For a long time, he rested in her glorious heat, luxuriating in her tight wet clasp on his throbbing cock.

Nothing could snatch this moment from him.

Grace was his at last.

The feeling was indescribable. She'd become part of
him and he'd become part of her.

"I'm hurting you, Grace," he said hoarsely. She panted
with distress and he read tension in her face.

"No," she muttered, although she gripped his shoulders
as if she clung to a rockface and she'd tumble into a chasm
if she let go.

He shifted to relieve the pressure on her, pulled out
slightly. The searing friction nearly blew the top of his
head off. She whimpered at the movement and arched up
so the tips of her breasts brushed his chest. Experimentally,
he rocked, working himself in again. Grace was sleek and
wet. This time he slid into her more easily.

He flung his head back and withdrew, then went in
harder. His world shrank to Grace and the scalding whirl-
pool of pleasure inside him. In a ferment of need, he began
to plunge in and out. With every thrust, his frenzy built.

He lost all sense of time and place. There was just Grace and his overwhelming hunger for her.

He slammed into the hot, mysterious depths. A dark whirlwind roared in his ears, made him deaf to everything but the furious pounding of his heart.

He withdrew on a shuddering groan then claimed her again. Heat. Darkness. Pressure. Paradise.

He picked up his rhythm, moving faster, more ruthlessly. The crescendo built and built. Finally it hit a dazzling summit. He could hold back no longer.

He jerked once, twice, and came.

White hot rapture seared him. The world turned molten with ecstasy. For an endless time, his body shuddered as he filled her with his seed.

Through all the thundering, shaking, scorching release, his heart drummed one word over and over.

Mine. Mine. Mine.

Chapter 15

Grace lay unresponsive beneath Matthew while he pounded into her. A hot liquid sensation flooded her womb. Her hands slid off his damp back to lie loosely at her sides.

Frustration chafed at her. She was jittery and feverish, as though someone had flung her high into a lightning-filled sky, then abandoned her on the edge of the storm.

Matthew groaned again. He'd left her behind long ago. She couldn't doubt his enjoyment but she shared none of it. Instead she felt pummeled and squashed. A muffled whimper escaped her, but nothing indicated he heard.

How much longer could this go on? Surely he must soon finish.

He seemed to shudder over her endlessly.

His weight and the force of his release jammed her deep into the mattress. His eyes were closed and lines of ferocious concentration marked his expression. The smell of his sweat was sharp in her nostrils.

He'd moved into a world that held only his own pleasure. He was unaware of her except as a receptacle for a lifetime of pent-up lust.

She winced as rarely used muscles between her legs

protested the hard invasion. Hoping to spur him to end sooner, she lifted her knees.

The fault for this disaster lay squarely with her.

It wasn't fair to blame Matthew. He'd tried to cling to honor. She was the one who had lured him on, even when she should have guessed this acrid disappointment waited.

She'd wanted more. When clearly no more was to be had.

Black bitterness filled her soul.

She'd given up so much for this.

For nothing.

What else had she expected? She was such a fool. She knew what the sexual act was like. She'd had nine years to get used to a man grunting over her. It wasn't like anything new happened tonight.

What made everything worse were those fleeting moments when she'd wondered if there might be more.

When he'd kissed her neck and an electric thrill had sizzled right to her toes. When he'd touched her breast and a profane part of her had longed for him to take her in his mouth. Most of all, when he'd first moved inside her and she'd felt the approach of . . . *something.*

Something miraculous.

The blazing instant had crumbled to dust.

Then it was just Grace Paget on her back while a man thudded into her. Exactly like those infrequent occasions when Josiah had asserted his marital rights.

She closed her eyes and prayed that the act would soon be over. Just as she'd prayed when Josiah took her. But the unshed tears behind her eyelids were new.

Eventually, finally, Matthew finished. With another deep groan, he slumped onto her. He buried his face in her shoulder so his sweat-soaked hair brushed her ear, her cheek, her neck. He trembled with exhaustion and his chest heaved as he struggled for air.

The smells of sex and well-exercised male swirled around them. She knew instinctively that he'd poured everything he had into her. The evocative thought made her raise her hands to embrace him. Then disappointment jabbed like a needle again and she let her hands fall back.

He was heavy, although not unbearably so. She sank down into the bedding. She was hot and sticky and felt uncomfortably stretched where he was joined to her.

He was a much . . . bigger man than Josiah. Her first glimpse of his nakedness had set her nerves buzzing with apprehension. She couldn't imagine that huge member fitting inside her.

His commanding size had heightened her excitement. Then.

Now she felt suffocated.

She desperately wanted dominion over her own body again. Briefly, she touched his shoulder. His damp skin was hot under her palm. "Matthew, I can't breathe."

Slowly, he raised his head. His honey eyes were sleepy and his expression made her think of a well-fed lion. A well-fed, very satisfied lion.

"Grace, you are a marvelous woman," he said thickly.

The compliment didn't please her, although she couldn't have said why.

"Even marvelous women need air," she said with asperity.

Oh, Grace, that was unworthy of you.

She watched his dazed fog of pleasure recede. Guilt lacerated her. She had no right to spoil this occasion for him. She hadn't expected him to demonstrate great skill. She'd wanted to make love to Matthew Lansdowne, not some practiced rakehell who knew how to touch her body but had no interest in her soul. Well, she'd got what she wanted. He was a man. He'd done what men do. Clearly he'd liked it.

Good for him.

She smothered the sour thought. She'd set out to give him pleasure. His delight should offer recompense. Perhaps it would have, if dissatisfaction didn't gnaw at her like a hungry dog on a bone.

He lifted himself on his elbows and studied her with what she'd dubbed his botanical look. She resented feeling like a scientific specimen. She resented that those clever eyes might look closely enough to discern the unhappy, inadequate soul she hid beneath her sniping.

"You're angry," he said neutrally.

"No, I'm not!" she snapped then wished she'd kept quiet as one black brow arched in disbelief.

"My mistake," he said in that same even voice. It sliced at her taut nerves like one of his grafting knives.

"Please get off me," she choked out. If she stayed under him much longer, she'd start crying. Then he'd comfort her and she'd feel even more like a peevish witch than she did now. A peevish witch and a failure as a woman. Self-hatred knotted her stomach.

He pulled free and rolled over to lie on his back. She took her first full breath in what felt like hours. Her throat was tight with tears she refused to shed. Gingerly, she sat up, aware of aches in places she'd forgotten.

Face it, Grace. The deed is done, however disappointing it was.

She'd irrevocably lost any right to call herself a virtuous woman. Her father's dire predictions when she married Josiah had finally come true. She'd given herself to a man who wasn't her husband. She was now a daughter of sin.

If only sin had been slightly more . . . *sinful.*

She glanced across at Matthew, expecting him to look annoyed or triumphant. But he stared at the ceiling and frowned as though he worked on a horticultural problem. She'd seen that expression when he tried to resurrect a rose that wasn't shooting with the vigor he expected. The memory was an unwelcome reminder that she genuinely liked the Marquess of Sheene. She liked his courage, his forbearance, his kindness, his curiosity, his honesty.

And heaven help her, even after what had just happened, she liked how he looked.

Lying against the pillows with a thoughtful expression on his striking face, he was every woman's dream. Her gaze traveled down his lean chest and his flat stomach to his member lying loose on his thigh, to the long, straight athlete's legs.

He shifted his regard from the ceiling to her. His organ wasn't quite as flaccid as it had been.

She blushed. She couldn't pretend she didn't admire his body and he returned her interest with interest of his own.

Then she recalled he wasn't the only naked person in this room. If she wasn't careful, he'd have her on her back again. Hurriedly, she scooped the crumpled nightdress from the floor and clutched it in front of her.

"I have to wash," she said nervously as he hardened before her eyes.

How could he recover so quickly? Apparently vigorous young men were less easily exhausted than tired old ones like Josiah.

"Then wash, Grace." Unbelievably he smiled, a slow curve of his lips. That sweet smile tugged at her, made her recall why she'd done this in the first place.

No!

This was what had got her into trouble last time.

Never again. Never, never again.

She wished she could say she walked to the screen with a queen's composure. But she knew she skittered for cover like an antelope sighting the lion she'd compared him to earlier.

She snatched the ewer of warm water and poured some into a bowl. Her hands trembled so badly that she splashed the wooden floor under her bare feet.

Calm, Grace, calm.

She picked up a flannel and soaped it with unnecessary violence.

Why had she imagined sex with Matthew would be better than sex with Josiah? Just because she wanted Lord Sheene in a way she'd never wanted her husband. Just because he was young and handsome and when he'd kissed her, the pleasure made her think she'd die.

Kissing must be where pleasure stopped for a woman.

A thorough wash removed the traces of copulation from her skin. Nothing removed the leaden weight from her heart, or soothed the ocean of thwarted desire churning in her belly.

She drew the flannel between her legs. She was tender there, although he hadn't hurt her. It was a long time since she'd taken a man into her body, and never a man so well endowed. Aches she'd never felt before lingered.

With a stifled sigh, she rinsed the soap off and threw the dirty water into the slops jar.

"Are you going to hide all night, Grace?" he asked softly. She hadn't heard him move so she guessed he still lounged on the bed like a sultan awaiting his favorite *houri*.

He was right. She couldn't skulk behind the dressing screen the rest of her life. She had to face him sometime. She just wished she had something more substantial than the cobweb-thin nightdress to wear.

"Grace? Have you drowned in the wash basin? Should I rush to your rescue?"

The lovely undercurrent of amusement in his question sent a traitorous rustle up her spine. She'd have thought her unenthusiastic response to his lovemaking would wound his masculine vanity. But he seemed in high good humor.

"No, I'm coming." Her voice was muffled in the folds of the nightdress as she dragged it over her head.

He'd just been inside her. Modesty was out of place. Still she folded her arms protectively across her front as she emerged from behind the screen. Thankfully, for her peace of mind, he'd drawn the sheet up to his waist. He'd heaped the pillows high and he lay on his back with his hands linked behind his head. Against her will, her eyes focused on his naked chest, tracing the subtle play of muscle and bone under the smooth, lightly furred skin.

That couldn't be desire stirring, could it? Not after tonight's fiasco, surely. That would be impossible.

His eyes sharpened on her as she stepped closer. "Come back to bed, Grace."

His deep voice curled around her, warmer and more inviting than a fire on a wet winter afternoon. She shivered and planted her feet on the richly patterned Turkish rug in the middle of the room.

"I suppose you want to do it again," she said flatly.

She hardly needed to ask. The gleam in his eyes was confirmation enough.

"Yes, I do." He shifted across and folded the sheet back for her. "This time I want you to enjoy it too."

"Women don't enjoy sex." Then an admission she'd never made to a living soul. The occasion required honesty, not face-saving bravado. "At least I never have."

"Perhaps you've never had the right lover."

She'd been wrong. He was indeed as vain as any other man. Old cynicism forced its way upward. "And you're that right lover?"

Her sarcasm was petty but something in her cried out

for a shouting match. Perhaps the persistent, provoking itch between her legs.

"I ask your forgiveness." Shamed color marked his cheekbones. "The experience was overwhelming in a way I hadn't expected."

She blushed too, remembering when he'd thundered into her like an emperor conquering a rebel city. No mistaking how lost he'd been to sheer physical sensation.

"There's nothing to forgive." Her voice shook and those annoying tears prickled again. "It's not your fault there's . . . there's something wrong with me."

His eyes lit with understanding as he patted the space at his side. "There's nothing wrong with you. You're perfect. Come back to bed and I'll show you."

"Said the spider to the fly," she retorted without budging. She focused on that tanned, long-fingered hand moving upon the pure white of the sheet. The gentle stroking was astonishingly . . . suggestive. Another spark of unwilling desire fizzed through her.

He still stared at her. "You said you trust me, Grace. Is that true?"

Was it? She didn't know anymore. She forced herself to give a stiff little nod. "Yes."

"Then prove it. Come back to bed."

Oh, why not? He'd take her again. She was more certain of that than that the sun would rise on the morrow. At least one of them would enjoy it.

Still, only with the greatest reluctance did she step forward and slip in beside him. "Should I take off my clothes?"

"Later," he said gently. "I rushed you last time."

"It wouldn't have made a difference." Her voice was thick with suppressed tears. "I've never been any good at this. I thought it might be otherwise with you, but . . ."

"It wasn't. I know I have amends to make."

She wished he wouldn't be kind. But he was a kind man. He'd been guilty of nothing more than excess enthusiasm at holding a woman in his arms at last. He'd tried his best to engage her participation before he took her.

His kindness and his awful loneliness, more than any wish to repeat the embarrassing, frustrating act, made her lie back. She tried to inject a note of humor into the fraught atmosphere. "Do your worst."

He gave a soft laugh. In spite of everything, that laugh shivered through her and made her hot and uncomfortable again.

"My darling Grace, give me some credit. This time I intend to do my best."

Chapter 16

$\sim\!\!\infty\!\!\sim$

Matthew twisted up on one arm to look down into Grace's face. The view, while exquisite, wasn't encouraging. Her expression was shuttered and her body vibrated with tension.

He was ready to embrace a radiant new world. She wanted to snap his head off.

He couldn't blame her. Jesus, what a lumbering oaf he was.

Making love had opened a dazzling dimension of experience to him. Experience beyond anything he'd ever imagined. In his loneliness, he'd spent a lot of time imagining.

But he'd been unprepared for the heat, the closeness, the way he inhaled his lover's sweat and breath and responses. The intimacy had been glorious. And astonishing.

He felt bound to Grace now. Forever.

Tonight's joy would always be a thread of bright gold woven through his life's ragged fabric.

He'd passed through a transforming fire.

She hadn't.

He'd blundered badly. He was merely human and he'd been drunk with elation at making her his at last. All his desperate yearning and aching frustration had erupted into an inferno of release.

Finesse had been too much to ask.

God help him, he needed finesse now. More than he'd ever needed anything in his misbegotten life.

Somehow he must awaken the passion that infused every drop of her blood, every ounce of her flesh. He must heal the wounds her husband had left to fester in her heart. Even if that bastard Paget hadn't harmed her physically, he'd wounded her soul. Perhaps mortally.

How was he to succeed? He was a novice. More a novice than she. And she was more a novice, he now realized, than he'd allowed for.

All he had were instincts and an almighty need to share the wild rapture he'd found in her arms.

Surely she was wrong about women never enjoying sex. Even as a boy, he'd known females interested in bed sport. And his school friends had been vocal about girls who were hot for it.

Not overwhelming evidence, but enough to raise doubts whether every woman endured the act merely for the sake of procreation or as wifely duty.

You're a scientist. Approach this with your brain, not your balls.

He sucked in a deep breath and tried to list the facts as he would before a botanical experiment. Grueling when his mind clouded with desire and the woman he wanted more than life lay quivering with uncertainty beside him.

He closed his eyes and bit back a groan. Her beauty lured him to discard good intentions.

Focus still eluded him. Denying himself the sight of her only made him more aware of her scent, her warmth, the soft huff of her shallow breathing.

Hell, everything about her was temptation.

He had to do this right. For both their sakes.

Think, man. Think.

Grace had enjoyed kissing. She'd also enjoyed his touch.

Things had proceeded better than expected until he'd spread her legs.

She'd said kisses were a good start. He opened his eyes to find her watching him with a troubled dark blue gaze. Her top teeth snagged her lower lip.

He bent to nip at her mouth until she released that poor tortured lip, then he settled his lips fully upon hers. She made a tiny sound of protest or surprise. He couldn't tell which.

Don't let her be afraid of him.

The thought was unbearable. He was on the verge of stopping when he felt an almost imperceptible relaxation, the faintest answer to his tentative kiss.

It was going to be all right. If he was careful. If he kept his head.

Christ, let him keep his head this time.

Slowly, slowly, he buffed his lips back and forth over hers, learning shape and texture and taste. Apart from the kiss, he didn't touch her. Beneath the undemanding caress, her tension slowly drained away.

From breath to breath, he lived through each minuscule change in her response. He knew he was winning when he drew away slightly and she angled after him to capture his mouth.

The kiss deepened, but not too much. He intended to beguile her into pleasure.

He continued the teasing, soft, tormenting kisses. She lay on her back and he leaned over her. It was almost a game. Or would have been if he wasn't blind with need. If he wasn't painfully hard with wanting her.

When her mouth was warm and supple under his, he

slid down in the bed. Carefully, he took her in his arms, turning her on her side to face him.

She jerked with sudden nervousness. The rigidity returned to her body. "Matthew, I'm not sure," she whispered, her breath a sweet drift across his face. "I'm not sure I can go through this again. Even for you."

Once more he cursed his earlier clumsiness. "I'll stop if you ask me to." He hoped to God that was true. He hoped to God she wouldn't test his promise. Delicious as this slow seduction was, his desire seethed closer to the boil with every second.

He kissed her again. His hand traced the frozen straightness of her spine. He kept his touch unthreatening. Up and down. Up and down. Learning the graceful, slender line of her back. Soothing each tight muscle.

Gradually her stiffness faded, increment by increment. She sighed and moved into his touch. The soft night rail brushed his cock.

His shuddering reaction almost made him yelp.

Easy, Matthew, easy.

He needed to cherish her like his most precious rose. He needed to coax her to bloom, to give up her beauty just for him. Patience would reap its own reward.

She no longer lay taut and unresponsive. Her body had regained its lovely sinuousness. Her breath came in excited little puffs and her breasts pressed, full and luscious, to his bare chest. Only the sheer nightdress separated him from her skin as they lay side by side.

He bit back a pained groan.

Jesus, this was impossible. He was mere inches from shoving her onto her back, ripping the rag from her body, and driving into her.

Control.

Holding himself back was more difficult than learning to walk after his madness, learning to speak, learning to read. This stretched his nerves to breaking. This twisted every sinew into a painful tangle of yearning. This threatened to fry his brain in his skull.

Somehow through the overwhelming need, he kept his kisses light, gentle.

This time when she bumped her belly against his cock, he knew she did it deliberately.

Triumph flashed through him.

Such a small concession. The first of many, he hoped.

He'd learned caution. He didn't mistake her hesitant cooperation for permission to rush to completion. He snatched at resolution. Close to impossible when her hot scent swirled around him and threatened to submerge him.

With a superhuman effort, he ignored his urges and focused on igniting hers. He remembered how she'd trembled when he kissed her neck. He tucked the thought away and closed his eyes, concentrating on her mouth.

Finally, when her body folded against his with the beautiful naturalness of a water lily opening on a lake, she gave a tiny sigh and parted her lips. Immediately, his tongue plunged inside.

She growled deep in her throat and slid closer. Her hands crept up to tangle in his hair. Her tongue rasped against his, ventured into his mouth in a quick exploration, then returned for a longer foray. Searing desire zigzagged through him.

He wondered if she even knew what she did. He doubted it. She was lost in kisses. Only reminding himself what was at stake prevented him from becoming similarly lost.

She'd trusted him this far. If he failed her, she'd never trust him again.

How excruciating to hold to his goal when she clung so tightly. Or when his tongue was so deep in her mouth.

Too intense. Too much. Too soon. Patience.

Damn bloody patience. He snapped and snarled at that restraining voice.

He needed her so much. He needed her now.

Even so, he drew back from the edge. Eased the pressure on her mouth. Broke the long succulent exploration into smaller, quicker kisses.

He burned to taste her everywhere. To find out if all of her was as sweet as that honey trap of a mouth. He shifted her onto her back and licked his way down her neck to the fragrant curve of a shoulder. She quivered and made a muffled sound of excitement. Her legs rubbed against his in a devilishly suggestive dance and her breath emerged in rapid gusts.

Oh, yes, his strategy worked, all right. It might even succeed if he didn't shatter into a million shards of frustration first. He nipped and sucked at her sensitive neck and tasted her shivers of surrender.

Only when she gasped and mewed with pleasure did he lift his head.

Flushed with desire, she sprawled against the white sheets. Beautiful. Her eyes were dark and heavy, the pupils so dilated, they almost swallowed the rich blue of her irises.

He slid his hand down to raise the hem of the nightdress, revealing long slender legs. Her intoxicating scent assailed him anew, made the blood surge in his veins.

Jesus, she'd kill him before she finished.

Somewhere he found the strength to rein himself in.

He uncovered the soft plain of her belly. The skin there was so pure and white. He couldn't help kissing it, dipping his tongue into her navel, nibbling a path from one hip to the other. She was his territory and he wanted to map every glorious inch. He nuzzled her hipbone where she curved so deliciously. His hand moved up and down her leg, learning the perfect shape of thigh and knee and calf.

Her different textures fascinated him.

What a magnificent mystery was a woman. Was Grace.

He didn't dare touch her sex yet. Even if the incense of her musky arousal promised to send him spinning to the sky.

She moaned again and moved agitatedly on the sheets. He prayed he goaded her into a fever of desire. He certainly goaded himself into one.

Through years of suffering, he'd learned discipline. He beat back the ravening beast inside him.

He bunched the nightdress higher, revealing the plump undersides of her breasts. The barrier of fabric, flimsy as it was, had become unbearable.

"Take it off," he growled. "Take it off or I'll tear it to pieces."

"Wait," she said breathlessly. She wriggled up against the pillows to tug the nightdress over her head.

No teasing fiddle with the ties this time.

Hell, if she teased him now, he'd damn well explode.

His blood pounded hot and heavy, louder than thunder. With a shuddering breath, he knelt over her, straddling her hips. He filled his hands with her breasts, luxuriating in their beauty, cupping their roundness.

When he bent to kiss one puckered raspberry nipple, her body jerked in startled reaction. But she didn't move away.

Invitation to continue. He took her in his mouth. She tasted like a perfect summer. He sucked gently, laving the whorled tip. Her gasp made him pause.

He raised his head. She looked confused, dazed. Luscious.

"Am I hurting you?"

"No." Then in a rush, "I . . . I like it."

"Good. So do I." This time he sucked harder, flicking at her with his tongue. She moaned and buried one shaking hand in his hair, urging him closer. He needed no further encouragement.

Although the command *patience* wore threadbare, he took his time.

He learned what made her shudder, what made her sigh. He became so attuned to her that every touch of teeth or lips or fingers offered pleasure.

She writhed in his arms, tangling her legs with his, fighting for air. He trailed one hand across her stomach to the soft curls that hid her sex.

She made a soft sound of desire and arched up.

He slipped his hand between her legs. The merest brush of his fingers in her moisture and she jerked in response. She was so sleek and hot.

Not being inside her was torture. But it was still too soon. Even while she shivered and quaked with reaction.

He found one particular place that made her cry out. He scraped his teeth over a tight nipple and touched her between the legs again.

Her spine bowed and she bit back a scream. A hot flood drenched his fingers. His nostrils flared as the scent of her arousal rose stronger, sharper.

How could she call herself a cold woman? She was living flame. She flickered and burned and glowed and her heat warmed him to the depths of his soul.

"Oh, Matthew," she said on a long sigh, opening herself wider to his hand. "Matthew . . ."

He loved the way she no longer hesitated over his name. He loved the way she moved restlessly under his seeking fingers as if she wanted more.

Perhaps at last she wanted him.

He rained kisses down her ribs and over her belly and across her thighs. Then he used his hands to nudge her legs further apart.

The flushed, plump folds of her sex were as beautiful

as any flower. More beautiful. As with any flower, his impulse was to bury his face in it, to inhale its essence.

He'd promised himself he'd kiss every part of her.

It was a promise he meant to keep, by God.

Grace lay back on the pillows, basking in the worship of Matthew's mouth and hands. The sweetness of what he did made the breath catch in her throat. She'd found a lover who set her blood singing. He touched her with such reverence, even when he pushed her to her limits. Who would have thought a man could subvert her control? What a grand and amazing discovery.

How strange that this untried youth taught the widow about sensuality.

She should put him out of his misery, tell him to take her. He'd given her pleasure beyond her wildest dreams. He deserved a reward.

But she loved what he did. She didn't want it to end, selfish cat she was. He made her feel like a goddess.

If the ultimate act offered nothing but endurance, she could bear it. As long as he touched her again the way he touched her tonight.

Those fiendishly skilled hands—where had he learned such things?—pushed her legs further apart.

Oh, heavens, was he going to touch her there again? She closed her eyes and braced for shivery delight.

Nothing happened.

His hands stayed tantalizingly close to where she wanted them, but not close enough. She bit her lip to muffle a frustrated moan.

Oh, Grace, you are a wanton. The angels despair of you.

She opened her eyes.

He was looking at her. At her . . . *there.*

She couldn't mistake the unalloyed yearning on his face as he knelt between her white thighs.

It should disgust her. He should disgust her.

But the idea of him seeing that hidden part of her made her shake with raw excitement.

A good woman would close her legs, roll away, cover herself.

A good woman wouldn't be in this bed in the first place.

His grip on her thighs tightened. His eyes blazed in his pale face and his cheekbones stood out in sculpted relief. Before she could speak, he moved further down the bed and bent his head. For one bewildering moment, she registered the heat of his breath on her cleft.

Then his mouth took her.

It was too much. For one long quivering moment, she lay unmoving. His mouth was hot, heat to her heat. She felt the probe of his tongue. Flame licked at her skin.

She couldn't let him do this. It was depraved.

With trembling hands, she reached down to push him away, trying to ignore the springy softness of his hair under her fingers. Her arms had the strength of jelly and she couldn't shift him.

Scrambling up against the head of the bed, she stared at him in shock.

He lifted his head and looked at her. To her horror—and reluctant fascination—his mouth glistened with moisture.

Her moisture.

She shivered, not entirely with revulsion. Although the thought that a man could do this, would even want to do this, had never occurred to her.

Goodness, until tonight, she'd had no idea a man needed to do anything other than shove his member inside a woman.

"You can't!" she gasped, raising herself on her elbows.

"Why not?" His eyes were brilliant with pleasure. How decadently beautiful he looked caught between her thighs.

"It's . . . it's wrong," she stuttered, knowing she sounded like a fool.

"Did it feel good?" the smiling devil asked.

"Not at all!"

He arched a cynical brow. "Really?"

"Really!" she said with breathless emphasis.

"Don't you want to try again and make sure?" He sounded ridiculously reasonable for a man who wanted to do . . . *that*. "Aren't you curious? I am."

"Curiosity killed the cat." She absurdly fell back onto the old proverb as if that answered anything. All the time, the curiosity she so derided built and built. What would it be like if he kissed her there? The brief instant when his mouth had touched her hadn't been unpleasant. Far from it, actually, if she forced herself to be honest.

Of course, no decent woman would countenance such a thing.

But she was no longer a decent woman, was she?

Tonight, she'd ceased being respectable wife, indigent widow, virtuous lady. Tonight, she'd become a madman's harlot.

A madman's harlot wouldn't shrink from an act just because it struck her as strange and perverse. A madman's harlot would embrace every indulgence her madman offered.

"You're thinking about it. I can see it in your eyes." He curled his fingers more firmly around her thighs and spread them wider. "I swore I'd stop if you asked. That hasn't changed."

"Don't you want to take me?" she asked almost on a wail.

His long mouth quirked with wry humor. "More than I want to breathe. But this time, you'll be with me all the way."

"You promise you'll stop if I say so?" she asked doubtfully, even while she lay down.

"I promise. Though never trust anything a man tells you when he's got his head between your legs."

Grace's giggle ended on a strangled moan when with a ruthlessness she'd never have credited to him, he tilted her hips up and buried his mouth in her. He made a low, deep sound of enjoyment. She shivered as his tongue and lips and teeth worked her.

The sensation was odd. She wasn't sure she did like it.

Until the first blast of pleasure scorched her.

She stiffened in astonished reaction and clenched her hands hard in the sheet. She swallowed a startled whimper.

Still, he must have heard her. He paused and stared up at her. "All right?"

Speaking was an effort. "No."

"No?" he asked skeptically.

Curse him for not taking her word. The strange cramping of her interior muscles subsided, leaving her wanting more.

"No!" Then, when she looked deep into his golden eyes, "Yes."

"Good," he said shortly and started all over again. His tongue flickered over her then he drew hard on her center of pleasure.

Until tonight, she hadn't even known she had a center of pleasure. She bucked under his mouth, not sure whether she wanted him to stop immediately or if she never wanted him to stop at all.

He placed one hand firmly on her churning stomach and increased the pressure on her sex. This time he didn't pause until she writhed and cried out. Even then, he didn't stop until the heat searing her turned into a ferocious disk of light that burned a path through her inhibitions then slung her into a sky of fire.

For a long shuddering interval, she remained suspended in that shining wilderness. Rivers of flame raced through her veins. She jerked and trembled under his mouth.

It was frightening. It was startling.

It was heavenly.

When the strange, dazzling experience subsided, sweat was cold on her naked skin. Her lungs heaved as she gasped for air. She felt wonderful. As though someone had combed every sinew in her body into smooth sleekness. She felt as if she could dance away the night. She felt more exhausted than she ever had in her life.

Grace opened her eyes to find Matthew braced over her with an arrested expression on his face. "What happened?" he asked in a shaken voice.

Talking was a strain. "I can't describe it. How did you know to do that?"

"I guessed." He placed tender kisses on each sloping breast.

"Can you do it again?"

"I don't know," he rasped. "Not immediately. Not if I'm to retain what little sanity I still have."

He'd shown her bliss but was yet to achieve his own release. After what he'd just done for her, only a selfish lover would deny him.

"Then take me, Matthew," she whispered. She anchored one hand around the back of his neck and prepared for the familiar, uncomfortable invasion.

Even enlarged and excited, he sank in with perfect smoothness. He settled hot and heavy inside her.

He didn't move. His breath was ragged in her ear.

She'd never felt as close to another human being. It was

as though the same blood pumped through their veins, the same heart beat for both of them. Heat and passion surrounded her.

This moment had always left her feeling trapped.

She didn't feel trapped now.

She sucked in a shaky breath. Experimentally she shifted, changing the pressure. The movement set off tremors of pleasure. His size still stretched her but the sensation was one of fullness, completion.

She hooked her hands over his shoulders. He was slippery with sweat. His musky scent was so pungent that the whole world smelled of his hunger. His hunger for her.

She squirmed with delight, making him groan. Her wriggling must test him. Some devil made her move again.

"Jesus, Grace," he gritted out. "You try my limits."

"I hope so," she purred. He felt so wonderful inside her. As if he supplied part of her that she only realized now she'd lacked. She bent her knees and tilted her hips so he went deeper. She ran her hands down the tense muscles of his back. He flexed under her touch.

"That felt good," she said breathlessly. "Do it again."

"If I start, I won't stop." His voice was rough.

"Start." She shifted again and felt him shudder.

"Grace," he grated out. He withdrew, then plunged into her. Her nails sank into his back and her womb clenched in welcome.

With deliberate slowness, he set the familiar rhythm.

Except none of this was familiar. Every time he settled in her body, he forged an emotional connection that nothing could sever.

On and on he went. Possession. Release. Possession. Release. Every thrust another link in the chain that bound her to him.

Eventually his inhuman control fractured and he drove

into her faster, more wildly. With every thrust, her excitement built. It echoed how she'd felt when he kissed her between the legs. That had been wonderful, astounding. But this was more powerful.

Because he was with her.

He pounded into her as though he meant to crush her. She didn't care. She never wanted this spiraling feeling to end. The storm swirled her higher and higher.

Ecstasy poised her on a knife edge. She cried out and rose to meet him. He changed the angle of his penetration and went even deeper. The pleasure edged close to pain. She tensed as he pressed hard inside her. Then her womb opened and she took all of him. Her inner muscles convulsed into spasms of delight and she screamed.

Violent rapture flung her against the doors of heaven itself. She was lost in a hot, dark world where nothing existed except Matthew. All she could do was hold him and pray she survived.

Through the tempest that blasted her, he reached his climax. He groaned and convulsed in her arms. For this moment, he was unequivocally hers and she reveled in the possession.

After an endless time, he collapsed in absolute exhaustion. His shoulders and chest heaved as he struggled for breath. He buried his head in the curve of her shoulder so his damp, soft hair tickled the side of her neck.

He was big, he was heavy, he was on top of her. And she never wanted to let him go.

Small quakes still shook her. Quivering reminders of the paradise she'd discovered. A paradise she hadn't known existed. Gradually, Grace's breathing returned to normal. Or as normal as it could be with Matthew squashing her. Even more gradually, torrid delight faded into afterglow.

She'd had no idea. She'd honestly had no idea.

With tender gratitude, she stroked his bare back, making idle patterns on his scarred skin, learning the hard lines of spine and shoulder blade.

She could touch him like this forever. She listened as his breathing steadied and his heartbeat slowed.

He grazed his chin against her shoulder. The bristles on his face scratched. She felt rather than heard him inhale. He turned his head to place a gentle kiss on her neck.

"I love you, Grace," he whispered.

Chapter 17

The soft words crashed into the charged silence like a declaration of war instead of a declaration of love.

As soon as he spoke, Matthew knew he'd made a mistake. His biggest mistake of all in this long, momentous night.

Damn his unruly tongue. Double damn his yearning heart.

It was too late to take back what he'd said. Even if he wanted to.

He wasn't sure he did. He wasn't ashamed of how he felt.

Jesus, his love for her invested every heartbeat.

Of course he loved her. He'd loved her from the moment he'd seen her bound, bedraggled and defiant, to that fiendish table in the garden room. Even when he'd mistrusted and reviled her, he'd loved her.

After what they'd just shared, she must know he loved her. Every touch, every kiss, every stroke of his body in hers had professed his love. Hadn't she felt it?

But she wasn't ready to hear vows of undying love. Even if he hadn't guessed that already, her horrified reaction now told him. Stiffness returned to the body which had curved against his in perfect trust. The hands that had played a delicate symphony on his naked back stilled as if turned to stone.

Her shocked paralysis faded and she struggled out from beneath him. "Lord Sheene . . . My lord . . ."

Only seconds ago, he'd luxuriated in an intimacy he'd never known. It hurt like the very devil to hear her try and distance him.

He raised himself on one elbow so he could look at her. "Back to *my lord* again?" he asked wearily.

"Matthew, listen to me." Color lined her slanted cheekbones. "You can't love me."

She sounded furious. How strange. He'd braced himself for embarrassment or, worse, pity. But her eyes sparkled with rage and something very like fear.

Why should his confession make her frightened? The thought nagged at the edge of his mind.

She pushed herself up against the pillows and fumbled to tug the sheet higher to cover her nakedness. Another barrier, he recognized with regret. No part of her remained in contact with him. The inches that separated them felt like miles of ice field. He had the absurd fancy that if he attempted to cross that gap, he'd stumble into a crevasse and freeze to death.

"Of course I can," he said with a hint of impatience. While all the time, the bitter fact of her rejection seeped into his mind.

"It's not possible. You shouldn't. It's not . . ." She took a deep breath. He watched the sheet rise against her breasts and fought the urge to rip it away.

She wanted to hide from this but he wasn't going to let her. He wasn't going to let her hide from *him*.

Then a vile thought plunged like a knife into his few remaining shreds of contentment. Even while his gut clenched in anguished denial, he made himself ask the question. "Did you sleep with me to save yourself from my uncle? If so, I appreciate your generosity, but there was no need. Sharing this room will convince him we're lovers. You didn't need to make the ultimate sacrifice."

"No!" She paled and her pulse set up an agitated beat in her throat. The hands clutching the sheet tightened until her knuckles shone white. "No, never, never think that. You know I want you. There was . . . there was no sacrifice."

"Your reaction leads me to think otherwise," he said in a wooden voice.

The anger left her expression and her face contracted with sorrow. "You took me by surprise. I spoke hastily. Forgive me. I . . . I wasn't kind."

Her pity was harder to bear than her anger. "I don't want kindness," he almost snarled.

Flinching at his tone, she raised her eyes to look directly at him. The compassion in her voice made him want to hit something. "Matthew, forgive me. I know this is difficult for you. But you make too much of what just happened between us."

"No, I don't," he said stiffly.

"Listen to me. You've been locked away since you were fourteen. The only female you've seen in eleven years is Mrs. Filey." Her voice was very steady. Damn her, he couldn't doubt her sincerity. Even if he recognized the words as arrant nonsense.

"I don't expect you to love me, Grace." He left unspoken his belief that a woman like her, fine, beautiful, passionate, could never love a lout like him. He still found it hard to credit that she'd given herself to him.

"Matthew . . ." she began, but he spoke over her.

"I love you." The words emerged as a challenge. "Whether you accept this or not, I love you."

"I'm flattered."

He fisted his hands to stop himself shaking her. "I don't want you to be bloody flattered."

"Well, I am." She hastened into earnest speech before he could snap at her again. "I'm not belittling how you feel. But this is your first experience of a woman. It's easy to mistake pleasure for love."

She stopped as if waiting for him to agree. He kept silent. Every particle of him vehemently denied what she said. Yes, he'd discovered what intercourse was like. Yes, it had been extraordinary, breathtaking, life-changing.

But it wasn't everything. He loved Grace whether he made love to her or not. Her every breath was precious to him. If that wasn't love, he had no idea what else it could be.

He heard her tattered inhalation. Her unnatural self-possession frayed. "I'm not surprised you're overwhelmed. I'm . . . I'm overwhelmed too. But one day, you'll be free and you'll meet a woman you truly love."

"You're wrong," he said stubbornly, flopping onto his back and staring up at the ceiling. He ignored her rosy depiction of his future. Freedom was an impossible dream. He'd long ago accepted that. "Give me patronizing explanations until Christmas. You won't change what I feel."

A difficult pause extended.

"I've hurt you," she finally said in a sad voice. "I'm sorry."

"No matter. We won't speak of this again." His response dripped damaged pride. He knew he behaved like a blockhead but he couldn't help himself.

Tentatively, she reached out to stroke his cheek. "I've spoiled our magical night. Please forgive me."

He closed his eyes, letting her touch radiate through him. It soothed his roiling anger and unhappiness. Desire, briefly satisfied, surged in on a hot tide.

He'd promised not to mention his love again. Nothing on earth could stop him showing her what she meant to him. Eventually she'd believe in his feelings. Believe in him. He'd batter at her resistance with passion until she let him into her heart.

Grace had a shocked second to register the change in his face. Only a second. He flung the concealing sheet back and wrenched her into his arms.

"God help me," he muttered in a tormented voice before capturing her mouth in a reckless, devouring kiss.

Clutching at his back, she strained up toward him. His loss of control didn't frighten her. It excited. His desperation fed hers.

He wasn't gentle. Heaven help her, she didn't want him to be. She wanted him to invade her. His touch conveyed power and savagery. Her refusal to believe his declaration had angered him. And hurt. How she hated that she'd hurt him.

For one radiant moment, the words, *I love you, Grace,* had settled warm, calm, sure in her heart. She'd almost done the unforgivable and said, *I love you, Matthew,* in return.

Almost. Before vile truth stung her like a cobra. She couldn't tie him to her with commitments he'd later regret.

While he wanted her, she was his.

Oh, Grace, lie to Matthew. Don't lie to yourself. You're his until the day you die.

He placed one hand around her throat, forcing her head up to his kiss. His anguished kisses made her shake. He tasted of desire, he tasted of passion, he tasted of need.

Almost roughly, he palmed her breast. She gasped and writhed, hooking her legs around his hips so she lay open to him. Blood pounded in her veins. She'd explode if he didn't take her. Take her hard. She moaned into his open mouth, snatching at his shoulders to drag him closer. She nipped his earlobe and felt his sex twitch against her belly.

A thrill raced through her. Where was demure Grace Paget? This wild wanton harpy was a stranger.

He drove himself into her to the hilt. For a long, panting moment, she lay pinned under his delicious weight. With a groan, he began to pound into her irrevocably, implacably. She rose to meet him, jerking with the force of every thrust.

This is lust, Grace. Lust. That's all he feels for you. That's all he'll ever feel for you.

But the heart she tried to silence cried out its love. And begged for Matthew to love her in return.

She clenched into climax, clutching at him, imperiously demanding he stay inside her. Still he rode her. Taking her higher into blinding pleasure. The blazing rapture sent her reeling. At the peak, she called out his name.

This time when her passage gripped him, she held on until he joined the glorious conflagration. She milked him until he was spent. Even then quivers of ecstasy shook her.

He groaned and pulled away to lie at her side, struggling for breath. She ached all over. She'd never felt so good. She turned her head to look at her lover. *Her lover.* Languor thick and sweet as molasses oozed through her veins.

She watched his lips curve in a weary smile, creasing his cheek. She loved his smile.

You love everything about him. You love him.

Dawn must be close. To confirm the thought, the first bird called from the orchard outside. Matthew drew her into his arms and kissed her softly. She breathed in his musky sweat and nestled against him with her hand on his heart.

Matthew emerged from sleep slowly, luxuriously. It must be nearly noon. He swam up from the depths of a calm warm sea. The glittering sea of the far south that he'd read about. A blue sea under a glorious sun. A sea full of pearls and exotic creatures and soft silky water.

And mermaids.

Indubitably there were mermaids in this sea.

His particular mermaid slept naked in his arms.

When he was inside her, she undulated in endless waves like a sea of pleasure. How startled he'd been when he realized she was capable of climax.

But then, he knew so little of women.

Perhaps he hadn't wasted those lonely years learning scientific method. After the hash he'd made of the first time, he seemed to have got the idea. He already planned further experiments. Perhaps he'd write a treatise.

He smiled.

A treatise in scholarly Latin for the journals that published his botanical work. A treatise on pleasing the woman you loved. That should make them sit up and pay attention.

Her essence lingered where he licked his lips. She tasted of salt and female. He wanted to taste her again. The thought made him hard. Or harder. He'd woken in a familiar state of arousal.

The room was a wreck. Bedcovers trailed on the floor, the mattress wasn't square on its frame. Clothes lay scattered where he'd thrown them.

He lay flat on his back under a crumpled sheet. His arm circled her bare shoulders and she turned toward him so her slender form shaped itself to his side. One hand rested on his chest. Her nails were uneven and torn from physical work. The calluses on her hands were silent testament to her familiarity with drudgery. The faint roughness of her touch had been erotic torture last night.

Difficult to believe she'd been married nine years. Sleeping with perfect trust in his embrace, she could still be sixteen. A gentle pink flushed her cheeks and her lips were red and swollen from his kisses. They were slightly parted, hinting at the dark mystery within.

Looking at her face, he noted the marks his shadow beard had left. He wanted to kiss her. He wanted more than that. He beat back burgeoning desire. She was exhausted.

A tendril of hair snaked over her shoulder to curl across her breasts. Her beautiful breasts. The nipples were full and pink, not the sweet hard nubs he'd suckled last night. It was the difference between a tightly furled rosebud and the softness of an open rose. The change fascinated him. As did the faint pattern of blue veins under her white skin.

His beard had left traces there too. He'd kissed her everywhere, hadn't he? The sensitive skin of her thighs must bear his mark too. The thought pleased. As though he'd secretly branded her his.

He wondered what she dreamt.

He could imagine. But perhaps he gave himself too much credit. He bit back a snort of derisive laughter.

My, aren't we proud of ourselves this morning? Quite cock of the walk.

Grace sighed and snuggled closer. The soft exhalation made his sex throb. It wasn't so different from the breathy sounds she made when he took her.

He'd loved hearing her lose control. He wanted to hear that again. And soon.

Not yet. It was too sweet lying in this sunny room remembering the night just past, planning the night to come.

And the day.

She stirred on the threshold of waking and buried her nose in his chest. A deeply voluptuous growl emerged from her throat as if she craved his scent like she craved breath.

He looked up from her breasts to find her staring sleepily at him. She looked rumpled and confused.

And happy. Surely he wasn't wrong about that.

"Good morning, Matthew." A smile curled her lips. His heart broke into a rattling gallop.

"Good morning, Grace," he returned gruffly, feeling like the worst kind of satyr. She'd only just woken, for God's sake, and all he could think about was tumbling her so thoroughly that she couldn't see straight. The way having her naked in his arms stopped him seeing straight. Although one part of him was painfully straight. And standing ready. Thank goodness, the sheet hid what an insatiable monster he was.

"Did you sleep?" she asked softly.

A banal question, made less banal by the downward slide of her hand from his chest.

Searing desire licked at him and he struggled to answer. "Yes."

Her smile broadened. "Good."

Down. Down. Down. Slow. Excruciatingly slow.

His throat clamped shut as she brushed his cock. No chance now of concealing his rampant arousal.

Another glance of that cool hand across flesh that was so very, very hot. A pause. She wrapped her fingers firmly around his sex. His heart shuddered to a stop and bright light blinded him.

"Jesus . . ." he bit out. Then the capacity to speak left him in a great whoosh as she rubbed him deliberately, up and down, up and down.

Her rhythm wasn't quite right. Which didn't stop every drop of his blood rushing to where she touched him.

Grace's fingers continued their amateurish, unsure, breathtaking seduction. Squeezing him. Sliding over him. Cupping his balls. The effort of control almost made him weep.

She rose and knelt over him. Her free hand swept the sheet away. He read curiosity and desire in her face. And a very female satisfaction when she saw what she did to him. Her touch became surer, more competent, more likely to shatter him.

As she leaned closer for a better grip, her breasts sheered across his chest. Fire blasted him and he jerked in her hand. Her nipples were tight with arousal now. He heard her suck in a deep breath.

"I must have you." With shaking hands, he pushed her onto her back.

Her hand fell away from his cock so she could curl her hands over his shoulders. She wrapped her legs around his waist. "You most definitely have me," she whispered and rose with beautiful ease to join him.

Immediately, he felt that amazing sense of connection. Pleasure and joy and belonging. For a man alone so long, this was intoxicating, addictive, heady. Nothing his uncle had done in eleven years had come close to defeating him. He already suspected, after only one night in her arms, that losing Grace would mean his destruction.

She sighed and bowed up, so he penetrated deeper. Almost reverently, he began to move.

He worshipped her. He adored her. He wanted her more than life itself. With every thrust of his body, he told her so. Even while he strained to keep the despised words locked away.

Her hips took up his rhythm. As if to every thrust that said *I love you, Grace,* her body replied, *I love you, Matthew.*

Only a fool would believe it.

He was a fool. God, he was a bloody madman.

Her crisis came quickly. How soon he'd learned to recognize the signs. Her face was naked with feeling. Tears weighted the thick lashes shielding her eyes. He reached down to stroke the sensitive place where he'd kissed her last night. He wanted her to achieve her quivering extremity. The most beautiful sight in God's green world.

He pressed between her legs and felt her immediate convulsive response. She tightened around him and the hands on his shoulders tensed into talons. Barbarian that he was, he exulted to think she marked him as he'd marked her.

Then thought itself deserted him as her climax forced his. He poured himself into her. The bitterness, the unhappiness, the loneliness, his unworthiness.

His love.

Afterward he felt clear, cleansed, whole. He felt like a man with a man's pride. And a man's ability to love. And to protect what he loved.

He tightened his hold on her and silently dared the devils haunting his life. They threatened his most precious jewel at their peril.

The world thought it held the advantage over Matthew Lansdowne.

He'd prove the world wrong.

Chapter 18

G race wandered through the sunlit woods in a daze of sensual bliss. She'd been Matthew's mistress for three days and her body ached delightfully from his frequent attentions. Each time they made love, the rich pleasure widened and deepened until now it ran like a broad river beneath everything she did.

Hard to believe her assured lover had never touched a woman before he'd come to her bed. Hard to believe she'd never considered herself capable of passion. Hard to believe she could draw such joy from irrevocable ruin.

She'd left Matthew to his roses half an hour ago. Reluctantly. But his experiments were at a crucial stage and her presence distracted him. The knowledge made her smile. She looked forward to this evening, when he worked out the day's frustrations on her.

"Aye, that's what I like to see." Filey emerged from the overhanging trees and stood squarely in front of her on the path. "A lass smiling with right ready welcome."

Grace's fragile well-being evaporated in an instant.

Fool, fool, fool.

How could she forget she was a helpless prisoner? How could she forget peril lurked around every corner?

She was alone and utterly defenseless. Matthew was in

the courtyard. Wolfram had stayed snoozing beside his master. She'd left her little table knife in the pocket of another dress. She'd become disastrously complacent.

Fear contracted her belly into painful knots and the hairs on the back of her neck prickled. The memory of Filey's rough, sweaty hands fumbling at her breasts rose in her throat like vomit.

"His lordship is just behind me."

She cursed the betraying tremor in her voice. Nervously, she backed away. Could she run fast enough to escape? She doubted it. And Filey was so strong, once he caught her, she had no hope of fighting him off.

Filey's gloating grin was so wide, she could see the dark gaps at the back of his mouth where teeth were missing. "Eh, no pulling the wool over my eyes, flower. I seen him digging at his garden. Bugger me if I'd leave a bonny lass for a parcel of dead sticks. Time you got a real man between your legs. And I got the horn for you right bad."

Revulsion bolstered her failing courage. She raised her chin in shaky defiance. "You have no right to talk to me like that. Monks told you to stay away until Lord Sheene tired of me."

"Aye, but Monks aren't here. Happen he's watching the gate. Any road, if the marquess is coddling his plants instead of poking his slut, I reckon that's proof enow he's had his fill."

"That's not true!" she said hotly, still edging away.

"Aye, well, even so, nobody misses a slice off a cut loaf."

Grace hid a shudder at the horrible analogy. "You're disgusting."

Filey took a menacing step in her direction. "Careful, lass. Happen I'll remember you said that when I fuck you."

Fury swamped her debilitating fear. "You'll never have me, you foul brute."

She whirled on her heel and broke into a panicked run. Panting, she dashed down the path toward the house. But she'd walked further than she thought. Acres of trees extended between her and the safety of Matthew's arms.

"Bugger the skittish bitch," she heard Filey mutter, then the thud of his feet as he set out after her. She gave a terrified sob and forced herself to a faster pace.

Wildly, she swerved around a bend in the path. The dry leaves beneath her feet slid away. She stumbled to her knees with a painful jerk.

"Dear God, help me," she gasped.

Precious seconds dissolved as she righted herself and launched into her careening flight once more. Filey's sawing breath was so loud in her ears, he must be only inches behind her. She didn't slow down to check.

She put on a last despairing kick of speed. Filey was close enough for her to smell fresh sweat over his usual acrid stench.

She swerved toward the trees.

Too late.

He lunged and grabbed her shoulder with bruising fingers. As he flung her down, she screamed. Her front collided with the dirt with such jarring force that her teeth rattled.

Filey threw himself on top of her. His weight crushed her. She'd forgotten how big he was. She tried to claw along the ground but he flipped her over to face him as if she weighed no more than a blade of grass.

She screamed again although there was nobody to save her.

"Button your bloody gob," Filey growled, shoving one filthy paw over her mouth and muting her cries. He trapped her between his knees so she couldn't wriggle away.

Suffocating blackness edged her vision as he covered her nose. She punched and kicked but it was like fighting a wall of solid oak. He was so large, he hardly seemed to notice her flailing beneath him.

She couldn't breathe.

Savagely she bit down on his palm until his blood filled her mouth.

"Shit!" Filey ripped his hand away. Grace had an instant to suck in a mouthful of reviving air before he smashed her across the face with his closed fist.

Agony arced through her head. Stars distorted her vision. She grappled back to consciousness and screamed. The sound echoed around the woods.

There was no answer. How could there be? Matthew was too far away to hear.

She must face this horror on her own. Tears poured down her cheeks as she struggled uselessly against Filey's massive bulk. He stank of onions and unwashed male and lust. She gagged as she gulped in enough fetid air to stave off fainting. She tried to knee him in the groin, but he caught her legs beneath his.

"Eh, none of that! Or I'll whack you good and proper. Makes no road to me whether you're awake."

"I'd rather be unconscious!"

"Aye, well, I'll knock you around if that's what you're after. There's lasses like a bit of that."

Grace's hatred surged anew. "The marquess will kill you!"

He snorted his contempt. "That namby-pamby nod-cock? Chance would be a fine thing."

His hands closed brutally hard on her arms as he rubbed his erection against her belly. He was sickeningly ready.

"What about Lord John?" She was willing to invoke the Devil himself if she had to.

"Aye, Lord John Lansdowne is another kettle of fish. But he'll reckon you was willing. He knows what trade you plied."

"I'm not a whore!"

"Well, you are now. I don't see parson blessing your fun with his lordship. Give over skriking and lift your skirts."

"Get off me!" She bucked but he was too heavy to shift.

Filey's rancid breath puffed into her face. "Eh, but you'll make a grand wild ride, lass."

She shrieked with outrage and clawed at his eyes. He jerked out of the way and she gouged his cheek instead. Her fingernails sank with revolting ease into skin and flesh. She snatched her hand free as four jagged lines sullenly began to leak blood.

"Fucking bitch!" He raised his fist again and clouted her on the side of the head so hard that her ears rang.

Filey's blow dazed her into paralysis. She didn't flinch when he hooked his hand into her low-cut bodice. Vaguely, she felt his thick fingers curl against the top of her breasts. Then a sudden wrench as he rent her gown to the waist.

The sound of shredding material wrested her back to awareness. Her bare breasts spilled free of the ruined gown. Through bleary eyes, she saw him lift himself on his elbows.

"By gum, lass, that's a grand pair of tits."

Grace's gorge rose as he smacked his lips together in moist appreciation. She scrabbled to draw the tattered edges of silk together but Filey batted her hands away with a careless swipe. Then he took both wrists roughly in one hand and forced them above her head.

Pride deserted her. Only choking terror remained. "Stop this, for God's sake," she pleaded, not caring any more whether she sounded brave and defiant.

"You know better than that," he almost crooned. Blood suffused his face, making the network of broken veins stand out across cheeks and nose. Saliva glistened on his thick lips. He bent to bite one exposed breast.

She cried out in agony and struggled to throw him off but her strength faded. She'd never before realized how powerless a woman was when a man straddled her. He yanked at the fastening of his leather breeches with his spare hand. She tried to scream again but all that emerged was a choked whimper.

"Eh, I'm right looking forward to this, flower." Filey chuckled salaciously. The sound chilled Grace to the marrow.

Far too quickly, his breeches fell open.

She told herself she wouldn't look. She wouldn't look.

Her horrified gaze dropped to where his member sprang from its nest of graying brown hair. "No!" she cried in a cracked voice. "No!"

Disbelieving shock flooded her as he stroked the thick, throbbing length. "Aye, that's grand."

He licked his lips again and spittle dribbled down to shine on his stubbled chin. Hurting her wrists, he dragged her stiff arms down and forced her clenched fists to brush his erect flesh.

"Let go of me!" She jerked in appalled disgust.

She tried to kick him but his bulk trapped her legs. He laughed and pressed his straining member into her hands. "Oh, you're keen."

"Don't touch me," she sobbed, trying to recoil.

"Eh, flower, I'm harder than a brass doorknocker."

She couldn't bear this. She couldn't.

Her cracked whimper was a wordless plea for mercy. But he didn't seem to hear as he shoved her skirts to her waist with clumsy enthusiasm.

She tried to roll to the side but he knocked her flat with a savage punch to the mouth, splitting her lip so warm blood trickled down her chin. She lay in wretched stillness as he ripped away her flimsy underwear. With a grunt of satisfaction, he spread her quivering legs and positioned himself.

Grace tensed as he drew back ready to thrust. At the last minute, she twisted to avoid the inevitable.

"Bide still, bitch," Filey muttered, steadying his heavy member with one hand and tugging her arms above her head with the other.

"I'll kill you for this," she panted, closing her eyes and waiting for him to drive into her. She was dry and he was large, so the pain would be excruciating.

Then unbelievably, a sharp bark resounded behind her.

Wolfram?

Had her prayers been answered?

She squirmed to see. But Filey pressed her down too firmly.

She heard a low growl, another bark. A shadow briefly covered the sun. Everything turned to chaos as a huge brindle shape hurled itself at Filey.

"What the hell?" he gasped.

The dog's momentum thrust Filey hard on top of her, squeezing the breath from her lungs. Wolfram growled and snapped. The man's shrinking member slid along her bare leg. She shuddered to think how close he'd come to ramming it into her.

She burst into a frantic babble. "Wolfram! That's right. Good boy!"

She shoved at Filey's suffocating weight even while he fought the dog and missed his target. He landed a sharp jab to her ribs and she cried out. Wolfram's teeth closed around Filey's swinging arm, inciting her attacker to a string of obscenities.

Across Filey's heavily muscled shoulder, she saw Matthew dashing up with a heavy branch in one hand. His face was incandescent with fury. He looked like an avenging angel chasing Lucifer from heaven. He looked like he could commit murder and not even bother to shrug his indifference.

"Wolfram, heel," Matthew said in a voice so quiet and intense that it seared. Instantly the dog obeyed, slinking back to crouch in bristling alertness at Matthew's side.

She read Filey's brief shock at hearing Matthew. Then the gloating smile returned and he turned his head toward the marquess. Clearly Filey thought he still held the advantage. "Come to watch, your lordship? Happen you'll learn summat about pleasing a lass."

"You're a dead man!" Matthew's eyes glittered like yellow fire and a muscle jerked in his cheek. Grace's breath snared with fear as he kicked Filey off her, then hefted the makeshift club high. He swung it down hard across Filey's back. A sickening thud as wood cracked on bone.

"Bugger me!" Filey gasped.

Grunting, Matthew lifted the log and hit Filey again before he could cower away. The brute lurched to the side, raising his arms to protect his head. "Leave off, will you, for Christ's sake?"

Grace scrambled free, clutching the remnants of her dress to her breasts. Her face stung as if a thousand bees had attacked it. She drew her knees up to her chin and huddled in a protective crouch beside the path. Convulsive shivers shook her as she tightened her arms around her raised legs.

New tears flowed over the sticky residue of the old. As they fell, they made the abrasions on her face smart. She'd been so certain there was no hope. Now she couldn't accept she was safe.

"You'll never touch her again." Matthew stood over Filey like a divine avenger. Her lover was almost unrecognizable. No trace remained of the kind, gently amused man. He hoisted the log above his head, ready to crash it down on Filey's head.

"Don't kill him, Matthew." Grace's plea emerged as a muffled croak. She struggled to her feet and stumbled to his side.

Wolfram growled as if expressing his opinion of her request. Matthew's lips tightened over his teeth in a similar snarl. He didn't look at her but kept his eyes fixed on the cringing Filey. "Why not?"

"Just a bit of fun, your lordship. No harm. You know what lasses are like." Then fatally, "Well, maybe your lordship don't know. But the tart was hungry enow for a poke from a real man."

"Roast in hell, you bastard!" Matthew's eyes shone blank with rage and his muscles bunched as he prepared to swing the log down for the killing blow.

With horror, Grace realized he'd moved beyond the constraints of reason. She caught at his arm. "Don't do this. If you kill him, your uncle will chain you up again. He'll use it as conclusive proof of madness."

Matthew still brandished the log. "He hurt you."

"Yes, he deserves to die. But not at the cost of all you've achieved."

"Please, your lordship! Please, lass, take pity on a poor wight." Filey's pathetic groveling was almost more disgusting than his bragging. Fumbling to fasten his breeches, he staggered upright. He winced theatrically with each movement.

Grace ignored Filey and spoke to Matthew in a low voice that trembled with conviction. She couldn't let him do this, even if everything within her screamed for revenge. "Don't give your uncle this ammunition against you."

Lucidity seeped into Matthew's eyes, tempering the blazing gold. He touched her bruised cheek while his mouth thinned.

She must look a mess. The pain was certainly bad enough.

"I'd like to smash him to pieces," he said fiercely.

As always, she drew strength from his touch. "So would I, but your uncle must never think the madness has returned."

Wolfram gave another growl. She turned to see Filey trying to limp away. He hadn't straightened from his awkward crouch. His face was a mask of agony.

He'd suffer from Matthew's beating. He deserved to. The bruises he'd given her still ached. Her head still pounded. Her stomach still cramped with horror.

"You broke my bloody back," Filey whined, darting a worried eye at the dog.

"Unfortunately, I doubt it," Matthew snapped in his best Lord Sheene manner. "Get out of my sight before I reconsider letting you live."

"Aye, my lord." Filey edged away from Wolfram. "Very good, my lord."

"Wolfram, chase," Matthew said softly.

The dog bounded after Filey, forcing him into a shambling run. "Bloody hell! Call off your mongrel! Shit! Get away from me, you mangy bugger! Leave off!"

Matthew placed one arm around Grace as the ungainly pursuit continued through the trees. She leaned gratefully into his strength. Her legs felt like they were made of watery custard.

"Will Wolfram hurt him?" Grace asked shakily when Filey's groans had faded to a distant echo. Talking tested her split lip. Her jaw throbbed where Filey had punched her.

"Not unless I tell him to," Matthew said grimly. He flung away the log with a disgusted gesture and tore off his coat to wrap it around her. She appreciated the warmth. She was deathly cold.

She grabbed Matthew's arm, using her other hand to

preserve what modesty she could. Silly, she knew, when he'd seen every inch of her, kissed every inch of her. But after Filey's depredations, she craved the frail armor of clothing as much for her soul as for her body.

"Christ, Grace. Look at you." His expression was savage as he studied her injured face. He wrenched a handkerchief from his pocket and dabbed at her oozing lip. "I should have killed the bastard when I had the chance."

She winced and spoke through chattering teeth. "Thank God you arrived. I thought he was going to . . . He was going to . . ."

Her voice faltered into silence. Ugly gulping sobs tore at her throat.

"Shh, it's all right." Very carefully, his arms encircled her, surrounding her with heat and his familiar scent.

Eventually, she raised tear-drenched eyes. "I'm sorry."

"Let's get you back to the cottage." With the easy strength that always surprised her in such a lean man, he swung her into his arms.

"I can walk." She wasn't sure that was true.

"I'll carry you."

She didn't have it in her to argue, so she rested her pounding head on his shoulder. "You make me feel safe."

"I shouldn't," he said flatly, striding along the path.

"You can't blame yourself for what happened."

"I blame my uncle." Then he added a bleak rider, "And yes, I blame myself."

His arms tensed and she flinched. Every inch of her hurt worse as danger receded and her body reacted to the beating. She tightened her hold around his neck. The brush of silky dark hair against her fingers was strangely comforting.

"I thought you were with your roses."

"I missed you," he said softly.

"If you hadn't come . . ." she said brokenly, hugging him closer.

"I did."

"Yes."

He was her rock. He was her surety. He was her beloved.

All they had in this terrible wilderness was each other. God help them.

Chapter 19

Matthew eased Grace onto the sofa. She stiffened when he put her down, even though he was careful not to jar or jolt her. Her battered face already started to swell and discolor.

Jesus, he should have killed Filey. Now he must await another opportunity.

That opportunity would come soon enough.

First, he must ensure Grace's security. Until then, he could do nothing to pursue long-overdue justice.

"I'll get something to make you feel better," he said when she seemed reluctant to release him. She wasn't a clingy woman but this afternoon's ordeal had tested her limits.

"All right." Her hands slid down to tug nervously at his coat, drawing the edges together to hide the white lushness of her breasts. The breasts Filey had mauled. Matthew bit back another surge of anger. Filey had trespassed fatally this afternoon. There would be a reckoning before this sweet spring turned into full summer.

"I won't be long." He leaned forward and kissed her mercifully unbruised forehead.

He headed into the kitchen to heat some water. Then he gathered what he needed from the shelves in the garden room. He didn't want to leave her alone long. He hadn't missed the flash of panic in her lovely eyes when he'd told her he was going, even if only into the next room.

Grace was sitting up, still clutching at the ruined gown under his coat, when he returned. No disguising her relief when he appeared in the doorway.

He laid out his supplies on a small table. He was deliberately methodical. It helped soothe the raging beast within that yowled to smash and rampage. "Tell me where you hurt."

"Everywhere." She tried to smile, but her swollen lip defeated her.

She was so brave, it cut him to the heart. Concern for her swamped even his titanic rage, although rage seethed, ready to ignite at the first spark.

He knelt beside the couch for better access. Tenderly, he smoothed bedraggled hair from her brow. "Filey didn't get what he wanted. And he won't. You have my word."

Her eyes were wide with dread. "Your uncle may retaliate."

"My uncle doesn't hold all the trumps in this game," he said with calm certainty. "You're safe."

After a long pause, she nodded.

He sucked in a relieved breath and gently pulled his coat from her shoulders. He bent to slide her slippers from her feet then roll down her tattered stockings. Finally, he unhooked the rigid fingers that curled into her bodice.

"Let me see, Grace," he murmured when she didn't immediately relinquish her deathly grip.

"No." She pressed against the back of the sofa.

Oh, God, she was frightened. Of him.

Filey would rot in hell.

"I'd never hurt you, Grace. You know that," Matthew said in the crooning voice he used when he treated an injured bird or animal. "You're safe with me."

Some of the tension drained from her face. Or what he could see of her face under the bruises. She relaxed her hold and the dirty yellow dress fell away. As he brushed the fabric aside, she whimpered and hunched her slender shoulders.

What was she hiding? He shifted to see but she wrapped her arms across her chest in a protective gesture.

"Grace?" he asked softly, carefully parting her entwined arms.

Then he saw her naked breast.

Filey's teeth marks stood out clearly, rimmed in purple and grazed red where he'd broken the skin.

Apart from that foul bite, bruises covered the pale skin on chest and ribs. The violence Matthew struggled to control swelled to choke him.

"Christ," he breathed, balling his fists.

Shame reddened her cheeks. "I couldn't stop him."

"No, but I will," he grated out, unable to tear his eyes from the signs of Filey's abuse.

She must have read murder in his face because she stretched out a shaking hand to clasp his wrist. "It's too late."

"Jesus, how can you say that?" Taking a deep breath to calm the crashing thunder in his blood, he slid her long sleeves down. Her arms were bruised and finger marks circled her wrists, mute testimony to how roughly Filey had handled her. The demon inside him jerked at its leash.

"I'm sorry, my darling." He noticed how she flinched with each movement. "You'll feel better out of this dress."

Surprisingly, her mouth quirked in a shadow of her usual smile. "I'm sure you're not the first young man to use that line."

He forced a smile although her courage made him want to weep. In his heart, he howled for Filey's blood. With the scissors he'd brought from the kitchen, he cut her skirt away. Then he removed the tattered drawers and corset and shift.

How it pained him to hurt her, but he couldn't help it. When she was naked, he let down her tangled hair and combed it with his hands so it fell loosely around her shoulders. Through the silky black tresses, her white skin shone like a pearl, where the bruises and abrasions didn't disfigure her.

He drew a rug over her then left briefly to collect a bowl of warm water from the kitchen. "I'll help you sit up," he said when he came back.

When she was upright, he wet a cloth and very, very carefully bathed her. Her body was slim and graceful in the late afternoon light. But as he traced each perfect curve, stroked each hollow, he didn't think about sex. Instead, a vast tenderness filled him.

With the gentleness he'd used throughout, he dried her. He laid aside the damp towel and removed the lid of a small jar. "Arnica, calendula, witch hazel help bruises to heal." As he scooped a handful of ointment, a fresh smell mingled pleasantly with the jasmine. "There are advantages to having a lover who spent his youth poring over herbals."

"Instead of touring the fleshpots?" she asked dryly, although she tensed with silent discomfort when he smoothed the mixture on the darkening marks around her wrists.

Filey would pay tenfold for every drop of Grace's pain. Matthew swore vengeance against his enemies even while he kept his touch light.

"Ouch." She grimaced when he began on the swollen, purple mess of her left cheek.

She'd been so sweetly stoic through what he knew was an agonizing process. He covered the last of her bruises with ointment and turned away, wiping his hands on a linen towel. "Rest now, Grace."

"Where are you going?" Her eyes were bright with fear.

He dredged up a smile that he prayed reassured. "Only to the kitchen. I'm brewing something to help you sleep."

She gave a visible shudder. "I'll never sleep again." Her hands shook as she tugged the rug up to hide her body.

"You'll get over this." Briefly, he touched her shoulder, feeling the tremors that racked her. "I won't be long."

In the kitchen, Matthew quickly made a tea of valerian, willow bark, and meadowsweet. It would dull her aches although she'd feel buffeted and sore for several days. She'd survive this ordeal and emerge whole and shining. He just wished to hell he could be there to see it.

He brought the laden tray through. "Do you feel any better?"

She looked up from her supine position and managed a smile. Or as much of a smile as her ruined face allowed. "Actually, I do."

He deliberately concentrated on practicalities. "I've got bread and cheese."

"I'm not hungry." Weariness shadowed her expression. Emotionally she reached her limits. As she raised herself awkwardly on the cushions, he handed her the steaming cup. She clearly felt the full effect of Filey's beating. Until now, shock had kept the worst of the pain at bay. She sipped and he couldn't help but laugh at her moue of distaste. "It's dreadful."

"You can't take opium. This was the next best thing."

Wondering amazement filled her eyes. Astonishing how expressive even her bruised face was. "You remember that?"

"I remember everything about you. Now drink up. Then try and eat something."

He waited for another argument. But she must have felt even worse than he thought because she finished the tea and food, then lay back in exhaustion.

"My head hurts," she mumbled into the cushion.

He was sure it did, even though the tea already had a narcotic effect. She hardly made a murmur as he wrapped the blanket around her, scooped her into his arms and carried her upstairs to bed.

After sharing this room for three days, he had no trouble laying his hands on her night rail. Not that she'd worn it much recently. He carefully dressed her, then pulled back the sheets.

"Don't leave me," she whispered even as her eyelids fluttered. She was barely conscious.

"Never," he said, although the word was a betrayal.

His false promise seemed to satisfy her because she relaxed against the pillows. Almost immediately, he heard her breathing take on the slow rhythm of sleep. He covered her with the blankets although the room wasn't cold.

He tugged off his boots and lay down beside her. She should sleep for hours, but he didn't want her to awake alone and frightened.

Grace gave a soft cry of distress. Immediately Matthew stirred to alertness. Somewhere in the dark hours, he must have fallen into an uneasy doze.

He wore a shirt and trousers and lay on top of the covers while she lay beneath them. He hadn't wanted to risk hauling her into his arms and hurting her while he was unaware.

They'd been lovers only a few days but already he'd become dangerously addicted to holding her through the night. Without her, he was bereft and lonely. As if his world no longer turned in the right direction.

Jesus, how would he survive without her? Not just for one night. Forever.

He suppressed the grim premonition of what hell

awaited and reached over to light a candle. "Grace, are you all right?"

The flickering light revealed new bruising on her face in spite of his efforts with the ointment. Pain and the ghost of fear shone in her dark blue eyes and tautened her swollen mouth. His resolve that Filey, and ultimately his uncle, would pay for this outrage surged anew. If heaven granted just that modicum of justice, he'd die a happy man.

"Yes." The drugs thickened her voice. "What time is it?"

He checked the silver pocket watch he'd left on the bedside table. "Twenty past three. Would you like some water?"

She smiled, then flinched as the movement tested her torn lip. "Yes, please."

He left the bed and filled a glass from the crystal decanter on the chest. "How do you feel?"

"Like a coach and four have run over me," she said wryly, lifting herself with difficulty and accepting the drink in a trembling hand. "Twice."

He managed a smile, although in truth her suffering made him too angry to feel much amusement. "Can I get you anything?"

"No." An unsteady breath. "I want you to hold me."

"I might hurt you," he said, even while he itched to comply. Not so he could make love to her, although desire charged the still air. It always would when he was with her. But desire, for once, wasn't the most urgent thing. Love, tenderness, care were what mattered now.

"Matthew, I . . . I need you."

How could he deny her? God, he'd die for her if she asked him.

He waited for her to take a few sips then removed the glass. With great care, he slid under the sheets, immediately feeling her warmth.

How cold his life would be without her. Like darkest winter. Like the grave.

He heaped the pillows behind his head and gently drew her toward him. She didn't need to tell him she was in pain. It was clear from the way she gingerly rested her head on his shoulder. She curled against his side and stretched her arm across his chest.

"That's better," she sighed, burrowing one hand beneath his shirt so it lay over his grieving heart. The sweet scent of Grace washed over him, sunshine, woman, jasmine soap. And a teasing hint of herbal liniment.

She was shaking. For Grace, terror still stalked this quiet room.

Since she'd become Matthew's lover, he'd existed in a brittle paradise. He'd always known his joy was precarious but he'd refused to recognize the risks he ran by clinging to his darling. Risks that today had exploded into violence.

"Do you know the worst part of what happened this afternoon?" she asked in a husky voice.

Unfortunately, he did. He'd been bound and beaten often enough. "The sense of utter powerlessness," he said grimly.

"Yes," she whispered as if mere acknowledgment eased her. She sounded drowsy. The drugs he'd given her lingered in her system.

"Sleep, Grace," he said softly. "I'll keep you safe."

The promise emerged from deep within. He'd protect her from Filey, Monks, and his uncle. Whatever the cost.

The cost was likely to be his sanity, if not his life.

For her sake, he must act. For her sake and his own, if he was to have any claim to be a man.

He stared out into the candlelit room while Grace slept. His brief paradise had disintegrated to dust. Cruel truth looked him straight in the eye.

Grace couldn't remain on the estate. Even if he managed to keep her out of Filey's clutches, too many other hazards lurked.

Matthew had long ago lost the chance for a normal life. But a woman like Grace belonged to the world. She deserved happiness with a decent man who would love her and care for her and give her children. That man could never be Matthew Lansdowne. Much as he'd barter his soul to say he was.

He had to come up with an escape plan for her. Then, once she was free and safe, he'd end his uncle's reign of evil forever.

Chapter 20

Ten uneasy days passed. Matthew cursed each second that Grace remained on the estate and in danger, even though anticipating her departure was like bathing in acid.

His determination to spirit her away never wavered. He only had to recall Filey's hulking body jammed between her bare legs and the sickening thud of the brute's fists on her flesh. Each moment she spent as Lord John's captive, she was at risk.

Filey slunk about, bruised, limping, sulking, sporting an increasingly filthy bandage on his arm where Wolfram's teeth had broken the skin. He seemed cowed, but Matthew didn't fool himself that the threat had passed.

Grace's bruises had almost gone and her grazes weren't severe enough to scar. Little other evidence remained of the frightened, tearful woman whose injuries he'd tended. The only long-term effects he noted were a new desperation in her passion and a reluctance to stray far from his side.

With every day, he loved her more. He wouldn't have thought that possible, but it was true. When he buried himself deep inside her, he felt they shared blood, breath, souls. So often the words *I love you* surged up to push at the back of his teeth. So far he'd managed to stifle unwelcome declarations. The memory was too vivid of how she'd recoiled when he'd told her before.

Grace called him a brave man, but he wasn't brave enough to risk rejection again.

She wanted him. She trusted him. She seemed to like him. She just didn't love him.

Which hurt like the very devil.

His eternally fascinating Grace sat opposite him now on the couch. Twilight drew in and they shared the hour before dinner. Her presence soothed his troubled thoughts, even if nothing could dispel them. He glanced across from his armchair near the unlit fire and marveled yet again that such a glorious woman should be his.

Because for now she was unequivocally his.

She reclined against the arm of the couch in an unconsciously seductive pose. One elegant hand held a half-full glass. Her crimson gown was tight enough to make a whore blush. The rich color made her skin look like new milk.

His eyes dipped to where the fiendishly low neckline barely covered her nipples. He licked his lips as if he already tasted their sweetness.

Soon.

Desire stirred lazily in his veins. Later, when he held her naked in his arms, it would blaze into a conflagration. In this quiet room, appetite was a gentle fizz in his blood, an alluring whisper of pleasure to come.

She'd piled her hair high, leaving silky tendrils to tease bare shoulders. How he longed to festoon that slender neck with cascades of rubies. Rubies, diamonds, pearls, emeralds. Never sapphires. Not even the finest sapphires could rival the beauty of her eyes.

He had no jewels to offer, only his longing, loving heart. To his aching regret, he knew she'd never covet that poor prize.

She raised her glass and sipped at the rich red liquid the same color as her dress. Such a simple thing to make the breath hitch in his throat.

She was everything he wanted. The prospect of her leaving pierced his guts like a saber.

He hadn't told her she must go. Until he had a firm plan, he saw no point in raising hopes of freedom. Of course she'd leap at the chance of escape. She'd be a fool not to.

A tiny frown contracted her fine dark brows. "What's wrong, Matthew?"

He forced himself to smile. He strove to hide his disquiet but she knew him so well. "That dress needs rubies."

She shrugged. "I don't care about jewels."

He knew she didn't. But that didn't stop him from regretting that he'd never bedeck her with glittering treasure. His mind conjured a breathtaking image of her draped in nothing except ropes of shining stones.

"What's that?" she asked, turning toward the window which sat ajar to catch the soft spring air.

"I just . . ." He wondered how she'd guessed the lascivious images slinking through his head. Then he too heard the carriage rumbling up the drive to stop in front of the cottage.

Only one man had unlimited entrée to the estate. Lord John's arrival was unwelcome but no surprise. Monks would have informed him of events last week. Matthew set his crystal glass down on a side table with an audible clink. Animal wariness banished his sensual imaginings.

"It's my uncle." He rose and moved to stand at Grace's side like a palace guard protecting his beautiful young queen.

"Your uncle?" she said breathlessly, beginning to stand.

"Courage, love." The endearment slipped out before he could stop it. He placed one hand on her shoulder, feeling the fragile network of bone and sinew under the satiny skin. "Don't let him see you're afraid."

"I am afraid," she whispered, subsiding under the downward pressure. Beneath his fingers, her pulse fluttered like a trapped bird.

A brawny lackey opened the door to the salon and his uncle swept in with a retinue of three footmen wearing the dark green Lansdowne livery. He stopped a few feet away from Matthew and the woman poised in rigid silence on the sofa.

"Good evening, Matthew." He removed his leather gloves and high-crowned hat and handed them to one of the servants who bowed and left.

"Uncle," Matthew said in an expressionless voice.

Lord John glanced around with the supercilious expression familiar from hundreds of previous visits. He waved his cane at the remaining two footmen. "Build up the fire, close the windows and curtains, then wait outside."

The servants bustled around the room, turning it into a stuffy greenhouse. When they left, the door's discreet click echoed loudly in the vibrating, airless silence.

"I am most displeased with you, nephew," Lord John said when it became apparent nobody was going to ask what he was doing here.

The power games were childish, Matthew knew, but they were all he had. Over the years, he'd become adept at unsettling his uncle. Now he bent his head in an insolent approximation of a bow. "My commiserations, Uncle."

As expected, his uncle ignored the sarcasm. Instead and with an unmistakable air of ownership, he lowered himself into the vacated armchair and rested his hands on the huge lump of amber set into the top of his cane. There was a prehistoric fly trapped in the gold. The spiteful symbolism had never been lost on Matthew.

His uncle's narrow mouth set in sour lines. "I was in

Scotland on the King's business when I received disturbing reports that you'd attacked one of your warders."

"One of my warders attacked this lady," Matthew returned coldly. Grace's fading bruises indicated what had happened eloquently enough.

Her chin tilted with cool pride. Her face was as pale and perfect as a marble effigy on a tomb. She hadn't risen to curtsy. His uncle would register the insult although he gave no sign he even noticed her.

Lord John paused. "Whatever the truth, I find myself concerned about developments. The wench has proven a disappointment. I should have realized that she wouldn't suit my purposes. I will replace her."

Aha, battle was engaged, Matthew thought with savage satisfaction. After an unusually brief preliminary skirmish. His uncle liked to toy with his victims, watch them run hither and yon in a futile bid to escape his fiendish nets. The abruptness of this attack indicated Lord John was more rattled than he appeared.

Excellent.

Matthew curled his fingers reassuringly upon Grace's shoulder. The muscles under his hand were tight. She knew what his uncle meant by the word *replace*.

"On the contrary, Mrs. Paget is all I could wish her to be," he said smoothly.

His uncle tried and failed to adopt a friendly man-of-the-world tone. "Come, lad. Believe me, she's a paltry milk-water chit. You need a woman who knows how to please a man. You have no grounds for comparison when it comes to a fuck."

Grace gave a tiny start and a shamed wash of pink colored her cheeks. It must pain her intolerably to realize that his uncle knew to the day when she'd started sharing Matthew's bed.

"Mrs. Paget stays," he said implacably.

These days John Lansdowne was unused to anyone defying him. Anger flashed in the arctic eyes and the thin hands clenched on the cane. As each year passed, he became more lordly, as though gradually he took on every trapping of the marquessate except the title. That the title remained forever barred to him was a source of infinite regret, Matthew knew.

"You'll forget her soon enough when a red-blooded jade warms your sheets. Mrs. Paget threw herself on my mercy last time I was here and begged me to remove her. My boy, you must see it's wrong to force a respectable woman to whore herself."

"I'm sure the guilt keeps you awake at night," Matthew said with heavy irony.

"You will never release me, Lord John." Grace's words sliced through the atmosphere of building animosity like a crystal knife. "I know too much. You mean to kill me."

Lord John's eyebrows, graying copies of Matthew's, arched disdainfully. "Madam, you overestimate your significance."

"I believe not, my lord." Contempt dripped from each word.

"You're very bold now you're my nephew's harlot," his uncle said equally coldly. "What of the virtuous widow?"

Grace flinched at the word *harlot* but she retained her regal manner. "Better a harlot than a bully and a fraud and a thief, my lord."

"Why, you insolent slut!" His uncle surged to his feet and raised his hand.

Before the blow made contact, Matthew lunged forward to stand as a barrier before his uncle. As he moved, Grace gasped and jerked back against the couch.

"Strike her and you'll regret it," Matthew snarled, leaning forward so his height dwarfed the older man.

Violence surged close in the overheated room. In eleven

years, the simmering hatred between uncle and nephew had never exploded into physical confrontation. Now the anger boiling in Matthew's blood blinded him to everything but the urge to kill. He could almost feel his hands squeeze the last poisonous breath from his enemy's throat. Rage was a searing, caustic taste in his mouth. His muscles bunched in readiness for action. The world shrank to a pulsing red pinpoint that held only his uncle's loathsome face.

Grace flattened her palm against his spine. The simple connection dragged him back from the perilous edge, reminded him what was at stake.

Jesus, what was he doing? He couldn't kill his uncle here. Lord John's henchmen outnumbered him and would inevitably overpower him afterward.

Then what would happen to Grace?

Grappling for control, he clenched his teeth so hard that his jaw ached. How he wanted to lash out, to destroy. He couldn't. Not yet. Satisfaction must wait until Grace was on the other side of the polished white walls.

"Good God, restrain yourself, man!" Lord John lurched out of immediate reach. "I wouldn't lower myself to touch the jade."

"See that you don't." Matthew fought to steady his breathing. Grace's touch on his heaving back was his only frail connection to reason. The warmth of that contact calmed the storm in his blood. Slowly he straightened from his threatening slant.

"I've seen enough. The whore goes tonight," Lord John growled. "I'll get you another woman. One mare is the same as another in the dark."

Matthew was aware enough now to hear Grace's shocked release of breath. "I don't want another woman," he said. "I told you—Mrs. Paget stays."

His uncle's overweening self-assurance already showed signs of reviving. "Proving yourself with a female has given you the mistaken impression you have some choice, nephew."

"There's always a choice," Matthew said austerely. Their battle was open in a way it hadn't been for years. Pray God he kept his nerve long enough to win. He tamped down the remnants of fury and fixed a level stare on Lord John. "You forget I hold ultimate power over you, Uncle."

Lord John responded with a scoffing chuckle. "Are you mad again in truth? How long before Monks has to strap you down and feed you like a puling baby and wipe the filth from your body while you cry and scream and babble nonsense?"

Matthew didn't react to the humiliating description. Instead, he spoke with a calmness grounded in absolute confidence. A confidence he'd never felt before when he confronted his uncle. Grace had made him a stronger, surer man. Her hand dropped away from his back but the warmth lingered, much as her image would linger in his heart till the day he died.

"If you harm Mrs. Paget, Uncle, I swear on my parents' graves you'll lose control of the Lansdowne fortune."

His uncle's scorn was palpable in the suffocating room. "Just how do you plan to achieve that, boy?"

Lord John could call him *boy* and *lad* a thousand times, but it didn't change the fact that the power balance had permanently shifted. With Grace at his side, Matthew was invincible. His uncle had made a fatal error when he'd sent his bullies to Bristol and they'd snatched this particular woman.

Matthew allowed himself a small, superior smile. "Why, with my life, Uncle. Your power hangs by one slender thread—that I stay this side of heaven. I die and you lose all chance to dip your greedy paws into the family money." His voice hardened. "Touch Grace Paget, steal her from me, injure her, and my days are numbered."

"No," Grace protested frantically from behind him. "This is wrong."

His heart ached for her distress but he didn't look at her. All his strength, his mind, his determination focused on vanquishing his uncle.

"Idle words from a useless popinjay." Lord John tried for a careless laugh but the blood had receded from his cheeks, leaving him even more pasty-faced than usual.

Matthew forced himself to shrug with a nonchalance he didn't feel. "That is my final power, Uncle. There are a hundred ways I could kill myself in this room alone. Then my cousin becomes Marquess of Sheene. Your access to the Lansdowne coffers ends unless you intend to bribe doctors to say he's mad too. I doubt you'd get away with this scheme twice."

"Cease your melodramatic drivel," Lord John snapped, although his effortless air of command noticeably frayed.

"Matthew, I'm not worth it," Grace breathed. "Don't do this. I beg of you."

He turned to meet her troubled eyes. "It's the only way, my darling."

"You offer to lay down your life for this whore?" Lord John said with disgusted incomprehension. "She's nothing but a cheap harlot. You'd buy her equal for twopence in any alley."

Matthew swung back to his uncle and bared his teeth in unconcealed threat. "Speak of this lady with disrespect once more and I'll ram your words down your throat."

"You imagine yourself in love. There's no point trying to make you see sense," his uncle sneered, although he took a step backward. Clearly, he hadn't forgotten the moment

Matthew had loomed over him with murder in his eyes. "I'll return when you've regained what pass for your wits."

He rapped his cane hard on the floor. Almost immediately, a footman opened the door. Matthew thankfully inhaled the blast of cooler air that rushed into the room. The heat left him feeling stifled. Or perhaps it was the evil that oozed from his uncle's pores like the stench of rotten flesh.

"Keep your slut for the nonce. Enjoy her while you can." Lord John stalked out without another word.

Matthew stripped his coat from his sweating body, threw it over a chair and strode across to pour himself a brandy.

Against all expectations, he'd won. He couldn't believe it.

He downed his drink in a single gulp and poured another. He turned to offer the glass to Grace, then froze in shock.

A torrent of tears cascaded down her ashen cheeks. She stood facing him, trembling so hard that her words emerged in staccato bursts. "I'm not worth your life, Matthew."

"Of course you are." He slammed the glass onto the sideboard so roughly that brandy spilled onto the richly polished wood. "You're heaven and earth to me."

Couldn't she see that? The forbidden words *I love you* surged up anew. He reached her side and wrenched her into his arms. Immediately her sweet jasmine and sunshine scent filled his head.

"I don't want you to die," she sobbed, burying her head in his chest. Her hands kneaded his back through his shirt.

"Foolish girl," he murmured into her soft hair. His arm tightened and he pressed her shaking body closer. She fitted against him as if made for his embrace. "You can rely on my uncle's greed if nothing else."

She pulled far enough away to wipe at her tears. "I hate your uncle."

The bitter realization struck that the time for prevarication had passed. "He won't stay defeated, Grace. You're not safe under his dominion. Make no mistake—everything on this estate is under his dominion."

"I can't help that," she said thickly.

"Yes, you can. You can leave."

Her gaze, dark with confusion, swimming with tears, flew to meet his. "I'm as much his prisoner as you are."

Oh, God, could he bear to tell her? He took a deep breath of the overheated air. "I can get you out."

She searched his face as if she suspected him of joking. "You've always said that's impossible. Why has that changed? How can we escape?"

He briefly closed his eyes in agony, although the image of her ardent, tear-stained face burned in his brain. "Just you, Grace," he said with difficulty. "You're going. I'm staying."

She withdrew slightly and frowned. He fought the urge to tug her back into his arms, if only because soon, she'd be too far away to hold. "I don't understand. If I can leave, why can't you?"

"I'd give anything to make things different, but anyone who aids me is sentenced as a criminal. It happened last time."

"I'd be with you. I can tell people what your uncle has done."

She sounded so eager, so hopeful, he hated to deny her. "Do you think I wouldn't sell my soul to be free and with you? But I'm a certified lunatic. I'm confined for the public good."

"You're not mad," she said vehemently. "You know you're not mad."

"For the past few years, no. But my doctors will swear I'm dangerous."

"Doctors your uncle bribed. He didn't deny your charge."

"That doesn't mean their diagnosis is wrong."

"It is wrong!"

"Grace, stop!" He leaned forward and kissed her hard. Tasting tears. Tasting desperation.

Heat exploded in his head, dazzled him with light. Her mouth was voracious. Even while he sank into delight, he had the strange idea that she argued with him even through her kiss. She ran her hands up his chest to link them behind his neck. Through the fine shirt, her touch scorched his skin. His arms encircled her, drawing her closer.

How the hell could he ever let her go?

Panting and distraught, she tore herself free. She was shaking violently and her face was pale with tension. She glared at him as if she hated him, while her mouth glistened with moisture from their fierce kiss.

"I won't go," she said in a raw voice. "You can't make me. I want to stay with you."

What lunacy was this? He shook his head to clear it. Surely he'd misheard. Circumstances had forced her into a madman's bed. She'd been abused and attacked and insulted. Any sensible woman would grab the chance of escape and run until she was a thousand miles from this estate and everyone on it.

Clearly Grace wasn't a sensible woman.

His heart clenched in bewildered despair. Perhaps she didn't understand. "I've worked out a way you can get away. This is your chance. You want to be free. You must be free."

"I don't want to be free without you," she said stubbornly. She lifted her chin and gave him the same defiant glower that had stolen his heart the first time he'd seen her.

He didn't dare read the message in her eyes. Tears streaked her cheeks but she wasn't crying anymore. "Whatever we face, we face together."

Matthew's heart kicked with shock.

Could this mean what he thought it did?

Could it?

Surely he wasn't wrong about the inevitable, life-changing truth forcing its way into mind and heart. His anguished, adoring heart.

He sucked in a deep breath and dredged up every last ounce of courage to ask the inevitable question. "Grace . . ." he began, then crashed into silence.

He drew in another lungful of air. Ridiculous, but he kept forgetting to breathe.

He steeled himself to speak. Christ, he'd confronted death and illness and torture, but forcing these few small words out took every ounce of courage.

He met her fathomless indigo eyes and braced himself to go on. "Grace, do you love me?"

His voice sounded rusty, like an old man's. His hands clenched and unclenched at his sides.

The silence that followed lasted an agonizing eternity.

Still she didn't speak.

Oh, Christ, he'd got it wrong. Somehow he'd got it disastrously wrong.

Yet for one brief, blinding second, he'd been so sure.

Despair like slow death trawled his veins. Self-loathing clenched his belly hard and tight. As if a woman like Grace Paget could love someone like him. Had he forgotten the cruel lessons of the last years? He was only half a man, condemned to live half a life. Sometimes, like now, that half life was all he believed he deserved.

She looked uncertain, unhappy. Of course she did. She wouldn't want to hurt him. He couldn't bear her pity, but what other response could she offer after the hellish mess he'd made of this? He cursed himself for his damned clumsiness. These last embarrassing minutes would poison the few days remaining to them.

"I thought I loved Josiah," she said slowly. Her eyes didn't shift from his face.

"You were little more than a child."

"I'm a woman now."

"Yes." Helplessly, his gaze ran over her body, tracing each luscious curve, each inch of creamy skin revealed by the crimson silk. His eyes returned to meet hers.

"I know my heart, Matthew. I know what I feel won't change." She took a shuddering breath and extended one unsteady hand in his direction. Her voice shook with intensity. "When I tell you I love you, that means I'll love you forever."

What does a man do when his dearest dream comes true?

Matthew stared at her outstretched hand. He'd never imagined this time would come. He wasn't prepared. Her words soaked into his soul, slowly turning the parched desert there into a verdant garden.

"You love me," he said slowly, wonderingly. Then with greater certainty, "By God, you love me." His astonished laugh ended on a choked note as he snatched her hand.

"So much," she said huskily. Her fingers curled hard around his. "So very, very much."

He dragged her back into his arms. "I can't believe it."

"Believe it," she whispered. She raised her hands to frame his face so she could look into his eyes. The blue was so pure that he saw right to her gallant, steadfast soul. "I love you, Matthew. I will always love you."

"And I love you, Grace."

Such simple words to change his life. Yet after tonight, he'd never be the same man again.

He pressed his lips to hers. As her mouth blossomed under his, the frenzy left him. Only gratitude and love remained.

Love above all.

"Don't send me away," she said brokenly.

"Hush," was all he said. He buried his face in her thick hair and wondered how he could live without her.

Chapter 21

❦

"**N**othing you say will make me go."

Since last night, Grace had repeatedly broached the subject of her departure. This morning she refused to let Matthew sweep her objections aside or distract her with kisses.

Kisses and other things, she thought with a blush.

They walked through the woods and she could tell from Wolfram's unconcerned nosing in the underbrush that Monks and Filey were nowhere near. Sunlight dappled the new leaves and lit Matthew with gold. That seemed symbolic. He was gold to her, pure gold. She didn't want to leave him. Ever. Even if it meant staying a prisoner.

Matthew sighed heavily. "You heard my uncle. We have no choice."

"Yes, we do." She stepped in front of him, forcing him to stop and give her his complete attention.

"Grace, listen." His voice roughened as he grabbed her arms in less than gentle hands. She wondered if he meant to shake her but he just held her. His touch was hot, even through her satin sleeves. "Your life is too precious to risk."

"Then come with me!"

"You know that's impossible," he said sharply. Anger sparked in his eyes. "There's no point arguing."

"If you can plot my escape, you can plot escape for both of us," she said with equal force.

"I'll die within these walls." His grip tightened as if to add physical emphasis to his words. "I accepted that last year when my uncle had Mary and her husband transported."

The desolation he lived with every day opened a jagged rift in her heart. "How can I go on without you?" she asked in a thin voice.

He lifted his hands away. His eyes were as flat as polished bronze and filled with so much love and pain, she had to bite back a cry of distress.

"You're too strong not to," he said softly.

How wrong he was. She wasn't strong at all. She blinked back tears. Heavens, all she seemed to do these days was cry. "I'm not strong."

"Yes, you are. You know you are." His voice was impossibly deep and she seemed to hear him in her blood as much as with her ears. "You stood up to your father. You stood up to Josiah. God, you even stood up to my uncle. My one comfort in sending you away is that I know nothing will break you."

"I won't go."

"Yes, you will. You know what it will cost me if my uncle harms you."

She glared at him. "That's not playing fair."

"I'm not playing fair, my love. I'm playing to win."

Furious denial surged. She wouldn't let him do this. "Two can play at that game."

She gripped his head between shaking hands and dragged him down until his mouth met hers. She'd tried to seduce him against his will before and failed, but now she knew how vulnerable he was to her.

He didn't fight, but his lips remained closed and his arms hung resolutely by his sides.

She wasn't going to let him win.

She curled her arms around his back, pressing herself brazenly to his lean form. Against her breasts, his heart pounded, belying his veneer of control. She had to break that control then she had to break him. Anything to make him abandon his cruel plan to exile her.

Desperately, she licked and nibbled at his lips, nipping his bottom lip until he opened his mouth. Her tongue darted into the dark interior, then lingered to taste and torment. He groaned deep in his throat and finally kissed her back, answering each incursion of her tongue with his. He hauled her up in a furious embrace and took charge. She could no longer tell who was the aggressor. His kiss held the same frantic passion she'd felt last night when she lay in his arms. She closed her eyes while heat and darkness engulfed her.

"Jesus, Grace!" Abruptly the kiss ended. "This proves nothing!"

She opened her eyes to see him staring down at her with turbulent despair. He tried to step back but she caught one of his hands before he could move away.

"Can you live without this?" she asked in a guttural voice. Without finesse, she shoved his palm against her breast. Her nipple immediately tautened to a yearning point under his hand. "Or this?" Roughly, she reached forward to cup the front of his trousers. He was already hard and eager. She stroked his sex and felt him swell under her touch.

Once she'd never have summoned courage to do this. Love made her bold. And desperate.

Briefly, he resisted then the hand on her breast curved to shape her flesh. She sighed and leaned into the familiar sweetness.

"No!" he said hoarsely, tearing himself away to stand a few feet distant. "I can't live with the fact that you're in danger." A hectic flush marked his prominent cheekbones and a muscle twitched spasmodically near his jaw.

She wrapped her arms around herself to counter the chill slowing her blood. "You can't fight this," she said in a frantic rush. "You can't fight me. I know you too well."

"Yes, you do." He raised a hand to prevent her headlong flight back into his arms. "Do you want to turn what we feel into a weapon? We'll end up destroying one another."

"I can't leave you." She wanted to sound strong, invincible, but the words emerged as a choked plea. "Don't make me go."

His face contracted with pain. "Let me save you, Grace. Give me this one gift." Then in a low shaking voice, "For God's sake, allow me this if nothing else. I have nothing else."

His last bleak statement cut through her resistance like a knife through butter. She fought back tears. She wouldn't cry. She wouldn't cry.

Acrid shame flooded her. Her defiance tortured him to his limits and he'd already borne so much. She expelled her breath on a muffled sob. "You break my heart."

He understood immediately that she'd acknowledged his right to banish her. He stepped forward to take her in his arms. "I wish to God it could be otherwise, my darling."

"When I'm free, I'll get you out of here," she said fiercely, tilting her head so she could see his face. It sliced her to her soul to leave him, but what else could she do?

His expression was stark with sorrow. "Grace, forget me. If my uncle traces you, our efforts are for naught."

"I won't abandon you."

"You have to," he said with bitter finality. "It's your only chance."

"No," she said just as obstinately. Before he could argue, and she knew he'd argue, she rushed on. "When do I go?"

"Tomorrow."

No.

Horrified, she jerked free. "You can't mean it!"

She'd only just reconciled herself to leaving. One more day? She couldn't bear it.

"Every hour you're here, the danger increases," he said somberly. "My uncle already schemes to take you away or kill you. By now, he'll have convinced himself my threats mean nothing. Every hour, Filey gains courage. There's a food delivery tomorrow morning. Monks and Filey will open the gates. It's how I escaped last time. I'll create a diversion and you'll slip out."

She wasn't going to cry. She'd cried last night. She'd cried this morning. She was going to be brave. For the sake of her own pride if nothing else.

"But tomorrow?" She struggled for composure.

"It's best," he said with implacable softness and passed her the handkerchief he fished out of his coat. "Now, here's what we should do."

As Grace joined Matthew for dinner in the salon, she was aware this could possibly—was likely—the last evening they'd spend together. Even if her vague plans of rescue came to fruition, their liaison was over once she left the estate. She harbored no foolish illusions that a happy ending awaited in the world outside.

Yet again, the painful reality stabbed at her that a great lord and a destitute farmer's wife had no future together. He must take possession of his power and prestige. She must settle to life as a poor relation with Cousin Vere and his noisy, ever-increasing family.

What about love? her heart cried in anguish.

Love. Yes, in this place, at this time, they loved each other. But while she'd love him until she died, his love was a hothouse plant that couldn't thrive beyond his prison. How could it when he'd seen nothing of the world?

She wished to heaven she could think of something to make him come with her. But her mind remained blank of everything but grief.

One thing alone kept her from breaking down. One frail hope. She was Matthew's only chance at freedom.

If she managed to evade their jailers. If Lord John didn't track her down. If she found someone to believe her bizarre story.

If.

If was all she had.

If. And tonight.

"Would you like more wine?" She reached for the decanter.

He shook his head. "No."

Her hand dropped to the table near her plate. Her crowded plate. Neither of them had done justice to Mrs. Filey's excellent roast chicken.

"I want you in my arms," he said in a low, intense voice.

He looked across the table at her, his eyes brimming with desire and understanding. He knew what it cost her to agree to go. Because he knew, she stifled her impulse to insist again that she stay. She didn't care what danger she faced as long as she faced it at his side. In this strange place, she'd discovered both herself and a man worthy of her love. But he was hers for a heartbreakingly brief time.

If only . . .

No, such thoughts weakened her. He fought as hard as she to maintain courage. She couldn't dishonor that struggle by playing the weak, hysterical woman. The memory of her tawdry behavior that morning made her cringe.

"Come, my love." He pushed his chair back and extended one hand in her direction.

She took his hand and leaned over the table so she could whisper, "It's so early. Do you think they'll suspect?"

Matthew smiled, but like all his smiles tonight, it was tinged with ineffable sadness. "They'll suspect I have an insatiable appetite for you. They'd be right."

"Show me." Could that husky purr possibly be hers?

His eyes darkened to the color of old brandy and his fingers tightened on hers. "My pleasure."

She left the salon on his arm with a decorum that lasted until they reached the shadowy staircase. Shaking with need, Matthew backed her against the newel post and covered her mouth with his. She gasped with shock at the carnal hunger she tasted on his tongue. His erection nudged her belly, solid, thick, seeking.

He needed her tonight more than he'd ever needed her before. The knowledge pierced her heart even as her body softened and turned liquid under his tempestuous kiss.

He speared his fingers through her hair to hold her head for his kisses. Long, searching, wet kisses that beguiled her soul. She ran her hands up and down his back, cursing the barrier of clothing between her and his naked skin. He was always ready for her, but this desperation whipped her blood into a raging fever.

"I want you," he growled into her lips.

He rubbed himself against her, leaving her in no doubt he was near the edge. The elaborate carving dug into her back but she didn't care, as long as he kept touching her. What did minor discomforts matter? No pain could compare with the pain of the separation poised over their passion like a warrant of execution.

"Mrs. Filey might see us," she moaned, even while her hand slid around his flank to touch his sex. He was massively aroused. She nipped at his neck. He wasn't wearing a cravat and the sight of his strong, bare throat had enticed her all through dinner.

"Christ, Grace, you drive me mad," he grated out, leaning his forehead against hers while he fought for breath. He tilted his hips so his hardness filled her hand. "Keep doing that and Mrs. Filey can go to the Devil."

"You're my devil," she whispered. All that male potency under her fingers would soon be hers. She needed him to make her his, to overwhelm her sorrow and fear with passion.

"Always, my love. Always."

He swung her up into his arms and climbed the staircase. His heart thundered under her cheek. His arms were warm and secure. She pressed her face into his chest, breathing deeply. He smelled of lemon and musk and clean male. She took another lungful of Matthew-scented air. She wanted his essence to permeate so deeply, it lingered forever. Because soon memories would be all she had.

Tears pricked at her eyes. Her hands tightened around his neck although she knew nothing would keep him with her.

He shouldered the bedroom door shut behind him and placed her on her feet with her back to the oak. She flattened her palms on either side of her, wordlessly offering herself. She needed him to hammer at her like a molten ingot on a forge and mold her into something of his creation.

He leaned forward and kissed her hard, using teeth and tongue, as he shoved her skirts up. He wasn't gentle, but she didn't want gentleness. There was a sharp ripping sound and her ruined drawers sagged to her feet.

His passion surged with a dark tide she'd never felt before. It was unbearably exciting. Her womb clenched hard with arousal and hot moisture pooled between her quivering thighs.

With careless elegance, he tossed his coat aside. He slid

his hand down and released himself from his trousers. He sprang free, hot and ready. She shifted restlessly against the cool wood as another bolt of need sizzled through her.

Then startled, she realized what he meant to do. "Here?"

"Here," he said with a ruthlessness that thrilled her. When he pushed her against the door, his touch held a savagery that made her tremble. He inclined his head toward the waiting bed. "And there. Later. Lift your leg and rest it on my hip."

She immediately obeyed, hooking her ankle behind his waist. She hopped to keep her balance. He was too tall for the position to be easy and her skirts bunched in a roll at her waist. "It's not very comfortable."

"Trust me," he said in a voice so deep it surged through her veins like a great wave.

He'd said that so many times in their sexual games. She stretched up on her toes toward his hardness. Not close enough. She wanted him inside her. Now.

"Lean back." He slipped his hand under her bottom and lifted her. Immediately the strain on her thighs eased.

He stroked the slickness between her legs. She shuddered and cried out as he pushed one finger inside her, then two. The pressure was glorious. Standing like this, she was open to him and he took full advantage. She quaked under his hand but didn't tumble over into climax. Tonight of all nights, she wanted him with her when she reached her peak.

He didn't prolong the preliminaries. She was so starved for him, she didn't mind. She couldn't doubt how he wanted her. Desire invested his every sawing breath.

He hoisted her higher.

"Matthew!" She gave a startled cry when she left the ground. She twined both legs around him as his sex bobbed against her belly.

"Hold on," he breathed into her ear. He crowded her

against the door and slid in with one massive thrust.

She had no control over his penetration. As her weight came down on him and she took his full length, she gasped. She gasped again with pleasure when he rocked her up and down, using both hands under her. She snatched at his shoulders, testing the coiled tension in his muscles.

He crushed her between his body and the smooth wood. Both were hard and unyielding. As he was hard and unyielding inside her.

Groaning into her shoulder, he drove deeper. Her sorrow, her regret, her longing, her love coalesced into one shining whole. This desperate, rough loving branded her his. Forever.

Passion rose fast. She cried out his name and clenched down hard. In a blinding cataclysm, her world exploded into scintillating light.

She clung to that ultimate height as long as she could. Even while rapture blasted her like wild summer lightning, helpless tears of loss and heartbreak poured down her cheeks. Vaguely, through shivering pleasure, she felt him pumping into her. Hot. Endless. Hers.

Only until tomorrow.

How could she leave him? Every time they made love, he became more a part of her. Abandoning him would be like having a leg amputated.

Exhausted, they slid to their knees. Under her palms, Matthew's shirt clung to his damp back. The sharp scent of their coupling surrounded her. With a weary gesture, he rested his forehead on her shoulder and sucked air into his lungs. She smoothed his tousled dark hair, a gesture of aching tenderness after their unfettered passion. As her heart slowed and strength filtered back into her limbs, she leaned into him in silence.

The bleak fact of impending separation swam up through Grace's dazed reaction.

How could she live without this? There would never be anyone like Matthew. Her hands curled into claws on his shoulders as if she dared anyone to take him away. Then deliberately, she relaxed her frantic hold.

What use defying a fate already ordained? They must part. That had been foretold from their first kiss.

Her body ached from his ferocious possession. Her face was wet with tears. She shifted to ease the pressure on her knees and touched his cheek. He'd shaved before dinner, but bristles already prickled her palm. By dawn, his face would abrade her skin like sand. She didn't mind. She wanted him to mark her. Tonight more than ever.

"I love you, Grace." He lifted his head and stared at her as though he etched each feature into his memory.

"And I love you," she returned, needing to join in the old dance of vows given and returned. She never should have told him she loved him. Now she had, she couldn't stop saying the words. "You make me forget everything but you."

She leaned forward and kissed him on the mouth. She wanted to seduce him with the same ruthless single-mindedness he'd just demonstrated. But anguish and love surged up too strongly. Her lips softened and her kiss became an expression of endless longing instead of a brand of ownership. He sighed into her mouth and returned her kiss with a sad sweetness that sliced to her soul.

Slowly, with a sense of wonder her time as his lover had never lessened, she rose on her knees. With trembling lips, she kissed his brow, his eyes, his cheeks, the hard angles of his jaw, the pounding pulse in his neck. She wanted to claim every inch as hers.

Usually he led when they made love, but for now, he seemed content to allow her sway. He clasped her waist but made no other attempt to touch her.

She took her time, inhaling his lemony scent, tasting

his warmth, listening to the slight hitches in his breathing as she anointed his skin with her mouth. This was their last night together and strangely that drew her to linger. She wanted this memory honed sharp as a new blade so it stayed with her for the rest of her life.

With each delicate touch, her heart whispered, "This I will remember. And this. And this."

She slid his shirt up and over his head and let it fall to the floor. Her eyes feasted on the lean strength of chest and shoulders. The pattern of fine black body hair. The long powerful arms. The gleaming, bare skin that stretched across his bones.

Tonight, when she knew how little time remained, his masculine beauty hurt her like walking on broken glass. She drew in a shuddering breath and pressed her lips to the ridge of his collarbone then moved to kiss each hollow and curve of arms and torso.

Slowly, Grace. Slowly. Polish every moment like a diamond.

His breathing roughened with each brush of her mouth. The spicy scent of his arousal grew more piquant.

Her gentle, inexorable exploration teased, made him burn. Still he knelt before her and let her continue. He cared enough to allow her this freedom. The thought only made her love him more. And lent her courage.

She breathed in a lungful of air redolent of Matthew and slid behind him. His hands fell away from her as she shifted.

The sight of his ruined back always made her stomach knot in sick denial. How had he borne this abuse yet emerged as the wonderful man she loved? It was a miracle.

She paused, gathering her nerve, then very deliberately placed her mouth on the obscene scar that curled from his left shoulder blade to his right hip.

He recoiled as if she hurt him, although the wound had long ago knitted. "Grace, don't," he hissed in warning.

She leaned her cheek into his back. "I want to do this."

"My scars should disgust you," he said hoarsely. His long muscles were hard as iron with tension and shame.

"Never," she said softly, her voice thick with emotion. "These are marks of bravery, Matthew. Wear them with pride. They make you the man you are, the man I love with all my heart."

She trailed away into silence. Words were such frail vehicles to convey her love. She kissed the whiplash again, following its length until she reached the hard edge of his hip. Then carefully, methodically, tenderly, she moved around him and pressed her lips to every welt. Scars from the scourge. Scars whose cause she couldn't identify. Scars that could only be burns. She dwelled over each patch of shiny white skin. It was as if by acknowledging his torture, she could leach away his pain, then and now.

With every kiss, her determination to save him firmed. Whatever it cost, she would defeat the fiends who had perpetrated this evil.

When she'd launched her act of homage, his body was stiff, resistant. But gradually, she felt him accept her touch, even move into it as though her love soothed his old agonies.

His ragged breathing, his beckoning heat, the taste of his skin stirred excitement low in her belly. She nibbled and licked her way across one shoulder to his bare chest. Her hand slipped forward to brush his nipple and she heard him bite back a groan. Under her palm, his heart raced in a crazy gallop. The slow seduction worked simmering magic on him as well as her.

With every kiss, forbidden curiosity tormented her. She'd kissed so much of him. Now she wanted to kiss all of him.

No! The idea was unholy. She'd never heard of such a thing. She couldn't do it.

But as her lips dipped to explore the taut skin of his belly and his earthy scent flooded her senses, she couldn't banish the outrageous images. Until she could no longer resist their urging.

This was her last night with him. She meant to test the boundaries of sin. "Lean back," she said in a throaty voice.

To her surprise, he immediately complied, supporting himself on his elbows and straightening his legs so he was spread before her like a feast. A feast she intended to devour. She blushed at the thought.

She crawled over him until she straddled his legs. He sprang impressively free of the opening in his breeches, vivid testimony to how he wanted her. His unwavering attention fixed on her and the ghost of a smile tilted his mouth. His eyes glinted deep gold through the lowered fringe of eyelashes.

Her heart lurched with sorrow that she must leave him. The lacerating awareness that she'd never have this chance again gave her the nerve to bend her head and kiss the engorged tip of his sex.

He jerked as the wet warmth of her mouth encircled him. Then he wrenched away. *"Jesus!"*

"Don't you like it?"

The question he'd asked her repeatedly since they'd become lovers. She crouched over his lap and studied him. Strangely, she wasn't nervous any more.

"Grace, it's . . ." He fought to put words together. His throat worked as he swallowed.

She took shameless advantage of his bewilderment to lower her head again and lick his length. He tasted musky and damp. He tasted of sex. She shivered to realize he must taste of her. Piercing need tugged at her womb.

She licked him again. He arched and groaned but didn't move away. She obeyed the clamor of her instincts and took him fully into her mouth.

He was large. And hot and silky against her tongue.

He'd often committed this intimacy on her willing body. It was his turn now. He trembled and cried out at the touch of her lips. A surge of feminine power rocketed through her. This strong, magnificent man was completely at her mercy.

Experimentally, she sucked. He strangled a curse and buried his hands in her hair, urging her on. She increased the pressure and squeezed the base of his sex with a relentless rhythm. Then her seeking fingers cupped his testicles.

"God, I love you," he groaned. His hands fisted against her scalp. "I love you, I love you, I love you."

Tenderly, carefully, she ravished him with her mouth. Listened to each groan, each shattered inhalation of breath. Felt him quiver. Waited for his control to break.

This was the most decadent act she'd ever committed. Yet she felt almost innocent. His love surrounded her, purified all sin, made the world glitter.

She loved him. How she loved him.

He reached down to drag her up by the arms. She knew from his throbbing tension that he was close, so close. She licked her lips. She'd never forget the taste of him.

His hands shaking with urgency, he positioned her over him then sighed with pleasure as she sank down. She closed her eyes, luxuriating in how he filled her.

Not just her body but her heart.

With a sureness that was now second nature, she moved on him. She basked in the stunned pleasure that flooded his face every time she took him inside her.

With one ruthless movement, he ripped aside the green silk of her bodice. She gasped when her breasts spilled free to the cool air. Her nipples pebbled, not just with cold but with excitement.

"Beautiful," he said with satisfaction.

He caressed her, weighing her breasts in his hands, testing the sensitive areolas. He brushed the hard tips with his fingers. Then took her more firmly, tugging and rolling until she shivered with need. Each minuscule change in pressure shot searing heat to her loins, made her tighten around him. He curved up and placed his mouth on her breast while the other hand continued to torment.

She loved the way he enjoyed her. Before Matthew, her body had just carried her through the day. Now every inch was imprinted with pleasure her lover gave her. Pleasure she gave him.

"Now," he growled and thrust up hard.

Their bodies were so in tune that rapture hit simultaneously.

She cried out his name as brilliance streaked through her. Waves of ecstasy buffeted her, sent her reeling. Only a tiny pinhole of light shone in the dark turbulence.

And the light was love.

She rode out one climax. Another. Then another. Each flung her higher. Each left her sure she could give no more. Then the next climax would hit and leave her shuddering in helpless reaction.

When it was over, she wilted in a limp heap onto Matthew's chest. He was her destiny. He broke her heart. But she'd never regret sharing these days with him. The radiance would glow, no matter how far apart they were.

Between her legs, she was sticky and she ached. It was a good ache. The best ache. She sighed and buried her nose in his chest to dam sudden tears.

How could she bring herself to leave him tomorrow?

* * *

Toward dawn, Matthew roused Grace from her restless doze. She'd hardly slept and in the candles' guttering light, exhaustion marked her lovely face.

He was a conscienceless beast. He'd used her ruthlessly, relentlessly, only giving her brief surcease. She'd be sore. He hadn't been gentle, to his shame.

They hadn't spoken of parting. Although impending separation hovered behind every touch, every sigh, every climax. He'd tried to make this night more than a sorrowful valediction. He wanted it to be a celebration of their love that she'd remember with a smile through the years to come. The years he couldn't be with her.

This was the last time they'd lie together. An elegy played in his heart as he cupped her breast. It fit perfectly in his hand. She was naked. They'd eventually shed the last of their clothes. He'd forgotten quite when. Somewhere before midnight, he was sure. Somewhere between carpet and bed. She must be a mass of bruises from him pounding into her on the floor.

She sighed—she wasn't awake although she wasn't asleep either—and turned toward him. Her nipple darkened and tightened. Her body recognized what was to come.

He bent his head and placed a tender kiss on that rosy peak. Then he turned his attention to her other breast, drawing it into his mouth and suckling it. His touch held a bittersweet softness.

The mark of Filey's vile bite was now only a shadow. It would fade and disappear. What they felt wouldn't.

"I love you," she murmured and stroked his hair.

She'd said those words so often tonight. But he wanted to hear them again. How many times were enough? Enough to lend an ember of warmth to the icy loneliness that awaited him?

He nuzzled the delicate skin under her breast and kissed

his way across her belly. She sighed and bowed up toward him. He raised his head to find her watching, her eyes dark with grief. The imminence of parting hung heavy between them. He moved over her and kissed her with all the adoration he felt. Her lips were pliant and silky.

She opened to him immediately, her tongue seeking. During the long night, they'd tested passion's fury. This was different. Sweeter, sadder, deeper. For all that their earlier couplings had been unions of soul as well as body.

Her legs fell open so he rested in the hot apex. He was hard, even after the night just passed. Very gently, for he wanted her to remember he cherished her as much as wanted her, he stroked her cleft.

She was dry. He'd tried her to her limit. It was a gift of love that she turned so willingly to him now.

He kissed her again, trying to store the taste and feel against the desolation to come. She could revive a dead man with her kiss alone. In his case, she had. For one insubstantial moment, he'd tasted life in her arms.

He sucked and licked at her neck and she rewarded him with a rush of moisture against his seeking fingers. He nibbled his way downward, planning on using his mouth to bring her to climax before he took her.

"No," she whispered, as he lingered at her navel. "I want you with me."

She was right. This was farewell. He should be inside her. He needed the joining as much as she. They'd shared pleasure all night. Now he must give her everything he had.

"Grace, you break my heart," he said rawly, raising himself on his elbows to see her face.

She was pale as the moon. Against her white skin, her lips were swollen and red. He'd remember her like this to his dying day.

She stroked his jaw. He pressed his face into the caress.

"Make love to me, Matthew. As though the world ends today."

The world did end today.

He knew what she wanted. She didn't want desperate passion. She didn't want the excitement of experiment. She wanted the two of them moving through eternity as though nothing could ever sunder them.

A bird called outside. Sunrise wasn't far away.

Very slowly, he entered her. Relishing every sigh, every quiver of weary muscles. He planted himself deep, so deep he touched her soul. Then he held still, breathing as she breathed, his heart beating in time with hers.

Her touch was ineffably tender as she traced his shoulders, his chest, his back. Her wandering fingers wrote a lifetime of love on his skin.

He took a deep breath so her scent filled his head. Only then did he move. He was slow, penetrating to her core with every thrust and holding himself there as he glimpsed heaven.

She gave herself up to him. She was his partner, his darling, his lover. He wanted this communion to last forever.

He'd worked off his fierceness earlier. He felt no driving hunger to conquer or subdue or possess. Just this moving toward and away, endless as the tide or the rising and setting of the sun.

He kept up the deliberate, tender rhythm for an inhumanly long interval. He thought of nothing but the woman in his arms and how he loved her. He couldn't speak. His feelings went beyond words. There was just darkness and sighs of pleasure and the soft sound of his body sliding in and out of hers.

He clung to that mystical closeness. But eventually his body bayed for satisfaction. He couldn't hold himself back.

Her climax started slowly and built and built. It was

like nothing he'd ever felt. The waves became a great crescendo that swept him with her into wild release. He gave himself up to her in a blinding burst of joy and love. Then held her safe as she slowly came back from the brink of the universe.

They would speak the words of parting later. But in his soul, he'd just said every farewell he needed to say.

Chapter 22

Grace crept into the salon and scuttled across to the elaborate desk that dominated one corner. It was still early. Mrs. Filey worked in the kitchen and paid no attention to comings and goings. Matthew had slipped outside to check on something with his roses.

She and Matthew wanted to present as normal an appearance as possible today. After the night's unbridled passion, there had been a poignant joy in talking quietly as they dressed. She always loved to watch him shave, but this morning, the pleasure had been tinged with sharp regret that it was the last time she'd share the small, precious intimacy.

They had touched constantly as they'd moved about the bedroom. Tiny, glancing contacts. She wondered how she'd survive without the gentle brush of his hand on her skin.

All the while, sorrow hovered unspoken, darkening the air. Matthew had infiltrated her very marrow. Every beat of her heart repeated his name. His scent was the air she breathed.

After such a night, how could she abandon him to his lonely prison?

She didn't just abandon him. She meant to betray him.

Quickly, she checked over her shoulder but the door remained closed. As once before, she rifled Matthew's desk. She wasn't sure what she'd say if he found her snooping through his private papers. Certainly anything but the truth.

Pigeonholes ranked across the top held writing implements and stationery and nothing else. Frantic with guilt and her need to get back to Matthew, she turned her attention to the drawers.

Here she found what she wanted. Or at least she hoped it was, she didn't have time to check. If Matthew knew what she intended, he'd never forgive her.

Hurriedly, she bundled handfuls of documents into her pockets and down the front of her dress. She grabbed another pile without looking and fled the room.

Grace prayed guilt wasn't written on her face when she entered the courtyard. Matthew looked up with a smile when she appeared. He'd seemed calm, composed this morning, but he'd learned to hide his deepest reactions in a cruel school. Biting her lip, she forced back tears. She had to be strong. For both of them.

"Come for a walk," she said huskily.

His marked black brows contracted in a puzzled frown. This wasn't part of the original plan. "Grace?"

She squared her shoulders as if she prepared for battle. Why not? She did. "Please."

She didn't know what he saw in her face but he set down his pruning shears and came to take her arm. "As you wish."

Wolfram rose and trailed after them.

Silently, they made their way through the sunlit woods. As if by agreement, both stopped in the glade where he'd first kissed her. That magical moment seemed so long ago. She'd lived a lifetime with him since. A lifetime in a little over two weeks.

"Are you afraid?" he asked in concern, brushing a few wisps of hair back from her face. She played the widow Paget today and she'd braided her hair tight around her head.

"Yes, I'm afraid." Then in a rush, "But I'm more afraid for you."

His eyebrows arched in surprise. "Me? What can they do to me that they haven't done before? I'll be fine. I told you—my uncle's control of the Lansdowne gold ends if I die."

Once she might have believed him. Now she knew better. She'd had time to consider all the implications of his decision to send her away. With an abrupt gesture, she pushed his hand from her face.

"I know what you intend," she said curtly. Wolfram whined at her tone and pressed closer to his master's side.

"I intend to get you back to the real world," he said in a grim voice, dropping one hand to the dog's head.

"Yes. Then you're going to kill Filey and arrange your own death. I'm not a fool, Matthew. You're only biding your time until you think I'm safe." Her voice broke, leaving her resolve to remain cool and pragmatic in ruins. "This may be the last time we speak to each other. We can't part on a lie."

"Grace . . ." He paused, looking stricken. This attack surprised him, she knew. "What happens to me doesn't matter."

"How dare you say that?" she spat. "Of course it matters."

"I'm not living like an animal in a menagerie until I die of old age. I refuse to let my uncle plunder my inheritance any longer. I can't escape this estate without harming the innocent. My only options are life in this prison or death. I choose death. That is my one freedom."

"Promise me you'll wait six months," she said steadily

even while her heart screamed denial at the cold accounting of his options. He couldn't die. She wouldn't permit him to die.

"Why?" he snapped, goaded into a flash of anger. "Nothing will change."

"I'm sorry," she whispered, her stomach cramping with nausea as she pictured the lonely hell she consigned him to.

His anger faded and his lips tilted in a smile, although his eyes were dull with hopelessness. "I'm not, my darling. I'll die seeing your face and remembering your voice saying you love me. There are worse ways to leave this world."

Her brief weakness fled. He sounded resigned to his fate and she wasn't letting him get away with it. She wouldn't give in on this, no matter how her heart keened for his misery. "I don't want you to leave this world!"

His smile vanished. "Jesus, Grace! Would you rather I sit in this cage like a prize capon until I become mad indeed? If you love me, leave me the liberty to choose my destiny."

The moment she'd dreaded since she'd guessed his plans had arrived. She straightened her spine and stared at him, reading his pain, reading his brave resolve to end his captivity in the only way he believed possible.

She bit her lip and strove for courage. Thank heaven he wasn't touching her. If he touched her, her resistance would crumble like chalk. Raising her chin, she forced herself to speak with merciless clarity.

"Unless you promise to take no action for six months, I'm not leaving."

The blood drained from his cheeks and an expression of ineffable hauteur masked his distress. "This is beneath you. I won't submit to blackmail."

"I'm asking for six months." She prayed she found help

before that time was up. She prayed she lived so long without falling into Lord John's clutches.

"For God's sake, don't endanger yourself to save me." His voice developed a taunting edge. "What do you imagine you can do against my uncle? He'll crush you with less thought than he'd give to swatting a fly. Have you learned nothing?"

He spoke directly to her greatest terror. Or her greatest terror after her fear that Matthew would die before she found aid.

She sucked in a deep breath. She could handle fear. She'd been frightened so long, it had become her natural element.

"I won't take stupid risks. But I may meet someone who can help." She'd always known her plan was flimsy. Hearing it aloud, it sounded insubstantial as a cloud.

"I'll never be free. You just extend my torture." He spoke as if he hated her. He probably did right now. She could imagine what it had cost him to decide to end his suffering. Now she thwarted his chance to retrieve his honor and stop his uncle's depredations.

"Just for six months, Matthew." She reached for his hand but he flinched away.

"You insist that your will prevails by giving me an impossible choice." He hadn't spoken to her so coldly since her first days on the estate. She shivered. She'd forgotten quite how astringent that tone was.

"I want your word you'll do nothing to endanger your welfare for six months."

Lord, what if she'd stuck to her original plan and asked for a year? Could she rescue him in six months?

He stared into the trees as if he could no longer bear the sight of her. She didn't need to see his expression to recognize his desolation or how angry he was.

After a long pause, he shrugged with a carelessness

she didn't believe and turned to her. His golden eyes were guarded as they'd been guarded when he'd first seen her. Even Wolfram's stare seemed an accusation.

Matthew's lips twisted in a caricature of a smile. "As you say, what's six months? Yes, you have my word."

She let out the breath she'd been holding. His honor was more precious to him than life. He wouldn't break his promise.

"Thank you."

"Now, are you ready to leave or do you have further conditions?" He presented his arm with an elegant flourish. He was at his most lordly, his deep voice clear and crisp. No trace now of her ardent, tender lover.

He was furious and hurt at what he saw as her betrayal. She'd had an unfair advantage. When she bartered his cooperation for her safety, she'd known she'd win. Now the sun rose high in the sky. Must rancor contaminate their last memories of each other?

She ignored his extended arm. She didn't want him to escort her back to the cottage like a stranger. "Matthew, is this how you want to say goodbye?" she asked in a small voice.

"Grace, you test me to my limits. You know what we're about to do. You know why we're doing it." He didn't sound angry anymore. Instead he sounded deathly unhappy, which was worse.

The guilt that had tortured Grace since she'd stolen his private papers twisted in her belly like a snake. This was for his own good, she assured herself desperately. She couldn't tell him the full extent of her plan or he'd stop her. She knew that as she knew she loved him.

"It breaks my heart to leave." She blinked away tears.

His smile became more natural and he reached out to take both her hands loosely in his. Beneath his smile, he still looked tired and sad.

"You have my promise. I'll do nothing to change my situation for six months. Now let us make peace, my love."

He'd always been so generous, even when he believed her his enemy. How could she bear it if she failed him?

If she thought about that, her courage would shrivel to nothing. She needed every ounce of courage to escape. Although not as much courage as he needed to stay.

"There will be no peace for me until you're free," she whispered, her heart brimming with misery.

His face sharpened with grief. "Don't, Grace. Run as far as you can and forget me."

She didn't bother arguing. What was the point? Nothing would deter her. "Kiss me," she said in a broken voice.

Very gently, he took her face in his hands. At first, his lips were cool but heat soon overcame restraint. He took his time, savoring her as if she were his last meal.

She trembled and opened her mouth. She couldn't bear this parting. She couldn't. Only the fragile hope that she could rescue him kept her from begging him to let her remain.

As his tongue drove into her mouth, he snatched her up against him. She twined her arms around his back and kissed him with equal hunger.

There was passion. And sorrow.

Above all, there was love. Love burning like a flame.

She wanted to stay in his arms forever.

It was impossible.

Danger awaited her. Untold suffering awaited him. He'd said little about the consequences of what he meant to do. She knew enough to guess. And he'd face the aftermath without her. She felt as though she deserted him on the field of battle to face an invincible enemy alone.

Gradually, the frenzy abated. The kiss ended as it had begun, in gentleness and regret. He drew away and she glimpsed tears in his eyes. Tears he was too proud to shed.

"I love you, Grace." It was a vow.

"I love you, Matthew."

"It's time." He looked as somber as she'd ever seen him.

"Yes." She stretched up and kissed him once more. Quickly. Because if she lingered, she'd never leave. "God keep you, my darling."

She turned and ran blindly back toward the cottage.

Matthew waited hidden in the trees near the main gate, Wolfram a silent, devoted sentinel at his side. Grace had left him half an hour ago.

Monks hammered at something in the shadow of the gatehouse. Filey was out of sight, although from hundreds of mornings watching them unload supplies, Matthew knew he wouldn't be far away.

Grim prescience was a leaden weight in his gut. Grace didn't know what she asked when she made him wait six months. He couldn't bring himself to tell her. Christ, he could barely put the thoughts into words himself.

He'd steeled himself to what would happen once she was gone. Barely. His uncle had ordered him constrained after his last escape. Any pretense that it was for his own good or to keep a dangerous madman under control had disappeared. His wardens had tied him to that cursed table in the garden room and savagely beaten him as punishment. No other reason.

The chastisement had only lasted a few hours. Enough to remind him he'd rather die than resume life as a poor chained madman.

Now he deliberately put himself into their hands. They'd tie him down, mock him, torture him. This time, they'd do it because they believed him mad indeed. Which meant his ordeal would be longer, tougher, more agonizing.

God lend him strength. Every time his captors treated

him like a madman, he was sick with terror that the madness would return in reality.

A twig snapped behind him and he turned to see Grace. She looked such a little Puritan in her black widow's weeds and severe hairstyle. It was strange to see her like this again. As though she was no longer the woman who turned his nights to flame. This woman was beautiful—she could never be anything else—but already beyond his reach.

"Are you ready?" He itched to snatch her into his arms one last time but if he touched her now, he'd never let her go.

"Yes." She nodded, her gaze unspeakably sad as it clung to his face. With one hand she clutched a bundle wrapped in a silk shawl. They'd spent a long time deciding what she'd take. In the end, they'd selected things she could barter for food or a ride in a cart. Handkerchiefs, a few bits of tawdry jewelry, shoe buckles. A little food. Water.

Actual cash was appallingly short. She only had the few coins she'd carried on arrival. Neither Filey nor Monks had thought it worthwhile to steal those. Just as they'd never thought to destroy her worn clothing.

"Has the supply cart turned up yet?" she whispered, crouching at his side.

"No. But it won't be long."

Matthew felt her hand slide around his. Her fingers were cold, although the day was warm and fine.

"It will be all right," she murmured. How like Grace, to comfort others when she needed comfort herself.

"Yes."

He suspected she knew he lied. He wasn't angry anymore. The suffering that awaited was the price he paid for the rapture he'd found in her arms.

He'd pay any price for that.

For a brief span, he'd been allowed to feel human. More.

Every time she told him she loved him, he'd felt like a god. Well, the god would come crashing down any moment. And gods, he was sure, were never as full of dread and regret as he was.

Jesus, where was the bloody cart?

The bell rang. As he'd suspected, Filey was nearby. He came around the house to help Monks lift the bar from the gate. The heavy doors opened with a rusty squeak and the laden wagon rattled in. These days, his uncle made sure two men drove the wagon. That made four men plus Mrs. Filey he needed to convince with his performance.

"Go, Grace. Go now," he whispered, grief piercing his gut like a stake. "Godspeed."

He pressed his mouth to hers in a brief but passionate kiss. He fought the urge to grab her close. What was one touch more when he craved a lifetime?

"Goodbye, my darling." Pain throbbed in her farewell. One longing look from indigo eyes burning with anguish and love, then she was gone.

Without thinking he stretched his hand out after her, as if to wrest her back. He only grasped emptiness.

He watched her make her way through the underbrush to a point where she was still hidden but close to the gate. She paused under the shade and turned to smile at him. Strangely, it was a smile without darkness, the same smile she gave him when he brought her to climax.

Her bravery stunned him. Inspired him.

She disappeared into the trees. The black dress served wonderfully as camouflage.

"Follow," he urged the huge wolfhound as he straightened. They'd decided Wolfram should go with Grace as protection.

The plan's success hinged on the next seconds. Could he do what he had to?

For Grace, he could.

He squared his shoulders and defied the ocean of fear that threatened to drown him. He took the pellet of herbs from his pocket and put it in his mouth. Immediately, a pungent taste filled his head.

Grace lingered on what could be her last glimpse of the man she loved. When she'd first seen him, his lonely beauty had struck her like the pure true note of a hammer on brass. Her last impression was no different. Any joy he'd found in her arms had been fleeting.

Breaking into her anxious distraction, Wolfram trotted up. She patted and praised him, knowing all the while that she took him from what he loved. They had that in common.

She fumbled at her waist for the short rope she'd brought to tie to his collar. She'd protested when Matthew insisted she take the dog. Now she was glad. If things went wrong, he'd keep Monks and Filey away. And outside the gates, Wolfram was a link with Matthew.

The dog stood obediently while she knotted the rope. She said a prayer of thanks that Matthew had trained him so well. At times, she thought Wolfram was almost human.

"Courage, my friend," she whispered. Even though it was she, not the dog, who needed courage. Fear made the breath stall in her throat. Fear not just for herself, but for Matthew too.

What if he miscalculated the dosage of the herbal mixture? Too much might kill him.

Dear God, don't let her escape end in tragedy.

She had to trust him. She'd seen firsthand his knowledge of plants. He'd said he'd only take enough herb to incapacitate himself.

She wouldn't think about what could go wrong. Instead, she had to watch for her opportunity to sneak out the gate.

Her hand clenched in the thick hair on Wolfram's neck. Very carefully, keeping her eyes fixed on the men, she rose.

In the late spring heat, her widow's weeds prickled uncomfortably. She'd become used to the light silks and satins of her risqué wardrobe. Now the thick black fabric scratched her sensitive skin and the high neck and long sleeves irritated her.

She watched as the men began to unload. The two draft horses stood patiently in harness as the men worked around them. There was a lot of garbled shouting and it was clear the drivers were wary of Monks. Which spoke volumes for their intelligence.

Matthew's guttural groan made her jerk her head around. He staggered out of the line of trees, clutching his chest as if his heart pained him. She suppressed a horrified gasp. He looked so ill.

For the first time, she really understood what he meant when he said he had a violent physical reaction to certain herbs. He doubled over and she heard his painful retching from where she hid.

If she'd known what he'd go through, she wouldn't have fallen in with his plan. She dug her nails into her palms to stop herself running to help him.

This was a charade. He was doing this so she could escape.

The words sounded hollow and unconvincing when she stood in impotent grief and watched her lover in such agony, he contorted with pain.

Wolfram whined softly. "Stay, Wolfram," she said quietly.

The big body under her restraining hand quivered with tension and his attention fixed on where Matthew struggled to stay upright. She couldn't blame the dog. Her stomach lurched with revulsion that she left Matthew in this state.

"Help me!" Matthew gasped, falling. Even at this distance, she saw he shook as though he suffered a fit. "Help me, for God's sake!"

"Shit!" Monks turned to see what was wrong. "Filey! His sodding lordship looks right to die!"

All four men raced across to where Matthew writhed on the ground.

It cut Grace to the bone to see that long, lean body twisting and trembling. Had his madness been like this? No wonder he lived in perpetual fear of his illness returning.

He went through this for her. She owed it to him to see he didn't suffer in vain. She owed it to him to escape so she could set him free. Inside these polished white walls, she could do nothing but share his burden.

"Come on, Wolfram. Let's go."

The dog whined and turned his head toward his master. He didn't move when she pulled the rope.

"Wolfram!" she said in her best imitation of Matthew.

She tugged the rope again. All attention focused on Matthew. He sounded in excruciating pain. Each strangled groan froze the blood in her veins to ice.

Wolfram barked sharply then bounded away through the trees.

She just stopped herself calling after him. If she alerted Lord John's henchmen to her location, the game was up before it started. Her heart thudded with foreboding. Already, the carefully plotted escape unraveled.

The huge dog ran up and began licking Matthew about the face. Monks and Filey tried to shove the shaggy beast away but to no avail. Chaos reigned on the grass.

She clutched her makeshift bundle tightly against her breast where her heart pounded like a crazy drum. She whispered a confused prayer for Matthew's safety and dragged in a deep breath.

Now, Grace. Now.

She picked up her skirts in fingers that were stiff with terror and dashed across the cleared area. She was so frightened, she noticed nothing but the bulk of the wagon in front of her. Breathlessly, she dived into its shadow.

Her chest heaving with fear, she crouched there. Had anyone noted her flight? She didn't think so. Nobody paid any heed to the wagon. Monks swore loud and long. Filey fought off Wolfram. The only people who tried to help the sick man were the drivers.

One had Matthew propped in his arms and the other wiped his face with the faded scarf he'd tugged from his neck. Yet again, guilt clawed at her that she left an ill man with brutes who had no idea how to treat him.

Goodbye, my love, she whispered in her heart. *God keep you safe until I return.*

Surely it was her imagination, but she thought she saw Matthew's head tilt in her direction. Just for an instant. She was too far away to see the molten gold of his eyes. But in her heart she did. Then he groaned and collapsed upon the younger driver's shoulder in shivering unconsciousness.

There was nothing more she could do for him here. It was time to discover what she could do for him in the world outside.

Slowly, she turned around to face the gates.

And came face to face with Mrs. Filey.

Chapter 23

~~~⚬⚬~~~

G race staggered back against the rough wood of the wagon and stifled a scream. With trembling hands, she raised her bundle before her like a shield.

How had she been so fatally stupid? Why hadn't she checked where Mrs. Filey was?

"Please . . ." she stammered. Then she remembered Mrs. Filey couldn't hear.

For a long appalled moment, Grace stared into Mrs. Filey's dull brown eyes. The woman's face was worn and wrinkled and impassive. She stood about a foot away, her arms full of household linen.

Grace was lightheaded from lack of air. She dragged in a shuddering breath while blood thundered in her ears. She forced her terrified mind to work past her visions of what Monks and Filey would do when they discovered her.

Still Mrs. Filey didn't speak.

Could Grace have found an unlikely ally? Mrs. Filey had never indicated she cared a jot about Grace's plight. Why should she risk her husband's wrath now?

The woman gave a tiny jerk of her head toward the wagon. Grace frowned, not understanding.

Again that gesture that almost wasn't a movement.

Grace looked at the tray of the cart. It was empty apart

from a few handfuls of hay which had cushioned the more delicate goods in transit.

Mrs. Filey shrugged as if she could do no more. She shoved the pile of dirty washing onto the wagon, then stumped inside to fetch more. She always walked as though life had defeated her, Grace thought, not for the first time.

Then she realized what had just happened.

Mrs. Filey must know what she and Matthew plotted. And she hadn't raised the alarm.

Grace considered the pile of laundry. It would cover her until she reached a village. Hurriedly, she flung her bundle onto the tray and scrambled up to hide herself under the sheets. They were the fine monogrammed linen from Matthew's bed. Immediately, the scent of their lovemaking surrounded her. Stale but unmistakable.

Her stomach still twisting with fear, she huddled down as Mrs. Filey pitched more laundry over her. Horses would take her further and faster than her own feet. Unless Monks and Filey realized she was missing before she got away. Unless they thought to check the wagon when it passed through the gates. Unless Mrs. Filey merely waited to point her husband to Grace's hiding place.

She held her breath while her heart hammered a terrified tattoo. She heard Mrs. Filey approach, then flinched as more washing covered her.

How was Matthew? Dear Lord, let him come through this. Gaps between the wagon's timbers allowed air to enter, but sounds from outside were muffled. Monks was still shouting. For once, she heard an uncertain note in his bluster. Usually he was imperturbable and confident. Matthew's sudden attack must have rattled him. Filey made increasingly desperate suggestions about what to do.

"Reckon we should take him to the house." She didn't recognize the slow, Somerset-accented voice.

"Aye," Monks said. "Aye, we'll take him to the house."

Then more loudly, "Woman! Shift your scrawny arse. Filey, you grab his legs."

"He's in a right taking," Filey said. "I seen nowt like this since he was a lad."

"Shut your gob, man," Monks snarled. "What is that halfwit bitch doing? Woman!"

"Eh, you know she hears nowt."

"Aye, fucking useless cow. Go and fetch the dozy jade."

Grace held her breath as she waited for Filey to come for his wife. Another pile of washing landed over her and she barely managed to smother a gasp of terror.

What if Filey became suspicious about the size of the load of laundry? What if he decided to check it?

"Monks wants you, Maggie." Filey spoke slowly so his wife could read his lips.

Grace hadn't been this close to him since he'd tried to rape her. The memory of Filey's reeking body pinning her to the ground rose like a miasma and she closed her throat against the urge to gag. If he dangled one of those thick hands over the edge of the wagon, he'd touch her. And Matthew wouldn't be able to save her this time.

"Aye, I'm a-comin'," Mrs. Filey said in a curiously flat voice. It was the first time Grace had ever heard her speak. "I got another lot of washing to get oot first."

"Eh, that's nowt to worry about. His sodding lordship's taken a right bad turn. Happen the laundry can bide till next time."

Grace struggled to stop herself shivering. Every muscle tensed to the edge of pain as she waited for them to go.

Or for Filey to reach down and toss back the sheets.

Filey and his wife moved away after what felt like an eternity. Only when they'd gone did Grace snatch a shallow breath into her air-starved lungs. The sick dizziness receded. Carefully, she relaxed each cramped muscle.

Could she chance one last look to see if Matthew was

all right? No, the risk was too great. Every beat of her heart was a frantic prayer for him to live. To live so she could save him from this hell.

"Should we stay and aid 'ee?" the unknown man, obviously one of the drivers, asked from near the front of the cart. "The nags don't like to stand so long in the sun."

"No, there's nowt more you can do," Monks said. "Happen we'll see you next week."

"Arr, well, I be off then. Is all loaded?"

"Fuck the laundry. His lordship can sleep in dirty sheets for the nonce. Mad bugger won't notice the difference."

"He don't look mad to I," the voice said. "Though he don't look blooming ayther."

"Arr, he b'aint well," another Somerset voice said very slowly.

"Aye, well, you're no sawbones, Banks," Monks snapped. "I'll take the quack's word over yourn any day. Now be off. Lord John doesn't pay you good brass to blather here."

Grace curled up in taut stillness as she heard the men approach the wagon. Would they check the laundry? She began to wish she'd followed the original plan and sneaked away to find cover in the surrounding area. But it was too late to change her reckless decision.

Her heart skipped a beat as the wagon lurched. Then she realized the cart moved because the two men took their places on the bench. Someone clicked their tongue to the horses and the cart jolted into motion.

She was on her way. Pray God next time she saw this cursed estate, she came to set her lover free.

"I want a piss real bad, nipper. How 'bout 'ee?" The older, more talkative driver spoke in a slurred voice.

Grace, who had fallen into a strange trance under the stifling weight of the laundry, stirred to full alertness. She wasn't surprised their bladders needed emptying. They'd swigged steadily since leaving the estate hours ago. Even from her hiding place, she could smell the sickly cider fumes in the hot afternoon air. Thank goodness, the horses seemed to know where they went because the drivers became more intoxicated with every mile.

"Arr." She'd already noticed that the younger man never said much.

The wagon juddered to a stop then shook as the two climbed down. She heard the older man's voice fade as he walked away from the cart.

Perhaps she should steal this chance to sneak out of the wagon. Very slowly, she raised one edge of the sheets so she could see. The drivers had their backs to her and faced the trees lining the road. Luckily, they were near the horses' heads.

With trembling hands, she grabbed her bundle and slid to the edge of the cart furthest from the men. Then she took a deep breath and climbed to the ground, keeping her head low so the wagon hid her.

Thick trees beckoned on either side of the narrow track. It hardly justified the name *road*. But of course, Lord John had chosen the estate for its isolation, hadn't he? He wouldn't want a highway running past the front gate.

She heard splashing on the ground and an acrid smell filled the air. She had to make a break while they concentrated on other things.

Silently, she dashed into the woods and crouched behind a moss-covered rock well back from the road. Her stiff legs protested the sudden movement, but she ignored the discomfort.

The older man turned and clapped the younger on the shoulder. "God, that Monks be a miserable bastard."

"Arr," said the younger, taciturn as ever. He faced the wagon and did up his rough trousers. Now she could see them, it was clear they were father and son.

"And speak of the Devil."

Through her heart's terrified pounding, Grace heard a horse approach. Dear God, they knew of her escape. Why else would Monks gallop in such a lather after the supply cart? Thank heaven the drivers had stopped and she'd taken the chance to leave the wagon. Otherwise, her fate would be sealed. The horrible thought chilled her blood to ice.

The wood burgeoned with late spring growth. She prayed it was thick enough to conceal her. Her fingers tensed into claws on the stone and she hunkered down on the leaf-strewn ground.

"Have you seen owt of a lass?" Monks shouted, still yards away.

The older man scratched his stubbly chin. "A woman? Nay, Mr. Monks. I seen nobody on this road. Never do. Why would we? It leads but one place and that's to his lordship. No reason a woman would go there, I reckon."

"Bloody idiot," Monks muttered and dug his spurs into the horse so it lurched up to the wagon. He reached over to pitch the laundry aside, casting sheets to the ground.

"Hey, watch what 'ee do there, Mr. Monks!" the older man protested. "I be called to pick that up afore I go on."

"Shut your gob!" Monks wheeled his horse around and urged it so close to the men that it nearly trampled them. The frightened beast whinnied and danced but Monks sawed savagely on the bit and forced it back toward the drivers. "If you see a lass, hold her and send me a message. She's a toothsome wench with black hair and tasty tits. Talks like the gentry but walks like a whore. There's a right fat reward if you find her."

"Arr," said the son and tugged his forelock as Monks cruelly forced the horse around and galloped back toward the estate in a cloud of dust.

Grace's pulse raced with a heady mixture of dread and relief as the pounding hooves faded into the distance. She'd been mere seconds from discovery. What if the drivers hadn't been so prodigal with the cider?

Monks hadn't said anything about Matthew. Was her beloved alive or dead?

Oh, not dead, not dead, her heart cried.

"That Monks be puggle-headed. A woman on this track," the older man said with a scornful snort as he lifted himself into the wagon. He'd quickly bundled the washing back onto the tray.

"Arr," said the boy, sitting next to his father.

"We never see a soul on this road. Let alone a woman. No use reckoning on a reward. He be chasing a mare's nest." He flicked the reins. "Walk on."

The wagon rolled away with a creaking rumble. Grace sucked in a breath to combat her dizziness. What if Monks had searched the woods?

But then, he didn't know she'd gone with the drivers. She could have taken any direction once she'd left.

Her lips curved in a triumphant smile. Monks was probably more terrified than she was. She'd hate to have to tell Lord John one of his captives had escaped.

No wonder Monks had sounded so furious.

Or was he furious because his other captive had died? She couldn't countenance the possibility. It might be foolish superstition, but something in her would know if Matthew was no longer alive.

Eventually, when she was sure Monks wasn't likely to double back, she rose from her cramped position. It was uncomfortably warm and sweat prickled under her arms and at her nape. The woods clamored with birdsong. The wagon had long disappeared down the rutted trail.

She took the bottle from her bundle and swallowed a

mouthful of lukewarm water. Before night fell, she wanted the security of people around her. She could get lost in a crowd. Out here, alone, she was noticeable. And there was always the risk that Monks might come back.

She began to walk briskly away along the deserted track.

Chapter 24

Matthew opened his eyes with excruciating slowness. His lids felt as though lead weights held them down. The first glimpse of light splintered his skull with jagged pain. He closed his eyes again on a long groan.

He knew where he was now. As expected, he was strapped to the table in the garden room. Sunshine still streamed through the windows so it must be early afternoon.

Before collapsing into a dead faint, he'd spewed copiously over Filey's boots. After that, he only remembered dim snatches of lacerating pain and harsh voices and rough hands.

He'd forgotten how extreme his reaction to comfrey was. His insides felt as though they'd been cleaned out with a rake. A rusty one. His skin was abnormally sensitive and the bands around his legs and wrists and chest were tight enough to hurt. He breathed as deeply as the strap over his torso allowed, then regretted it when his abused muscles protested.

Agonizing as they were, his various discomforts only occupied a tiny space in his mind. Instead he focused on one burning question. Had Grace got away? He'd seen her dart across to the wagon before his physical crisis prevented him seeing anything at all.

Was she still safe? What if his rash scheme only sent her into greater danger?

He'd known when he came up with his plan that he'd likely never learn her fate. Only now did he realize how that ignorance would eat at him until the day he died.

In six months.

Although given how bloody foul he felt right now, he might die sooner. His head ached as if red hot metal wires circled it. His belly still cramped painfully. A sour taste filled his mouth and his lips were dry and cracked. He desperately wanted some water.

Common sense and experience insisted his current miseries would pass. His animal self didn't believe it. His animal self wanted to skulk off to some dark corner and lie there until he expired.

Christ, he stank. Of rank sweat and stale vomit. His nostrils flared in distaste. He still wore his filth-encrusted clothing from this morning.

Was it this morning? He could have been here for days. He wouldn't know any better.

His only comfort was the hope that Grace had made it. And that now she fled from anything to do with the estate, including his sorry self.

"I know you're awake, nephew." Lord John's voice dripped over him like bile.

This time when Matthew opened his eyes, he kept them open in spite of how the glare shot blinding pain through his head.

Had he slept? Or had his uncle watched him throughout? That thought made him shudder.

"Uncle," he croaked, surprised his voice worked at all. The rake that had scraped out his innards had been particularly busy in his throat. "Could I have a drink?"

"Presently." His uncle stood at the head of the table out of Matthew's view. "First I want to talk to you."

Just talk? Matthew had expected a beating at the very least. Perhaps his uncle feared compromising his captive's health. He wanted his prize capon in prime condition.

The bitterness of this reflection leached away some of Matthew's disorientation. He became aware of his surroundings. It must be late afternoon. Direct sunlight no longer poured into the room. But was it the afternoon of the day he'd first regained consciousness?

While he struggled for clarity, his hands clenched in the straps that fastened his wrists to the table. His pride revolted at the repulsive picture he must present. His fetid rags were stained with illness and reminded him too vividly of his real madness. He'd much prefer to conduct this interview in clean clothes and when he didn't feel as though a herd of elephants had trampled him.

Still, what couldn't be helped must be endured. He kept his face expressionless. "I don't feel much like a chat."

It was a childish riposte, but it would annoy his uncle. He liked that. He liked that very much.

He heard Lord John's cane tap as he rounded the table. Then his uncle stood at his side, blocking the light. Matthew was grateful. His eyes stung like the devil.

"Pity. I find myself in the mood for conversation." Lord John theatrically produced a lace handkerchief and pressed it to his nose.

Matthew hid a flinch of humiliation. Round one to his opponent.

The room was shut against fresh air as every room his uncle entered was always shut. Even so, the older man wore a fur-lined coat. In the smothering warmth, Matthew was dizzy with the pervasive stench of his own dirt.

"Actually, I hadn't expected the pleasure of your company

so soon," Matthew said silkily, although it cost an effort. "You must have broken the speed record from London."

"I was in Bath when Monks's message reached me. An annoying journey but not onerous. Yet again, you prove an irritation, nephew." Then in a voice totally different from the smooth cadence he'd used so far. "Where is your slut?"

"Mrs. Paget?"

Matthew fought to conceal the savage joy that coursed through him. She had got away. *Grace was free.*

Puzzlement was his safest response. After all, his illness and her escape mightn't be connected. He kept his voice deliberately unconcerned. "Upstairs? Walking in the woods? Please find her. I'd like to see her."

"Oh, so would I. But I've got an army of men combing the grounds and so far, we've found no sign of the jade."

"I'd help you look, Uncle. But as you see, my circumstances are somewhat restricted." Another childish crack. He almost enjoyed himself. The news about Grace worked better than a tonic on his assorted aches. "Perhaps she was so frightened by my seizure, she's hiding."

"And perhaps this was a ruse to distract your keepers while your whore scarpered."

"Believe me, Uncle, I couldn't feign what I went through. Ask Monks or Filey if you don't think I was genuinely ill. If Mrs. Paget saw her opportunity, you can't blame her." Then the ultimate hypocrisy, "I'm devilish sorry. I'll miss her."

"Tell me what you and the chit cooked up and I'll be lenient. I'll even bring her back to warm your bed after I've pointed her foolishness out to her."

"Uncle, you see conspiracy where none exists. You know I'm prone to fits. You know I wanted the lady to remain with me."

That at least was true. A scalding memory rose of the

turbulent emotion in her face when she'd said goodbye. He'd nearly weakened and begged her to stay. Thank God she'd turned away before he could speak.

His uncle still sounded unworried although Matthew knew he must be desperate to catch and silence Grace. "No matter. I've sent for the Bow Street Runners. They'll track the troublesome jade. You're familiar with their efficiency."

Matthew wasn't the only one prone to making unworthy jibes. The Bow Street Runners had discovered him mortifyingly quickly after his second escape attempt.

Now the Runners were involved, Grace's ability to fade into a crowd was more crucial than ever. Foreboding filled him. Could a beauty like hers escape notice? Even when he'd first seen her, sick, frightened, and wearing shabby black, her loveliness had pierced him to the quick.

Lord John just needed to describe a woman with a face that stopped your heart, a widow who dressed like a pauper and spoke like a duchess. The Runners would find her within days.

Oh, Jesus, Grace. I've sent you to your death. At least here I could have tried to keep you safe.

"I hope you do find her," he said while his heart snarled, *You'll rot in hell, John Charles Merritt Lansdowne.*

"It shouldn't be too hard. The trollop is quite distinctive, isn't she? Not in the common way at all. No wonder you made such a fool of yourself. I find myself intrigued. If I can stomach the idea of using your leavings, I might sample her myself before I bring her back."

Matthew didn't react although rage seethed under his skin like lava boiling in a volcano. The idea of his uncle's cold white hands touching Grace made his belly contract with sick fury.

His uncle lifted his stick to watch the light gleam off the lump of amber in the handle.

Lord John had often struck him with that stick when he'd been a boy. The transgressions had always been minor, sometimes nonexistent. Matthew remembered the pain. He wondered if Lord John intended to hit him now. But his uncle just twirled the stick round and round and studied the fly trapped inside the gold.

Eventually, Lord John broke the charged silence. "You always turn into a blasted fool when your protective instincts are engaged. You're as bad as your damned useless father. Born to be a country doctor, not one of the kingdom's greatest magnates. The title was wasted on both of you."

Lord John's jealousy of his oldest brother was too familiar to rouse anything but weariness. "I honestly don't know where Mrs. Paget is. My fit has passed, Uncle. As you so politely pointed out, I need a wash and change of clothing."

"You do at that." His uncle's lips stretched in a superior smile. "But I haven't finished with you yet. Where is the slut?"

"I told you—I don't know." Matthew's hands fisted tighter.

"Wrong answer." His uncle raised his stick high then slammed it hard over Matthew's ribs.

The world shrank to a black tunnel illuminated by bright shards of excruciating pain. The breath left him in a great gasp that shredded his stinging throat. His body tensed against the blinding agony but escape was impossible. His bonds held him stretched out and helpless.

He might have lost consciousness again for a few seconds. He didn't know. When he opened his eyes, Lord John was studying him with the same dispassionate gaze that he had recently devoted to the dead fly suspended in amber.

"Killing me won't achieve your ends," Matthew managed to say, even though every word hurt.

His uncle's lips curved up in a faint, chilly smile. "You know better than that. I am skilled at inflicting maximum pain with minimal permanent damage. You'll have some bruising but you'll mend quickly enough. Now, once again, where has the slut gone?"

"I don't know."

This time Matthew was prepared for the blow. Or he thought he was until the dizzying pain shot through him. He tightened every aching sinew against the scream that rose from his belly and battered against his closed lips. If the beating continued, he knew he didn't have a hope in hell of keeping quiet. He'd screamed before on this table, he'd scream again. But he wanted to delay offering his uncle the satisfaction.

"You know . . ." He paused to draw in enough breath to speak. After his collapse, he was in no fit state to withstand much more and he suspected his uncle realized that. Still he struggled to maintain the remnants of his defiance. "You know violence doesn't work on me, Uncle. You've tried it before. Even if I knew where Mrs. Paget is, I'm less likely to tell you with every blow."

"Yes, you're a dumb ox under torture." His uncle hit him again, harder.

"I told you I don't know where the bloody girl has gone!" Matthew shouted, writhing uselessly against his bonds. Although eleven years of captivity had taught him he'd never break their deathly grip, no matter how he struggled.

"Yes, but I don't believe you," his uncle said in a quiet voice.

"I don't know where she is, you bastard!"

"Temper, temper." Lord John's lips curved in a chilly smile.

Matthew's powerlessness was a physical pain in his gut. Every muscle coiled tight enough to snap. He gave up his futile attempts to break loose. A red hot rope of pain extended across his torso. Even the shallow breaths that were all he could manage threatened to hurtle him into unconsciousness.

Through the scarlet haze, he heard his uncle continue speaking. "You'll be easy enough to break, nephew. You're soft. You've always been soft. You hate to see creatures suffer. Especially creatures you love."

"What do you mean?" Matthew gritted out through closed teeth.

"I wonder how long your air of heroic and silent suffering will last once your dog is howling with pain."

Bitter nausea filled his mouth while his dazed mind tried to comprehend what his uncle said. Horror swamped even his physical distress.

Over eleven years, he'd watched his guardian test the boundaries of evil but this, this was beyond anything Matthew had ever imagined. Lord John couldn't mean to torture Wolfram. Not if he still claimed any trace of humanity.

He injected every ounce of the contempt he felt into his voice. "Uncle, even you must shrink from abusing a dumb animal."

"I don't cause the pain, you do." Then more sharply, "Tell me where the jade is or face the consequences. I can smell a plot a mile away. This plot stinks worse than you do."

"You can't do it," Matthew said, even while he reluctantly accepted that his uncle would balk at nothing. "The dog has never harmed you."

"In war, the innocent always suffer, don't they?"

"Don't do this, Uncle. For the love of Christ, don't do this." He hadn't begged Lord John for anything in years, not since he was an ailing boy and unaware of the depths of his guardian's evil.

"Tell me where the wench is and you have my word the

dog remains unharmed." Lord John paused. "You know, I would have thought you'd learned your lesson about defying my will the last time, when I had your nurse and her husband transported."

Oh, yes, he'd learned his lesson. He'd learned this life wasn't worth living. He'd learned he'd do anything to end this travesty and wrest control of the Lansdowne fortune away from his uncle.

Six months. . .

Grace, you don't know what you ask.

Wolfram had been a loyal, undemanding companion. Since the day he'd arrived as a hairy, ungainly puppy seven years ago, he'd offered Matthew nothing but devotion and trust.

Now Matthew must betray that trust.

Because he couldn't betray the woman he loved.

He kept his voice expressionless. "I don't know where Mrs. Paget is."

"I'm sure witnessing Filey and Monks at work on your dog will jog your memory. You remember how . . . *thorough* they can be."

Lord John gave his stick a peremptory tap on the flagged floor. The door opened and Filey sidled in, cradling a freshly bandaged hand to his chest. He'd clearly been waiting just outside.

"Aye, your lordship?"

Matthew sucked in a breath of the fresh air that poured into the room. It cleared the mist of pain from his head, even though his ribs still felt like they were on fire. He needed to do something to save Wolfram. But what?

Christ, he loathed his uncle.

"Fetch me the mongrel." Lord John lifted the collar of his coat against the faint breeze through the open door.

"Aye, your lordship. Right away, your lordship. He's skulking in the woods somewhere. Bit me when we was holding down . . . *looking after* Lord Sheene." An expression of shifty pride crossed his jowly face. "But happen I put a bullet in his sorry tail as he took off."

"You shot my dog, you bastard?" Matthew shouted, struggling yet again against his bindings and just as uselessly.

Hatred rose to gag him. His muscles tensed to agony. If sheer rage could free him, he'd be knocking Filey's teeth down his neck right now. He pulled so hard against the leather ties that the skin of his wrists split and hot blood trickled down over his hands.

"Aye, happen I did. And not before time, my lord." The undercurrent of satisfaction in Filey's voice made Matthew vow yet again to kill him. But promises of vengeance wouldn't halt the coming abomination. If Wolfram was still alive to be tortured. He sent up a brief prayer that his dog was dead. Even while the thought made his heart kick with angry grief.

The idea of Wolfram crawling off into the undergrowth to suffer a slow, miserable death turned his stomach. Although given his uncle's abhorrent plans, it would be better if Wolfram died before Filey found him. Acrid sorrow flooded Matthew as he recognized that his dog was yet another innocent victim of Lord John's iniquity.

An expression of chilly anger crossed his guardian's face. It was the most emotion he'd shown since Matthew had opened his eyes. "If the cur is dead, I will be most displeased, Filey. Most displeased."

Filey's pasty face developed a sickly hue. "Aye, your lordship," he muttered. "Were only a bit of fun."

"Burn in hell, Filey," Matthew said in a low vicious voice, then looked at his uncle. "Let me up so I can look for Wolfram. You can't leave him out there hurt and alone."

"Of course I can," Lord John said indifferently. "Although of course I'll bring the dog in for your tender ministrations, if you tell me where the slut is."

His fists clenched, slimy with sweat and his own blood. Hoping against hope that Grace had remained true to their plan and headed toward Wells, then for London, Matthew said in a flat voice, "She has family in Bristol. I assume she went there. She didn't tell me she was going. She must have seen her chance with the gate open and me out of my wits."

Lord John frowned, as if considering what he heard. Did his uncle believe him?

"That's where Filey and Monks found her. Ask him," Matthew added desperately.

"Bristol?" Lord John said slowly. "It's possible. It would make sense to find a place where she could mix with the populace. A woman like her could always earn a coin on her back."

"She's no whore!"

"If she wasn't when she arrived, you've made her into one," his uncle said without emphasis.

"Eh, I'm not sure about Bristol, your lordship." Filey scratched his head with his good hand. "If I remember rightly, the lass said she was lost when we took her."

"She has family there," Matthew said. "That's all she told me. Now let me up to find my dog."

"Your madness has returned and you must be controlled." His uncle had the temerity to smile, a brief baring of teeth. "Surely you recall that much from previous fits."

"I'm not mad. I had a temporary physical relapse that has now passed," Matthew snapped. "You know that as well as I."

"How can we be sure?" His uncle's voice was smooth as oil. "I've sent for Dr. Granger. He'll give us his diagnosis when he arrives."

Matthew bit back an appalled curse. Dr. Granger was the more brutal of the two physicians who had certified him. For three miserable years, Matthew had endured beatings and purges and bleedings. He was lucky he'd survived.

His uncle permitted himself a small satisfied smile before he turned his attention back to his henchman. "Filey, set the search parties on the cur's trail. Woe betide you if he's dead. He'll be a useful lever if Lord Sheene has lied to us and we need to force the truth from him."

Filey bowed. "Aye, my lord."

"Then you and Monks will take two men and ride to Bristol. Someone will have seen the jade on the road if she went that way. Check for Pagets in the city. Check the area where you found her. If you pick up no trace by tomorrow, leave the men to continue searching and come back." Lord John turned to Matthew. "What was her maiden name?"

Matthew said without a word of a lie, "I have no idea."

His uncle nodded, for once believing him immediately. "No matter. We have enough to go on. I shall return, nephew."

By now Matthew's throat was so parched, he felt as though he'd swallowed the Sahara. And he desperately wanted to rinse the repulsive taste of stale vomit from his mouth. "You're just leaving me?"

"For the moment," Lord John said with obvious indifference. "Filey, you have your instructions."

They closed the door behind them, abandoning him to an airless room and a heart brimming with guilt and futile rage. There was nothing he could do for Wolfram. There was nothing he could do for Grace. There was nothing he could do for himself.

He was so damned helpless, he wished to hell he were dead.

* * *

Dusk had fallen and Grace still hadn't met anybody by the time the narrow track joined three roads. She looked up at the signpost marking the crossroads, squinting to read the words.

Slowly, she made out the faded lettering. And nearly shouted aloud for joy.

Matthew had always been vague about the estate's location and she'd been unconscious when she arrived. But it turned out she knew exactly where she was. Or at least where she went.

Marked clearly on one arm of the signpost was a village a few miles away whose name was almost as familiar as her own.

Purdy St. Margaret's.

Her cousin, the Reverend Vere Marlow, was vicar at Purdy St. Margaret's.

For the first time in months, since well before Josiah fell sick, her heart leapt with genuine hope. She forgot her weariness and her blistered feet and the way her heavy dress irritated her sticky skin.

If she reached Vere, she was safe. If she reached Vere, she could find help for Matthew.

A joyful bark behind her made her turn in surprise. She squinted into the sun and raised one hand to her eyes to shield them from the dazzling light.

A huge brindle shape hurtled up the track toward her.

Wolfram?

What was he doing here? How had he escaped?

Then she remembered that the gate had been open for the cart to depart. Perhaps his jailers' panic over Matthew's illness meant they'd been too distracted to shut it again. Either that or he'd escaped when Monks had ridden in pursuit. He must have followed the scent of the wagon or of Monks's mount, then picked up her trail from where she'd climbed down.

What if he'd caught up with her at that moment? Her belly clenched with horror as she imagined what could have happened if he'd run up when she'd hidden in the woods. Her bid for freedom would have been over before it had begun.

"Wolfram! Good boy," she said, crouching and stroking his shaggy coat. He licked her face and butted her with his blunt head and whimpered with delight. He was dusty and panting and almost pathetically happy to see her. The rope she'd tied to his collar still dangled from his neck.

"Good . . . *What's this?*" Wolfram flinched as her fingers brushed a wet patch of hair near his haunches. When she lifted her hand, it was sticky with drying blood.

"Wolfram?" Heavens, what had happened after she left? Had there been some kind of brawl? Had Matthew been injured? Killed? He'd promised her that his uncle would do anything to keep him alive. But who knew what could happen in a crisis?

No, she had to believe he was still in this world. Or she couldn't bear to go on.

Very gently, she explored Wolfram's injury. From what she could see, the graze wasn't serious. There wasn't even a lot of blood. Wolfram whined and pressed his trembling body closer to her. She automatically put her arms around him.

"You poor darling. We'll get you help. Don't worry." She spoke to comfort herself as much as the wolfhound.

Her heart lurched with a sudden pang of yearning for Matthew. She'd give anything for one last chance to feel his embrace and to hear his deep voice whispering her name. Missing him had been a constant sharp ache in her heart from the moment she'd said goodbye. But crouched on this lonely road, the stark reality of his absence stabbed at her like a steel blade.

Bending her head, she buried her face in Wolfram's coarse coat. She didn't cry. She'd cried so much already and tears had done her no good. For a long time, she knelt there, praying for her lover's safety, praying for strength, praying for her own survival so that she could accomplish the impossible task ahead of her.

Finally, she drew in a deep breath and stood on legs that quivered with exhaustion. She straightened her backbone, gripped the rope attached to Wolfram's collar and lifted her chin to the east as if daring life to defy her.

She would free Matthew or she would die trying.

The sound of the hallway door opening woke Matthew from restless sleep. Darkness surrounded him. It must be the middle of the night.

"Have you found Wolfram? Is he all right?" Matthew asked groggily as his uncle came in.

He tried to sit up then subsided with a painful grunt when his bruised ribs met the leather bindings. For a moment, he'd forgotten he was tied down. He was stiff and sore and thirsty. Around sunset, his uncle had sent Mrs. Filey in to give him some water. The cool liquid had been sweeter than nectar on his throat and on his chapped and splitting lips. But that must have been hours ago.

His uncle didn't answer but spoke to the servants who followed him into the room and began to light the lamps. "Release him but keep a close hold when you do."

Matthew maintained an appearance of weary apathy while they untied him and brought him to his feet. The instant the hands on his arms loosened, he broke into a frenzy of fighting and punching and struggling.

He'd reached such a pitch of anger that if he got his hands on his uncle, he'd kill him. Then gladly face the consequences, whatever his promise to Grace. For the sake of his own manhood, he couldn't stand docilely like a bullock awaiting the butcher's ax.

He was weak after his bout of illness and the beating, and clumsy from lying strapped to the table so long in this stifling room. He managed to clout one thug over the face before they caught his arms with embarrassing ease and wrenched them behind his back. The damaged flesh over his ribs tightened in agony and a groan escaped him.

Chest heaving and convulsive shudders running through his aching muscles, he hung from the men's grasp. Failure tasted sour in his mouth.

"There's no point to this, nephew," his uncle said frigidly, not looking remotely worried at the sudden violence.

"If I manage to kill you, there is indeed a point," Matthew gasped, breath scraping in and out of his lungs.

"When I've come to reward you for your cooperation? Surely not. If you can restrain your madness for the nonce, I'll allow you up to bathe and change your clothing. And Mrs. Filey already prepares a meal for you."

Matthew refused to express surprise or curiosity. Even broken and defeated and weak, he wouldn't surrender.

"Don't you want to know why?"

Matthew remained silent.

After a pause, his uncle pursed his lips with disappointment. "The doxy was seen in a village on the road to Bristol. Filey returned to inform me while the others continued on. They'll catch her before she reaches the city."

No! Jesus, no!

He thought he'd screamed his anguished denial aloud. But he mustn't have because his uncle still stared at him with a gentle expectation that didn't fool him.

Was what Lord John said true? Or a trick to draw him out about Grace's whereabouts? Bristol was in the opposite direction to Wells. Had she decided at the last minute that the larger city offered greater protection?

Oh, God, Grace, if they catch you, all hope is gone.

Chapter 25

Grace curtsied deeply as Francis Rutherford, Duke of Kermonde, swept into the library of Fallon Court. She hadn't been inside this beautiful paneled room since she was a girl of eleven. She hadn't seen the duke since she was fifteen, when she'd attended his fiftieth birthday at this house with her family.

Would he remember her? And if he did, would he deign to speak to her? He'd always been kind when she'd come to him as the spoiled daughter of his best friend. Now she was poor and desperate and needed his help. She ardently wished she had something other than her faded widow's weeds to wear. They proclaimed her poverty and put her at immediate disadvantage.

Goodness, what did her appearance matter when Matthew's fate hung in the balance? She stifled the stiff-necked pride that had forbidden her from seeking help from her family's connections before.

At her side Vere bowed, clutching his document case close to his narrow chest. He'd requested this audience without telling the duke about Grace's arrival at his vicarage yesterday.

She wasn't sure surprising one of the nation's most powerful men was a good idea. But she'd been too tired and frightened and sick with worry over Matthew to argue. And by the time she'd reached Purdy St. Margaret's, Wolfram had been limping badly and he'd demanded her immediate attention.

Thank goodness his injuries weren't serious, but he was exhausted and obviously fretting over his master's absence. They'd locked the hound in the stable while they came to the manor. He'd been howling fit to break a window when she left.

"Reverend Marlow?" The duke paused before them. Grace felt him studying the crown of her bent head. "What's this about?" Then she heard his sharply indrawn breath as she rose.

"Good morning, Uncle Francis," she said calmly, holding her head up and daring him to scorn her. She was a Marlow. Her blood was as blue as his, however empty her purse.

"It's . . . Good God, it's little Grace! I'd know those eyes anywhere," he said in astonishment. "Lord, I haven't seen you in ten years. Bless me, you've become a beauty."

Then he gave a delighted laugh as though her visit presented the greatest treat and held his arms wide. "Come here and say hello properly!"

She'd expected any reaction from wary curiosity to immediate banishment. Open and unhesitating welcome hadn't been on her list.

Fighting tears, Grace threw herself into his embrace. She'd always adored her godfather. Throughout her girlhood, he'd descended upon her at irregular intervals, bringing extravagant gifts and laughter. He'd always treated her as a cherished daughter. His wife had died young and childless and he'd never remarried.

"Oh, Uncle Francis! I've missed you so much," she eventually stammered in a choked voice, drawing away.

He bombarded her with questions, questions she answered as well as she could without long explanations. Any delay extended Matthew's ordeal. Was he even alive? The harrowing memory of how ill he'd been when she left gnawed at her like hungry rats. More hung on this meeting than a reunion. Although she couldn't help asking the one thing that had haunted her. "How are my parents, Uncle Francis?"

Vere had told her what he knew once he'd stopped apologizing for the carriage accident which had prevented him reaching Bristol. So banal a cause for all that had befallen her. But Vere hadn't seen her mother or father for years. The duke had been her father's friend since Eton.

By now, she and her godfather were seated on a leather couch near tall glass doors opening onto the magnificent garden.

"You know about your brother, of course." Kermonde's narrow face was somber. With his long nose and tawny hair and sharp pale blue eyes, he'd always reminded her of a fox.

"Yes. I saw it in the news sheets." She took a shaky breath. Talking about Philip always filled her with a crippling mixture of shame and sorrow. Her own criminally irresponsible behavior had hurt her family so much. Then they'd endured the loss of their only son in circumstances that brought humiliation to a proud name.

"Things haven't been . . . good. Your mother gave up her social engagements and retired to her room as an invalid. Your father throws himself into parliamentary work in a way that worries me. I sincerely believe they'd love to see you, Grace."

She remembered her father's final, unequivocal dismissal. "No, they wouldn't. Although I can't help but wonder about them."

"Since Philip's death, your father has reconsidered many things, not least his treatment of you."

Vere spoke, interrupting the heavy silence that fell. "Sir, Grace has brought an urgent matter to my attention which I believe only you can resolve."

"Do you need help, Grace?" Kermonde looked at her curiously. "My coffers are at your disposal."

She shook her head, wishing her requirements were so simple. She asked for more than gold. For Matthew's sake, she wanted Kermonde to pledge his name, his influence, perhaps his very reputation. "The help isn't for me but for a man who suffers injustice of the worst kind."

"Go on." Suddenly, her godfather didn't sound like her indulgent Uncle Francis but like the great Duke of Kermonde. Good. It was the duke she needed. Lord John was a powerful man and his crimes were hanging offenses. Perhaps her long-lost Marlow connections could save her lover.

Although not for her. Never for her.

"I have papers here, Your Grace." Vere tapped the document case. "The story they tell beggars belief. That's why I brought Grace to you. Although after all she's been through, she needs rest to recover."

"I don't need rest. I need justice," she said sharply. Vere showed an unfortunate tendency to coddle her. He was only six years her senior, but he already acted like a fussy old man. She wondered, not for the first time, how she could bear to live with him and his managing wife and noisy brood. And what could she do with Wolfram? Vere's wife Sarah already complained vociferously about having the huge hound running tame in her house.

She had nowhere else to go.

She dismissed the troubling thought. Her future wasn't important here. Matthew's was.

"Tell me," Kermonde said. "I'm intrigued."

* * *

Her godfather heard her out with few comments, then turned to the documents she'd stolen to prove Matthew's sanity. Drafts of articles for scientific journals. Letters in several languages to botanical experts across Europe. Correspondence from Lord John. His lordship had been careful not to confess any wrongdoing in writing. Nonetheless, the letters were a stinging indictment of greed and cruelty. They also set out names of doctors, treatments Matthew had undergone, other details that confirmed her outlandish tale.

When he finished, Kermonde looked up from his desk with a dazed expression. Afternoon drew toward evening. Grace waited nervously on the edge of the sofa.

Dear God, just let Matthew still be alive.

Vere had left on parish business after luncheon but he'd returned a short while ago. He now stood at the doors watching the light fade over the formal gardens.

"I can hardly credit it." Her uncle removed his spectacles and rubbed his eyes. She'd been surprised when he'd taken them from his pocket. She remembered him as fit and vital. His weakening eyesight was an unwelcome reminder that he was now over sixty.

"It's true," she said shortly.

He smiled at her. "I don't doubt it. I know Lord John's handwriting from parliamentary business. He's made himself a big noise in the world since he became his nephew's keeper. I'd always thought he was a sound chap. Now I find the fellow should be horsewhipped then hanged."

She'd come prepared to argue, persuade, plead. "You believe me?"

"Of course I do, my dear."

"And . . ." She paused to suck in a breath. Her heart raced with wild hope. "And you'll help free Lord Sheene?"

"By God, yes. This villainy must end. But it won't be as

quick as you'd like, Grace. I'll need to gather evidence and place what I know before the authorities."

"Isn't there enough here?" she asked urgently.

"No. Although you were clever to bring this material."

"How long will you need? Time is of the essence." She hardly cared that she badgered a duke of the realm much as she'd have haggled with a neighboring farmer over a ewe.

Even Kermonde looked slightly startled at her directness. "Months, probably."

"Months." The rioting happiness in her heart eased to a limping trot. In six months, Matthew's promise to her ended. Then he'd wreak revenge on his tormentors and break his captivity the only way he could. With his own death.

Compassion filled the duke's face. "Patience, my dear. Lord John has friends in high places, although not as many as he thinks. The case must be unassailable before I proceed officially. This will be Sheene's only chance. If we foul it up, he'll be held as a madman the rest of his life."

"I couldn't bear that," she whispered, then hoped her uncle didn't read anything significant into what she said. She'd tried to give the impression that her friendship with the marquess hadn't proceeded beyond the bounds of propriety.

"Lord John's greed is understandable if far from laudable. The Lansdownes were always confoundedly plump in the pocket. We do this right or it's not worth doing. At present, we know where the marquess is and we know what Lord John is up to. If we signal our intentions, he could steal Sheene away, lock him in a public asylum under a false name. Then we'll never find him."

"Lord Sheene has suffered so long." Grace rose on trembling legs and stood before her godfather's desk like

a petitioner. Why not? She was. She'd go on her knees if it
would help. Love had crushed her Marlow pride to dust.

That clever vulpine face took on a thoughtful expression as he considered her. Perhaps her advocacy had been
too passionate. But any delay stung her like needles piercing flesh.

Oh, Matthew, stay alive for me, her anguished heart
cried while the laden silence extended.

Kermonde gave her a faint smile. "I remember Sheene's
father. Fine fellow. Clever as a tree full of monkeys. Not
surprised his son inherited his brains. Very sad day when
he and his marchioness died. Went to the funeral. Remember the boy spoke bravely at the service. He must have
been ten or eleven, I'd say. Nice-looking youngster. He'd
be about twenty-five now."

He paused to send Grace another speculative glance.
Clearly, she hadn't concealed her personal interest. How
could she? She was on fire with love and fear. Still, her
reputation was at risk and she wanted no hint of scandal
to prejudice Matthew's case. Nobody must ever know how
joyfully Grace Marlow had whored herself to a madman.

"Uncle Francis, I'm doing this because I hate to see
someone abused and imprisoned," she said stiffly. "My
husband died only a few weeks ago."

"But your husband was much older, wasn't he, my
dear?" Kermonde's lips twitched. She'd told him little
about Josiah, but obviously enough for him to guess much
she hadn't said. "Dashed bad show this happened to young
Sheene. I should have taken an interest but I hadn't heard
anything against his uncle. Then news circulated that the
boy was out of his head and I haven't given the poor chap
a thought since. I was proud to call the late Lord Sheene
a friend. If I save his son further torment, it's the least I
can do."

"So what are Your Grace's plans?" Vere asked from behind her. She'd almost forgotten her cousin was present.

"I go to London where I'll put qualified men on the case. Discreet men who can ferret out information without alerting Lord John we're onto him."

"So when do we leave?" she asked eagerly.

Kermonde frowned. "Grace, I can't take you with me."

"But I'm the one . . ."

The elegant hand he held up was weighted with the ducal signet. "If everything you've told me is true, and I believe it is, you're in grave danger. Lord John has already threatened your life. You can't swan around London under his nose. If you're seen in my company, he'll know the game is up. I gather he has no idea of your connections."

She allowed herself a grim smile even while her heart protested that she and only she could save Matthew. "Lord John believes I'm a prostitute who works the docks at Bristol."

Her uncle looked shocked. She supposed he was unused to such free speech from a woman. Or at least from a woman he considered a lady. He remembered her as a sheltered young girl. How could he know the ways life had changed her since?

He cleared his throat. "Yes, well, it's imperative he has no idea where you are or who you've spoken to. I'll keep you informed. But I insist upon you remaining here."

"At Fallon Court?"

Vere spoke quickly. "No need to inconvenience yourself, sir. My cousin was on her way to take up residence at the vicarage when this unfortunate incident occurred."

"I can protect her better here. My two aunts occupy the tower suites so there's no impropriety about my bereaved goddaughter staying. John Lansdowne will quail at snatching you from a ducal residence. Should he even think to look here. He seeks Grace Paget, indigent widow, not Lady Grace Elizabeth Marlow, only daughter of the Earl of Wyndhurst."

She hadn't heard her real name in years. It seemed unfamiliar, as if it belonged to someone else. Lady Grace Marlow seemed an altogether more refined creature than practical Grace Paget who kept her sheep run and nursed her husband through the indignities of his final illness.

Vere bowed. "I'm sure my cousin appreciates your kindness."

Kermonde had spoken his will and it would be done, much as God's was. On the Kermonde estate, God and the duke were interchangeable.

Her godfather ignored Vere and surveyed her with a frown of displeasure. "We'll have to do something about your clothes."

She flushed with chagrin. "There's no need to treat me as a charity case. Nobody will see me."

"It won't do, Grace. It just won't do. That rag isn't fit for a dish clout. Good God, my scullery maids dress better. You'll be the laughingstock of the servants' hall."

"I'm in mourning," she protested, feeling like the greatest hypocrite who ever lived. Only two days ago, she'd rested naked and satisfied in Matthew Lansdowne's arms.

"Order a few black dresses if you must, but make sure you buy some pretty ones too. Sounds to me like you've paid penance the last nine years. About time you regained your place in the world, girl."

She couldn't argue, not while he was being so kind. Not while with him on her side, she might save Matthew.

When she didn't speak, Kermonde gave a *hmph* of approval. "Fetch your belongings from the vicarage. We'll dine at seven. Marlow, bring that wife of yours."

"Thank you, Your Grace," Vere said with another bow. "Mrs. Marlow will be honored."

The duke turned to Grace. "Tomorrow I'm for London. Keep your head down, young lady. Newly widowed. Makes sense you want time to yourself. I'll tell the aunts to leave you be. Those two can talk the leg off a chair if you encourage them."

Grace vaguely remembered the aunts from her last visit. They'd squabbled through the afternoon, paying no attention to anything except the sweets table and what the other did wrong.

Grace dipped into a curtsy. "Thank you, Uncle Francis. I can never repay you, but you have my undying gratitude."

Her worldly godfather looked uncomfortable. "Oh, tosh, girl. Always wondered what happened to you. If your father wasn't so stiff-rumped, he'd have handled you better and you'd have made a marriage befitting your station. I'd be dandling your babies on my knee now instead of rescuing your young man from this confounded mess he's tangled up in."

"He's not . . ." She fell silent as the duke cocked a disbelieving eyebrow. Clearly, nothing—*nothing*—in her story had escaped Uncle Francis. She suddenly remembered he was known as the terror of the House of Lords.

"As you wish, Your Grace," she said sheepishly and allowed Vere to lead her out of the library.

Chapter 26

After a fortnight, Grace was frantic with worry about Matthew. When he'd presented his plan as a *fait accompli*, she hadn't realized how lack of news would wear her nerves.

Had he recovered from his self-induced illness? Was he even alive? Had his uncle punished him for what he must immediately recognize as a well-organized plot? Lord John had beaten and tortured his captive before. The scars on Matthew's beautiful body bore mute testimony to that.

Was Lord John searching for her? Matthew's uncle wouldn't give up easily. Especially to ensure his safety and reputation. While Grace was at liberty, both were at risk.

Did Matthew yearn for her the way she yearned for him? Or was he in too much pain? Had the herbs triggered his madness?

That was her worst fear. He'd clawed his way back to sanity through will alone. She couldn't bear to think he might lose his mind again. Perhaps forever.

In the silken luxury of her bedchamber, she cried herself to sleep every night. She was so lonely for Matthew, she felt she'd die.

What if she never saw him again? What if all she did now came to nothing?

By day, it was easier to cling to optimism. Wolfram offered undemanding company and a link to her lover. But at night, as she lay watching the moon cross the sky, then dawn rise from the east, it was harder to hope. Lord John was clever and ruthless. The outcome of her battle was far from assured.

It was almost worse when sheer exhaustion plunged her into a restless doze. Dreams of Matthew tormented her. Dreams of him abused and starved. Dreams where he looked at her with the same cold gaze he'd leveled on her when she first arrived on the estate. Dreams where he reviled her for deserting him.

Even worse were the dreams where he made love to her. His touch was so real. His powerful body thundered into hers or took her tenderly and slowly. The rapture rose and rose inside her.

Then . . . nothing.

She'd wake with tears on her face and empty arms.

Oh, Matthew, Matthew, come back to me soon.

Silence was the only answer.

A week after her escape, proof arrived that there would be no child. Although she thought she'd long ago reconciled herself to barrenness, she'd cried all day in her room. Her courses had been late and a tiny seedling of hope had begun to unfurl, which only made her disappointment crueler.

She tried telling herself that a baby would add an impossible complication to an already fraught situation. But her sorrowful heart didn't feel like that. Her heart felt as though every day another thread of connection frayed between her and the man she loved.

Kermonde was in London. She knew he worked on Matthew's behalf but waiting tortured her worse than knives flaying the skin from her body. He sent regular letters, even if they usually came in his secretary's hand. Her godfather's latest note had just arrived and it contained news exciting enough to justify him setting pen to paper himself.

For what felt like the first time since she'd arrived at Fallon Court, she smiled as she dropped the closely written page to her lap. She looked up and noticed it was a perfect day. For the last fortnight, she'd existed in a gray cloud and the outside world hadn't impinged.

Now she realized the bench where she sat was in a pleasant glade near a fast-flowing river. While she'd been locked in wintry worry and despair, summer had arrived. Sunlight broke through thick green leaves and sparkled on running water. Birds twittered and flew among branches that arched above her head.

There was beauty in the world.

One of Matthew's doctors was in public disgrace. Dr. Granger was, by all reports, an out-and-out quack. The duke's men now scoured the country for him in the hope they could get him to admit he'd accepted a bribe to certify Matthew insane.

Hope.

She clung to the word the way she'd hold a candle up against a black night.

She looked down to where the letter with its marvelous news rested on the skirt of her pretty dimity dress. The village dressmaker had supplied her with a wardrobe more elaborate than anything she'd worn since leaving Marlow Hall. Unless one counted her whore's dresses on the estate.

She remembered the flame that had kindled in Matthew's golden eyes when she flaunted herself in those outrageous outfits. It had been a game, in a place where playfulness was an act of courage, a defiant gesture against darkness.

She prayed the darkness hadn't engulfed him. Closing her eyes, she whispered a plea for his safety.

A twig cracked on the path and she opened her eyes to see one of the maids. "Begging your pardon, my lady." The girl curtsied and cast a nervous eye behind her.

"Yes, what is it, Iris?" Grace folded the precious letter. Most of the servants left her alone unless she summoned them. She suspected her godfather had given orders to that effect.

"You've a visitor, ma'am."

"A visitor?" That was unusual enough to bring her to her feet. Perhaps it was Vere although he tended to wait for her to call. "Is it my cousin?"

She hoped there was no trouble. Vere had four children already and Sarah increased again. Pregnancy made her even more ill-tempered than usual. This was one reason Grace hadn't exactly been a regular visitor to her cousin's neat stone vicarage next to the glorious medieval church, St. Margaret's.

"No, it's your father," came a voice she hadn't heard in nine years. A tall gentleman dressed in black moved slowly into view behind the maid.

Grace raised a shaking hand to her breast. Her heart pounded as if it fought free of her chest. What did the earl's arrival mean? Had he come to demand she leave her godfather's house? Had he come to denounce her?

She wasn't ready for this. She'd never be ready for this.

"The Earl of Wyndhurst to see you, my lady," the maid said, curtsying again and backing away.

Awkward silence descended.

Grace had last seen her father in a towering fury. Then he'd been a powerful and frightening figure. Over the years, the memory of that awful afternoon in his library had eclipsed other memories of love and kindness and generosity. She'd been a spoiled little girl. Too spoiled, as her headlong descent into ruin had demonstrated. She'd learned to consider consequences too late.

The man who stood before her wasn't the bitter, angry monster who populated her nightmares. The earl walked with a stick and deep lines marked his face. There was more gray than black in his thick hair.

He was her father, yet not her father. Then the familiar ironic smile flickered briefly and he wasn't a stranger any more.

She straightened her shoulders and met his eyes with a direct look. She had a right to be here, even if he wanted to banish her back to obscurity. But bravado didn't disperse the haze of uncertainty, grief, guilt, and resentment in her heart. And love. In spite of everything, love lurked too.

For a charged moment, they stared at each other, father and daughter. Only a few feet separated them, but it might as well have been a chasm a mile wide.

"Have you no greeting for your father, girl?" He didn't sound angry and his stare seemed questioning rather than accusatory.

Unthinkingly, she sank into a curtsy. "Good afternoon, sir," she said in an unsteady voice.

When she rose, she was dismayed to see tears in the dark blue eyes that were faded copies of the ones she saw in the mirror. She'd always favored her father's looks, with her dark hair, pale skin, and indigo eyes.

"Sir? Is that the best you can do, Grace? After all this time?" he asked hoarsely. The hands he placed on his stick trembled. He'd always moved quickly and vigorously. It was a shock to see he used the stick for support, not fashion.

"I don't . . . don't know what you want."

She heard him draw in a shuddering breath. "First, a warmer welcome than I've received."

"As you wish." Hesitantly, she approached. He was stooped enough now for her to reach up and press a kiss to his cheek. It was a brief salute. Once, she'd have thrown her arms around him in an extravagant hug. But those days were gone.

"I'm glad to see you, Father." It was true, although the changes in him cut to her soul. Even after a few minutes of his company, she could see this man was different from the one she remembered. For a start, he was willing to unbend enough to speak to his errant daughter. She stepped back. "Did Uncle Francis tell you I was here?"

He'd closed his eyes when she kissed him as if the gentle salute hurt. Now he stared fixedly at her. She wondered what he saw. At least she was dressed like a lady, not the beggar she'd looked when she'd arrived at Fallon Court. That in itself made her feel a fraud. She was a beggar.

"No, Vere wrote to me at Marlow Hall. Thank God he did. I came as soon as I got the letter. I've looked for you for the last five years, child."

Her father had looked for her? None of this made sense. When he'd barred her from his house, she'd had no doubt that his decision was set in marble.

Yet now he said he'd sought her out.

Bewildered, she wondered what had changed, when *he'd* changed. Was it after Philip's death? Although neither had mentioned her brother's name, the tempestuous, beloved ghost hovered so tangibly, she could almost touch it.

But no. Her father said he'd started to search for her five years ago. Philip had been alive then and galloping head-long toward ruin in the fleshpots of London.

The earl had relented for Grace's sake, not just because

he'd lost his only son and turned in desperation to his one remaining child.

"You said you never wanted to see me again." She couldn't stifle a hint of bitterness. Her marriage had been irresponsible, reprehensible, she recognized and regretted that. But her beloved father's implacable rejection had opened a wound that had never healed.

She saw him whiten at her tone. "I said many things that afternoon. At the time I meant them but I quickly repented of my harshness. Within a year, I came to York and approached Paget about helping you both, finding him a position on one of my estates so at least you could live in some comfort. But he threw my offer back in my face."

Her father had swallowed his pride to the point where he'd extended the hand of friendship to Josiah? Grace felt lost in a world that bore no relationship to the one she thought she inhabited.

She spoke through a throat tight with distress and twisted her hands in her skirts to hide their trembling. "You didn't ask to see me?"

"Your husband said you'd turned your back on your family forever and looked forward to a new and better life with him. He said you despised the Marlows and everything we stood for."

She could imagine how self-righteous Josiah had sounded when he'd told her father those lies. "And you believed him?"

The earl's mouth turned down. "I had no other option. You hadn't written to us since your marriage or tried to see us."

She'd always imagined that if she ever met her father again, he'd be angry, as he'd been angry after her elopement. But instead, he was just so wrenchingly sad and she didn't know how to react. His sadness weighed down her heart until it felt like a massive stone inside her.

"You told me not to," she said, fighting the urge to touch him, comfort him.

A faint smile crossed his face although the deep sorrow remained. When he dredged up a touch of the dry humor she'd loved as a girl, she thought her heavy heart would break. "So obedient at last, daughter. You were never the most biddable chit. A pity this was the one time you should have ignored my command."

"You sounded like you hated me," she said in a hollow voice.

"I was angry, disappointed." He took a step in her direction. "But I never ceased to mourn the break with you. You'd always been my favorite, you know."

Yes, she had known. She'd mistakenly assumed that her father's indulgence would extend to forgiving her unfortunate marriage, but she'd been tragically wrong.

Except that her father had forgiven her, it seemed.

Josiah had never told her that the earl had tried to make peace. Perhaps her husband had been afraid she'd abandon him and return to her earlier life. Perhaps they'd both have been better off if she had. They'd never known a moment of true happiness in their marriage. Her love for Matthew shone a stark light on the sterility, emotional and physical, of her life with Josiah.

The earl was still speaking with an urgency she'd never heard from him before. "Then five years ago, I tried to make amends again, hoping your resentment had softened with time. But you'd disappeared. The shop in York was derelict and none of your neighbors knew where you'd gone. I've searched high and low, had my men asking after you in every bookshop in Britain. I've even had my agents checking in America."

"I was in Ripon," Grace said. "Until a few weeks ago, anyway."

"Ripon . . ." The earl paled until he was the color of new paper and staggered back as though she'd hit him.

"Are you all right, my lord?" Grace surged forward to support her father but at the last moment, hesitated. Would he want her help?

He quickly found his balance but she noticed that the hands on his stick were white-knuckled with tension. "You were only thirty miles from Marlow Hall? All this time?"

"Yes, on a farm. Sheep." Grace's mouth flattened in a wry line as she spread her hands in front of her so her father could see. "Here are the scars."

"Heaven curse me." His face retained its unhealthy pallor while his voice was gruff and shaking with emotion. He clutched the stick as though it was all that kept him upright. "My little girl with a workman's hands. I'd brought you up fit to become a duchess. What have I done? *What have I done?* How can you ever forgive me, child?"

How she hated to see her father like this. And the fault, after all, was hers. She twined her hands together in front of her and forced herself to speak.

"I think . . ." She mustered all her courage and went on. "I think it is for you to forgive me, Father." This time, the word *father* emerged without strain.

His face contorted with emotion. "Oh, Grace, my dearest girl, I forgive you with all my heart, as I hope you will in time forgive me. I've been such a fool but I hope the years have made a difference to the man I was. I hope they've taught me wisdom." He paused and extended his arm. "Walk with me back to the house, daughter?"

Grace caught a flash of painful vulnerability in his face. She was astonished to realize that even now, he was far from confident she'd accept his escort. The Earl of Wyndhurst she recalled from her girlhood had always been utterly sure of himself.

She took a deep breath, knowing the rest of her life hinged on what happened now. A smile would reassure her father but she couldn't summon one, no matter how she tried.

The earl had made mistakes. So had she. Both of them had paid a heavy price for their sins, if what she saw now was any indication.

When she spoke, her voice was calm and sure. "I'd be honored, Father."

The bedroom was dark as Grace crept inside. Perhaps her mother was asleep, although it was only mid-afternoon. On the long carriage journey up from Somerset, she'd learned from her father that the countess spent most of her days dozing in her closed room. It seemed such a tragic contrast to the vibrant, vital woman Grace remembered.

Quietly she shut the door behind her and immediately the stuffy atmosphere became a terrifying reminder of Lord John. Her heart raced and the breath caught in her throat. She fought the trapped feeling that threatened to suffocate her.

Then the familiar scents of roses and beeswax surrounded her and dissipated the choking panic. The combined scents transported her back to childhood and brought tears to her eyes. Because she had moved a thousand miles beyond that spoiled, innocent girl who was lost forever.

The smell made the past so close, so tangible. She took a deep breath and leaned against the door. It was too dark for her to see the beautiful inlaid pattern of musical instruments in different woods. But the child inside her remembered the violins and flutes on the back of the door. Just as the child remembered the soft blues and pinks of the floral carpet on the floor and the blue silk hangings that shrouded the high, elaborately carved bed on its platform.

"Who's there?"

Even her mother's voice was different. High-pitched and querulous. She was only fifty but she sounded like a frightened old woman.

Grace couldn't speak over the grief clogging her throat. *This was wrong, so wrong.*

The bedclothes rustled as her mother shifted nervously on the mattress. "Who is it? Is that you, Elise? If you've come to dress me for dinner, I don't think I'm up to going downstairs tonight."

Her mother never ate meals in the dining room anymore. She'd heard the bewildered love and sorrow in her father's voice as he described his wife's behavior since Philip's death. Learning of her mother's total retreat from life had filled her with guilt and piercing sadness.

It was worse standing in this room now and seeing for herself.

"Elise?"

"It's . . ." Grace stopped and tried again. "It's not your maid, Mamma."

The figure in the bed lay so still that Grace could almost touch the silence. Then, so softly that she hardly heard the word, "Grace?"

On trembling legs that she wasn't sure would support her, Grace stepped forward. "Yes, Mamma. It's Grace."

"My little Grace . . ." Another rustle of the bedclothes. Then in a stronger voice. "I'm dreaming, aren't I?"

It was so hard to force words out. "N-no. I'm really here." Her strange paralysis shattered and she dashed across the carpet to fall to her knees beside the bed. "I'm really here, Mamma."

"I don't believe it." Her mother rolled over onto her side and reached out to stroke Grace's face as if only touch could confirm her presence. When Grace felt the dance of those loving fingers across her cheek, she closed her eyes.

She was home again.

Grace sucked in a shaky breath. Even through the shadows, she could see how sunken and pallid her mother's face had become. The scraggly strands of long hair that escaped her cap were gray and lifeless. The last nine years hadn't been kind to the Countess of Wyndhurst. Little trace remained of the celebrated beauty who had married the earl and reigned from Marlow Hall as queen of county society.

"I thought I'd never see you again," the countess whispered in a broken voice.

"So did I." The words emerged thickly, indistinctly.

"Why didn't you come when . . . when Philip died?" A trace of anger. "I needed you, Grace, and you weren't here."

Why hadn't she come? Josiah would have forbidden her but she could have disobeyed him. In her heart, she'd defied him for so many years by then, disobeying him in reality wouldn't have made things worse between them. She'd thought her father hated her, but she should have been brave enough to face his anger. *She could have at least tried.*

She'd been wrong. And cowardly. And cruel.

"I'm sorry," she said in a broken voice. "I'm so sorry."

"I miss Philip so much." Tears began to fall from the countess's dull eyes. "I've missed you."

"I know, Mamma, I know," Grace murmured, rising to sit on the edge of the bed. Curled up under the covers in her delicate white nightgown, her mother seemed as small and fragile as a sparrow. Very gently, Grace encircled the frail body with her arms and cradled her mother against her.

For a moment, her mother's thin form was tense, as

though she were unused to human contact. Then she bent her head to Grace's shoulder and burst into an exhausted fit of weeping.

Grace's hold tightened and she leaned her cheek against the lace of her mother's cap. She had so much to say, there was so much she wanted to know. But she stayed silent.

She'd always loved her mother—she'd loved her whole family, although it had been a thoughtless, selfish love. What she'd learned about love from Matthew gave her the wisdom to know that for the present, silent comfort was what her mother needed.

Eventually, her mother stopped crying and raised her head. Grace was so used to the gloom by now, she had no trouble reading the expression on the countess's face. She looked tired and sad, but there was a peace there that had been missing before.

"Open the curtains, Grace. I want to see my daughter."

"Yes, Mamma." Grace rose and threw back the heavy draperies so that bright light flooded the room, banishing the darkness.

Chapter 27

Kermonde's carriage lumbered along the track to the estate Grace had fled four months ago. In the Morocco leather interior, tense silence reigned. Grace was masked and sat opposite the duke. Beside her, her father stared broodingly out into the twilight.

She nervously twisted her gloved hands in the skirt of her dark green merino traveling dress. Her heartbeat drummed so loudly in her ears, it drowned out the carriage's endless creak. The cloudy sky and thick trees crowding the road turned the evening into deepest night. She shivered, trying not to read the darkness as an omen of looming disaster.

What had happened since she'd last seen Matthew? Was he fit? Was he unharmed? Was he alive? Dear God, let her not be too late. Four months was a long time, even for someone who hadn't counted every frustrating minute as an hour.

When the duke's men had finally found Dr. Granger, the sham physician confirmed he'd seen Matthew recently. He'd said nothing else to ease her fears. Reading the doctor's testimony included in her godfather's letter, she'd choked with sick, impotent anger. Dr. Granger had boasted of beatings, purges, bleedings, and blisterings he'd administered to the adolescent marquess. The memory of Matthew's ruined back tormented her. Now, graphic knowledge of the abuse he'd suffered as a youth sent nightmares to shatter what little sleep she snatched.

Dr. Granger claimed he'd only examined his patient on his latest visit. But had Monks and Filey continued the doctor's cruel methods under Lord John's orders?

She'd begged her godfather to send someone to spy on the estate, but Kermonde had been reluctant. If Lord John caught a whiff of the plot against him, he could spirit Matthew away beyond chance of rescue.

"Peace, child. Everything will reach a satisfactory conclusion." Her father placed one large hand over her restless fingers. He must have watched her long enough to guess the dizzying swirl of dread and doubt inside her.

She turned her head and met his eyes in the dimness. "I hope so."

Once she'd have scoffed at the suggestion that her father would support her through her quest. But many things had changed, including her status as a penniless and friendless widow. Now she was openly acknowledged as the wealthy heiress, Lady Grace Marlow. Even poor Josiah's name had faded into oblivion. The thought made her sad, as if her husband was the same failure in death that he'd been in life.

But Josiah's ghost was a pale insubstantial shadow. Its melancholy whispers were inaudible beneath her clamoring anxiety for Matthew.

"Grace, I'd rather you waited in the coach where you'll be safe." Kermonde clutched a leather strap as the vehicle lurched into another pothole.

This argument had gone on for weeks but Grace had remained obdurate. After so many months receiving secondhand news or no news at all, she needed to see Matthew with her own eyes. Her only concession to her godfather was that for discretion's sake, she'd agreed to wear a mask and keep silent. The world must never discover Lady Grace Marlow had been mistaken for a common harlot.

"Francis, let the chit be." Her father pressed her hand then let her go. "We've gathered more men than Wellington had at Vittoria. Can't you see she's set on having her way?"

Behind Kermonde's luxurious equipage traveled a dozen horsemen and two coachloads of armed retainers. Bringing up the rear, another carriage contained two royal physicians. King George had been furious when he learned of Matthew's ordeal. The late Lord Sheene had been a great friend, advising him on his art collection. What had clinched His Majesty's interest, though, were the brilliant botanical articles. Thank heaven she'd stolen them.

How her father had changed, that he was prepared to defend her so openly. Behind the mask, tears prickled her eyes. But the warmth was fleeting. Fulfilling as her reunion with her mother and father was, her thoughts never strayed far from Matthew. She wanted to look into his eyes. She wanted to hear his deep voice with its undercurrent of wry amusement. She wanted his scent. She wanted to touch him. Only his physical presence would silence the demons howling in her heart, insisting she couldn't save him.

She was exhausted and elated and worried and frightened. She bit her lip as dread rose to choke her. Could they edge so close to victory and still fail?

She sat up straight and uncurled fingers that had tightened into stiff claws in her skirt. She must be strong. For Matthew. For herself.

The carriage turned toward the gates and she braced herself for what was to come.

* * *

"Where did the bitch go?"

Matthew didn't bother lifting his head to answer his uncle. *I don't know* had worn down through repetition. He sagged in his shackles, resting the weight on his arms to ease his aching legs. He was tired, so tired.

Soon, they'd release him from the chains that bound him to the garden room wall. Only to tie him to the table where he could catch a few hours' sleep. The pattern had become horribly familiar since Grace's escape.

And she had escaped. His uncle still sought her but after all this time, Lord John must know she was long gone.

That thought alone sustained him. Somehow she'd eluded her pursuers. Even the legendary Bow Street Runners had admitted defeat. Thank Christ, once she'd got out, she'd realized Matthew was beyond help. He'd been sick with worry that she meant to mount some futile rescue attempt and willfully place herself within his uncle's reach.

"You're a fool, boy," Lord John said coldly from the armchair set before his chained captive. His voice was the sole thing in the room that was cold. Matthew wore only a shirt and light trousers. Still, he sweated profusely in the greenhouse atmosphere.

After four months, he should be inured to the stifling heat. But he lived for the hour in the morning and the hour in the afternoon when they let him exercise outside. That and three meal periods a day constituted his allotment of freedom. He cooperated to keep his strength up. In eight weeks and two days, his promise to Grace ended and he'd kill his uncle. What happened afterward, he didn't care.

"The slut has forgotten you, taken another lover." Lord John rested his hands on the top of his stick.

Matthew told himself that he hoped Grace had found someone else to care for. And knew himself a damned liar. Corrosive jealousy burned him at the idea of her in another man's arms, of another man touching that silken skin, bringing her to sobbing pleasure.

That other man was a lucky devil. To be free. Luckier still to be with Grace.

Matthew must have failed to hide his reaction. His uncle laughed low and salaciously and his fingers tightened over the smooth yellow knob. "She's a peach, isn't she? Sweet as honey. And quick to spread her legs."

Matthew didn't respond. The taunts were too familiar.

"When we find her, I'll try her myself before I give her to Monks and Filey. And my other men."

Matthew raised his head and glared at his uncle. If hatred could kill, Lord John would be in his grave instead of brushing an invisible fleck of dust from his heavy brown velvet coat sleeve.

His uncle still mused on what he intended to do to Grace. "Perhaps I'll let you watch. To revive fond memories. I might even permit you a slice before we finish her."

Sour loathing rose like vomit in Matthew's throat but he clenched hard against it. He must appear docile, beaten, or Lord John would never release him. And he must be free to kill.

From experience, Matthew knew this inquisition could continue for hours. His uncle called on the estate at erratic intervals to question him. Although he must by now admit nothing, not exhaustion, not pain, not anger, would make Matthew reveal what he knew.

"Of course, there is another way, nephew." His uncle checked his fingernails as if discussing the weather. "Tell me where she went and you'll have her back in your bed quick as a snap of your fingers."

"I don't know where she is," Matthew said in a voice rusty with disuse, although he knew it was fruitless to reiterate his ignorance.

He changed the angle of his body to ease the strain on his arms. His lank hair flopped around his face. For four months, his daily grooming routine had been restricted to a shave and a quick wash in a basin. He knew his uncle's strategy was to break his spirit, but that didn't make him any happier to know he looked the worst kind of ruffian. Since recovering his wits, he'd been fastidious about his appearance. Dressing like a gentleman had been a gesture of defiance against the shrieking specters of madness, captivity, and hopelessness.

"A pity we never found the cur," Lord John said negligently. "He would engage your cooperation, I have no doubt."

The mention of Wolfram stirred the rage that had roiled inside Matthew since that horrific afternoon. Matthew assumed he'd crawled into some hidden hollow to bleed to death from the bullet wound. It was better than Lord John torturing the hound to death, but not much. He tamped down his flaring temper and concentrated instead on the blazing ache in his shoulders.

Anger threatened his control and without control, he couldn't defeat his uncle. Now Grace was safe, his only remaining purpose was Lord John's downfall.

Without much interest, he heard movement in the hallway. His jailers must have finished checking the grounds as they did every night. He wondered with dull curiosity if his uncle would order them to beat him. Since Grace's escape, Lord John had only rarely subjected him to violence. But he sensed a frustration in his uncle tonight that could spill over into brutality.

Matthew didn't stir as the door opened, although the faint breath of air from outside fell on his sticky overheated skin like balm.

"Release that man immediately!"

Matthew's head jerked up in astonishment. *What the hell* . . .

What in God's name was happening? He shook his head to clear his vision. The sudden explosion of noise and color and movement after the quiet wretchedness of the last months left him disoriented.

He frowned and fought to make sense of this chaos.

Who were these strangers? What were they doing here? He didn't recognize the man who had spoken and who now placed himself in a position of authority at the center of the room.

But he was heartbreakingly familiar with the slender figure in dark green who jostled past the men pressing through the doorway and dashed to his side. Softness scented with sunshine and delicate flowery perfume suddenly supported his weight.

Grace. . .

Damn. Damn. Damn.

With appalled disbelief, he stared down at the masked lady whose arms encircled him. Her mouth trembled into a joyful smile. Under the mask, tears shone in her indigo eyes.

"You're alive. You're alive." She whispered the words like a prayer. She sounded so happy.

He wished to Hades he felt the same.

"What in Christ's name are you doing here?" he snarled in angry despair. How the hell could she put herself in danger like this? Had he endured four months of torment for nothing?

Her hold tightened. In spite of his anguished fury, her touch felt so good. Briefly he closed his eyes and struggled for control, although her nearness made control nigh impossible. Still he tried. He'd need all his wits to bring her out of this disaster.

Oh, Grace, why did you come back? Why did you risk everything? Why? Why? Why?

She pressed into his side and even through his anger, he felt life spark inside him for the first time since she'd gone. "I'm here to rescue you," she said softly. "Look."

Dazedly, he opened his eyes. All he could see was her beloved face, pale beneath the mask. He wrenched his attention from her to take in the room. The suddenly crowded room.

Against one wall, Monks and Filey stood in the custody of four brawny men armed with horse pistols. Monks was disheveled and shackled, and drying blood smeared his mouth. He'd clearly put up a fight. Filey must have been as spineless as usual because he wasn't chained like his crony. Four other men in livery ranged around the walls.

Now Matthew's bewilderment receded, he realized that the long-faced, gray-haired man who demanded his release was vaguely familiar. Next to him stood an equally authoritative-looking man who bore a strong resemblance to Grace. Two middle-aged men of great self-importance stood to one side. After eleven years of acquaintance with the breed, he had no trouble identifying them as doctors.

"Your Grace?" Lord John surged to his feet, shock eating into his usual sangfroid. "What is the meaning of this?"

"Unshackle Lord Sheene," the first man, apparently a duke, said.

Lord John's self-possession revived. "You have no rights here. Your Grace, Lord Wyndhurst, I protest this intrusion."

Matthew's bewilderment mounted. Why was the Earl of Wyndhurst here? Was he some relative of Grace's? Was the duke? She'd said she came from a wealthy family but these men were among the greatest in the land.

"Protest all you like." The duke made a lordly gesture toward the men who held Filey and Monks. "I said I wish this man released."

Filey drew out a key and shuffled toward Grace and Matthew. The stench of his sour breath and stale sweat briefly suffocated Matthew as the brute stretched up to unlock his irons. Grace huddled closer and he felt her tremble with anger or revulsion or fear. Probably all three. He couldn't read her expression under the damned mask.

None of this made sense. Why had these people come to his aid? He stifled a groan as blood rushed painfully back into his numbed arms. The piercing agony made him lightheaded and he swayed against Grace.

He felt stiff and ungainly after standing so long. Without his chains to hold him vertical, he was humiliated to discover his legs wouldn't support him. Grace staggered under his weight, then suddenly Wyndhurst shored up his other side.

"Courage, man," he muttered. "We'll see you safely out of this."

He'd never met the earl. He couldn't imagine what he'd done to deserve the almost affectionate encouragement. Nonetheless, he nodded and fought to regain his balance.

"Oh, Matthew," Grace said in a choked voice. "What have they done to you?"

"My lady, you promised silence," the duke said curtly.

Matthew watched delicate color wash over her face. The lush mouth he'd dreamed about for four long months flattened. He wanted to kiss her more than he wanted to take his next breath but their audience made that impossible.

Why must she be silent? Why was she masked? What were these men to her?

Surely she wasn't the duke's mistress. Call him a fool but he was convinced she still loved him. He heard it in her voice. He saw it in her eyes. He felt it in the hands she laid with such tender strength on his body.

"We need to examine the patient, Your Grace, my lord," one of the doctors said in an officious voice.

The earl helped Matthew to an upright position. At least this time his legs didn't buckle. He gingerly rolled his knotted shoulders and stretched his tingling arms as feeling and movement returned.

"The marquess is a raving madman," Lord John snapped.

The earl shot him a contemptuous glance and released Matthew. "Nonsense. I can already see he's as sane as I am."

"Wyndhurst, you're hardly qualified to judge," Lord John protested, his chin taking on a belligerent jut. "I insist this dangerous maniac is constrained."

"My lord, you may insist upon nothing," the unknown duke snapped, his tawny eyebrows drawing together in aristocratic displeasure. "I am here on the king's business. That business includes your arrest."

Lord John's response was no less haughty. "I find myself at a loss, sir. Upon what charges?"

"Abduction, deprivation of liberty, fraud, larceny, assault. I could continue."

"On the word of this slut?" Lord John was clearly in no doubt of Grace's identity, despite the mask. "I don't know how she enlisted such exalted interest in her lies but I stand prepared to prove my innocence. Should these absurd accusations ever reach a court of law. Which I doubt."

"This lady's testimony will not be required," the duke said coolly. "We have Dr. Granger and Dr. Boyd in custody. We have concrete proof of your dishonesty. We have Lord Sheene."

"A certified lunatic," Lord John snapped, although his complexion was waxy and the hands clasping his cane shone white-knuckled with tension. For the first time ever,

Matthew saw a line of sweat above his uncle's lip.

The duke remained unimpressed. "A man who suffered a fever in youth and who has been unjustly imprisoned ever since. These men are the king's doctors. They will provide a true diagnosis of his sanity. But like Lord Wyndhurst, I see no evidence of madness. Although I see much evidence of crime."

"There is no crime, damn you! I've been a good and watchful guardian over my poor deranged nephew."

Matthew was steadier on his feet but he kept his arm firmly around Grace. Who knew when she might be ripped away from him? These men offered the astonishing promise of liberty but he couldn't yet trust they'd prevail.

He straightened and squared his shoulders. It was time he became more than a spectator. "I'm not mad and you know it, Uncle." Matthew's tone was caustic. "You've been a grasping and self-aggrandizing guardian to the Lansdowne fortune, more like."

"Don't fight a hopeless battle, Lord John," the duke said in a persuasive tone. "Come quietly for the sake of your family. Believe me when I say the game's well and truly up. I offer you my word I'll do my best to help your wife and your girls if you give yourself into custody."

"Damn you, I will not be tried as a common felon." Lord John's cheeks were bloodless now and his hands trembled so violently that the amber-topped stick clattered to the ground.

The duke studied the cane as it rolled across the flagged floor, then smiled at Lord John with a hint of pity. "Yes, you will. Because you are a common felon."

"I'll see you in hell first." Still facing the duke, he backed toward Matthew. He fumbled at his pocket and pulled out a beautiful little pistol with a pearl handle.

With rough urgency, Matthew shoved Grace behind him although his uncle wasn't aiming in her direction.

Over Lord John's shoulder, he noticed the armed escort was ready to intervene. The men had the bearing of trained soldiers and were obviously used to dealing with trouble. But in this small space, violence could spiral out of control and in the fracas, Grace might be hurt.

"You can't win, Lansdowne. You must know that," the duke said calmly without shifting.

"I can win! I've always won!" Wildly, he lunged toward Matthew. "I should have been Marquess of Sheene, not you, you rotting stump of useless lunacy!"

No trace of the assured tyrant remained in this shaking, desperate man. The conscienceless beast who had always inhabited his uncle's body under the social polish was at last naked to the world. Spittle marked his lips and spattered Matthew. Without shifting his eyes from the gun, Matthew wiped one hand across his face.

The scent of impending bloodshed sharpened the atmosphere. Matthew heard Grace's low sound of distress and his protective grip on her tightened.

"Put down your weapon!" the duke barked.

"For pity's sake, Lansdowne!" Lord Wyndhurst approached Lord John, keeping a careful eye on the pistol. "This has gone far enough!"

"Be careful!" Grace cried out, lurching forward. "Be careful!"

Matthew thrust her out of the way. "Uncle, it's over," he said quietly, trying to stem the building crisis. "What use to cause further pain? Think of your daughters. Your wife."

Lord John cocked the pistol, the sound echoing eerily in the quiet room, and waved it in the air. "Don't preach and prate, nephew. You've always been a bloody parson at heart. What do you know about what a real man wants?"

Matthew ignored the jibe, as he'd ignored so many of

his uncle's jibes. He kept his voice steady, reassuring, as if he spoke to an injured animal. "I know a real man doesn't destroy his family just to save his vanity, Uncle. A real man accepts the consequences of his actions. You reached high and came to disaster. There's no one else to blame."

His uncle sneered even as the gun swung in Matthew's direction. "For God's sake, spare me the lecture, you self-righteous worm. You think you've defeated me. You haven't. Nobody bests John Lansdowne. My one regret is I didn't fuck the bitch then kill her when I had the chance.'"

Quickly, before anyone could stop him, he raised the gun to his temple and fired. The report resounded around the closed room. A dull thud followed as his body hit the floor.

Behind Matthew, Grace inhaled on a shocked gasp. He felt her hide her face in his back. Nobody else moved as the hot tang of gunpowder and the metallic stench of blood mingled in the stuffy room. The bluster of Lord John's final words jangled like untuned bells in the close air.

The man who had tormented Matthew for eleven years was dead. He should feel triumphant. He felt nothing. Numbly, he stared at the still figure lying in its expanding pool of blood.

"Good God," Lord Wyndhurst said eventually.

The doctor who hadn't spoken knelt at Lord John's side. He raised his head and said, "He's dead."

"A coward to the end," Grace said shakily. She broke free of Matthew's hold and stepped toward Lord Wyndhurst. "My lord, are you all right?"

Matthew immediately missed her warmth. The absence reminded him too vividly of her absence during these long lonely months. Longingly, he gazed after her.

His distraction lasted a fatal moment too long. Monks broke free of his captors and sprang forward.

"Matthew!" she screamed. She whirled back toward him. He dived to drag her to safety.

Too late.

Monks flung his beefy arms over her head. The chain of his shackles tightened brutally around Grace's slender neck.

Chapter 28

"I'll break her neck easy as I'd wring a hen's," Monks snarled, jerking the chain to wrench Grace closer. Her terrified eyes sought Matthew's, silently pleading for help.

Matthew felt like someone had punched him in the gut. Cold creeping fear turned his blood to ice. How the hell had he allowed this to happen? He should have foreseen that his jailers would snatch any chance to escape justice. What in heaven's name had possessed Grace to come here tonight? He cursed her gallant soul, even while his heart filled with overwhelming love. And dread.

"Don't mistake that he means it," he snapped, gesturing everyone else in the room back. One false move and Grace would be dead.

He assessed Monks for signs of weakness and as so often before, found none. He balled his fists against his sides as he fought the urge to fling himself on the brute and strangle him with his bare hands.

"Stay where you are," the duke said to his men who surrounded the room.

"Aye, that's right canny." Roughly, Monks tugged Grace around so his back was to the French doors and she faced the room like a living shield. "Nobody follows."

"What about the lady?" the duke asked.

Monks laughed unpleasantly and Matthew saw Grace shudder at the sound. Her face was pallid with terror.

Monks sneered. "She's no lady. She's a poxy whore."

"No!" Grace gasped.

"Button your lip, slut!" Monks grunted and tightened the chain so she coughed against the pressure. He glared at the duke. "Do nowt to stop me getting away and I'll let the lass go."

That was a lie. Monks was in a towering fury and he'd vent that anger on Grace when he had her to himself. If he was caught, a hanging already awaited. What difference another murder?

Against every instinct he possessed, Matthew steeled himself to say what he must. "Release the girl and you have my word as Marquess of Sheene that you may leave unhindered."

He ignored the duke's movement of protest. Grace's life was more important than revenge or punishment.

Monks edged toward the doors, forcing Grace into a stumbling backward walk. "Eh, and pigs might fly. I'm not daft. Happen I'm summat better off keeping the lass as a bargaining piece, your lordship. Collect her at the gate in half an hour."

Collect her dead, Matthew knew.

If his beloved were dead, what use was freedom?

This had gone on long enough. He turned and seized a pistol from the nearest of the duke's men.

"Let her go, Monks." His voice rang in the silent room. Silent except for the uneven gasps of Grace's breathing against the chain.

"You'll not risk shooting the lass," Monks sniggered.

"I won't shoot her." With a surprisingly steady hand, Matthew cocked the gun and aimed between Monks's eyes.

"Don't be a blasted fool, man!" Lord Wyndhurst whirled toward him. "You'll hit her!"

The cool weight of the gun was familiar, even after all these years without touching a weapon. In his boyhood, he'd shown blazing talent as a marksman and had promised to become a crack shot. He hoped to hell his hours of pitching rocks at trees had kept his eye in. It seemed a fragile basis for confidence but as he leveled the pistol, he had no doubt he could do this.

He loved Grace too much to fail.

"Matthew, please," Grace begged brokenly then fell silent as Monks twisted the chain. The harsh metal links rubbed the skin on her neck raw, Matthew noted with grim anger. Monks would pay for that. And so much else.

"Stay absolutely still," he said softly to Grace. If she made a sudden movement or jerked Monks out of position, the bullet could go wild.

The lout towered above her, presenting an easier target than he realized. Strangely, everything in the room was uncannily clear as if illuminated by bright light. Matthew took a deep breath and said a silent prayer.

"You're right full of hot air, my fine lordship," Monks scoffed. "You'd no more have the gumption to shoot me than you would to swim to America."

Matthew leveled the pistol. "I've always enjoyed swimming, Monks."

Without hesitation, he pulled the trigger. The bullet entered squarely between Monks's thick eyebrows. The mud-colored eyes widened with shock. Then glazed in swift death.

Monks tumbled to the floor without a word, taking Grace down with him. She screamed as she fell, a jagged high-pitched shriek of terror. The sound broke the odd paralysis that gripped everyone in the room.

Wyndhurst burst into movement and rushed over to disentangle her. "Are you unharmed, child?"

"Yes. Yes, I am," she said shakily. At the admission, some of the painful tension drained from Matthew's shoulders.

"Bugger me," Filey gasped, staring in open-mouthed surprise at Matthew. "I seen nowt like it."

Matthew's heartbeat quieted as his agonizing fear for Grace receded. Thank God his father had taken the time to teach him to shoot like a sniper. Thank God he'd kept up his target practice with whatever lay to hand in his prison.

Slowly, his arm lowered until the pistol dangled at his side.

He'd never killed anyone before. He'd imagined the act would be harder, more emotional. But he looked across at Monks's motionless body and felt only a vague satisfaction.

His eyes slid over Lord John's body. Then as he always would, he looked up and sought Grace. Drawn and shaken, she huddled in the Earl of Wyndhurst's arms. Once more, her strong resemblance to the older man struck him.

Why did she turn to someone else for comfort? Couldn't she see that Matthew starved for her merest touch? She must know how he longed to hold her.

"Egad, Sheene, that's the best damned shooting I've ever seen!" the duke said. "I take my hat off to you."

"I couldn't let him harm her," Matthew said in a flat voice. Jesus, he *felt* flat.

With a deliberate movement, he set the gun down on the table to which he'd been bound so often. It gradually seeped into his mind that nobody would restrain him again. The thought seemed distant, unimportant, as though it applied to someone else.

Lord John was dead. Monks was dead. Filey would face

justice. Matthew should be shouting to the skies.

When he'd imagined his release, he'd pictured himself incandescent with joy. But his emotions felt frozen.

"Remove this rogue. The law will deal with him," the duke told the men who held Filey.

"I were but Lord John's servant, Your Grace. I did nowt but what I were told," Filey said in his cringing way. He wasn't wasting any grief on his employer or his long-term colleague, Matthew noted sardonically.

"That's not true. He's guilty and I will see he's punished." Matthew had promised himself he'd kill this brute. Now his taste for spilling blood had faded. As far as he was concerned, the courts could decide Filey's fate. If the evidence against Lord John was as convincing as the duke claimed, Filey would hang.

He hardly cared. All that mattered was Grace. He fought the urge to rip her from the earl's grasp.

After the armed men hauled Filey away, the duke glanced around the room with displeasure. "I can hardly breathe. Newby, open the windows. Fenwick, find some clothing for Lord Sheene. He can't appear at Windsor in his shirtsleeves. He can wash and shave when we change horses."

Windsor? What was this? "Your Grace, what are your plans?"

The duke glanced at Matthew then over to where Grace huddled in the Earl of Wyndhurst's arms. "I'll explain on the road. Time is of the essence. His Majesty awaits. Jones and Perrett, remove the bodies. It's a confounded charnel house. Then I require privacy with Lord Sheene, Lord Wyndhurst, and this lady."

The servants cleared the room. Cool air rushed in and teased at the edges of Matthew's strange detachment. He struggled to accept the startling truth that he was free. His enemies were routed. His nightmare was over.

When they were alone at last, he extended his hand to the duke. "Sir, I thank you for your intervention. May I know to whom I owe my gratitude?"

"Of course," the duke said, shaking Matthew's hand with hearty strength.

"Lord Sheene." Grace stepped away from the earl and toward him. Still not close enough to touch, though, damn it.

The formality of address struck him as discordant even while her husky voice fell on his yearning soul like balm on a wound. He supposed like her mask, her use of his title was designed to preserve her reputation.

No, that couldn't be right. The men present must know who she was.

Bafflement surged anew. What game was she playing? He forced himself to concentrate on what she said even though his deepest instinct was to snatch her up and kiss her until she stopped treating him like a distant acquaintance.

Her mouth turned up in a faint smile as she gestured to the duke. "Allow me to introduce my godfather, the Duke of Kermonde."

Her godfather? His father's old friend Kermonde? He'd had no idea her connections stretched so high.

Grace turned to the other man. "And my father, the Earl of Wyndhurst."

Astonishment held Matthew silent. In a night of surprises, this was perhaps the greatest. His indigent widow belonged to one of the grandest families in England. He could barely believe it. Even while he managed a creditable bow, he struggled to make sense of everything. His muscles, still stiff from his long captivity, protested the movement but he ignored the twinge of discomfort. "Your Grace. My lord."

"Are you hurt, Sheene?" Kermonde clapped him on the back and he almost groaned. "No need to test your sanity.

Any man who shoots like that doesn't have bees in his brain box. We have doctors here if you want them. They can poke and pry at you in the carriage if you feel need of their services."

Doctors? He didn't want doctors. He wanted Grace. Grace who already glided away to take her father's arm. Grace who he noticed was dressed in the height of fashion. Grace who had touched him briefly when he was in chains, but who now left him bereft.

He didn't understand. He was free. She was here. Why the hell wasn't she in his arms? "Grace?" he asked dazedly.

But it was Kermonde who spoke. "You must see Lady Grace cannot stay. The risk of scandal is too great if her link to this matter becomes public."

She paused at her father's side and tilted her head toward Matthew. The blasted mask still hid her expression. A sullen trickle of blood seeped from the wound at her throat, reminding him how close he'd come to losing her.

So why did he feel like he was losing her now?

"Goodbye, Lord Sheene," she said huskily.

Goodbye? What bloody nonsense was this? "Christ, Grace! You can't go! Not like this!"

She turned away. "I must. I came to free you, my lord, and to see justice done. Now all matters between us are at an end. I wish you every happiness."

"Grace, no!" He staggered forward, reaching for her even as she moved with her father toward the door. "Wait! What in God's name are you doing?"

She looked back and the full lips he'd kissed so often curved in a sad smile. "I'm returning you to the world, my lord. A world I can never share."

"That's not true! What do I want with freedom if you're not there to share it?" She plunged a knife into his vitals then twisted it.

She shook her head in wordless denial. She trembled.

He couldn't doubt she suffered. But why was she doing this?

Her voice broke. "Don't, I beg you. Matthew, don't make this worse than it is already. I knew from the moment I met you that anything more between us was impossible. Please . . . just let me go." She bent her head and let her father lead her from the room.

"Grace! Grace, stop!" Matthew called, but she didn't pause.

This couldn't be happening. He wouldn't let it happen. He forced his leaden feet into clumsy pursuit.

Kermonde grabbed him before he'd taken more than a step. "Let her go. This isn't the time."

It mightn't be the time but it might be his only time. He shook off Kermonde's restraining hand and set out after her.

Grace was pathetically grateful she had her father's arm to cling to as she stepped into the night. Her terror when Monks had grabbed her still crashed through her blood like thunder and her legs felt as though they'd crumple. Her mind replayed that horrific moment when he'd jerked her into his massive chest and scraped the chain across her neck.

She barely credited Matthew's astounding feat of marksmanship. Then had followed the nightmare instant when Monks's lumbering body had dragged her down with him.

Death's cold bony fingers had brushed her tonight. Monks had meant to kill her. His murderous rage had been palpable.

But worse by far than Monks's attack had been telling Matthew goodbye.

She'd seen him for the last time. As she'd promised herself four long months ago, she'd liberated him from his uncle. Now she'd liberated him from her.

She couldn't bear it.

Tears stung her eyes, dampened the horrible mask. She stumbled blindly, hardly aware where she went. Hardly caring. Without Matthew, there was nowhere she wanted to go.

"It's all been too much for you, Grace." Her father frowned with concern as her step faltered again. "Kermonde was right. You shouldn't have come."

"I had to be here," she said in a muffled voice. She swallowed to ease the lump of misery that choked her and winced at the pain in her bruised throat.

"Grace, wait!" she heard Matthew shout from the house.

Her stomach cramped with wretchedness. Matthew was a fighter. He'd doggedly fought for his sanity and his freedom and his pride through the last eleven years. Misguided as the attempt was, he'd fight for her.

Of course he wouldn't just farewell her with an acquiescent nod of his dark head. Although it would be kinder to both of them if he did.

"Take me home, Papa," she said brokenly.

What a coward she was to hope she could rush away before she had to confront Matthew. She couldn't summon courage to stay and endure his pain. She rejected him for his sake but he wouldn't understand that until he'd tasted the world he'd never known.

"Just a word, Grace," Matthew said with a bark of command from behind her. She'd forgotten how quickly and how quietly he could move. His hold was implacable as it closed on her upper arm. He swung her around to face him. "Surely you can spare me that much."

Yes, surely she could. She bit her lip and reluctantly lifted her head until she met his eyes. Her father released her and stepped away.

The open doorway and the carriage lamps allowed her

to read the fury and incomprehension in Matthew's face. His beloved face. Hungrily her gaze traveled over his features, testing the changes four months had made. His disheveled hair was long enough to touch his shoulders and he needed a shave. His cheekbones stood out prominently and there were deep hollows above the sharp angles of his jaw.

"Lord Sheene . . ." she began, then glanced away because she couldn't bear to witness the misery underlying his rage.

"Be damned to that! You know my name," he growled, hauling her away from her father.

"I'll wait in the coach," the earl said.

"Father!" she called helplessly. How could he abandon her when she needed him most? For once, she wanted him to play the despot, order her off this estate with its memories of death and pain and captivity.

And love. Always love.

"Come when you're ready." Her father shuffled toward the line of carriages where armed men waited with the shackled and cowed Filey.

"There's no point to this," Grace said in despair.

"Well, there's something we don't agree on," Matthew said grimly. He ignored her resistance and dragged her around the side of the cottage until they had privacy. They were directly outside the garden room. Lamps within shed enough light for her to see his impatience. Not that she needed to see it. It was vividly apparent in his voice and in the hold he kept on her arm.

"What the hell is this about?" he snapped.

She wrenched away with a shaky jerk. "You haven't got time. You've got to go with Kermonde. The king commands your presence."

"Damn the king. He's waited eleven years for the pleasure of my company. He'll wait another half hour. Why are you running away?"

"My father . . ."

"Will wait too." The awful night became even worse as he encircled her with his arms and hurt confusion softened his tone. "Grace, aren't you happy to see me?"

"Of course I am," she admitted before she could stop herself. For one blissful second, she leaned her head on his chest. Under the stained linen of his shirt, she heard the race of his heart. How she'd craved his touch. His rich scent filled her head with poignant memories.

No. She couldn't afford to weaken.

"Let me go, Matthew." She tried to sound firm, resolute, determined, but her words emerged as a choked whisper.

"It's been an eternity. I want to hold you. Grace, let me hold you." His voice was velvety with yearning. Every hair on her body prickled as that seductive tone brushed across her skin, lured her to surrender.

"I . . . can't," she said through dry lips. This was like having her skin scraped off. She couldn't take much more. With a muffled sob, she struggled out of his arms.

At first, she thought he wouldn't let her go, then he lifted his hands with an ironic gesture. The eyes that had haunted her for four endless months were opaque as polished golden glass. He studied her as if he read her every secret. He probably did. In their short time together, he'd come to know her so well.

When he spoke, his voice was level. "Won't you take off the mask? I've only had dreams to keep me company. I want to see your face."

"The servants," she said huskily. If she took off the mask, he'd know how she cried.

"As you wish." He smiled at her, the sweet, tender smile that was manna to her soul. His voice gentled and he took her gloved hand in his. The warmth of his touch through the soft kidskin was a piercing reminder of all she sacrificed.

She should pull away but nothing could make her surrender this one last contact. "Kermonde is under royal decree to bring you directly to Windsor."

"Very well." Matthew's jaw took on a determined line. He'd worn the same expression when he told her she had to escape. "It's not how I wanted to do this. But then, I never thought my chance would come."

"Chance?"

To her horror, he fell to his knees, still clinging to her hand. "Grace Paget, will you grant me the transcendent joy of agreeing to become my wife?"

Everything she wanted. Everything principle insisted she couldn't accept.

Oh, Matthew, Matthew, don't do this!

With a savage movement, she tore herself away. She stopped a few feet from him. "I can't marry you, Matthew," she said rawly, wringing her hands in wild distress. "It wouldn't be fair."

He frowned as he absorbed her refusal. "Are you afraid of my madness?"

"No! No, never think that," she said frantically. How could he imagine that was why she denied him? "You're not mad. You were sick. Now you're cured."

With a slight stagger, he rose to his feet. He was even thinner than he'd been when she first saw him. Knowing his uncle, she guessed Matthew had been chained since she left. He needed rest and sustenance and a chance at happiness, not this fraught encounter with a former lover.

Automatically she reached to help him but he drew apart with a trace of hauteur. "You told me you loved me. Was that a lie?" Then the brief coolness evaporated and his voice cracked. "Have your feelings changed, Grace?

Because as God is my witness, mine haven't. I love you. I will always love you."

"*Stop!* For pity's sake, stop!" she cried out, lifting one shaking hand in his direction to keep him away, although he hadn't touched her. She saw so clearly that they had no future together. Why couldn't he see it?

He looked even more bewildered. Her chest constricted with guilty anguish. This should be the most joyous day of his life and she ruined it. Her father was right. She shouldn't have come here. It was cruel and self-indulgent.

"Do you love me, Grace?" he asked with the stark honesty that always reached right to her marrow.

She wrapped her arms around herself to stop her convulsive trembling. She'd known this time had to come, she'd known from the first time she kissed him. But the reality was so much more painful than her painful imaginings.

"Grace?"

He wasn't hiding behind pride. She owed him equal honesty. "Yes, I do love you." Perhaps she was unwise to tell him but she couldn't lie.

"Then why?"

Kermonde rounded the corner of the house and stopped as he observed Grace and the marquess together. "Sheene, I can delay no longer. His Majesty awaits."

Matthew didn't shift his gaze from her face as he replied. "A minute's patience, sir."

In other circumstances, Grace would have laughed at the well-bred surprise on Kermonde's face. Dukes weren't used to people telling them to hold their peace.

"A minute then." It was clear Kermonde meant sixty seconds precisely. At least he moved far enough off to give them an illusion of solitude although not far enough to let them think he meant to wait much longer.

Matthew's eyes were unwavering. "Tell me, Grace."

She sucked in a shaky breath. She was right about this.

She knew she was right about this. He was so intelligent, surely she could make him understand too.

"You haven't seen anything of the world. You think you love me but . . ." She lowered her voice so the duke wouldn't hear. "I'm the first woman you've bedded. I'm almost the only woman you've seen in eleven years. Anyone would mistake the significance of his feelings. You want to make promises. You're a decent man. But when you resume your rightful position, you'll regret any commitment. You'll regret it even more when you fall in love with the woman fit to stand at your side."

He was genuinely angry now. "Unlike the Earl of Wyndhurst's daughter."

She flinched at his sarcasm then lifted her chin and faced him down. "Unlike the poor widow Grace Paget who was your mistress."

He drew himself up and spoke in a low growl. "So you think I'm too stupid to know what I feel and too weak to keep any vows."

"No, never that. But what we shared was part of your captivity. It's time to start life as a free man. I can have no role in that life."

"You are that life," he said with a snap.

"Lord Sheene," Kermonde called. "I insist we leave."

"Are you coming?" Matthew extended his arm as he'd extended it so often when she'd shared his imprisonment.

She shook her head. "I promised my father there would be no scandal. For his sake, no hint must emerge that you and I have been lovers. You go with Kermonde and I go home to Marlow Hall in Yorkshire."

"Then I'll come to you after I've met the king."

"No. You have to stay in London and prove your sanity publicly. You have to take your place as Marquess of Sheene. You must make it clear there's no taint of madness." Then the harshest words of all. And still harsher because they were true. "It's over, Matthew. There is nothing more between us. We part here and now."

Still he refused to surrender. She'd been right to call him a fighter. "That's not good enough."

"Lord Sheene!" Kermonde's tone was peremptory.

"I'm coming." But he didn't move. Instead, he reached out to take Grace's hand again. She knew she should pull away but she couldn't. If he kissed her, she'd shatter into a thousand pieces. But he merely looked at her with his familiar grave attention. He spoke very slowly. "If I prove my worthiness over a year, will you believe in my steadfastness?"

"A year?" She hadn't expected to haggle. She wasn't sure what she had expected. He'd never been likely to say yes and go meekly away.

"Yes, a year," he said curtly. "Will that convince you?"

"You've already given up so much of your life," she stammered. "Don't waste another year on a futile bargain."

"You're the one setting conditions, Grace. I'll marry you tomorrow and let the rest be damned. I have no doubts, as long as you love me."

Outwardly he was calm but she knew he hid a titanic storm of emotions. How could he not after tonight? His sudden release. His uncle's death. The shooting of Monks. Now this clash with her. He'd been through so much. Too much.

"Sheene!" Kermonde said sharply. Clearly ducal tolerance had reached an end.

Matthew didn't even blink. "Grace?"

He had to go. Powerful men worked on his behalf. She couldn't allow him to jeopardize that. She gave a jerky little nod. "If you feel the same in a year, ask me again. Don't consider yourself bound. I told you, Matthew—you're free. Of your uncle. Of your bondage. Of me. If you think of me with occasional gratitude, that's all I ask."

A pathetic lie. And one she could see he didn't for a moment believe.

"A year then." He spoke as if he closed a financial transaction.

"There can be no contact between us." While she died slowly of loneliness and he discovered he wanted a world that contained no trace of Grace Paget. The inevitability made her belly twist with anguish.

"Agreed." His voice was clipped. "I won't write or try to see you. You have twelve months to mourn Josiah and decide what you want. You have your bargain. But never imagine for an instant that this is ended. You and I have unfinished business, Grace."

With focused ruthlessness, he lifted her hand and quickly stripped away the glove. She should protest. This moment would just become a bitter memory to taunt her.

When he bent over her hand, his long hair fell forward to hide his face. He pressed his lips to her bare palm and she couldn't stifle a sigh of pleasure. Impossible not to remember nights when he'd kissed each inch of her. Every cell of her skin remembered his possession. Every cell of her skin longed for him to take her again. But it could never be.

Tears blurred her last image of him as he lifted his head and stepped back with a formal bow. How she loved him. She would never love another.

He turned away and at last strode across to Kermonde. He held himself straight and moved with an unhindered confidence she'd never seen in him before. This was a man ready to embrace his challenges. Embrace and conquer.

Only when Kermonde's carriage left in a clatter of hooves and wild cracks of the whip did she realize he'd taken her glove with him.

Chapter 29

A pool of afternoon sunlight warmed Grace on the cushioned window seat inside Marlow Hall's Chinese summerhouse.

She stirred from her troubled doze. She'd dreamed. The dream that still visited with heartbreaking frequency although almost a year had passed since she'd seen Matthew. The dream where his long, powerful body drove into hers, where his arms lashed her close, where his deep voice whispered love.

She whimpered. Her cheeks were sticky with tears. How she hated to wake to a cruel present and the desolation that ran beneath her new life. The grief never faded. Slowly, reluctantly, she opened her eyes.

Matthew stood between the open red lacquer doors at the top of the summerhouse steps. Under one arm, he carried a slim mahogany box.

She exhaled on a soft startled gasp. Graphic, carnal images from her dream flashed behind her eyes and sent heat rushing to her face.

His intent, unblinking stare didn't shift from her. How long had he watched?

His physical impact was astonishing. In their year apart, she'd forgotten quite how handsome he was. A slight breeze ruffled his thick dark hair, now cut in a fashionable style. With a pang, she remembered his wild black locks drifting like warm silk across her wrist while he'd kissed her hand in farewell. She couldn't imagine this dauntingly elegant man clutching her with such desperation. She couldn't imagine him clutching her at all.

After months of thinking of him, dreaming of him, longing for him, now that he was here, he seemed a stranger.

Awkwardly, she sat up. She felt ill at ease, at a disadvantage, sluggish with sleep. She swiped a shaking hand across her cheeks to hide her humiliating tears. She forced her lips into an uncertain smile of greeting.

"Matthew . . ."

Why did he have to find her like this? Unprepared. Vulnerable. Yearning.

Taloned dragons carved into each door reared up like heraldic bearers to frame him. But Matthew was the one who looked ready to breathe fire. His face was hard and expressionless and his eyes were dark as burned toffee. A line of color marked his cheekbones and his body vibrated tension.

He didn't return her smile. Foreboding shivered through her. What on earth was wrong? He looked angry. Aggressive. And utterly in command.

"Matthew?" she said even more tentatively. Her smile faltered and faded. "What are you doing here?"

He didn't act like a man on the verge of a marriage proposal. *Of course he didn't.* She was a fool to imagine he still wanted her. He'd had a year to discover that Grace Paget's charms were tawdry currency.

Had he come to tell her he'd formed another attachment? If so, she owed him a calm reception and a generous farewell. Even while her heart shattered into a thousand jagged shards.

She'd braced herself for this, known it must come. But

nothing primed her for the chill that crept through her blood as though she died from the inside out.

She'd avidly followed his progress in the newspapers and from letters her mother received from the London friends with whom she'd recently resumed correspondence. Ever since Matthew's triumphant return to society, rumors had flown of his engagement to any number of well-bred beauties.

He must have finally made his choice. What other reason could bring him here in such obvious disquiet?

Oh, lucky, lucky girl. Grace couldn't stifle a surge of bitter envy as she thought of the unknown woman Matthew decided to make his marchioness.

She raised her chin and met his eyes squarely. Dear God, let him say it fast and put her out of her misery.

For a taut instant, they stared at each other like combatants.

"Grace."

He drew out the word so it became a long, deep, guttural growl. A sound as primitive as a lion's roar for its mate. Her skin prickled with animal awareness and the breath caught in her throat. Every drop of moisture evaporated from her mouth. Low in her belly, blood began to beat slow and hard with anticipation.

Her face must have betrayed her unfurling arousal. Or perhaps, like her, he reacted to the sudden charge in the air, as electric as the pause before a lightning strike.

Still without shifting his fierce focus, he set down the box he carried. Then he reached to close the doors and slide the bolt across.

Any doubt as to his purpose fled. A delicious thrill rippled through her. The summerhouse was raised on a platform so the windows opened above eye height. With the doors locked, it was a bower designed for private sin.

Sin was clearly his aim.

Now she looked more closely, she realized it wasn't anger that tightened the skin over the bones of his face. It was incendiary hunger.

She should protest. Question. Demand he tell her why he was here. But overwhelming need kept her silent and pinned to the window seat.

Her pulse pitched into a drunken race as she watched him lift his hands to untie his neckcloth. Carelessly, he discarded the length of linen. The soft drift of the white strip to the parquetry floor made her shift restively on the silk cushions. She was already ripe for him. Her sensual dream had left her moist and ready. A year's frustrated desire crawled through her veins.

The angles of his face sharpened. His glance flickered to where her thighs clenched together under her pale blue muslin skirts, twisted revealingly tight after her disturbed sleep. Molten gold flared between his luxuriant black eyelashes.

Oh, yes, she knew that look. She knew what that look promised.

Delight. Surrender. *Love?*

With a smooth movement that stirred her volatile senses, he shrugged out of his beautiful dark blue coat and flung it down near his crumpled neckcloth. All the time, his eyes seared her with such heat, she felt greedy flames licking at her skin. She shivered with another surge of wicked excitement.

He now wore only a cream brocade waistcoat, a fine white shirt, and buff breeches tucked into high black boots. Now he'd discarded his coat, she could see he'd filled out during the year. For the first time he didn't seem too thin for his height, although he'd always be a lean streak of a man.

Her eyes traveled over his broad shoulders, across his powerful chest and down to his narrow hips. Her already heated cheeks burned as her attention finally settled on the bulge in his breeches.

No question he wanted her.

Her head jerked up as he muffled a groan. Her wanton focus on where his sex swelled and hardened had broken some barrier in him. Swifter than a hunting lion, he crossed the polished floor, casting off his waistcoat on the way.

Keeping one foot on the floor, he rested a bent knee on the garish gold cushions patterned with willow trees and scarlet peonies. This close, his radiating heat lured her. The hoarse susurration of his breath was harsh in her ears. His face was stark with longing. He looked like a man at the end of his endurance.

She didn't know who reached out first but in an instant, she was in his arms. Shamelessly she rose on her knees to press herself against him. For a fraught moment, he stared down into her face as if it offered the answer to every question. Then his mouth crashed onto hers. She tasted passion and hunger and power. His arms crushed her as the blazing open-mouthed kiss sent her spinning into dazzling passion.

He tasted wonderful, nourishment for her soul. She'd pined for this for a year. Frantically, she arched up. She only lived when he was near. Without him, her world was gray, cold oblivion.

She curled her tongue around his in ardent welcome. His teeth scraped over her lips. His breath filled her lungs. She lost herself in his savage heat. This was more war than seduction. She didn't care. He touched her. She wanted nothing else.

"Christ, I've missed you," he grated out, lifting his head and staring at her out of glazed eyes.

"And I've missed you. So much."

He pressed his mouth to hers again. Eager. Ruthless. He shook with unfettered desperation. She ran her hands up his flanks, feeling the shirt bunch under her touch. Beneath the material, the muscles of his back flexed as he kissed her face, her eyes, her neck in a fever of caresses. Soon, soon, he'd slide her skirts up and part her legs and take her. She couldn't wait.

She shivered with delight as he nipped at her throat. She made a low sound and rubbed herself against his erection. He seemed larger, hotter, more powerful than ever.

His hand slid across the slope of her chest, tormenting her with its slow progress. The delay built her need until she trembled with sensual anticipation. He teased the embroidered edge of her bodice. Then he slipped under the loose curve of the neckline to palm one nipple. The crest immediately tightened.

She hissed with pleasure as he rolled the nub in his fingers, pulled it, squeezed it. Each touch sent a spike of arousal to her loins. By the time his attention moved to her other breast, she writhed on the silk like a trapped animal.

Leaning over her, he parted her thighs with his knees. His arms supported his weight, encasing her in a space of his making. He was close enough for her to see the wild gold kaleidoscope of his eyes.

Familiar scents of lemon and Matthew surrounded her, made her dizzy with desire. Then she was dizzy indeed as he tumbled her back against the slippery cushions and came down between her legs.

He shoved her skirts to her waist and placed his hand firmly on her center. She bucked under the pressure, flooding with heat and moisture. Within seconds, her drawers were on the ground. Shaking with urgency, he released himself from his breeches.

He was seconds away from taking her. In her father's

summerhouse. The reality of who she was and where she was squeaked vaguely from the back of her passion-soaked mind.

"We shouldn't," she forced out, even while she raised her knees to bring him closer to where she wanted him.

"We should," he said gruffly. He braced his arms on either side of her. "I've locked the door. Nobody can see us."

Then even such few words as those deserted them when he nudged her entrance. For a delicious second, her passage resisted his intrusion. She was slick with arousal but it had been over a year since she'd taken a man into her body and her intimate muscles defied the incursion. He pushed again with a confidence that took her breath away, flexed his hips, and settled into her full length.

She gasped at the joining, so much richer and more intense than her vivid lonely dreams. He groaned her name and buried his head in her shoulder.

Her body took time to adjust to his size and weight after so long without him. He stretched her inner passage and her muscles clenched around him.

Tears sprang to her eyes at the incredible feeling. He was hers again. Even if just for now.

Tentatively, she reached up to stroke his damp hair, pressing his face closer. All the love she didn't dare speak invested her touch.

Oh, Matthew, never leave me. I love you.

She bit back the pathetic cry before it escaped.

The sweet stasis couldn't endure. His back tightened, then he began to move deeply, surely, possessively. She moaned and lifted herself to meet him as the glorious rhythm reigned.

She was so ready, the friction quickly pushed her over the edge. Without warning, her body convulsed on a sun-bright peak. For a small eternity, rapture blasted her, turned the air around her incandescent with pleasure.

She tasted the salt of her tears on her lips. Aftershocks still quivered through her. Tenderly, she ran her hands down his lean hips to knead his firm buttocks. Part of her clung to the ecstasy even as the blaze subsided to a gentle glow.

The physical delight hadn't faded. If anything, it was sharper, deeper, more profound. Matured through suffering and loss and deprivation.

She expected him to finish but he wasn't satisfied yet. Implacably, he tilted her hips and continued to ravish her. Shocked, she realized he hadn't found release in that shivering culmination. She'd been too lost in her own pleasure to register his responses.

Before her last climax subsided, another more shattering crisis ripped through her. She raised her hand to her mouth and bit down hard to muffle a scream. Uncontrollable ecstasy gripped her in claws of flame. It was as though the dragons on the doors had breathed their fire into her lover.

Still he didn't relent. Almost roughly, he reached down to stroke the swollen folds between her legs and this time she did scream. She arched up to kiss him using teeth and tongue. Her touch held no tenderness. Although in her heart, she felt an endless lake of tenderness for this man she loved so dearly.

Another wave hit her and she shuddered, blind with the violent onslaught of sensation. Time itself was suspended as she lost herself in ultimate pleasure.

Matthew groaned from deep in his throat as he at last gave himself up. While liquid heat spilled into her womb, she clutched his shaking body.

Slowly, inevitably, she made the dazzling descent from heaven. She closed her eyes and let pleasure ebb through velvety, electric darkness. He lay on top of her, heavy, beloved, welcome.

For a long breathless time, they stayed linked in the aftermath. Then through her boneless exhaustion, she felt him shift and withdraw.

He lifted himself until he sat with his back against the wall. Painted Chinese bridges and gardens framed the pure male beauty of his face. He dragged her up to rest against him. Under her cheek, his heart pounded wildly and his chest heaved as he struggled for breath.

He'd taken her as if the world ended today. She'd loved every moment of it. She raised her head and studied him. His mobile mouth was curled in a smile. He looked calm, satisfied. His frantic need was banked, although bright embers still glowed in his eyes.

She lay back and waited for her heart to steady. She felt as though he'd wrung every ounce of passion from her. Her womb quivered with the force of his volcanic possession. She felt stretched, well used, replete.

She might have dozed. Matthew did, propped up against the wall with his legs stretched out along the bench.

Gradually she became aware of the outside world. The faint creak of the elaborately carved shutters in the breeze. The warmth of sunlight. The distant honk of a graylag goose on the lake. Her mind slowly returned from its dazed journey to ecstasy.

Just what was Matthew doing here? Why had he left London for the wilds of Yorkshire?

Not just for a quick rut with a willing wench, surely. There must be women aplenty in the capital happy to oblige the great Marquess of Sheene. He'd become a sensation, the darling of society.

He'd been through so much in the last year. First there had been the scandal of Lord John's death and the revelations of his crimes. The public validation of Matthew's health and sanity. The trial and hanging of Filey and the venal doctors. Matthew's unstinting support for his aunt and cousins who had faced destitution and disgrace. The triumphant return from New South Wales of the family servants who had risked so much for their master.

So what now? Had Matthew made this arduous journey to tell her he'd selected another woman as his bride?

Something in the frenzied anguish of his touch told her he'd hungered for her as she'd hungered for him.

Perhaps she was a fool. But she couldn't help believing that for now, Matthew was still hers.

Goodness, he'd just flung her on her back and taken her as though he'd combust to ashes if he delayed another second. What more evidence of need could she have?

She smiled as he sighed sleepily and slid his arm around her waist to hold her closer. Incredibly, he was here. That was all the favor she begged from fortune for the present.

"I flatter myself you missed me," Matthew said in a rusty voice above her head.

Grace stirred from her blissful inertia. Her back still pressed into his chest and her head tilted against the broad security of his shoulder. She must have slept again.

Speech seemed almost strange after the perfect communion of their bodies. How long had they rested in radiant peace? Long enough for the sun to move below the hill behind the summerhouse.

"Flatter yourself indeed." She gave an exhausted laugh and ran her hand along the strong forearm that circled her waist. She'd presented him with all the resistance melted butter offered the knife and they both knew it. "I let you tumble me like the most round-heeled wanton."

"You're my wanton. Come here," he said rawly and tugged her around and up for a long kiss.

Hungrily, their mouths met and clung. He tasted like

sex and yearning. He tasted as though he still loved her.

Oh, let it be so, her aching heart cried.

She drew away slightly and pushed her skirts down. They frothed around her thighs in wicked abandon. Almost as much wicked abandon as she'd shown in his arms, she thought with a blush. What would the world think if they saw the usually subdued and decorous Lady Grace Marlow now?

"I've brought you something," he said huskily. He disentangled himself and rose to collect the box he'd left beside the doorway. He fastened his breeches but left the rest of his clothing lying where he'd thrown it.

With a reverence she couldn't help but notice, he lifted the box and carried it across. He sat beside her, his untucked shirt settling loosely around his lean hips. Sheer cambric gaped at the neck, offering glimpses of the firm planes of his chest. She licked her lips as she remembered tasting him there.

He groaned and tore his gaze from her mouth. "Stop it, Grace. We can do that later. First we have to talk."

"Later?" she said breathlessly. It was the first hint that he intended more than just an afternoon's sport.

"Yes, later." He gave no indication that he knew one word had changed her world. He drew in a shuddering breath and spoke more evenly as he laid the box in her lap. "This is for you."

She didn't want presents. She just wanted him. More, she wanted him to tell her that he was here to stay.

But clearly whatever the box contained was important to him. She made herself reach for it then she looked up. A lock of his fine black hair fell across his forehead and a ghost of a smile hovered. Her heart lurched with a wayward surge of love.

"What is it?" she asked in a low voice.

"Open it and see. The catch is on the side. I'm rather proud of the design. I came up with it myself." He sounded relaxed, confident, in a way he never had before. Always before, his uncle's evil had darkened the air. She only realized how much, now the shadows had lifted.

After a little fumbling, she raised the lid. Underneath was a frosted glass cover. She slid away the plate to reveal the contents.

"Oh, Matthew," she whispered, moved to tears.

"I called it *Grace*. I hope you don't mind." For the first time, his manner held a hint of shyness, disconcerting in a man who had just made love to her without hesitation or reticence.

Gently, she curled her hand around what was inside the box and lifted it to the light. "It's your rose."

"No, it's *your* rose."

A heady fragrance filled the air. With one shaking finger, Grace touched a flawless pink petal. The color was unforgettable. It was the most beautiful rose she'd ever seen. Impossible to credit that those unpromising stalks in his courtyard had produced this exquisite bloom.

"It's perfect," she whispered. "It's a miracle."

He was a miracle. How could she not love the man who conjured this beauty with hands and imagination?

The faint smile broadened. Had he worried that she'd reject his gift? Foolish, darling Matthew. The question was whether the rose was a promise of a future or a token of parting.

"I worked on it whenever I could. This last year has been busy."

An understatement, she knew. The Marquess of Sheene had been a ubiquitous presence in London since his release. Everywhere he went, society feted him as a hero. She'd read of the string of honors he'd received, the friendship with the king, the invitations to join scientific boards and societies.

Echoing her gesture, he reached out to touch the petals. The sensitivity of his fingers on the flower reminded her of his hands on her skin.

"I did most of the basic experiments when I was a prisoner, but I couldn't get it right." He glanced up with an expression that combined pride and diffidence in a breathtakingly attractive mixture. "This is the first bud, Grace. It appeared almost a year to the day after I promised to wait. It seemed a sign."

"And you brought it to me," she said softly, staring at the flower. The anniversary of his release didn't occur for two more days. That date was etched on her longing heart.

Reverently, she set the rose back in its container. The glass kept the air inside moist and cool. No wonder Matthew was pleased with his design.

Then she noticed something else.

"My glove," she said blankly. With unsteady hands, she reached in and withdrew a light green kidskin glove from a recess carved away from the damp. The buttery leather was crushed and worn from incessant handling. "Have you kept it all this time?"

"Of course." He wasn't smiling any more and his eyes deepened to a rich, rare gold. Beautiful, unwavering, somber.

"You make me want to cry." Her voice emerged so thickly, she didn't sound like herself.

She laid the box on the bench and tightened her grip on the soft leather until her knuckles whitened. What was he trying to tell her? What did the rose mean? The glove?

Had he carried her glove into his new life like a knight wore his lady's favor into battle? The thought sent choking emotion to her throat.

"You are crying, my love," he whispered and reached out to brush away a tear. His stare held a message but she was too keyed up to read it with any certainty. She needed a declaration but now that the time had come, she was too afraid to hear words that could crush her dreams.

Without really caring about his answer, she asked the first question that came into her mind. "How did you know where to find me this afternoon?"

"Your father told me," he said quietly, not shifting his gaze from hers.

This was surprising enough to pierce her despairing suspense. "My father?" She blushed furiously as the implications sank in. "Dear heaven, he could have followed."

"I don't think so. He's a sensible man. He knew I required privacy. I've just received his permission to pay my addresses to his daughter."

"Well, you did that," she said on a cracked laugh as she remembered how uninhibited those addresses had been. Then finally words she hardly dared say. "Are you asking me to marry you, Matthew?"

"Of course. Why else am I here?" His jaw set in a determined jut that indicated this was an argument she wouldn't win. But she was too speechless with joy to muster any objections. He brought her hand to his lips and kissed the marks where she'd bitten her palm in extremity. The glove slid unheeded to the floor.

"You've had your year, Grace. You must know I've stayed faithful. No other woman can hold your place in my heart. I love you." He paused and his fingers tightened around her hand almost to the point of pain. "The question is do you love me."

Matthew's every muscle tensed with dread as he waited beside her. Nervous sweat prickled at the back of his neck.

The last time he'd asked her to marry him, she'd refused. He didn't think he'd survive another rejection.

She looked troubled, not at all like a woman ready to embrace a glowing future with the man she loved. Fear worse than he'd ever known spurred his heart into an unsteady gallop. Jesus, don't let her have changed. He'd thought when she greeted him with such fervor, that she must want him too.

But passion didn't always mean love, as a year in society had taught him. His unjust incarceration and dramatic release meant the ton's ladies had treated him like a prince from a fairy tale. He'd lost count of the lures, licit and illicit, cast his way.

"Only you make my heart sing, Grace," he said with every ounce of conviction he felt.

"Are you sure this is what you want?" Her voice was so quiet, he barely heard her.

"I knew you were the woman for me from the first moment I saw you. Through illness and suffering and solitude, I've learned to be very sure of my decisions, my darling."

She shook her head and avoided his eyes. "I don't come to you with an unblemished past. I've done bad things, hurt people, hurt myself. I'm not virtuous, Matthew. I'm not pure. And I'm likely barren."

"Your past made you the woman you are. I'd never change that. Whether we have children is in God's hands." Then more urgently, because she still hadn't answered the most important question of all, "Do you love me, Grace?"

He heard her draw a shaky breath. "You must know I do."

He'd hoped, but hadn't known. Not after this separation. Many things could change in twelve months. She hadn't spoken of love during their wild encounter. Then neither had he. Deliberately. He hadn't wanted to frighten her off.

"Is that a yes?" He pressed her hand hard between his as though he could convince her through touch alone.

At last she managed a smile, even if a tremulous one. Tears glittered in her shining eyes. "Of course that's a yes."

His heart caroled hosannas and hallelujahs even if he only breathed one word. That word was the most exquisite sound in the world. "Grace . . ."

He wrenched her into his arms and kissed her hard, passionately, without surcease.

He'd never get enough of her. She was in his bones and his blood and his mind and his heart. The year without her had been endless hell, whatever outward success he'd achieved. She gave meaning to everything he did. Without her, he was nothing, lost, trapped, as much a prisoner as ever.

She kissed him back as if she felt the same. An astonished corner of his mind edged toward accepting that she did feel the same.

When they drew apart, there were tears on her face. Not all hers, he admitted without shame.

She gave a watery laugh and brushed a trembling hand across her cheek. "I'm so happy."

"So am I," he said in an equally choked voice.

The indigo gaze studied him as if she could see right through to his soul. If she could, she'd know one word was written there. *Grace.*

That word would be there until the day he died.

Perhaps she did see because her beautiful smile brightened her face. Her voice was husky with feeling. "This story deserves a happy ending. Let's do our best to give it one."

"Come, darling Grace." He stood and offered his hand. "We have a wedding to arrange."

She clasped his hand and stepped without hesitation to his side. He took a deep breath of clean country air and felt the chains that had bound his heart fall away.

Love had at last set him free.

Avon Romantic Treasures

Unforgettable, enthralling love stories, sparkling with passion and adventure from Romance's bestselling authors